AN ENCHANTING ENEMY

His eyes were the deepest blue she had ever seen, almost the color of midnight. His skin was dark and smooth except for lines around his eyes. He looked like a seafarer.

Again Taras felt his magnetic pull. She *wanted* to surrender. Without effort he dampened her will to fight. What wizardry did her enemy possess? It was far greater than her own, she feared.

"Wherefore have you come to the forest, wench?"

"That—that is my affair."

They were alone. She needn't worry about evading the others. That improved her chances of escaping this one. She sat up and reached for her knife. The sheath was empty!

"You are looking for this?" he asked, opening his hand. Her dagger looked like a child's toy in his palm.

Rage broke the sensual cords binding her. Like a leopard she pounced at his face, hooking her claws to tear out his eyes. He caught her wrists and pinioned her arms behind her back, crushing her to his chest. He slid one hand down her buttocks and forced her to step into him, then clasped her legs between his own. She could feel every hard, male inch of him.

Wrapping her hair around his fist, he pulled her head back and pressed his mouth to her throat. "You belong to me now," he said.

Spell Weaver

Roxi Ashe

LEISURE BOOKS   NEW YORK CITY

A LEISURE BOOK®

December 1999

Published by

Dorchester Publishing Co., Inc.
276 Fifth Avenue
New York, NY 10001

ISBN 0-8439-4649-0

The name "Leisure Books" and the stylized "L" with design are trademarks of Dorchester Publishing Co., Inc.

Printed in the United States of America.

*To weavers of fairy tales, myths, and epic poetry;
may you forever enchant your listeners.*

*Thanks to the skald, Stan Helton,
for the use of his epic poetry.*

Spell Weaver

Chapter One

Strong men might die for such a love potion. The dark forests beyond London had yielded to her their most precious herbs—mistletoe and monkshood, belladonna and woodruff—agents to ignite sexual desire.

Taras of Widnes trickled pale red liquid into a pewter vial. Trying not to breathe the evil vapors, she forced a wooden stopper into the container's mouth. She was afraid of this thing she had created. Biting her lip, she lifted her gaze to Sir Osric. He reached across the table, but she swept the vial beyond his grasp.

"I think, *think*, mind you, that I've finally discovered the right potion," she said. "This may make her fall in love with you, but I can make no promise."

"I'll try it now, my lady," Osric said, stretching again for the vial.

Once more Taras held it away. She couldn't bear the desperate eagerness in his homely face. Why did she raise his hopes when the outcome was so dubious, so perilous?

"Give me time," she said. "I must test it first."

"Test it? On yourself? Nay, if it is lethal, I'll not have you die in my stead."

Taras held the vial against her breast. "I warn you, more than a spoonful a day might slay you. The monkshood alone can—"

"I'll gladly risk my life." He reached into his purse and extracted a coin. "Come, let me taste the draft. For three years I've longed for this moment."

"For three years I've filled you with decoctions, yet your lady still loves another," Taras snapped.

She sprang from her chair and shoved aside a swag of dried herbs in the window. She saw knights in the court-yard below throwing spears through wooden rings. Osric should be practicing his battle skills instead of lingering here in the tower, seeking what might kill him. Why in the name of all the saints must she ply such a deadly art? She wasn't fitted to it. Her mother was the herbalist and alchemist, not her. If she lived a thousand years, she might never get it right.

"I cannot understand your faith in me," she said, slap-ping her thick auburn plait over her shoulder. "My love potions win you nothing but bellyaches and an empty purse. I'm ashamed to take your money."

"You may have it all! What good is money when the woman I desire thinks me ugly as a frog?"

Again Taras bit her lip. With his bald head and wide mouth, his short stature and thick waist, Osric was no handsome prince, yet he was her only friend in King Ethelred's court. The vial trembled in her hand. She ought to throw the blasted thing out the window and tell her mother she'd never again decoct so much as a flaxseed.

"I fear this chemistry," she said. "I've never before used such poisonous plants. If you drink too much, I may never see you again."

10

"I'll take only a sip." Smiling, he came and rested his hand on her shoulder. She turned away and for a long moment stared down at the knights.

"I don't trust my skill. You should ask Mother's help," she finally said. "She understands earth lore. Ethelred even thinks she'll one day render gold from a plain rock. I'm nothing but an apprentice, and an unlucky one at that. Just ask Mother."

"Bah, your lady mother has no time for a ragged-arse knight—she cares only for the king. Her medicines are for him alone."

"Ethelred needs medicines no more than I do," Taras snapped. "He's a cowardly little grass spider, that's all, ensnared by his own webs. His belly wouldn't gripe and burn if he ended this war."

She shut her eyes for a moment. Osric was Ethelred's knight; it was foolish of her to belittle her second cousin, the king of England. What if Osric passed along her words? She wasn't afraid of Ethelred's wrath falling upon *her* head, but she had to think of her mother, Lady Gwendolyn. Without Ethelred's protection they would still be at Widnes Keep, just across the border from the Danelaw, easy prey for the rampaging Vikings. Since her father's death last year on the battlefield of Manathilim, only King Ethelred stood between them and being ransacked by Vikings. At least, that's what Mother said.

Osric suddenly wrenched the vial from her hand and fled. "Here, take my coin!" he cried, tossing his purse back at her.

Taras struck the purse aside; silver coins showered the floor rushes. "Wait! Osric, come back!" By the time she reached the doorway he was already clattering down the winding staircase. Sweet Mary, in his desperation the lovesick fool would likely swallow the vialful.

"Osric, take only a sip! Just one! Swear to me, or I'll tell the king!"

His voice echoed back at her: "Aye, only one today. Tomorrow I marry!"

Taras awakened to a thunderous knock, then her chamber door slammed open and Lord Camlann swept into the dark room. Bearing a rushlight, her mother followed on his heels.

"Get up, cousin," he commanded. "The king wants you in the throne room. Up, I say!"

Taras scooted against the headboard, dragging the furs with her. "How dare you charge in like this? Mother, what's this knave about?"

"Just do as he says. You're in grave trouble!"

"What happened?"

"I'm not sure, but can you not hear the commotion downstairs? Oh, what have you done?" Lady Gwendolyn reeled against a bedpost and clung to it with both hands. "After all I've done to ensure our place at court, Ethelred will cast us out! This is your fault, you inept young thing!"

Taras stared at her in astonishment. A terrible idea sprang into her mind. "Has something happened to Osric?"

"Osric? Have you been giving him philters again?"

"Enough of this prattle!" Camlann snapped. He grabbed Taras by the wrist and jerked her out of bed. The furs slid to the floor, leaving her standing in nothing but her thin white chemise. Ignoring her shriek of outraged modesty, he dragged her from the chamber and through the upper halls to the staircase. Her mother wept aloud as she hurried to catch up. As they descended the staircase, the crowd gathered below shocked Taras.

The nights looked menacing in the great hall's feeble light. When Camlann started down the staircase with Taras they fell quiet for an instant, then one shouted, "Witch! Enchantress! Get her!"

Brandishing swords, three men surged up the staircase.

Camlann thrust Taras behind him and drew his own sword. "Nay! The king would see her alive!"

Taras caught her mother's arms and shoved her up the steps. "Run! Get into your chamber and bar the door. Hurry!" She heard steel clang behind her and knew they'd engaged Camlann. Unwilling to let him fight her battle alone, Taras spun against the wall and ripped a ceremonial spear from its hooks.

"Enough!"

King Ethelred's bass voice rumbled through the smoky air. Flanked by his personal guards, he stormed into the hall and bellowed again. The knights lowered their weapons and retreated. Sweating, Camlann leaned against the stone balustrade and rested the tip of his sword on the step. Taras hovered just behind him, gripping the spear and panting so hard, she thought her heart would burst.

Ethelred folded his arms across his wide chest and gazed up at Taras without expression. Then his beard parted in a sly smile. "Come, kinswoman, we must speak."

She didn't want to give up the spear, yet she couldn't very well approach her liege with a weapon. To reach him, she had to pass through the angry, silent warriors. What if they disobeyed the king and attacked again?

"Go to him," Camlann said. He snatched the spear out of her fists and pushed her roughly ahead of him.

To her surprise, the knights fell back when she stepped onto the flagstones. Several crossed their breasts and regarded her out of the corner of their eyes. Others stared at her in dismay. Their strange reaction alarmed her more than their aborted rage.

When she reached Ethelred she dropped to the rushes on one knee and lowered her head. She wished she had a mantle to cover herself; her chemise left her feeling bare before the roomful of hostile men.

She expected Ethelred's wrath, but he caught her hand

and raised her to a chair. She folded her arms across her chest and waited a long, uncomfortable minute while he leaned back in his chair and twirled his mustache.

"What did you do to Osric?" he finally asked.

Guilt flushed her from head to toe, then her insides went weak as water. She asked in a faint voice, "Is he—" She couldn't frame the awful word, *dead*.

Instead of answering the question, the king reached under his mantle for a dagger. "We found this beside him. He used it to mark the letter T on his pillow. It's the first letter of your name, Taras. He was accusing you."

"I—I do not deny it, my liege."

The king's eyes gleamed with undue pleasure. Taras's gut twisted into a small, hard knot.

"You admit you gave him the potion? Who made it— you or your lady mother?"

"I did." She scanned the throng until she found her mother leaning on Camlann's arm. Lady Gwendolyn's cheeks were bloodless, her eyes deep hollows of fear. Dear God, surely the king wouldn't hold Mother accountable, too. "She had nothing to do with it."

"I know that," Ethelred said with a cold smile. " 'Tis as Sir Osric's squire said: Osric drank from the vial just before the feast last night. He told the squire you'd concocted the potion."

"I knew I shouldn't have given him the draft." The damning words tumbled from her lips, but she couldn't stop them. She'd killed her friend. "Did he drink it all?"

Ethelred sat forward and seized her wrist, clenching tightly. Within seconds her hand throbbed and her bones seemed ready to split. She did not try to withdraw. In the year she'd lived in his castle, he'd sometimes hurt and shamed her. It was his way and she hated him for it.

He thrust her arm away. "What is to be done with you now, Taras of Widnes? What is to be done with the king's

14

own kinswoman, distant in birth though you are?"

"What is to be done with anyone who kills another, my liege?" On shaking legs she rose from the chair and stared at him out of burning eyes. Then she extended her naked arms and crossed her wrists. "I bow to the king's justice."

Lady Gwendolyn sobbed. Taras didn't spare her a glance. This was her burden alone. She'd killed a knight and now she must pay the price.

But King Ethelred burst out laughing. He shoved to his feet and roared, "Squire! Fetch our precious Sir Osric!"

In disbelief, Taras twisted around to see Osric's young squire push through the crowd, cradling something in his mantle. Tears dribbled down the boy's face to stain his tunic. Where was Osric?

Ethelred moved to stand beside Taras. The squire dropped to one knee and unwrapped the mantle. A huge bullfrog gazed up at Taras. It let out a croak.

Taras's knees gave out. Ethelred caught her before she fell and clutched her against his side. "Look at your handiwork, enchantress!" he roared. "You have transformed him. Ho, what a grand day this is!"

"Nay!" Taras shrieked. The swollen frog writhed against the squire's hands. "It was a love potion—a draft to make him more desirable. I used no herbs to transform him. I know of nothing to render a frog from a man!"

Ethelred seized the frog and swung it onto Taras's bosom. She screamed at the touch of the cold, slimy thing and broke from Ethelred. Two knights caught and held her fast. Holding the frog, Ethelred walked slowly toward her.

Taras fought to free herself, but it was no use. Standing rigidly in their arms, she stared at the frog in horror. Ethelred dangled the creature mere inches from her face. She could see every bump, every piece of slimy, odorous skin. Its webbed feet paddled the air between them, then its wide mouth parted in a ghastly smile.

"Don't shrink, enchantress. He's your friend."

"Oh, dear God," Taras panted. "Oh, dear God—Osric, what have I done to you?"

"A miracle!" the king said with a great laugh. Sweeping the frog high overhead, he spun in a circle. The knights erupted into terrible shouts. For a moment Taras thought they would tear her apart; then she heard the king bellow, "You've done a miracle! Because of you, I shall defeat my enemies."

He handed the frog to the squire, then pressed his mouth to Taras's ear. "I shall defeat them, starting with Cynewulf of Amandolar. Come, Taras, to the throne room. I shall tell you my plan."

Chapter Two

It's a plan forged in hell, Taras thought as she rode the path behind her cousin Camlann's huge destrier. They were five days out of London and Camlann wasn't sure when they would reach the mountains of Amandolar. If they ever got there, she was to enter Lord Cynewulf's castle, gain his confidence, and give him the terrible potion. When he was transformed into a frog, she was supposed to kill him.

She remembered the dreadful interview with the king after she'd transformed Osric. She hadn't needed to hear his speeches about the danger Cynewulf posed; the Wolf of the North had existed in legend for all the years of her memory. Mothers told their children that if they didn't behave, the Wolf would sweep down and gobble them up. Her own mother had told her that very thing, and now here she was, riding straight into his jaws.

She mustn't think of herself. If Sweyn Forkbeard's foul Vikings overran England, life would be over, anyway. The brutes hadn't spared her father and his men, nor any of the thousands of Britons both young and old, male and female, who'd crossed their paths over the dozen years since the war began.

But did she actually have the power to bring down the greatest of Forkbeard's chieftains? How strange that God would deliver him into her hands through a fluke of fortune. If Sir Osric had not hungered so for love, she would never have brewed that potion. She wouldn't now be on the road to Amandolar. The whole thing seemed outrageous, a prank gone awry.

"Ethelred is quite mad, you know," she told her cousin. When he didn't reply, she urged her mare up beside his warhorse. "Quite mad to hatch such a plot."

Camlann shifted in the high wooden saddle and scowled down at her. The vertical scar on his right cheek twisted his mouth into a permanent sneer. He doffed his helm and shook out his dark hair. "I tire of that constant refrain. I've heard naught but your blithering the better part of a week. Osric the Frog would make better company than you. Now keep your mouth shut."

"You sound like my mother."

"The dame has more sense than you, little cousin. If we don't kill Cynewulf this year, he'll rejoin Sweyn Forkbeard in the spring. How long do you think England will stand when the damned Wolf comes back with fresh warriors to swell Forkbeard's army?"

Shivering, Taras pulled her snood close about her head. The air was chill this morning, the colored leaves quivering in the wind, but her own shivers had nothing to do with the cold. Through her mantle she touched the small pewter vial between her breasts. The fate of England hung from the cord around her neck.

The Wolf of the North. The name sent a shiver all the way to the roots of her hair. She stiffened her spine. She wasn't afraid. Nay, not at all, even though they said he couldn't be killed, that half the English army had tried and failed. That's why Ethelred was counting on this enchantment.

She wasn't afraid, she told herself firmly. She was . . . bedeviled. She could scarcely believe she'd changed poor Osric into the slimy creature his squire now kept on a pillow. And how could she change a man-wolf into a frog?

She chewed her bottom lip and thought about Lord Cynewulf. He called himself *lord* rather than *thane,* even though he was Danish. She supposed he'd lived in England long enough to adopt an English title. His name was not English, though, sounding somewhat like *kine wolf.* Her mother said it meant *cunning hunter.* She didn't like the sound of that.

She didn't like being compelled to destroy a man, either, enemy or not. But her mother insisted that she obey Ethelred. Not only did England teeter on the edge of a knife, Lady Gwendolyn said, but so did the family lands. Widnes Keep still belonged to Gwendolyn, as did the huge estates farther south. Even Lord Camlann's mighty fortress was in jeopardy, close as it was to the Danelaw. All would be lost if Sweyn Forkbeard wrested the crown of England from Ethelred's head.

Taras did not care so much for the lands, but for the people farming them. It was her duty to stop the wolf in his tracks. "I'm not given to lying," she said, causing Camlann to turn with another frown. "He'll surely wonder why I've come—"

"You've come to buy herbs," Camlann interrupted. "You know what you're to say, blast you!"

Taras narrowed her eyes. Of all Ethelred's vassals, why had he chosen this churl for her traveling companion? Mayhap Ethelred had considered their blood ties, but she didn't see why that made any difference. Camlann didn't intend to enter the castle, only to get her there unharmed. Any knight would have served as well.

"I know what to say, Camlann. But to actually induce him to drink this foul-tasting potion . . . I don't know how it's to be done."

Camlann reined in and grabbed her roughly by the shoulder. His nostrils flaring, he slewed his towering horse against her leg and forced her off the path.

"If a woman of your looks doesn't know how to addle a man's pate by now, perhaps I should throw you down and give you a few lessons. I've wanted to for long enough!"

"Try it and I'll take a knife to you!" Taras said, wrenching her shoulder free.

"Ha!" He reached down and caught her bridle. "We waste time. Dismount and lie in the leaves!"

But Taras yanked aside her skirt, snatched the short knife strapped to her calf, and slashed her cousin across the knuckles. Roaring, he let go of the bridle and jerked his destrier away before she could cut him again. He stared down at his bleeding hand for an instant, then grabbed the hilt of his longsword.

"Little bitch, I'll hack off your head for that!"

Knowing she could neither outrun nor fight him off, she drove the mare backward with her knees and wrenched the pewter vial out of her bodice. She cut the cord with her knife, then pulled the stopper with her teeth.

"All I need do is splash you with this potion, Camlann, and I'll dine on frog legs tonight!"

Camlann's hand froze on the sword hilt. Wide-eyed, he backed into the bushes on the other side of the path. His superstitious fear seemed to affect even his warhorse. The beast reared, its hooves pedaling the air. Camlann's bloody hand slipped off the reins. With a cry he tumbled to the ground.

"Peace, Taras! I claim the Peace of God!" he cried, rolling onto his hands and knees. "Don't transform me!"

Taras curled her lip in scorn. "The Peace of God has nothing to do with our quarrel. I bid you go," she said in a voice shaking with rage. "Go before I change you into the miserable, crawling thing you truly are."

"Close the vial," he begged, using his horse's tail to clamber to his feet. Panting, he edged around his horse to use its body as a shield. "Pray, let us have no more trouble!"

Making no move to push in the stopper, Taras held the vial in one white-knuckled hand. "Go, cousin. I don't need you. I'll find my own way to Amandolar."

"But the king said—"

"The king said I was to go kill a man. He did not say *two*. Now go, lest I disobey him."

Camlann made one last attempt to dissuade her, but when Taras only sat her horse and studied him, he mounted and swung off down the trail. Over his shoulder he cried, "The day will come when I'll get you, bitch. I swear by all that's holy, I'll get you."

Taras sat like stone until the sound of his hoofbeats receded into the distance, then with trembling fingers she pushed the stopper back into the vial. After retying the cord around her neck, she dropped the vial between her breasts. Only then did she start to breathe again.

For the rest of the morning she traveled north. In midafternoon she entered a deep gorge cut by a swift, narrow stream. Gradually the path opened onto a basin formed by the walls of a cliff. A waterfall plunged into a green pool.

She reined in when she caught sight of a sod hut. Raising her voice over the noise of the falls, she announced her presence. When no one came out, she dismounted and led the mare to the open doorway. It was empty.

Half-disappointed and half-relieved, she stooped

through the doorway to look for food since Camlann had galloped off with the provisions. She found nothing but a badly tanned deerskin stretched across the back wall.

Growing hungrier by the minute, she tied the mare near a clump of dry grass and unsaddled her. Checking to make sure she still had her knife, she started into the woods. Long ago her father had taught her to set snares for small game; she was confident she could catch her supper. As she walked, she unplaited her hair and pulled free the binding string. Within a quarter of an hour she found a game trail. Rabbit tracks criss-crossed the path. A stream trickled along the far side.

She cut three long switches from a linden tree and bound them into a springy snare, tied a loop in one end of the binding string, and covered the works with dry leaves. Then she looked around for a hiding place.

There was a sound like distant thunder and the ground quaked beneath her feet. Hooves. Camlann was coming after her!

She couldn't see him through the trees, but she heard the hoofbeats coming closer. The undergrowth wasn't thick enough to hide her. She splashed across the stream, clawed her way up the bank, and slipped under a fir tree's spreading boughs. It was dark under the tree's dense branches. Camlann wouldn't see her.

The hoofbeats pounded like war drums. Now she knew there were more than one horse. If not Camlann, then who was coming? In an agony of fear she strained to see.

Silver and gold flashed through the trees, then a warrior on a black destrier burst onto the path. Behind him rode half a dozen men.

Scarcely forty feet from Taras's hiding place, the leader snapped one gauntleted fist into the air and dragged his warhorse to a halt. The riders skidded to a standstill in a great cloud of dust. Taras prayed they would trample her snare into oblivion before they saw it.

With catlike swiftness, the leader dismounted. As he glanced around he unclasped a silvery wolfskin mantle over his left shoulder. His long byrnie of chain mail swung against his thighs as he tossed the mantle over a bough. He did not doff his winged helm. Light reflected off his thick golden braids and smooth brown skin. He looked forged of sunlight.

Taras sucked in her breath and held it. He grabbed the destrier's bridle and led it to the stream, stopping just before the edge of his mail coat brushed the water. Taras wanted to jump up and run away, but so close, she could smell the steam rising from the warhorse. She forced herself to keep still, knowing he couldn't see into the deep shadows where she lay.

And then he looked up and stared straight at her. From either side of his noseguard his fierce, glittering eyes penetrated the shadows. She felt his gaze bore into her soul.

He was a Dane. She could not mistake the bronzed cheekbones, the patrician nose, the eyes dark blue as an icy lake at twilight. The Viking was her enemy, yet she trembled under a sudden terrible urge to crawl forth and surrender to him. Shivering in every limb, she dug her nails into the ground.

For half a minute he continued to stare, then his eyes traveled on. He hadn't seen her after all, thank the Blessed Veil!

The Viking left his horse and waded out of the stream. The other men led their mounts fetlock deep into the stream; then they flopped down to noisily slurp water. Taras hardly looked at them. Their leader stood watching from the path, his arms folded across his mighty chest. Taras prayed he wouldn't see the rabbit snare.

The black destrier was the first to lift its head and trot

back to the path. It pressed its dripping muzzle to its master's neck. The warrior wiped him down with a twist of grass, then crouched to examine his hooves. Taras watched him lift each massive hoof as though it weighed no more than thistledown. She needed no soothsayer to guess the power he wielded over the great golden sword at his hip.

He dropped the last hoof, straightened, and clapped his hands. Before his men could react, he swung into the saddle and galloped up the trail. With a great deal of splashing and cursing, the riders hurried out of the stream and raced after him. In a few moments the forest was peaceful again.

Immediately, Taras bolted out of cover and slid down the bank into the stream. She jumped and splashed across, then sped off like the wind itself, her mantle sailing behind her.

Her mare jerked in alarm when Taras rushed into the camp she'd set up. Gasping for breath, Taras hurled a blanket onto the animal's back and hoisted her saddle. She knew it was foolish to travel with night coming on, but she dared not stay. She stood a better chance on horseback than sitting here like a plucked duck.

She'd been too quick to send Camlann away. How was she to get to Amandolar when fighting men prowled the forest? Remembering the look in the Viking's eyes chilled her. Pray God she wouldn't run into him again! With men like that warring on England, no wonder Ethelred was losing.

A new, stronger desire to reach Amandolar flared within her. She had to vanquish Cynewulf. Ethelred believed his death would break the backs of Forkbeard and his chieftains. If changing him into a frog and grinding him beneath her heel would save her country, she would do it without compunction. The vial pressed hot as driven nails between her breasts.

Lord Cynewulf, you need drink only one spoonful. Just one.

24

"I see you've come to spy." The deep voice came from behind her. Taras dropped the saddle and spun on her heel.

Silently the Viking stepped out of the shadows twenty feet away. Now he wore nothing but a sleeveless hauberk and braies of black leather. Golden bands encircled his wrists and biceps.

Taras realized he had seen her hiding under the fir. He must have seen the snare and her tracks—that's why he'd halted his men. "You must think yourself a cunning fox, Viking."

He did not answer immediately. The vertical clefts in his cheeks deepened as his eyes traced her curves. She itched to draw her short knife but knew she must let him come within range first. If the knife didn't convince him, she'd have to threaten him with the potion. She didn't want to waste it, though. The potion was for Cynewulf. This Viking would likely taste steel, instead.

The mare glanced around and whinnied. Taras wondered if she could cut the reins tethering the animal and mount before the man reached her. "What do you want, Viking?"

"To look at you suffices for now," he said with a foreign inflection. He set one sandal-shod foot on a boulder and rested his forearms on his knee. "In all my wanderings I've never beheld a wench of such ripeness and beauty."

"I am no bedwench—you shall not treat me so!"

"I shall treat you as I see fit," he said in tones matching the sudden frost in his eyes. "You're a Briton come to spy on us. Know you the penalty?"

"I haven't come to spy!" Dear heaven, what could she say to convince him to leave her alone? "We were hunting game. My companion became lost. I—I wandered here amiss."

"Ah, such a sad tale. I thought at first you'd come here

on purpose, but now I see it was simply for the lack of wit peculiar to Britons."

In surging anger she jabbed her finger at his face. "You cannot claim even the most beggarly portion of wit, sir, but only the craftiness common among thieving, yellow-haired barge-rowers! Now begone from my camp!"

He lunged over the boulder. Caught offguard, Taras didn't have time to draw her knife or mount the horse. She turned and leaped into the pool. Kicking with all her might, she swam into the current and plunged, clothed, downstream.

The cold, swift current swept her far beyond his grasp but she saw she'd made a deadly mistake as her mantle twisted around her legs and trapped her arms. The harder she fought to pull it off, the more entangled she became.

The torrent shoved her over a ledge and underwater. Pinned against a boulder, she couldn't move, couldn't breathe, couldn't escape.

She felt hard hands catch her under the arms and knees. With a thrust of his powerful arms, the Viking jerked her out of the stream. He laid her in the ferns along the bank and stripped off her sodden mantle, saying nothing while she coughed and gasped for air.

"You are a stupid child," he said when she could breathe again.

"Leave me alone!" she cried, trying to sit up.

He draped his arm over her breasts, holding her against the ground. "Leave you alone, when it is so rare to find a sprite in the forest? Leave you alone, when you'll doubtless drown yourself?"

His eyes were the deepest blue she had ever seen, almost the color of midnight. His skin was dark and smooth except for lines around his eyes. He looked like a seafarer.

Again Taras felt his magnetic pull. She wanted to surrender. Without effort he dampened her will to fight. What wizardry did this enemy possess? It was far greater than her own, she feared.

"Wherefore have you come to the forest, wench?"

"That—that is my affair, damn you."

"You will not speak with such venom when the lord tries your case," he said. "But perhaps he will show mercy if you reveal the truth to me. Perhaps I may temper his wrath."

"Who is your lord?" she demanded, but he only grinned. She knew he played with her. "Where are your men?"

He cocked a brow. "So interested? Do you seek to bed them, as well?"

"I'll bed no one, you dodipole! Get off me!"

To her surprise, he swung to his feet and stood looking down at her. "My men rode on; they have other matters to attend," he said at length. "I needed no help to capture a spying Briton."

So they were alone. She needn't worry about evading the others. That improved her chances of escaping this one. She sat up and reached for her knife. The sheath was empty!

"You are looking for this?" he asked, opening his hand. Her dagger looked like a child's toy in his palm.

"Give it back, thief!"

"So you can stab me?"

"So I can protect myself." Wincing, she slowly climbed to her feet. "My bones are broken."

"Shall I stroke you until your bones knit and your bruises fade into memory, river nymph?" His powerful gaze laid claim to her, melted her, and she squirmed. She felt the lodestone power of him.

"Begone!" she said in a voice so weak that it shamed her.

"And leave you to spy? I think not." He stepped close and

ran his fingertips up her arm. She felt her pulse leap. "You shall come with me to pay the price of your foolishness."

Rage broke the sensual cords binding her. Like a leopard she pounced at his face, hooking her claws to tear out his eyes. He caught her wrists and pinioned her arms behind her back, crushing her to his chest. He slid one hand down her buttocks and forced her to step into him, then clasped her legs between his own. She could feel every hard, male inch of him.

"You belong to me now," he said in a low voice. Wrapping her hair around his fist, he pulled her head back and pressed his mouth to her throat. "Only to me, trophy wench."

Chapter Three

Taras fought his iron grip, but he pulled her head farther back and tongued her throat. Despite her own peril, she remembered the vial dangling from the cord around her neck and feared more that he'd take it from her. Instead, he claimed her breasts through her wet bodice, licking until her nipples tightened and her breath came fast.

She forgot the potion. Against him she had no weapon, no defense, no hope. He had come out of nowhere to whirl her in a passionate tempest. Trained from childhood to abhor the very mention of Vikings, she was learning that all the tales were true. She shivered in his hot grasp and wept.

The Viking lifted his head, his eyes snapping with anger. Or was it desire? Would he throw her to the ground and have his way with her?

He stared hard at her for uncounted moments, then he muttered something in Danish and released her. Too humiliated to meet his gaze, she crossed her arms over her chest and bowed her head.

"You are a maiden?"

Was he a knave that he could not tell by her reaction to his lustful touch? Trembling in every limb, acutely aware of his nearness, she took a step backward. If he grabbed her again, she would cast the frog potion in his face. Ethelred could find another way to destroy Cynewulf; she would not suffer herself to be raped by this savage. She grasped the vial and pushed at the cork with her thumb.

Before she could loosen it, he snatched her up, threw her over his shoulder, and set off. She pounded his back and kicked him, but he strode on as though she hurt him no more than a flea might.

The ebony mantle of night had dropped over the forest, yet the Viking walked on as though he possessed cat's eyes. Several minutes later Taras heard the waterfall. He set her on her feet before the sod hut at which she'd camped.

"Your mare ran away," he said.

"Your Vikings probably stole her."

"Ach, that nag's not fit for dog meat." He put his fingers to his lips and whistled. His destrier trotted out of the woods and came to him, whickering at Taras and switching its tail.

"Eboracum, old devil, be silent!" the Viking commanded. He began to unsaddle the beast. Taras saw his now doffed armor tied to the saddle.

"Go into the hut and make yourself comfortable for the night, woman," he said. The saddle thudded to the ground.

"Comfortable? How can I be comfortable with you here? Begone with you, Viking!" But even as she railed at him, she realized her foolishness. What good would it do to argue? She was wet and cold, her mare was gone, and she couldn't see ten steps in front of her. When the moon came out she'd try to escape.

"Your thoughts are easy to discern," he said. "The moon will not help you. I have captured you, and there is no escape."

"And what will you do with me?" she choked. It was a stupid question, she knew, yet she could not hold it back. What else would a Viking do with a woman he'd captured, but ravish her and maybe even kill her if she fought?

He took a long time in answering. She tried to see his face but the darkness hid all but the cruel gleam of his eyes. She felt a brush of wind, then his fingers pressed under her chin, lifting her face. "You are a Briton. There may be some use for you other than the obvious one." He chuckled softly. "Now go into the hut as I commanded you, lest I lose what little mercy I still retain for one of your god-cursed race."

She snatched away from his fingers, lifted the tattered cloth door to feel her way into the darkness, and settled down against the wall. Her teeth clacked with cold. She heard the Viking moving around outside, then steel ringing against stone. After a few minutes, sparks danced just outside the doorway and a tiny flame sprang up. By its light she saw that the Viking had donned his chain mail. It sparkled as he bent to blow on the fire. He added tinder, then small sticks. At last he cast on a large branch.

The Viking looked into the hut. "Give me your clothes."

"Nay!"

"I mean to dry them, Briton. Unless you want to freeze tonight."

"Oh . . . Turn your back. Don't look at me."

"There is little to see in such a scrawny wench—nay! Do not attack me again. This time I may not fight you off. There is more than one way to keep warm on a cold night."

He turned and sat down with his back to the doorway. Taras angrily slipped out of her clothing and tossed it outside. Then she hunched against the chilly sod wall and drew her knees to her chest. She shook her hair around her body, but it was too wet to provide warmth.

"Here, I do not intend to let you sit like a naked sparrow chick."

Taras looked up in dismay to find him leaning through the doorway. His stare washed over her in fiery waves. He tossed her his wolfskin mantle. "Cover yourself," he said harshly. "Hurry."

She didn't have to be bidden twice. Wrapping herself in the fur, she pressed her forehead to her knees and prayed he wouldn't come in.

"I'll sleep by the fire," he said. "Your clothing will be dry by morning. Sleep well."

She held her tongue. The less she spoke to the barbarian, the better. Damned Viking.

She was cold though, even wrapped in wolfskin. After awhile she peered through the doorway and saw the Viking's dark shape stretched between the fire and the hut. Beyond the fire, Eboracum tossed his head and snorted.

Perhaps she could slip outside and sit by the fire. If he was fast asleep, she could don her clothes and steal the warhorse. She'd ridden mean horses before. Let the Viking find her little mare and chase her!

She tiptoed outside and edged along the wall. He lay only a few inches away, his slow breaths steaming in the cold air. She pulled the mantle hard against her to keep from brushing his face as she passed.

Suddenly he shot out his hand, grasped her ankle, and flipped her into the dirt. She managed to kick him in the face, then he mounted her stomach and pinned her arms over her head. Her mantle fell away from her breasts.

"Damn you, Viking, leave me be! I wasn't trying to run!"

His face looked devilish in the firelight. He stared down at her breasts, and for a moment she thought he would taste them. Instead, he held her wrists in one hand and took the pewter vial between his fingers.

"What is this, Briton?"

"Nothing."

"An amulet, perhaps?"

Would he take it away from her if she agreed? Vikings believed in luck, she'd heard. Maybe this one collected good-luck charms. God help her if he stole it.

Still, if she denied its worth he would almost certainly believe her a liar. Taking a chance, she said, "Aye, it's an amulet. My mother gave it to me to ward off enemies."

"Like me?" he asked in a deep, quiet baritone.

His voice made her belly tingle. She wanted to feel him speak again. This was madness. "Yes, like you. . . . I fear it doesn't work."

He smiled without mirth, then nestled the vial between her breasts. His callused palm chafed her left nipple, making her arch against him. Blushing, she forced herself to go still. His smile deepened. "You came out here to feel the fire, didn't you?"

Of which fire did he speak? She didn't like his tone or the hot gleam in his eyes. "Please, sir, let me go. You're crushing me."

He lowered his face and gently kissed her just under the ear. She arched again, violently. "Please, sir!"

"This time, little Briton. But do not rouse me from sleep again. I am not kind when my dreams are broken." He raised himself and watched her roll free.

Taras scurried to the far side of the fire and sat. Trying not to look at him, she examined her garments drying on sticks before the fire. When she finished looking at them, she feigned interest in the stars pricking the sky near the rising moon.

"You are hungry," he said.

She didn't answer.

"Eboracum destroyed your rabbit snare. I owe you food." He got up and went to the saddle. "Here, it's dried venison. It isn't much, but my warriors and I don't pause to hunt game when we're hunting Englishmen."

It was a horrible thing to say. He wanted to distress her on purpose, she could see it in his fierce gaze. She should reject the strip of dark meat he dropped into her lap. She ought not accept anything from the murdering pillager.

The Viking resumed his place beyond the fire. Hating her weakness, Taras began chewing the tough meat. When her jaws grew tired she said, "So you were raiding."

"Eh?" He propped up on one elbow and stirred the fire until flames painted his face red. "We were patrolling, if that is what you mean. Someone has to keep the damned English off our lands."

"Your lands? You claim the king's forest as your own? But why should I be surprised, when for years Vikings have stolen our land?" Taras knew she spoke recklessly, but she couldn't stop. It galled her to sit here as his captive when she should be on the king's business. "Stealing is part of your murderous way of life."

"It has been many years since we last went a-viking, wench. This land is ours. We sustain ourselves."

"Your breed sustains itself on others' misery."

"Ha! You are too ignorant to know our history."

"I know enough to name you the ill-begotten race of plunderers you are. How often you've swept down from the north upon us"—her voice broke as she struggled to finish—"to enslave us and usurp our lands!"

"And what of Ethelred the Unraed's bent for murder?"

The Viking stopped leaning on his elbow and straightened, erect and hard as an oak. He was terrible in the moonlight, his brows drawn over wolfish eyes shadowed with pain and anger. "Did your English king not attack us, his neighbors in the Danelaw, these twelve winters past? Did he not drench the earth with our blood?"

"It was to secure the borders of England from your predations—to free our country from the danegeld, a tribute too grievous to be borne!"

"You know not what you say, Briton."

"I know all I need to about your King Sweyn Forkbeard. My father told me all about him!"

"Your father? And where is this prince of men now, when you need him? Is he afraid to wrest you from me, or doesn't he care what fate befalls you?"

"You son of a sea devil, how dare you speak so of him? My mother laid him in the ground not a year ago. He fell under the ax of a Viking beast like you."

"Would that I had slain him myself," the Viking said. He leaned forward over the fire, his eyes blazing like hell itself.

Too enraged to fear him, Taras said, "Would that I could slay you. What is it you call blood vengeance? The weregeld? Aye, that is what I would exact from you. I could die then and smile."

"And you *would* die if you laid steel to me, wench. Or would you slay me with your sharp tongue?"

Taras hooked her fingers into talons, wanting with all her soul to try again for his eyes. Hatred sparked between them sharp and bright. Without thinking, she grasped the vial around her neck.

"Your amulet? You would kill me with your amulet?" He threw back his head and laughed. "That I would see. Go ahead, try it." He spread his arms and waited.

Taras caught the cord and tried to break it. The leather

cut into the back of her neck, bringing her up short. What was she doing? She dared not waste the potion on this wretch. Shaking with ire, she let go and stood up.

The Viking didn't move. He watched her out of narrowed eyes as she yanked her damp clothing off the sticks and stomped past him into the hut. Not caring if he watched, she dropped the wolfskin and pulled on her clothes. She'd be drawn and quartered before she'd sit naked under the man's furs a moment longer.

He looked into the hut. "What is your name, Briton?"

She gathered her hair into her hands and furiously began plaiting it. When they fought again, her hair wouldn't hamper her attack.

"I asked your name." His voice held a dangerous inflection.

Taras knew she'd trapped herself in the hut. To keep him from coming in to extract the information, she said, "Taras. Lady Taras of Widnes to you."

"Tar-as," he said. Somehow he made her name sound as though it were his to bestow. "What is its meaning?"

"That is none of your concern. . . . What is your name?"

"That is none of *your* concern. Where is this Widnes, your home?"

"On another world it seems," she spat. She resumed plaiting her hair. When the braid reached her waist, she flung it over her shoulder, covered herself with her mantle, and marched outside. Eboracum snorted when she flounced down near him. "When will you let me go?"

The Viking uncoiled from the ground and stood listening. His nostrils flared, taking scent. Then he sprang at Eboracum and threw the saddle on his back. "Taras, mount quickly!"

"Why?"

"Are you deaf? Wolves."

She jumped up but could hear no sound. "Shouldn't we take refuge in the hut?"

"With no real door? How long could we withstand them? And I will not leave Eboracum in the open. Come, mount!" He leaned down and seized a branch from the fire, then leaped into the saddle, clapped on his helm, and pulled her up behind him. "Fly, Eboracum!"

The great warhorse plunged onto the shadowy path. The moon slid behind ragged clouds. Cold wind rattled the branches and moaned through the forest. Or was it the howl of wolves?

"Where are they?" Taras murmured in the Viking's ear. "I can see nothing."

"They're coming." Urging the horse to a greater speed, he twisted in the saddle and stared behind them. Taras held tight to his waist and strained to follow his gaze, but the flaming branch made the surrounding darkness more intense.

And then she saw a huge body spring onto the path next to them. Before she could shout a warning, the Viking thrust the branch into the wolf's face. It yelped and shrunk back. The Viking shoved the branch into Taras's hand and drew his sword from its sheath. "Odin's breath, here they come!"

The predators ran silently out of the darkness, their fangs and eyes glittering in faces black as death. Taras hunched low to give the Viking sword room.

"You bring me bad luck, Briton," he said.

"I? What have I done?" She jabbed the torch at the pack. There were eight of them—lean, hungry brutes. Their leader's jaws gaped inches from Eboracum's heels.

The wolf burst around the horse and leaped at Taras. Before she could strike with the torch, the Viking smote off its head. A great howling went up from the pack and they slowed.

37

"They've gone mad," the Viking said. "This is not their way. They don't even fear the fire. What witchery have you wrought?"

"Don't lay the blame at my feet!" Taras shouted. "They're trying to eat me, too!" Perhaps the wolves were not mad, but ravenous, to hunt in a pack like this. "You might blame your Viking pillagers instead of me—but for your wars there would be game in the forest!"

Eboracum began to slow. Foam flew from his mouth and his haunches were so sweaty that Taras could hardly keep her seat. If she lost her grip on the Viking, she'd fall into the wolves.

Eboracum screamed and twisted hard to the left. Taras fell off the horse and hit the ground, losing the torch. Immediately the Viking pivoted and slashed two wolves springing at her. He jumped out of the saddle and snatched her off the ground. "Mount up! Go!"

In terror she scrambled onto Eboracum's back, seized his mane, and rammed her heels into his flanks. But instead of fleeing, she turned him straight into the wolves and dragged hard on the reins. Emitting a deafening scream, the battle-trained charger reared and churned his hooves. Taras hung on for dear life as the horse plunged toward his master, biting, kicking, crushing wolves. The Viking fought his way to the horse and leaped up behind Taras.

Their will broken, the wolves pursued only a few moments more. As Eboracum bolted down the path, their howling faded into the air.

Taras leaned back against the Viking and let him guide the horse. She was too weak to struggle against the touch of his body, the protective arm he clasped around her waist. She could still smell blood and death. It was a miracle the three of them were alive.

"Good Eboracum," she murmured. "Good, brave stallion."

"Keep still and ride, green-eyed warrior wench," the Viking said against her hair. And then, "Why didn't you flee when you had the chance?"

She set her jaw and gave no answer. She had none. She was a fool, that was all.

Chapter Four

When morning dawned, the Viking urged the horse into a meadow and helped Taras dismount. After leading Eboracum to water and unsaddling and wiping him down, he tied him near a frosty clump of grass. Yawning, the Viking dropped his helm on the ground and rubbed his bloodshot eyes.

"You need sleep," Taras said.

"Not yet."

"It was a long night."

"No longer than the three before it."

So he hadn't slept in four nights. Taras thought about that. His shoulders weren't so square this morning; it wouldn't take much to put him to sleep. She'd make him warm and comfortable, and perhaps sing him a lullaby.

She went to the edge of the forest to gather branches. Among the roots of an old linden tree she found a cluster of balm mint. Smiling inwardly, she picked a handful and returned to the Viking, who was clearing a spot on the ground. Taras squatted beside him and made a pyramid of sticks, then began shredding inner bark for tinder. She pushed the fluff under the sticks.

"Have you steel, Viking?"

"Damfertigénen will suffice." As he drew his sword and laid it on the grass, Taras saw bloodstains on its edge. The Viking began to strike the fine steel with a piece of flint.

Taras held a bit of shredded bark to catch sparks. She dared not look at the man, whose nearness made her tingle. She focused on his strong, dark hands. Those hands had killed just hours before, yet she knew they could give pleasure as well.

"Hold the tinder still, Taras. You're shaking."

"I'm not shaking. I'm cold," she lied.

"There are faster ways to warm you," he said, flashing her a look. Taras pretended not to notice.

When at last the bark began to smolder, Taras pushed it into the pyramid and blew until the fluff ignited. The Viking gradually added branches.

Taras rose to stand beside the Viking, who continued to feed the fire. She crushed the mint in her hand, unleashing its sweet aroma. The Viking glanced around, sniffing, but did not comment.

Balm mint put people to sleep. Taras's mother had often calmed her fidgets with the stuff. She held it a little closer to the Viking's head and squeezed until juicy droplets burst onto his mail. Pretty soon he rubbed his eyes and gave a great yawn. Taras dropped the crushed leaves into the grass beside him. The Viking yawned again, then got up and staggered over to a tree. He sat down heavily and closed his eyes.

Taras watched him for signs of restlessness, but he seemed utterly relaxed, his hands draped over his crossed legs. She turned and tiptoed over to Eboracum.

"Going somewhere?"

His voice came from just behind her. She spun around to find him inches away, arms akimbo. He didn't smile, but light danced in his tired eyes.

"I thought you were asleep," she said in an accusatory tone.

"I was for a minute."

"You shouldn't have woken up."

"Perhaps your balm mint wasn't strong enough," he said. "It relaxed me, though. My thanks for the brief respite."

So he'd known what she was doing all along. Scowling, she pushed past him and sat down by the fire. She should have hit him over the head with a branch. *That* would have induced a deep sleep.

He went back to the tree and settled against the trunk. This time he didn't sleep, but cleaned his sword on the grass and began to hone it on a black stone. From time to time he tested the edge with his thumb. Taras saw blood well up, but he only grunted and resumed sharpening. Finally he took out a piece of doeskin and polished the golden hawk's head pommel and hilt. Encrusted with emeralds and onyx, the crosspiece sparkled in the sunlight.

Unable to restrain her curiosity, Taras said, "By what name did you call your sword?"

He slid the weapon into its gold-encrusted scabbard before looking up at her. Fire crackled in his eyes. "Damfertigénen."

"That has a very old sound."

"It is a very old sword."

"What does its name mean?"

"Slayer of the Damned," he said low.

Taras's blood ran chill. No doubt he'd slain many Britons with that sword. Trembling, she heaped wood onto the fire.

"You'll smother it, wench."

43

He warned her too late. The flame disappeared under a blanket of smoke. She flicked away branches and bent to breathe onto the embers. When she raised her head, the Viking was gone. She got up and looked into the forest. Silence.

He moved too quietly to be mortal . . . was he some terrible Viking war god? *Damfertigénen. Slayer of the Damned.* A name of antiquity. Maybe it was his name, as well.

"Fool! He's naught but a man of flesh and blood!"

At the sound of her voice, Eboracum snorted and flicked his tail. Taras got up and went to him. Would he let her mount him again? She knew she couldn't lift the heavy saddle onto his back. She'd ride without.

Catching his mane, she tried to vault onto him, but he danced sideways. Taras lost her hold on his mane. "Stand still!"

But Eboracum pushed his nose between her legs and tipped her onto the ground. She upbraided him until he thrust his muzzle against her neck and blew. Softening, she plucked a handful of grass and got up to wisp him.

"My Lord Wolf-biter," she cooed to the horse, "I suppose you are too tired to run anymore today. Be still and let me curry your filthy coat."

"What spell have you woven about my warhorse that he behaves like a tame sheep under your hand?"

He'd slipped up on her again, blast him. She turned and looked for him, but he remained hidden in the shadows. "I have woven no spell," she snapped.

"His docility belies your protest. He savages grooms who dare approach him."

"It's a miracle he's stayed healthy for so long then, don't you think?"

"I groom him myself." The Viking stepped out of the

darkness. He did not smile, but approval shone in his gaze. Taras didn't want his regard. She walked back to the fire.

"I've brought food, spell weaver." He dropped a rabbit beside her and sat down.

"May you enjoy it, sir."

"May I choke upon it, you mean."

"Aye, inhale it whole as befits a Viking savage."

"The meat is for you." He used the knife he'd taken from her to dress the rabbit.

She wanted to nettle him, but she'd run out of verbal barbs. She gazed at his hard body, watching the play of muscles beneath his short-sleeved byrnie. A red, swollen gash just above his left elbow caught her attention. She touched the wound. He glanced at her in surprise, then shrugged her off and returned to his work.

"You were bitten last night," she said.

"It is nothing."

"It festers."

"Bah." He skewered the meat and propped it over the fire. Rubbing his eyes, he lay down. Before long he began to snore softly. This time there was no mistake. He was sound asleep.

Taras cut her eyes at Eboracum. The horse's ears pricked forward. Perhaps he would let her mount him now. On his back she could be five miles away before her captor awakened.

But when she looked at the Viking, she noticed sweat on his brow. Sweat on a frosty morning? Was a fever from the wolf's diseased jaws upon him already? He might die if she left him alone.

Nay, he wasn't her concern. She had to be about the king's business. This man had stopped her long enough. Besides, the Viking had said the wolves might be mad. If they were sick and the poison was already in his system,

45

there was nothing she could do about it. She knew no cure for the foaming madness that seized men bitten by wild animals.

She eased toward the horse. Eboracum tossed his head and snorted. The Viking stirred in his slumber but did not awaken. She caught the horse's reins and fumbled with the knot. Her fingers stilled.

You're a fool, Taras of Widnes. A lop-eared fool.

She dropped the reins and marched back to the fire. Removing a charred stick, she ground it between two stones until soft black powder remained. Then she spat into the charcoal and mixed it to black paste. She added the balm mint she'd crushed and with trembling fingers smeared it into her captor's wound.

"You are weaving other spells, I ken," he said without opening his eyes.

"Spells that will keep you alive, though only the blessed Apostles know why I trouble myself."

He chuckled. She bounded to her feet and went into the trees to collect spiderwebs. When she had a handful, she grabbed leaves from the linden tree, then went back to him and lay the webs over the charcoal paste. She covered the poultice with linden leaves—medicinal in their own right—and bound it with strips torn from her chemise. If he'd go to sleep now, she could escape with a clear conscience.

He was looking at her, his eyes wary. She knew he'd guessed her thoughts. Before she could withdraw he caught her hand. "Wherefore do you minister to me, an enemy?"

"You kept the wolves from killing me last night."

"It was the other way about, Lady Taras. Had you not come back I would have fallen to them. You owe me nothing, yet you nurse me when you ought to flee. Wherefore?"

"It—it would be a sin to leave you to die of fever."

"Why a sin?"

Feeling trapped, she could only gaze back at him. Despite his weakness he looked virile as a devil. His expression sapped her strength to fight. She hated the sudden heat in her loins. He made it worse when he glided his thumb back and forth over her wrist.

"Is it not a greater sin to give your enemy power over you?" he whispered.

"I've given you no power, Viking." But she bit her lip and looked away. She didn't try to pull her arm free.

"What is that mist in your eyes, lady? Do you lament staying with me.?"

She blinked back her tears. Faint heart! She was foolish to stay, and more foolish still to let his demeanor lull her senses. His fragile crust of civility could break in an instant to reveal the barbarian underneath.

"I have reason to regret staying," she finally said.

"Mayhap." Slowly he traced her arm to the crook of her elbow. She tried to steel herself to his caress, to the burning touch of his eyes. All too well she remembered his lips on her breasts, the feel of his iron manhood against her. She did not wish it again.

To divert his attention, she asked, "Where are you taking me?"

"You shall see."

"When?"

"Very soon."

"Why do you toy with me?" she cried. She jerked her arm free. "Can you not see I can't bear this torture? Why are you doing this to me?"

His eyes darkened and his face grew granite hard. "Because you are beautiful. Because I desire you."

"That is all your reason? May a scabrous pox descend upon you, sir!"

47

"Such vulgar language from noble lips," he mocked. "One might take you for a scullery maid rather than a woman gentle-born."

Taras slapped him hard across the cheek. As she drew back to strike again, he rolled her onto her back. "We have done this before, I trow," he said. "Shall I kiss you into submission again, vixen?"

"Unhand me!"

"Only to feel your fists? Where has flown the angel who so carefully tended my wound but moments ago?"

"That sentimental blearwit is gone, never to return!"

Through clenched teeth he said, "I bid you be silent. Do not speak so again lest I teach you the manners you and your kind so sorely lack."

"A Viking pillager would teach me manners?"

"Someone needs to."

"And you think yourself equal to the task."

He released her and sat up. "I think any man equal to the task. Any Dane, that is. Your English masters neglected your training. You would be no maiden now had they trained you properly."

"I have no masters! How I despise the sight of you!"

"I know. It causes me no sadness." He reached into the fire for meat. "Eat this."

"I will not. I would starve before supping with you."

"As you please."

"And you will ride on without me."

"Very well. You will walk behind the horse, bound."

Taras balled her fists but dared not strike him again. She knew better than to get too close. Instead, she bent on him her most hateful glare.

"I supposed you were a stupid chit last night when I pulled you from the river," he said after a long silence. "But I little dreamed you'd spite yourself to this degree. Soon you will be too weak to even try to escape."

Taras snatched the meat out of his hand and ate it. The Viking put the remainder in his pack and went to saddle his horse. "Put out the fire, Taras," he said.

"Nay. I'll stay here, barbarian."

The lines of fatigue deepened around his mouth. "Were I an English carl, I would feed you dirt to humble your tongue."

"Were you an English carl, you would not abuse me so, you godless savage."

He stalked over and kicked dirt on the fire, showering Taras's clothing with ashes and dust. She jumped back, but he caught her arm and escorted her to the horse. There he released her. "Do not think of running, Briton."

She offered him a contemptuous smile and took his hand. "I would not dream of running in the frost."

He snorted and lifted her into the saddle, then vaulted up behind her. Eboracum's hooves crunched down frozen pedestals of dirt as he found the path. Taras scowled at the frosty red and yellow leaves lighting the forest. She could see no beauty in it.

Many hours later, they dismounted to walk up a steep, narrow mountain path. Taras had to grasp the horse's tail and let him pull her along. Even so, her breath came fast in the cold, thin air. Halfway to the top, the Viking pointed and said, "Look at the gyrfalcon."

Taras followed his finger. A big white bird soared out of the clouds and stooped on a dove, smashing it out of the air. It tumbled hundreds of feet to the ground. "An excellent kill," the Viking said. "I must mark the location of her nest."

"So you can trap her? In England only kings fly gyrfalcons. Plunderers like you fly naught but kestrels, as befits their lowly rank."

He smiled coldly. He seemed to grow in stature until Taras felt very small. He spoke to her in Danish.

"I do not understand your pagan tongue!" she cried.

"You will come to in time." He shifted his gaze back to the bird.

"You're like that falcon," Taras said. "You're a merciless hunter who delights in crushing the helpless."

"You consider yourself weak, she-lion?"

"Weak in body, mayhap, but strong in mind."

"We should join our flesh, then, and produce a child in whom intellect and might are one."

"I would never join with a pagan!"

"Pagan? Do we not both worship the Allfather?"

"Vikings worship nothing but their weapons, and maybe a bloodthirsty war god or two."

"The Icelander Althing converted to your Christian god before you were born, wench, as did my kindred at Discoftomb in the Danelaw."

"But a barbarian like you likely keeps to his heathen practices."

He pulled Eboracum into motion behind him. "What is heathen to you was a true religion to my ancestors. We each worship what brings us luck."

"Then you are a pagan."

He shrugged. "Call me what you will if it brings you comfort. Mayhap your mind will ease to know that Britons live among my people. You saw some riding with me yesterday."

Taras didn't want to hear such things. "Why should they ride with you?"

"They've sworn fealty to the Lord of Amandolar."

Taras dropped the horse's tail and caught the vial at her chest. The Viking cocked a brow "Have I spoken amiss?" he asked.

"Amandolar? Is that where you're taking me?"

"You are there already. Every tree upon these mountains belongs to Lord Cynewulf."

Taras could scarcely hide her jubilation. Her captor was

taking her exactly where she wanted to go, thanks to the holy saints who'd kept her from running away! The image of Osric the Frog leaped into her mind. Lord Cynewulf the Frog joined him, hopping in circles.

The Viking stared at her as though seeking her thoughts. She forced down her excitement; it wouldn't do for him to guess her plans. She spoke of other things. "These Britons—I do not understand their loyalty to a Viking."

"It is too much to explain to you. You'll have to ask them yourself."

"I won't speak to traitors of the king."

"You think so much of Ethelred the Unraed?"

"I should. He is my kinsman. My second cousin twice removed."

The Viking opened his mouth to speak, then snapped it shut. A muscle twitched in his jaw. Frost glittered in his eyes. Alarmed by the hatred she saw, Taras retreated a step. Eboracum neighed and pawed the ground. She patted his rump to quiet him.

Her action seemed to make the Viking even angrier. He turned his back and dragged Eboracum up the hill. He didn't bother to check whether she followed.

What if he left her here in this desolate spot? What if she couldn't find her way to the castle after coming so far? What if he'd guessed her plan? She ran after him and yelled, "I have nothing to do with the wars of men. You have no right to punish me!"

"You are a Briton, kinswoman of my enemy."

"Your own hatred is your enemy!"

He rounded on her. "Sweyn Forkbeard of Denmark is my king. I have sworn to punish all who oppose him. It was your misfortune to fall into my hands, Ethelred's cousin."

"Nay, it is *your* misfortune. Beware that you do not fall asleep a third time!"

"The threats of an ignorant wench fail to move me."

She thrust away from him to the edge of the path. "You call me ignorant, when your own lack of wit shines like a dead mackeral under moonlight and renders the very air foul?"

His jaw muscles vibrated under the skin as he said, "You are more intelligent than other Britons I have known, but it would not astonish me to find you burning your bed to kill a flea."

"Son of a Viking plunderer, in what slaver's stinking bilge did your mother beget you?"

His eyes caught fire. Taras packed every dram of hatred she possessed into the glare she returned to him. She forgot about Lord Cynewulf, forgot about her mission. This Viking embodied the enemy who had killed her father at Manathilim. With vengeful recklessness she seized the vial of potion and flung off the wolfskin mantle.

The fur hit Eboracum in the face, who screamed and reared. Taras jumped back and realized her danger too late. Stones slid under her feet, hurtling her toward the precipice. She flung out her arms and shrieked in mortal terror as she began to fall.

Chapter Five

The Viking threw himself at her, slid to the edge on his belly, and caught her hem. For an instant both hovered on the brink of death, then with a mighty heave he yanked her up onto the path. Taras fell flat on her back, stunned.

"Odin's beard, wench, do you truly prefer death over me?" he asked between gasps. He hauled himself to his feet. One of his braids had escaped its thong and the wind now whipped hair around his shoulders. Blood marred his cheek where he'd scraped it upon the stones.

Taras lay where she had fallen, hearing blood thunder in her ears. She wasn't sure if she could rise. She had no choice but to listen to him rage.

"First you throw yourself into a river, then you hurl yourself off a mountain," he said. "It seems your feeble wit has utterly deserted you."

In a blind rage Taras rolled to her knees and threw a handful of gravel into his face. Some of the stones peppered Eboracum. The destrier began to buck, his gyrations carrying him near the ledge. The Viking leaped to catch his bridle and steady him.

"By the old gods, Taras, I'll teach you a lesson you'll never forget!"

"Keep your hands off me, Viking, or I'll bite them off!"

He snatched her off the ground and slung her belly-first over the saddle. Ignoring her screams, he trussed her hands and feet. She writhed and screamed curses until he smacked her hard across the buttocks. She shrieked in shock and then, sensing he'd strike her again, bit her tongue.

"You learn fast," he said. He tucked the wolfskin mantle around her. She tried to bite his hand, but he pulled back in time. "And then, perhaps not too fast."

"Don't strike me again!"

"Temper your waspish ways, then." He helped himself to the waterbag, then wordlessly led the horse up the mountain.

Taras dangled from the saddle like a bundle of wash, her cheek bumping the horse's flank, her long plait nearly brushing the ground. She was afraid Eboracum would step on it and scalp her. She started thrashing again, but the thongs only cut deeper into her skin. She finally gave up and shut her eyes in misery. It took nearly an hour to reach the summit.

The Viking stopped on a pinnacle to survey the lands north. Above a long, narrow valley the mountains of Amandolar framed the top of the world. Their heads shrouded in vapor and smoke, the giant mountains plunged rocky feet into sapphire lakes and evergreen forests.

Taras didn't like the view. She was terrified to hang over the horse's side so close to the clouds. Blood pounded like hammer blows in her brain. The pewter vial dangled free on its cord and struck her face with each of the horse's movements.

The vial! What if the stopper fell out and the potion splashed her in the face? What would the Viking think when she turned into a frog and sprang over the cliff? Oh, why hadn't she realized her danger until now? The stopper was probably loose. At any moment the potion might spill. She wept and fought to hold her head up and away from the poisonous thing.

The Viking placed his hand on her back and bent to look at her. "What is your trouble now?"

"I cannot breathe!"

"You could if you stopped raging."

"Dear God, deliver me!" she cried. "From the fury of the Norsemen—"

"—deliver us, O Lord," he finished for her. "I fear your god has ceased to listen to that priestly litany. And he spurns the vain repetition of your black-robed priests."

The Viking's terrible blasphemy nearly made Taras forget the potion. His words would surely damn them both. "Nay—don't speak so! He'll send down lightning on our heads!"

"He would not hurl a bolt at me with you so close," he said.

"Don't tempt the Maker of Heaven and Earth."

He took her face in his hands and with his thumbs brushed away her tears. The clefts in his cheeks deepened. "Have I convinced you that it's futile to fight me?"

"Unbind me!"

"Swear you will not throw yourself off the mountain. I won't save you from yourself again—I've too many bruises as it is."

"I hate you with all my soul!"

"My regrets will rob me of sleep," he said with a great deal of sarcasm. "Now let us have done with this quarreling before I lose all patience."

She remembered his palm against her backside and

knew he could mete out worse punishment. "I won't fight you, Viking."

"Until you get your breath back, I suppose," he said with a heavy sigh. He untied her and helped her sit up. Taras thrust the vial to safety between her breasts. She didn't speak again until they reached the bottom of the mountain.

The Viking led her into a small clearing where water cascaded from a rocky escarpment. He lifted her from the saddle and held her in front of him, regarding her out of dark, serious eyes. She stared back, determined not to react to the touch of his hard body.

"You are beautiful—like the most glorious falcon," he said at last. His voice strummed a chord within her, vibrating in her most secret place.

Even with his hair tumbling wild and blood drying on his jaw, he was the most magnificent man she'd ever seen. She thought of the knights of King Ethelred's court, the prideful peacocks arrayed in silk and velvet and silver. None could compare with this enemy warrior, this savage conqueror.

She didn't want to make comparisons. Never in her life had she desired a man—any man. Her father had delayed giving her to wife; the men he would have chosen had been off fighting the war. Ethelred, now her closest kinsman, had selected two or three, but she'd rejected them. She'd ignored her mother's railing, insisting that she'd only marry for love.

But now tears of hot, shameful desire filled her eyes as her body simmered with need. As much as she despised this man who'd so sorely used her, she wanted to feel more than his lips and hands. She wanted him inside her, possessing her as only a man of his strength could. Damn and blast him.

"You weep, my lady?"

"I am not your lady." If there was any justice, the earth would open and swallow her this instant. It would probably do her no good, though; this man would doubtless go down and get her. Fighting her body's betrayal, she whispered, "Please, sir, let me go."

He opened his fingers one by one, relinquishing his hold on her arms. Even when she was free, Taras couldn't force her limbs to move. She saw his chest rising and falling, heard his breath hiss between his teeth. He finally stepped back and stabbed his finger at the forest. "See to your needs, damn it. Hurry if you know what's good for you."

She turned and ran into the bushes. For several minutes she leaned against a tree, hugging herself while tears of humiliation coursed down her cheeks. What was the matter with her, to entertain such desires? Was she no better than a bedwench, after all? She couldn't bear to think of herself like that. She was a lady gentle born. She must remember that.

When she returned he was sitting on a boulder, combing his tawny hair with his fingers. He pulled it back from his forehead, parted it, and began to braid it. "The meat is over there," he said, nodding at a flat boulder. It was the rabbit from breakfast.

She sat down and took a piece. Did he remember the way she'd looked at him a few minutes ago? Had he guessed her emotions and felt her heat? She must restore some distance between them. If she spoke of other things, perhaps he would forget. "Does—does your wound still pain you?"

He struck off the poultice and kneaded his arm. Giving her an odd look, he said, "It is as though the wolf never bit me. You have wrought magic. My household will benefit from a spell weaver."

"I won't join your household! When will you let me go?"

"I will never let you go."

57

"But you can't just keep me!" If he kept her under his heel, how could she get to Lord Cynewulf? "I'm a noble-woman."

He stared at her without expression as he knotted leather around his second braid and flipped it over his shoulder. "Not any longer."

"You are the most dishonorable man I've ever known."

"Were I as honorable as other men," he growled, "you would be no maiden now."

She threw the meat into the dirt and went to the water-fall. She scrubbed her hands and face to get rid of his touch, his smell, his taste. If she'd had the strength and opportunity, she would have held his head underwater until he drowned.

She felt heat on the back of her neck. Twitching about in alarm, she found him standing over her, a pulse jumping in his throat. He was braided, helmed, and armored for battle. Yet when she looked into his eyes she saw not enmity and lust, but pain. It was the pain that held her in place.

"By the head of Thor," he murmured, "you are lovely as moonlight on winter's first snow. In all my wanderings I have never beheld another so fair."

She tensed her muscles to stop them trembling. "What game do you play now, sir, that you caress me with word and gesture when you know I despise you?"

A muscle throbbed in his cheek. "I do not believe you find me so displeasing."

"Your heart swells with conceit." She forced her gaze from his handsome visage. She dared not think of him as a man of thought and emotion. He was an enemy, that was all.

There was a deep, curved scar on the ball of his thumb. She almost touched it before she remembered that she didn't care about his pain, no matter how old. She supposed it was a battle scar. If he didn't let her go soon, he'd bear more wounds than that one. Or perhaps she'd turn him into a frog. If she used only a smidgeon of the potion, she might have enough left for Lord Cynewulf.

He must have read the revulsion in her eyes, for he turned suddenly and stalked to Eboracum. The destrier tossed his head and whickered.

"Silence, old fool." He seized a handful of grass and started to rub the horse's withers. Eboracum snaked around and bit his mailed shoulder. The Viking swore and whacked him on the nose. The horse began to curvet and scream like an unbroken colt.

"One arm torn by a wolf, the other by a horse!" He rubbed his shoulder and cursed again. "By the wrath of the Valkyr, what more do I need?"

"Mayhap a groom," Taras said, "since you can't handle this fine stallion." She walked close to Eboracum and spoke his name. He stopped kicking and thrust his muzzle under her chin.

The Viking's countenance darkened. "It is time we rode on." He caught the horse's bridle. "That is, if you can make it to the stable, you spavined old wretch."

"He's a good, dear lad, much too good for a spavined old Viking."

"Spavined, is it?"

"Aye, and broken-winded, too. Now help me mount. That is, if you've strength enough in your wretched old arms."

He bowed with mock stiffness. "This doddering old fool shall try not to tumble you into the stream."

They rode out of the trees a few minutes later. Taras caught her breath. On either side of the path, blue mountains gored the sunset sky. Streams tumbled down the slopes to fill tarns and lakes. Sheep grazed on hillsides, and bees darted in and out of flaxen fields.

As darkness descended on the valley, cold wind swept down from the heights and tugged at the riders. Taras pulled the wolfskin close about her and relaxed against her captor. He curved his right arm around her like a shield.

A stone wall protected a group of longhouses on the shore of a lake. Light glimmered through a doorway, and for an instant music and laughter filled the night, then the door shut and the world became dark and quiet again. Taras closed her eyes and let the Viking hold her.

Hours later, Taras awoke as the Viking breathed her name and gently shook her. She gasped in fear and astonishment. A massive fortress commanded the summit of a savage, moon-washed fell. Above battlements and towers, pennants snapped in the mountain wind.

She hadn't imagined the Viking would take her to a fortress. Sweet Mary, could it be the castle of Lord Cynewulf, himself? She had to know, yet she dared not say the name. The Viking was suspicious enough of her already, judging from his talk of spells. If he realized she knew of Cynewulf, he might guess her ill intent. He might take the potion and lock her in a tower where she could do no harm.

"What is this place?" she whispered.

"Castle Ilovar."

She shut her eyes in disappointment. Ilovar. King Ethelred had said nothing of Ilovar. She wouldn't find Lord Cynewulf here, after all.

"The castle is fashioned after those of the Saracens," the Viking said. Taras didn't care. She squeezed back tears.

They rode through a village at the foot of the mountain, then the Viking dismounted. He bade Taras remain in the saddle while he led the tired horse. The steep road twisted back and forth like a snake's coils. Taras knew that an army trying to attack the castle would have to advance in thin ranks, making it easy prey for the defenders. With every clop of Eboracum's hooves, Taras's heart grew heavier. The castle would be hard to escape. Mayhap impossible.

When they reached the last turn a shout went up from the walls. The castle gates creaked open. The Viking mounted behind her and urged Eboracum through the gates to the circular barbican. Shouting in Danish, warriors crowded around to clasp hands with the Viking. Some took advantage of the confusion to squeeze Taras's thighs. She kicked their hands away.

"Stop kicking," the Viking said.

"Tell them not to touch me, then. You may keep your hands off me, as well. Let me down!"

"You wish me to drop you into the laps of these fighting men?"

Taras ground her teeth. She had failed Ethelred, failed her mother, failed England. She'd even failed herself. It was all *his* fault. "You scurrilous knave," she said, twisting to glare at him. "How I detest you!"

He flashed her a smile as he reached for someone's hand. "So you claim, Taras."

"It is true, every word of it."

"I must try to bear up."

"Always the jester, aren't you?"

"Not always." He cupped her chin and dropped his voice to a husky whisper. "It was no jest when I held you in the ferns and tasted your lips."

She slapped his hand aside. "You dishonor me when before these men you say such things."

"Only a few of them understand your barbaric English tongue. Your secret is safe with me."

"My secret? I have naught to hide. 'Twas no lovers' tryst that brought us together, but your brutal conquest."

"Have I made a conquest, Taras?"

His soft question compelled her gaze more surely than

the touch of his fingers. She felt unable to turn away, weak inside, as though he'd sapped the very marrow from her bones. All that remained to her was hate. "May God damn you to eternal fire, Viking."

"It is better than spending eternity naked on an ice floe."

Eboracum clattered onto the stone bridge. Taras heard a waterfall roaring in the dark void below. The bridge shook under the weight of the crowd. Taras buried her fingers in Eboracum's mane, praying the bridge wouldn't collapse.

They reached the outer bailey and the Viking guided the horse under an iron portcullis's bristling spikes. Within the inner bailey a stone keep reared into the sky, its turrets scraping the crystal stars.

One of the men took Eboracum's reins. The Viking eased out of the saddle and helped Taras dismount. A dog as large as a wolf leaped baying through the crowd and planted its forepaws on the Viking's chest.

"Good Warf!" the Viking said, thumping its ribs. "I've missed you, too. Back to your post now."

As the dog bounded off, a grizzled warrior rushed out of the keep and down the steps. He hurled men aside as though they were cut from linen and, roaring like a bear, lifted the Viking several inches off his feet. He wept in unabashed joy.

"I'm glad to see you, too, seneschal," the Viking said, laughing. "Now let me down before you break another rib."

Taras chewed her bottom lip. Everyone acted as though the Viking were master. What if he were the lord of the castle? How could she hope to find an ally to help her escape and get to Lord Cynewulf?

The Viking, giving her a solemn look, extended his arm to her. She took it and let him walk her upstairs to the keep. The seneschal hurried past them to fling open the iron-bound doors.

"Come into the great hall of Ilovar, Taras," the Viking said. "Come into your new home."

Chapter Six

He led her into a vestibule, where several tall warriors clad in bearskin and leather stepped aside to make a path. On legs as numb as posts Taras walked under a stone archway into the largest hall she'd ever seen. Rainbows broke from curved iron sconces festooned with crystal prisms. Light danced upon the walls to flirt with tall, narrow windows of colored glass. She gained a brief impression of pictures in the glass before her gaze riveted on the hall's noisy occupants.

Warriors and ladies with hair the color of ripe flax crowded long trestle tables. Standing almost in the fire inside several monstrous fireplaces, cooks turned spits laden with venison and boar, while maids hurried to add to the mountains of roasted meats, bread, cheese, and honeycomb on the groaning boards. In a high gallery, musicians played horns and flutes, pipes and drums. A juggler tossed a flaming torch into the air and had to leap onto a table to catch it. He stepped into a platter of sweetbreads before someone pushed him off.

Taras stood in amazement only a second or two before the seneschal gave a great bellow. There was sudden silence; then everyone jumped to their feet and bowed. They rose again with a thunderous shout.

The seneschal roared a phrase in Danish as he hurried across the hall and grasped the Viking's right hand, dropping to one knee for an instant before rising to shout once more. All Taras understood was the last: "Lord Cynewulf of Amandolar!"

In horror she stared up at the man who claimed her. He smiled at her, then raised his arms and shouted in Danish. The cries of the people fairly shook the vaulted roof.

Taras stumbled against the archway. The varlet had deceived her! Nay, she had deceived herself. From the very beginning she had known he was no housecarl.

"Blackguard!" she screamed over the noise. He swung his head to look at her. There was no kindness, no repentance there. "You made a fool of me!"

"You made one of yourself when you entered my lands, woman."

She flung off his wolfskin mantle and lunged at his face. Before she could claw him, the seneschal snatched her off the floor. She ground her heel down his naked shin, scrolling off flesh. Bellowing, he flung her to the granite floor and raised his big fist.

Lord Cynewulf knocked his arm aside. In English he said, "Seneschal, enough!"

"The Briton needs taming, lord!"

"You shall not be the one to do it."

"Neither shall you, you lying scoundrel!" Taras railed.

But the Viking turned his back on her. He stalked like a great wolf through the hall, nodding, clasping hands, laughing with his people; then he seated himself on the dais and beckoned to a serving maid. "Ardeth, see that Lady Taras has food and a place by the fire."

"I need nothing from you," Taras said in a voice roiling with ire. The folk laughed, then they turned away as though she were of no account and resumed their merrymaking.

The seneschal caught her arm and propelled her across the hall. He pushed her down on an empty bench before a fireplace in a deserted portion of the room. When she tried to jump up he clamped his huge fingers into her shoulder until she wept with pain. "You will stay there, Briton. Your master bids it."

Across the hall, Lord Cynewulf studied his captive. She was a strange one, stiff and proud, yet capable of great sensuality. He wondered at his reaction to her. It wasn't like him to put off gratification; many captive wenches had quenched his battle lust ere they reached the slaver's block. This one, though, was different. Briton or no, he wouldn't sell her. She angered and amused him.

Yet there was another, more compelling reason to keep her. She was King Ethelred's cousin. Better if she was his sister, but a kinswoman was enough. There might be a use for her. He would have to think upon it.

He watched Denholm the Seneschal shoulder his way to the dais. He was holding the wolfskin mantle. "It stinks of the Briton," Denholm said.

"She doesn't stink," the Viking said. "The nymph smells of cedar and sweet herbs."

"Bah, you bedded her so much your brain is addled."

Cynewulf opened his mouth to deny the charge, then closed it. The old war dog would laugh if he knew the truth. He might think he'd gone soft. Cynewulf was too tired for verbal sparring.

Denholm pushed away a cup of nabid that a serving

wench offered and commandeered her carafe instead. He quaffed deeply, belched, and said, "I was concerned when your messenger said you'd left the patrol to go a 'wenching. 'Tis not safe to ride alone in these troubled times."

"Ah, the English army poses no more threat to me than the maiden yonder," Cynewulf said.

"Beware of pride, lord. Many a warrior falls who underestimates his enemy."

Cynewulf eyed Taras. She was staring into the fire, ignoring the trencher someone had set beside her. "I do not underestimate any man," he said.

"Or woman?"

Cynewulf snorted. "She is a child, a foolish Briton."

" 'Twas no child I touched but moments ago," the seneschal said with a chuckle, raising the carafe to her in a silent toast. "Her breasts are plump as partridges—"

Cynewulf caught Denholm's forearm and slammed it down on the table. The carafe crashed to the floor with a noise that turned all heads. At Cynewulf's fierce look they glanced hurriedly away. "The wench is mine, seneschal," Cynewulf growled. "Touch her at your peril."

Denholm's mouth split in a grin. "Methinks the young pup is in love!"

"Bah, you are growing dottery with age." Cynewulf thrust aside his arm and took a long pull of nabid.

Much as Denholm annoyed him, he was glad to be home again after a month of riding and fighting. He would fight again next week, but this time it would be for pleasure. The Viking warlords owing him allegiance were coming to Castle Ilovar for the *moot*, the assembly, as they did once a year. Together they would lay battle plans for the spring, then, after the business was done, they'd have a tournament. It would be good to break spears for amusement for a change. Amusement or not, Cynewulf intended to win weapons, armor, and horses.

Sensing his thoughts, Denholm said, "The tournament will give you a chance to prove yourself before the wench."

"There is no need."

"Humph, you hold her heart in your palm already, then," the older man said with a laugh.

"What do you wist of women, Seneschal?"

"Who brought you your first wench these many winters past, eh?" When Cynewulf only shrugged, he demanded, "What will you do with this one?"

"Enjoy her."

Denholm tugged his beard. "Did you enjoy her attempt to tear out your eyes just now?"

"She was angry."

"She is dangerous." Denholm dropped his fist to the table and eyed his lord with disapproval. "I feel in my bones that she is no ordinary wench. This one would kill you."

Cynewulf swung his gaze to Taras. She was looking over her shoulder at him. Even from a distance, Cynewulf could see the stain of anger in her cheeks. "Laying claim to her is worth the risk. Owning her is worth any hazard."

"Will you say so when she carves out your liver?"

Scowling, Cynewulf leaned back in his chair and shut his eyes. Denholm chuckled and said, "By the old sea gods, I never thought to witness you in this state!"

"What?"

"Why, the unholy state of emasculation. The chit has bound you to her skirts, I trow."

Cynewulf opened his eyes and looked askance at his seneschal. "You underestimate my powers, old man."

"Methinks you underestimate hers. You are a prince among men, but, perhaps, mere putty in her hands."

"She is my prisoner, Denholm. She controls no part of me. I toy with her because it pleasures me to do so. When I tire of her, I'll sell her back to the cursed Britons who spawned her."

"Will you, my lord?"

"Bah! You will never change your nagging ways!" Catching up his mantle, Cynewulf shoved out of his chair and crossed the hall to the winding staircase. His path brought him close to Taras.

"Why did you not tell me that you are lord of this place?"

Her soft voice arrested him in his tracks. He set his hand on the banister and said, "Given your clumsiness near rivers and cliffs, I feared to further alarm you with my true identity, lest some calamity befall you."

"Indeed? It wasn't that you doubted your capacity to kidnap a simple maid?"

"There is very little simple about you."

"So I am dangerous, then." For an instant her fingers strayed to the pewter vial, then she dropped her hand to her lap. "Do you lock me in the dungeon now or save time and hang me?"

Cynewulf rubbed the bristles on his chin as though contemplating his answer. "I shall consider the question while I bathe. Join me?"

Taras bit her tongue to still an angry retort. Every word battle with him made her look like a cloud-witted bumpkin. She felt the air move as he turned to make his way up the staircase, but his feet made no sound.

Maybe he would drown in the bath. She wished she could pour boiling water over his head. She squirmed with shame when she thought of the opportunity she'd missed this morning. Blast it, she could have trickled the potion into his mouth while he lay feverish from the wolf bite. Instead, she'd nursed and coddled him. Fool! Imbecile! She could imagine Ethelred's thundering anger if he ever found out. She dropped her face to her hands and sat for a long time, berating herself.

"My men killed this boar not far from where I captured you," Cynewulf said.

Taras started. She had not heard him return. He was squatting beside her, holding a wooden charger full of meat. Water dripped off his hair onto the mantle pinned at his left shoulder. A bead of blood glistened on his now clean-shaven jaw. She must have been lost in her musings for longer than she'd thought.

"Begone with you, Viking," she said, but her voice lacked conviction. Her heart fluttered like a bird in her breast. His comeliness mesmerized her, made her weak and breathless. She'd never seen such cobalt-blue eyes.

"You're hungry," he said. He touched her bare forearm with one finger.

She winced as though he'd touched her with a branding iron. "Why should the Lord of Plunderers serve *me?*"

A muscle tensed in his jaw. "It would be a sin to starve a creature taken from the wild."

"You speak as though I were naught but a newborn falcon to be trained to your gauntlet!"

"You are." His eyes deepened in shade. He raised a morsel to her lips. "And I will teach you to feed from my hand."

Taras dashed the meat to the floor and jumped up. Cynewulf reached his feet first, and stood frowning down at her. "You could sooner teach the wild gyr on the mountain!" Taras said. "She might eat."

"Meaning you will not? Perhaps I will force you."

"Try it, and I will kill you!"

"With what? Your claws, or your sharp tongue?" He thrust the charger into her hands. "Eat."

She hurled it against the fireplace with such violence that it broke in half. Cynewulf's lips drew away from his teeth in a wrathful smile. "You grow more spiteful by the hour, my foolish little Briton."

"Insult me as you will. The jibes of a scral-topped knave matter not to me!"

"Then why do your cheeks burn like the setting sun?"

Taras turned her back on him. As her gaze fell upon a warrior quaffing ale, she said, "They wassail at your expense."

"Would you have me starve my own people? Methinks your temper would improve were you to wassail a bit, yourself."

Taras forced a small smile and settled onto the bench. "You may be right, lord."

She saw uncertainty flash in his eyes, then he snapped his fingers. "Ardeth, fetch wine!"

A maid hastened over to set her tray on the hearth. She splashed wine into a cup and thrust it at Taras, then, lingering, she poured wine for her master. She shimmied a little, forcing her breasts nearly out of her bodice. Even a blind man could see what she was offering.

Taras fought a powerful impulse to snatch Ardeth by the hair and beat her against the fireplace like a rug. Dear heavens, what emotion was this? Jealousy?

Ardeth gazed up at him, then set aside the carafe and brazenly ran her fingers over his ribs. "Warring has kept you strong and hard, my lord."

He tilted back his head to drink. Ardeth pressed her bosom against him and whispered, "Mayhap you crave a bit of softness now that the victory is won."

Cynewulf lowered the cup and stared down at her out of smoldering eyes. "The victory will not be won until King Ethelred lies dead upon the bare ground. Go, offer your softness to those who desire it."

"Yea, lord." As she picked up her tray she threw Taras a glance of animosity. Taras glared back. Her fingers curled and uncurled, yearning to snatch out those lovely yellow tresses. Instead, she seized the carafe off the tray and plunked it onto the bench. She didn't know how much Cynewulf had drunk from his cup. She didn't want him to run low before she could poison him.

"I see I am not the only woman you mistreat," Taras said.

"Had I rutted with her on the floor at your feet, would you have considered her better treated?"

"You will surely roast in the devil's fire for your insolence, sir."

"Ah, the spell weaver decrees my fate yet again."

"I am no spell weaver!" She denied the accusation with fervor.

Cynewulf kicked aside the broken charger and sat down on the hearthstone. Resting his forearms on his knees, he leaned close enough for his breath to stir her hair. Taras held her ground.

"Why do you fear to be called 'spell weaver,' Taras?"

It was the last question she'd expected him to ask. She almost touched the vial. Twisting her fingers, she wondered how she could pollute his wine without him seeing her. Her hands began to tremble.

"Why?" he repeated.

She didn't want to give the answer. To say it aloud might make it come true for her. The last thing on earth she wanted to be was a spell weaver. Her mother had taken the terrible oaths of alchemy, but not her. She had only tried to give solace and help through herbs. She'd never dreamed she could transform a man into a frog. Her mother's sorcery must have rubbed off.

"The church cleanses witches by fire," she said low.

"Ah, then you are a witch."

"Nay! I am an ordinary woman."

"Then why do you fear my jest?"

"To the church, the charge of witchcraft is enough to consign one to the flames."

71

Cynewulf chuckled. "And you called *me* pagan. Not even the terrible Thor demands the blood of man or maid for such a charge."

"The worship of Thor is false."

"The worship of priests who condemn innocents to die for sorcery is false, my lady, yet you would throw yourself on the pyre were they to demand it."

No, indeed she would not. She would run and hide like a craven little mouse. Unable to look at him lest he sense her thoughts, she dropped her gaze. Through her bliaut she saw the outline of the vial. His mouth was but a breath away. If only she could propel the liquid to his lips and get it over with.

The sudden image of those handsome lips becoming a vulgar, wide green mouth made her recoil. She edged away from him along the bench and leaned over to pluck at the rug before the fire. Her hand shook so hard, she barely managed to tear a thread from the weave.

"You would not harm my property if you knew the cost," the Viking said. "The rugs in my hall come from the East."

Glad for the interruption to her thoughts, she snapped, "Cost? Surely you speak of the cost in lives, since a Viking plunderer scarcely buys such adornments with money."

"You wound me, wench. I bought them at a marketplace in Byzantium years ago. No blood was spilled."

"None on that particular occasion, my lord pillager."

Cynewulf pressed his fist to his forehead. Taras wondered if she had shamed him before his people. Everyone in the great hall was watching them although they feigned disinterest. "Do you try to act a crosspatch," Cynewulf said, "or does it come naturally to you?"

Once more, anger overwhelmed all other emotions. She ought to uncork the vial and dash it in his face. He thought she was nothing, an amusement. Little did he know how quickly she could kill him, how glad she'd be to crush his hopping green body under her heel. She couldn't bear his insolence. How dared he, a filthy Viking, speak so to the king's own cousin? Her mission didn't matter as much as reclaiming her honor.

"You do not know in how much peril you place yourself, speaking so to me," she said.

"Indeed? Perhaps you will tell me, that I might be properly warned."

"I'll tell you naught!"

He reached out and snatched her off the bench, forcing her to the floor between his knees. She tried to strike him in his vulnerable spot, but he caught her wrists in one powerful hand and held her fast. "Tell me, Taras," he murmured, leaning close to her face. "Tell me how perilous you are."

"I could kill you in an instant!"

"Mmm, that I believe. Tell me more."

If he would let go of her hands, she'd show him more, by Heaven. "My own cousins fear me," she said, struggling. "They said they would hang themselves if I did not hie to the forest."

"And so you honored their pleas."

"I did not honor them. They had to run me off with hounds."

"I fully understand how they felt."

He didn't believe her, she could hear it in his voice. Everything she'd told him was true. The only part she'd left out was that she'd been ten summers old at the time. "I—I came back one night and threw one of them out of the keep in his undertunic!"

"Indeed?"

"And then I commanded the servants to drag him into the hog wallow and hold him there while the beasts trod upon him."

"Nay!"

"And some of the hogs escaped into the fields and trampled the young wheat, while the others rushed into the hall and overturned the lamps, catching the rushes afire!"

"In all my travels I have never heard such things," he said, gazing at her with respect. "You are a most fearsome wench, one that the mightiest warrior might dread."

She could hear laughter beneath the surface of his words. He searched her eyes until she began to squirm. She suddenly felt like a child of ten.

"If the penalty for weaving spells is death by fire," Cynewulf mused, "what price do your priests exact for lying in so dismal a fashion?"

"I didn't lie." She tried to jerk her arms free.

He let go with an abruptness that sent her crashing backward.

"Would you like to go to Byzantium?" he asked, as though he hadn't noticed her accident.

"Would you like to go to hell?" she said, gritting her teeth.

"As I mentioned the last time you cursed me, hell has certain advantages over an ice floe."

"Then may God encase you in ice, instead, since you prefer fire. Now go away, Viking." She would have to wait until later to poison him.

She felt his warm fingers brush her cheek. She trembled but did not pull away. "Now is the time for truth, Lady Taras," he whispered. "Tell me, why were you in the forest?"

What had Camlann told her to say? That she'd come to buy herbs? He'd never believe that feeble excuse. "Just go away."

"Lie down," he said. "Stretch out upon the rug."

She squinted at him in alarm. "Why? So you can mistreat me on the hard stone floor as you wished to do to Ardeth?"

"I would not mistreat an untried falcon. Now lie down."

She did not want to obey, but she hurt too much to resist.

He gently pushed her onto her stomach and began to rub her back. His fingertips burned through her gown like hot wax.

"You are very tense. Let go." He massaged her more deeply.

Her headache disappeared and she knew she was drifting into sleep. She didn't want to, not with the Viking's hands on her. She tried to keep her eyes open but soon she drifted off. She had plenty of time. She would turn him into a frog tomorrow.

Chapter Seven

She slept at last, but Cynewulf continued to caress her back. He wanted to slip his hand over her firm buttocks. He restrained himself only because people were watching. He finally took off his mantle, wrapped her in it, and lifted her. She stirred but was too exhausted to awaken.

As he started for the staircase, Denholm pushed through the crowd. In a drunken fog he roared, "You are taking her to your chamber at last! I thought you'd never get round to it."

"Lower your braying voice!" He mounted the stairs with the seneschal close behind him. Halfway to the top, Cynewulf turned on him. "Where in the name of the Asir are you going?"

"I would come along to watch your back."

"I need neither a nursemaid nor a voyeur. Now go."

The seneschal stopped, but his laughter followed Cynewulf up the steps. "Be sure to remove all sharp objects from the she-lion's reach, my lord, paying special heed to her claws!"

Cynewulf glanced down at the sleeping maiden. "Goose-capped Viking," he murmured. "I have no intention of declawing her."

Reaching his third-floor chamber, Cynewulf laid her in his high, carved bed and covered her with furs. She moaned and wet her lips.

"By Odin's sword, you are lovely beyond imagination," Cynewulf whispered. He hung his wolfskin on a peg by the door, then drew up a low stool carved like a dragon's head. He rested his elbows on the bed and his chin on his hands. The firelight cast a dim glow over Taras's face. "You need a strong hand, wench, lest you come to grief."

Yawning, he rubbed his eyes and settled his head onto the furs beside her. Just before he fell asleep, he reached under the furs for her hand. He would protect her just as surely as his falcons. And like them, she would learn to heed his call.

Light slanted through an arched casement window onto Taras's face. She opened her eyes and stared up at the ceiling beams, trying to fathom where she was. This wasn't her chamber in Ethelred's palace. She rolled her head on the pillow and saw Cynewulf lying halfway out of bed. Holding her hand, he was breathing on her neck.

She bolted upright and hit him on the side of the head. "You filthy-minded Viking pillager, how dare you crawl into the furs with me?"

With clumsiness born of exhaustion, Cynewulf sprang up and stumbled over a stool, crashing onto a white bearskin rug. He cracked his skull on the hearthstone. Taras launched herself on top of him and pummeled his face.

"Desist, you crazed shrew!" He spun her onto her back and straddled her hips, pinning her arms over her head with one hand. He touched a swelling bruise on his left cheekbone and fingered the back of his head. "Are you devoid of all reason?"

"Are you devoid of all decency, to assault me while I slumbered?"

"I never touched you, wench. You are too stained with travel to excite my lust."

"Stained!" Endowed with fresh strength, she wrenched her arms free. He dropped full-length upon her. She began to screech and writhe. She couldn't budge him, but her gown rode up to her waist.

"Yea, that is good, Taras," he said. "Thrust your bareness upon my sword again."

"I hate you!"

"Good. It would be a sad thing if you began to love me too soon, for then I would tire of you."

"Hellhound! Get off me—leave my chamber!"

"Nay, there is something we must do first." A wicked smile curved his lips as he dragged his hand down her side and gripped her hip, pressing his burning length against her. All the while he stared into her eyes with hawk-like intensity, tearing down her strength to resist. "Yea, there is but one thing to do before I leave this chamber."

"I shall do nothing with you!" She tried to reach the pewter vial, but he clamped her hands against her sides.

"We can do it like animals," he said, "or we can do it like civilized beings, but be warned, do it we shall." She felt herself warming to his suggestion, though she knew she should not.

"Do what?"

"Why, prepare for the day. There's work to do." He rolled off her and thrust to his feet, dusting his tunic. His lustful expression changed to a paternal smile.

"By Saint Titus's garters!" Taras said, yanking her gown down over her hips. "You take a child's delight in making a fool of me. I've never hated anyone so much in my life!"

"So you've told me several times already."

"It won't be the last, I assure you."

"The day will be long," he said. "Amuse yourself with what speech you will." After setting the stool back on its clawed feet, he sat down to gaze out the window at the ragged mountain spine off in the northwest.

His indifference after their wild tussle on the floor galled her. He stole her composure and made her a plaything to pick up or discard according to his mood. He was capricious and cruel, a barbarian despite the fine trappings with which he surrounded himself.

She picked up a fireplace iron and contemplated attacking him, but he only smiled and propped his shoulder blades against the bed before returning his gaze to the mountains. She rammed the iron into the embers and stirred until a flame shot up. "You've broken every bone in my body, Viking."

"You should disrobe. I'll gladly minister to your hurts."

"I'll care for my own injuries. Begone from my chamber!"

"Your chamber? You desire to nest with me, fledgling?"

"Nest with you?"

"There is room." He patted the bed. "I'll not begrudge you a corner, so long as you do not kick and snore."

"I slept in *your* bed last night?"

"I did not mind sharing, though it amazed me to find so slight a wench hogging the entire bed. You're larger than you look when you're asleep. It must be those spells you weave."

"Oh, I detest you!" She hurled the iron into the fire and stomped to the door.

"You'll doubtless find Denholm just outside."

She stopped with her hand on the latch. "You intend to keep me prisoner here?"

"Only as long as it takes me to wash you." Unlimbering,

he went to wrench open the door. Denholm was nowhere in sight. He yelled down the gallery, "Ardeth, fetch hot water for a bath!"

"I'll not bathe in front of you," Taras said. She tried to slip past him, but he slammed the door.

"You'll do as you're bidden."

"We'll see about that." Storming to the casement, she froze with one foot on the ledge. There was a fifty-foot drop down the castle wall to a jagged, unscalable cliff comprising the northern battlement.

"Jumping is not a good plan," Cynewulf said. "Unless, of course, you have wings in your little vial of sorcerer's tricks."

Taras wrapped her fingers around the pewter vial, but when he made no move to take it, she let her gaze drift to the low hills between the castle and the distant mountains. Silvery lakes reflected the mountains and clouds. Bordered by stone walls and streams, an ocean of grain riffled in the wind. A curious sense of calmness stole into her soul.

Cynewulf padded over and placed his hands on the ledge on either side of her. His breath warmed her shoulders as he leaned down to whisper, "Have you seen aught like this before?"

"Nay, lord." Her calmness fled, exorcised by burning excitement, a sensual arousal of her inner core. She did not even try to understand her shifting emotions, for she knew she could not. She almost leaned back into his arms.

The chamber door opened. Taras ducked under Cynewulf's arm and stood against the wall. Ardeth and a small army of servants marched into the room, each bearing a steaming kettle. They pulled back a curtain, revealing an alcove where a brass bathing tub stood.

Cynewulf caught Taras's eye, his gaze holding a silent promise. Steeling herself to the villain's charm, she folded her arms and regarded him coldly.

"You are not as haughty as you'd have me believe," he said. "Cold wenches do not writhe so exquisitely."

"They do when crushed beneath an oaf's fearsome weight."

"You will soon grow used to it, Lady Taras of Widnes." He brushed her cheek with his fingertips. Before she could strike him, he crossed to the alcove to watch the servants fill the tub.

Taras raised her hand to her cheek and considered his tall, princely form. Despite her intentions, she was finding it hard to think of him as a barbarian. In truth, he was kinder than either Ethelred or her cousin Camlann.

Cynewulf's eyes flashed like blue lightning. "Your bath is ready."

"I have no intention of bathing."

Cynewulf spoke in rapid Danish. The servants moved toward Taras, giggling. She backed to the fireplace. Cynewulf said, "You have naught to fear, Taras. Even a Briton doesn't melt at the touch of a soapy cloth."

Taras pushed the women aside and strode to the tub. "I'm aware of the merits of soap and water, but I'll not ply them until all of you are gone."

"Very well." Cynewulf dismissed the servants.

"I said *all* of you, sir."

"Perchance you need help with your garments."

She yanked the curtain closed, stripped, and stepped into the hot water. As she lowered herself, she had to drag in sharp gulps of air to endure the heat.

"You forgot the soap, my lady," Cynewulf said, parting the curtain.

Taras snatched the soap out of his hand and kicked water into his face. "Begone while I bathe!"

"You only play at bathing." With one sweep of his hand he ripped the curtain from the rod and sprang into the tub.

Taras tried to shove his head under water, but he rolled her onto his chest and controlled her with a firm hand.

"If you need instruction on bathing," he said, "ask me to disrobe before inviting me into your bath."

"I didn't invite you! Let me go!"

"Not until you are clean." He gazed down at her breasts pressed against his tunic. "I'm glad to see not all of you was bruised during the journey."

She tried again to thrust him off, but he slid his hands down her hips. "What are you doing down there?" she cried.

"Seeking the soap. It seems to have slipped between your legs."

"That's not soap—stop touching me!"

"But I cannot find it."

"Stop! I'll get it." She groped in the water between his thighs.

"What you've found is hard and wet, but methinks it will not lather," he said with a devilish grin.

She snatched her hand away. "You are contemptible!"

Cynewulf's grin deepened as he held up the soap. "True. I have had it the entire time, but if you would rather rub the other bar, I won't complain."

"Blackguard! I'll not stay here another second!"

"Have you never been bathed before?"

"Not by a man."

"Ah. Have you ever bathed a man?"

"Certainly not."

Cynewulf clicked his tongue. "When I've traveled in your barbaric country, the lady of the house always bathes the guests."

"Neither my lady mother nor I ever bathe anyone. I won't start with you."

"You're missing one of life's great pleasures. Be still now; I do not wish to trouble your sore spots."

Holding her around the waist, he glided the soap down her spine, over her buttocks, and up and down the back of her thighs. She squirmed against his arm, then gave up in despair. She might more easily break an iron band. If only she could distract him long enough, she'd open the vial and fix him for good.

He glided the soap inside her thighs. She cried, "Stop! You have no right!"

"I have every right." His breath licked her like a dragon's tongue. The desire in his eyes terrified her. When she tried to pull away he gripped the back of her neck and pulled her mouth to his. She squeezed her eyes shut as if to make him disappear.

"Kiss me, Taras," he murmured. "Your lips are warm and sweet as wild roses. Open your petals to me."

"Please . . . nay, nay . . . please."

His mouth closed over hers to wage intimate warfare, teasing, tantalizing, until she throbbed with every beat of his heart and couldn't bear his exquisite rasping against her belly. She writhed when he dropped the soap and caressed her slippery thighs and hips with his bare hands.

As Cynewulf pressed himself hard against her, he imagined how she'd feel wrapped around him. But for the leather between them, he would whirl her in a wild storm of lust. She was a snared falcon and he the falconer.

When he stared into her deep green eyes he read the same desperation he'd seen in the forest. The image of a falcon he'd injured in his youth flashed into his mind. By Thor's red hammer, he could not do it.

Swearing, he thrust her off his chest and swung out of the tub. Water streamed down his tunic to puddle on the flagstones. His manhood jutted large and rigid against his leather braies, and he ached to finish what he'd started. Nay, by the gods—he'd be ruled by his mind, not his flesh.

He was not barbarian enough to rut with a helpless woman. Not anymore.

"Damn it, wench, you madden me."

"How can you play such games, then blame me for your passion?" she asked in a cracked whisper. "Don't you ever touch me again."

"You feel shame, Taras?"

"I? You're the one who should feel shame!"

"So I must temper the wind to the shorn lamb, eh?"

"What is that supposed to mean?"

"It is a Norse proverb. It means I must take your shame upon myself."

"I have none to take. Your shame is your own, you misbegotten son of the devil! Now begone from here!"

"No one orders me from my chamber, wench."

"Then I shall throw you from your chamber after I've bent the fire iron over your thick skull!"

"Beware trying something you have not strength to finish."

Taras slid lower into the water and fingered the pewter vial. "You cannot watch your back all the time, Viking."

Cynewulf snorted. His muscles rippling like a lion's through his wet tunic, he strode to a chest near the window and extracted a pair of knee-length linen braies, an undertunic, and a many colored tunic of wool.

Taras looked away when he began stripping off his wet clothing, but when she heard his garments plop onto the floor she stole a glance. His back was wide and tanned deep bronze, his buttocks pale and muscular. She clapped her hand over her eyes.

Detecting her small gasp of surprise, Cynewulf smiled grimly. The wench was curious, was she? Perhaps he should turn around and let her see exactly what she had wrought. His swollen flesh had decreased not one jot in size.

Why should he choose this time in his life to develop tender feelings? Women were pretty toys to be used and discarded according to his need. He was the master here—why place this woman in a crystal box? She was his enemy, after all. A kinswoman of Ethelred deserved no quarter.

Muttering, he yanked on his clothing and buckled a wide leather belt around his waist. He sat on the bed to pull on his long woolen stockings. He tried to ignore the titillating feel of the furs against his thighs, the womanly scent clinging to the bed. With sharp tugs he laced his sandals over his calves.

His eyes briefly touched Taras as he buckled his baldric over his shoulder and hung his sword. He crossed to the fireplace to look into a brass shield while he scraped whiskers from his face with a sharp knife. He nicked himself twice but persevered; he'd never favored wearing a beard as other men did. The damned things itched and got in the way of his sword arm.

He pinned his mantle over his shoulder with an amber brooch, then returned to the chest for a white, long-sleeved woolen chemise with pleated skirts, and a bliaut narrowly striped in heather, moss, and violet. Another minute passed while he unearthed a silver girdle set with black pearls, and a long silver necklace adorned with dangling amber gripping beasts. He laid the finery on the bed.

"Get dressed, Briton."

"Turn your back."

"And have you stick a knife in it? Get out of the tub ere I come in and get you."

Taras slowly clambered out and splayed her hands over her groin. Ashamed or not, she raised her chin to a haughty angle. "Have you not the decency to give me a towel?"

He stared at her breasts. "Cold?"

She tossed her head.

"Come and dry yourself by the fire. Come."

"Come? *Come*, as if it is easy to parade past you clad in my skin!"

"It is easy for me to watch you."

"You're a devil," she said, ice crackling in her tone. "I hope an angel flies you to the very gates of Heaven—"

"A pleasant place, I'm sure."

"—and St. Peter hurls your black soul down to the flaming hell where it belongs!"

"You could use a bit of eternal fire yourself, judging by your nipples. My, how cold you are. How nice for me."

"I hate you more than I have words to express."

"Mayhap I will teach you my tongue, then, to increase your wordskill. Now hie to the fire ere I drag you."

Anger lent her a sort of brazen courage. Making no further attempt to hide her body, she strode to the fireplace. If the barbarian wanted to stare, let him stare. *May your eyes pop like a frog's, you heathen wretch.*

Cynewulf seated himself on the window ledge and gazed at her without expression. She turned this way and that, lifting her hair to the heat, ignoring his existence. She felt like a sparrow playing games with a hawk.

"Comb your hair. I find mops displeasing," Cynewulf said. He tossed her a silver comb and watched her use it. "You are a beautiful one, Taras."

She dropped the comb and turned her back. His hot gaze licked her spine. If she didn't turn him into a frog soon, she'd surely lose her wits. She couldn't bear this shame another hour.

"You have yet to pay for venturing into my forest," Cynewulf said. She stiffened but did not reply. "If you are finished drying yourself, perhaps you would like to dress . . . unless you wish to pay your penance now."

"I'll never pay penance to you!" She spun around and raised her fists.

Desire smoldering in his gaze, he left the window and slowly walked toward her. Stopping, he hooked his thumbs in his belt and rocked back on his heels. "Shall I make you kneel and swallow those words?"

She sidled past him to the bed and snatched on the chemise and bliaut, girding it at her hips. She tugged the bodice up to cover more bosom.

"Leave it," Cynewulf said. "Put on the necklace."

Taras looked at the silver necklace on the bed. Holding their amber heels in their forepaws, the barbaric little gripping beasts laughed up at her.

"I'll not wear your pagan relics," she said, but her voice shook. He was too close to her, too warm and big and powerful. She lifted her hands to the vial and carefully began to pry out the stopper.

He caught her shoulders and spun her around. His heated touch penetrated her to the bone. With one tug of his hands he could bare her. Her fingers fell away from the vial.

"Obey me, Taras," he whispered, "or I'll take my due now."

Chapter Eight

She had no choice. He was as motionless as a lynx on a cliff, and his hand was hanging on her shoulder. He would not wait forever. If she tested him again, she would surely pay the price.

Mayhap she wanted to pay it. That thought frightened her most of all. "I'll put on the necklace," she said.

He let go of her and stepped back. Her skin where his fingers had brushed felt hot and wanting, aching for another touch. Frustrated, she dropped the necklace.

Cynewulf picked it up. "Lift your hair."

She realized he'd planned to adorn her himself, after all. In commanding her to put it on, he'd asserted his power over her again. Damn and damn!

She almost refused him, but his eyes promised burning ravishment. She remembered how his naked back looked, and could almost feel its might. She was powerless against such strength. She couldn't defy him again without bringing down his wrath. Trembling, she gathered her hair on top of her head and waited.

As though he were considering whether to buy her, he walked around her, tapping his cheek with his forefinger. Taras lifted her nose and viewed him out of half-closed eyes. She wanted to rip him with her nails.

He stopped behind her. She felt the hairs lift on the nape of her neck, but she was too proud to turn to look at him. She drew herself up another half-inch and tried to quiet the staccato hammering in her spine.

He touched her neck. She caught her breath in suspense. She heard the clinking of amber and felt the gripping beasts' cool, round bodies kiss her bosom. He clicked shut the clasp.

Cynewulf spun her toward him, pressing hard fingers into her shoulders. She saw a muscle vibrate in his cheek. There was no kindness in his eyes. After all this, she still displeased him.

"You are beautiful," he said. "I've waited a long time to place that necklace on a woman. It becomes you."

She didn't know what to say. She sensed no lightening of his mood. He still looked angry and dangerous. She could be dangerous, too. He didn't know the fire he played with.

Before she knew what was happening, he caught hold of the leather thong around her neck and snapped it. The pewter vial swung in his fist. Crying out in alarm, she tried to snatch it back, but he held it out of reach.

"What is so important about this amulet? Why does your face blanch with fear?"

"I'm not afraid. Give it back!"

"What does it contain?"

"Nothing." Because she could see he didn't believe her, she said, "Some herbs. For the toothache."

"Your teeth are white as snow. You have a toothache?"

"Nay, but I may get one. My mother says it's best to prepare for the worst."

A corner of Cynewulf's mouth lifted. "Did your mother look into the future and see me, then?"

"She was thinking of other toothaches."

Cynewulf chuckled. For a moment Taras thought he'd give her the vial, but he thrust it into his tunic and caught her wrist. "Come, let us go down and break our fast. My stomach growls like a lion."

He hurried her out of the chamber and along the gallery to the staircase. Although the hour was early, folk crowded the great hall. "Does anyone in this castle do anything but eat and drink?" Taras muttered.

Cynewulf smiled and escorted her to the dais, where he took the chair and ordered Taras to a stool on his left. Several warriors rose to honor him, briefly touching their foreheads and hearts. Some women seated below the salt rose to curtsy.

Cynewulf nodded. "Continue your meal."

Maids hastened to set broiled fish, dried fruit, and sops in milk before them. Taras picked up her knife and prepared to eat; then, noticing Cynewulf's gaze, she set the knife by her trencher. She supposed he expected her to wait for him to take the first bite.

"Toothache?" he asked.

"There are worse pains than a toothache, my lord," she said, looking him up and down as though he were a growth of some kind. "And worse places to have them."

He reached into his tunic and brought out her vial, setting it beside his plate. The thing lay like a viper, sleek and cold and deadly.

Cynewulf helped himself to dried apricots, then sat back in his chair and rested his foot on the opposite knee, considering her. "I may be a pain to you, but will you not eat?"

"I've lost my appetite." Somehow she had to reclaim the

vial and administer the potion. When the maid came to refill his trencher, perhaps he'd be distracted and she could pour the poison into his cup.

"You will soon grow too bony to work," Cynewulf said. He stretched out his finger and gently pushed the vial, rocking it.

Taras thought she'd faint. If he knocked it over and the stopper came out and the potion spilled, she would never be able to transform him. She reached for the vial, but he set it beyond her grasp.

"Eat, that you might work," he said.

"I do not intend to work."

"In Ilovar, everyone works."

"Not I."

"I see. You Britons prefer the pleasures of the bedchamber to honest toil. Mayhap we will make pleasure your duty."

She threw him a glance to freeze his very marrow, but he only smiled at her. "Yea, you are well fitted to the task I would set you, vixen. I shall personally train you in your duties."

"I would rather scrub floors and empty slops than lie with you!"

"That is your choice?"

"Aye!"

"Then you have decreed it." He slammed his feet down on the floor and stood up. "Ardeth!"

The maid hurried over with a jug of sour ale. Cynewulf stopped her from filling his cup. Taras looked longingly at the pewter vial.

"I do not wish drink, but your help in training my thrall to her tasks."

Ardeth turned wondering eyes on Taras, surveying her fine clothing and jewelry. "Which tasks would those be, lord?"

"The hall is filthy after last night's wassail. See that she scrubs every nook and cranny."

"I will not!" Taras said.

"If she troubles you, beat her." Cynewulf dropped the vial back into his tunic and strode across the hall. A servant opened the door and he went out, his mantle billowing behind him.

"You heard the master," Ardeth said. "Get up and come with me lest I beat you to a pulp."

Taras sized her up. The maid was short and soft. "I will not take orders from a serf."

"But you will take orders from me," came a deep voice. Arrayed in furs and mail, Denholm stalked across the room, balling his fists at his sides.

Remembering his bone-crunching grip last night, Taras said, "It seems the pair of you leave me no choice."

"You were never offered a choice at any time, wench," Denholm said. "Do as you're commanded."

"Fetch that pail over there and follow me," Ardeth said, gesturing at a wooden bucket at the far end of the hall.

"Fetch it yourself."

Ardeth cocked her fists, but Denholm stepped between them and yanked Taras off the stool. Over her bitter protests he trotted her across the hall and forced her fingers around the bucket's cold metal handle. "Either you choose to obey," he said, "or I will drag you about your duties."

She jerked the bucket off the floor and stormed outside. Ardeth strode ahead of her to the outer bailey, where dozens of folk engaged in daily chores.

"The cistern is beyond Beldor's forge," Ardeth said. "Mark its location, for we use its water for cleaning. The well just outside the keep is for drinking."

Taras peered at the shops set into the thick castle walls. Each was fitted with an oak door girded with iron. There were no windows, so the shopkeepers opened the doors for

93

light. There was a bakery and a kitchen, a brewery and a fruit-drying shed. Outside, a launderer stirred clothing in a huge iron pot while his assistants rinsed and hung garments on poles to dry. A wizened man sat just inside the armory, joining small iron links to fashion a coat of mail.

Half a dozen housecarls lazed in front of the stable. Ardeth skipped through their midst, giggling. Taras plunged after her and instantly regretted it when hands shot out to fondle her. When a big fellow shoved his hand into her bodice, she smashed the bucket onto his knee. He cried out and clutched his injury.

The bucket banging her thighs, Taras fought her way out of the pack. As she passed the blacksmith's shop, she glimpsed a giant inside, pounding a red-hot sword. Sparks showered his head and shoulders with every blow.

Taras dashed around the corner and collided with Ardeth, who was coming back to look for her. The maid shouted, "I've a mind to whip you!"

"Try it and I'll ram your fists down your throat!"

Ardeth punched her chin, fast and hard. Taras grabbed her braids and yanked her into the dirt. Within seconds they were rolling over and over, hitting, scratching, and tearing out hair. Taras hadn't engaged in such a glorious catfight in years. She got astride Ardeth's waist and boxed her ears.

Cheering, the loafers from the stable ran over to encircle them. Everyone was happy until the sensechal came along. "By the shield arm of Odin, what goes on here?"

He batted aside the men and snatched Taras off Ardeth. The maid jumped up and began kicking Denholm's shins. He had to release Taras in order to defend himself. The men howled with laughter.

Taras stepped back, dusting off her skirts, and saw coins piled on a mantle. Ardeth was still kicking Denholm. An onlooker shouted her name and threw a piece of silver onto the heap. In a flash Taras realized they'd been wagering on the fight. Incensed, she grabbed the mantle by its corners and dashed toward the smithy. She heard the carls shout and knew they were after her. It was too late to repent.

She hurtled into the smithy just as the blacksmith plunged a fiery sword into a bucket of water. "Help me!"

The blacksmith didn't hesitate. He punched the lead housecarl in the eye, tripped two others, and belted a fourth in the mouth. Taras slung the bulging mantle into the forge.

"You brazen slackwit, I'll break your neck for playing us such a trick!" someone shouted in English. He rushed at her, fists swinging. A second later he was sprawled in the cinders under the blacksmith's boot.

Glaring at the crowd, the blacksmith jabbed his finger at the door, then ground his huge fist into his palm to underscore his meaning. His sweaty, naked chest bulged like a mountain of dolomite.

"The wench stole our coin, Beldor!" one of the men yelled. "It is yonder, melting in your forge!"

Gold and silver glinted in the smoking remains of the mantle. Beldor seized a flat-bladed shovel and scooped the pile of coins into a bucket of water. Steam engulfed his head as he bowed over the bucket. After a minute, he tipped the bucket, and out rolled a shapeless, steaming lump. For one stupefied instant the men stared at their money; then they turned on Taras.

Beldor stepped in front of them, shaking his fist. He jerked his head at the door. When they snarled, he picked up the shovel and raised it overhead. Several men drew swords.

"Leave them be!" Denholm said, materializing in the doorway. "The chit belongs to Lord Cynewulf. Touch her at the peril of your lives."

"Can you not see what she's done, seneschal? Look at our coin!"

"I see. You've lost nothing. Leave the wench and take your money away."

"She's melded it!"

"It can be melted, weighed, and each man given his measure. Now get out before I break your heads."

They rolled their precious lump of metal into a cloak and carried it outside. Beldor patted Taras's shoulder. She took his hand and said, "My thanks, champion."

"Do not expect him to reply," Denholm said, levering himself onto a bench beside the forge. "He cannot speak."

"Some illness?"

"Nay. You do not wish to know. It concerns your kinsman, Ethelred the Unraed king."

"Then I want very much to know."

"Know, then, that Ethelred's bastard son, the Knight of Solway Moor, cut out Beldor's tongue these twelve winters past."

Stunned, Taras stared at Beldor. He looked back at her without expression, then ducked under a doorway into a back room.

"They unmanned him at the same time," Denholm said. "Ethelred looked on and laughed."

"The king would not condone such evil!"

"There is no mistake. Ethelred's personal guard captured Beldor on his farm in the Danelaw. They slaughtered his wife and children before his eyes. Their deaths were neither easy nor swift."

She sank onto the bench beside him and buried her face in her hands. "Tell me no more."

"Foolish girl, it will do you good to know the true nature of your precious Unraed."

"He is my lord."

"Nay, Cynewulf of Amandolar is your lord."

"Never! I will never swear fealty to him!"

Denholm stood. "Aye, you will, Lady Taras. All who

dwell in Amandolar have sworn to serve him until the last drop of their blood leaves their body. You will do so, as well, I think."

Taras began to weep. Denholm stalked to the doorway and looked back at her. "You will not always be so stubborn. I must be about my work. Ardeth has gone back to the hall. It will go hard for you if you fail to join her soon."

Taras sat with her elbows on her knees, her forehead in her palms. Coals hissed in the forge behind her, but she felt cold. She wanted nothing to do with these Vikings, nothing to do with their tales of horror. Nothing to do with the warfare between them and Ethelred. She felt not pride, but shame in being the king's cousin. She thought of her potion, of the Viking she was pledged to kill, of Beldor watching his family slain. Of Ethelred laughing at Beldor's torment. If she used the potion, she would be no better than Ethelred.

Dear God, how could she go through with it? But perhaps the matter had been taken out of her hands. Cynewulf possessed the vial now. Surely he would not taste its contents.

If he did, it would not be her fault. She wouldn't accept the blame. He had taken the vial from her in a moment of cruelty. If he turned into a frog, the blame would fall on his shoulders alone. From this moment on, the matter was out of her hands. All she had to do was escape. What happened to Cynewulf wouldn't matter at all.

Wouldn't it? She rose and left the forge, the question tumbling over and over in her mind. If he became a frog, he couldn't join Sweyn Forkbeard in the spring, and Ethelred would stand a better chance against the Vikings. The war might end at last.

Wasn't it worth destroying one lone Viking to end the war? No matter what Ethelred had done in the past, it was the ongoing war that caused the most suffering. Twelve years was long enough for men to fight their stupid battles. If it took a woman to end it, then God's will be done.

She must induce Cynewulf to drink the potion. She must. She hadn't any choice. That meant she couldn't really be blamed for doing wrong. Didn't it?

She flinched from the answer.

After three hours of scrubbing, Taras had covered only half the great hall. The floor stretched before her like a tournament field. Inch by weary inch she pushed the brush across the stone squares. Sickness grew in her head and belly; she should have broken the fast this morning. She'd gotten no noon meal, and it was a long time yet until supper.

She pushed her hair off her forehead and gazed up at the windows. She'd never seen anything like them before, not even in cathedrals. Scintillating, vibrant, unearthly, the windows' beauty surely rivaled Heaven itself. Fearing that she'd committed blasphemy by comparing this pagan house to God's, she closed her eyes against the grandeur.

But when nothing happened after a few seconds, she looked up again. The sun beamed through a window she hadn't noticed before. In a stained-glass depiction of a valley, a golden-haired falconer raised a gyrfalcon on his gauntlet. "Cynewulf," Taras whispered. How like the prideful Dane to inscribe his image in the window. She did not look up again.

The light dimmed before she'd finished her task. Servants lit tapers and rushlights. The household wandered in for supper. Taras pushed to her feet and went to a fireplace to dry her skirts and rub her sore knees. She grimaced as she caught sight of herself in a shield hanging on the wall. With her hair a tangled mop, her face soot-smudged, and her clothing tattered and soaked, she bore no resemblance to the haughty maid who'd gainsaid her master at the morning meal.

"No one bade you stop working, you lazy chit," Ardeth said. She dropped a bundle of logs on the floor. "Stack the wood and be quick, then lay the rugs."

Too tired to argue, Taras stacked the logs haphazardly on the hearth. She tossed stray scraps of bark into the fire, then unfurled a rug. The logs shifted and rolled apart. She sat down on the floor, defeated.

"Such a valuable chambermaid you are," Cynewulf said from behind her. "I don't know how Ardeth has gotten on all these years without you."

He stood ten paces away. He wore his wolfskin over a blue fustian tunic. Armlets set with emeralds encircled his biceps. As always, Damfertigénen hung from his baldric. Taras's pulse quickened with an emotion she hoped was anger.

He swept his hand at the logs. "You are blessed with the dexterity common among Britons."

"And you with the gallantry common among Vikings, to mock me in my extremity."

"I see you've lost none of your venom. Your day was too easy."

Determined not to show how much the effort cost her, she thrust to her feet and tossed her hair over her shoulders. "Aye, the day was easy."

"Then you do not regret working rather than frolicking in my bed?"

She yearned to slap his face. Instead, she set her hands on her hips and strutted toward him. She stopped when her breasts brushed his chest, and smiled wickedly at him. She didn't miss his intake of breath and the sudden pulse in his throat. It proved her womanly power over him. That power would be his downfall. "The course I chose was far more palatable," she finally said.

"You would choose it again for the morrow, and the morrow after that?"

"I—I would."

"So be it. If you want to be a slave, I'll treat you as one." He stepped around her to warm his hands at the fire. Without looking at her, he said, "I see you've destroyed the garments I gave you this morn, and lost the amber necklace."

Her hand flew to her breast. The gripping beasts were gone. An odd sadness overtook her anger. She spoke quickly to hide her emotion. "It was the fault of your men and that maid, Ardeth. She attacked me."

"Do not blame the wench. Her actions were in keeping with her station. What of yours, my fine lady?"

"I defended my honor."

"By melting my men's coin?"

She was a little chagrined at that.

"Oh. You heard."

"Of course."

"Then do you recognize you've sorely used me?"

"I merely insist that you pay your debt to me."

Conscious that many were eavesdropping, Taras lowered her voice to an angry purr. "Did you not obtain it early this morn in my bath, sir?"

"I have not yet begun to exact my price in that way."

"Indeed you have, for you'll never again lay your hands upon me!" She turned her back on him, avoiding the anger she knew she'd see. She'd done it now. How in the world would she obtain the pewter vial? She had sought to catch the fly with vinegar instead of honey. Her cousin Camlann had been right—she knew nothing of how to use her womanly power.

When she turned to peek, Cynewulf squatted down and restacked the logs. "It is a shame to waste your talent on menial labor," he said at last. "Especially when you perform it so piteously."

She rounded on him. "Why, I scrubbed the floor until my knees turned black and blue!"

Cynewulf's gaze traveled to the water on the floor, the overturned bucket, the rugs heaped upon the benches.

"I didn't have time to finish," Taras said, once again feeling chagrin.

"Mayhap you should finish now. My people are ready to sup and rugs claim every bench."

Scowling, she marched over to a bench to hurl a rug onto the floor. A log rolled out from underfoot. She stumbled backwards. Cynewulf caught her on the way down.

"Aye, it is a waste to train such a clumsy wench."

"Let me go!"

"Never," he said coldly. "I own you, body and soul. Now get back to work." He strode off.

Chapter Nine

Cynewulf pretended to ignore Taras the rest of the evening. He saw her cast him many dark looks as she struggled with the rugs. For a time he thought she'd come over to rail at him, but once she'd laid the rugs, she helped the servants fetch and carry food. She didn't complain, though the same could not be said for those she served. Denholm's pheasants ended up in the ashes and Nivendel's beer in his lap. She spilled soup, causing a servant to slip and drop a gilded suckling pig.

Cynewulf watched in bemusement. Was she really so clumsy, or did she seek to show him what a miserable servant she could be?

When she started for the scullery carrying a stack of dirty dishes, Cynewulf nodded to Denholm. The seneschal took the stack, handed it to a servant, and dismissed her.

Hours later, Cynewulf entered his chamber to find his straw mattress bare. Curled on a pallet made of his bed furs, Taras slept by the fireplace. Her hair spread over the furs like a coppery fan. She held his silver comb in her hand.

Cynewulf squatted beside her. "Beautiful falcon," he whispered in Danish, "have you learned yet whose hand holds the jess?"

Desire surged into his brain in a sudden hot tide. He groaned within himself. To act upon his need would win him her eternal hatred. He didn't wish to embitter her by rough handling. In a distant corner of his soul he feared she would somehow fly off, never to return.

Such strange emotions. No other woman aroused this odd mixture of lust and regard. Was he coming to cherish this enemy maid? Surely not. How could he value the kinswoman of his most bitter foe?

Denholm still feared she would kill him. The seneschal had saved his life more than once, and Cynewulf had learned to listen to him, but in this thing he was a foolish old woman. With one finger Cynewulf touched the hair at his captive's temple. She was incredibly soft. Yet Denholm believed she was an assassin.

Cynewulf moved to the bed and began to strip. He needed to go to bed, to sleep without dreaming, to forget the wench . . . if only for a few hours. In his haste to doff his mantle, he stabbed his thumb on his brooch. He rolled a string of silent curses around on his tongue.

As he stared at the blood oozing from his thumb, his attention shifted to the scar below it that he'd borne for many years. One day as he helped his father pull an eyas falcon from a snare, in his clumsiness he'd pulled too hard and broken her wing. Despite his father's skill, the wing didn't knit, and the bird never flew again.

"How came you by your wound, lord?"

He turned to find Taras looking at him from the furs. She wasn't looking at his hand, but at a scar across his ribs. "I thought you were asleep," he said.

"I was . . . Is that a sword stroke?"

"Yea. A token from the field of Manathilim. I was careless."

His own voice sounded foreign in his ears. He heard a catch in his breathing that, until now, he'd experienced only in combat. Jove, how the wench moved him! He sat down on the bed.

"Does it pain you?"

"What? Oh, the scar. Nay."

"A shame."

"For you, mayhap."

He saw her shiver and surmised he'd frightened her. She wasn't a maid easily alarmed, but then, she wasn't used to being closeted with a man. He knew he was looking at her too hard. He heard a wolf howl somewhere in the blackness.

"The creature's song is mournful," Cynewulf said. He didn't know why he felt compelled to make conversation. He ought to wrap up in his mantle and go to sleep. Or mayhap he should crawl into the furs with her and prove just how little her feelings mattered.

"That creature's song is mine," Taras said.

"You're melancholy?"

"Since I've been enslaved, how would you expect me to feel? Joyful, like that slavering wolfhound you keep around the place?"

"You haven't been treated ill."

"Nay? Then how did I come by this?" She whipped the pelts off one leg and showed him a bruise. She didn't realize how much thigh she'd revealed. Fresh heat leaped into Cynewulf's gut. "And where did I receive the others marking my body?"

"*I* placed none upon you." Then he remembered tying her over Eboracum's back. "Save for the one on your southernmost end."

105

Flushing, she yanked the furs over her leg and glared up at the rafters.

"In truth, my lovely young thrall, you have meted out far more bruises than you've obtained. I've scores upon my shins and chest, and Ardeth showed me where your fists struck her."

"So that's what the slubberdegullion was doing while you supped tonight—displaying her bruises."

"Aye, and rendering her account of the fight. She said you nigh broke her eardrums."

"You expected me to bear my afflictions like a helpless kit?"

"Nay." He dropped his voice an octave as he said, "I expected you to bear them like the lioness you are."

"Lioness? Then I am a beast in your eyes?"

"If a beast growls and spits and claws, what but a beast might she be?"

Taras bent on him a fearsome scowl. He could see she wanted to fly at him. The idea made him smile. It took no effort to summon the memory of her firm, wet body against him in the bath. He wanted to mold her breasts to his hands, to flick his tongue into her mouth and bend her to his rule. *Come, Taras, fly at me. I'll lay your hot little body down and make you fight.*

The scowl left her face, replaced by dismay. Did she know what was in his mind? Could she feel the pulsating fire that all but consumed him?

"I won't do it," she said. She lay down and pulled the furs up to her chin.

Cynewulf yanked his mantle over his lap and lay down, turning to rest his head on his elbow. She rolled toward the fire. Even through the furs her lush curves beckoned him. It was a long time before he trusted himself to speak again.

"Denholm tells me you can read."

She made an impatient gesture with her hand. "Denholm talks too much."

"Funny, he said the same of you."

"I won't bear my suffering in silence. You know that."

"All too well. Denholm says you demanded to know why a lettered person must scrub floors. I didn't tell him you'd made the choice."

She twisted around to glare at him.

"Can you read, Taras? Is it true?"

"I never lie."

He didn't deign to refute her. "How is it that a woman can read?"

"My mother paid a monk to train me in the scholarly arts. She said I must be able to write down my—never mind." She looked away, but not before Cynewulf saw a glint of fear.

His nostrils flared in suspicion. It was plain she was hiding something. Had it to do with Ethelred? He ought to press her but decided against it. There would be a better time to extract answers. She would tell him whatever he wanted to know whenever he required it.

The straw mattress crackled as he rolled onto his back and clasped his arms behind his head. Firelight danced across the ceiling. He heard an ember pop, scattering gold- and ruby-colored sparks. "Taras."

"I haven't disappeared, much as I'd like to."

"Your talents are wasted scrubbing floors."

"Aye, but I'll not go to the furs with you."

"Your work is such that ten servants are needed to clear up your mishaps. Denholm was angry when you dropped his pheasants."

"The gluttonous knave required me to bring him five birds on a charger barely large enough for two. 'Twas an unfortunate mishap, but he deserved to eat birds covered in ash."

"And then you spilled a cask of nabid onto Nivendel the Briton."

"The dastard tweaked my behind. I cooled his nether regions."

"Ah, then it was no accident."

"A maid has a right to defend herself from varlets, even those of her own race."

Cynewulf leaned on one elbow to look at her profile. "It would seem you stand in need of other employment or, Thor guard us, you'll bring the keep down in ruins upon our heads."

"What would you have me do, then, great lord and master?"

He ignored her sarcasm. "It is harvest time. I need a scribe."

She was silent a long moment. "You would not require anything . . . else?"

"We'll try your hand at scribing first."

The word *first* hovered in the air between them. He didn't try to ease her apprehension. A slave needed no comfort, no security. This one needed to learn that he was master.

Desire twitched his nerve endings and brought renewed heat to his belly. Cursing silently, he snatched the mantle up to his shoulders and shut his eyes. It was a long time before he slept.

The cock had not yet crowed when Cynewulf yanked the furs off Taras and hauled her out of bed. "Come, lazy-bones. Time to be about your duties."

"I'd hoped to find you gone like a bad dream," Taras said. She didn't like the way he stood over her, his fingers encircling her wrists like manacles. How could she turn him into a frog when he could so easily overpower her?

And what had he done with the potion? If she couldn't

win it back, she'd have to find the right plants and somehow decoct them. She didn't know where monkshood
grew, nor any of the other herbs she needed. She wasn't
even sure how much of each decoction she needed for the
deadly liquid. Besides, where could she make it without
being caught? Anyone would know she wasn't brewing
ale; they'd guess she was weaving spells.

"You're deep in meditation," Cynewulf said, bending
close. She turned her face away. Had he guessed her
thoughts?

He guided her to the curtained alcove. "See to your
needs."

She came out a few minutes later to find a sleeveless
linen chemise and a moss-green bliaut on the bed. A pair of
sandals and long woolen hose lay on the hearthstone.
Cynewulf was gone.

Watching lest he return and catch her naked, she peeled
off her tunic and dressed at lightning speed. After drawing
on the hose and lacing the sandals to her knees, she girded
her hips with the silver belt she'd worn yesterday. She
combed her hair, then brushed her teeth with powdered charcoal and a green stick, rinsing until her teeth were white.

On her way to the door she glanced at the fireplace.
There on the mantel lay the pewter vial. She dashed over
and snatched it up. Liquid splashed inside when she shook
it. Sagging with relief, she tied the cord around her neck
and dropped the vial into her bodice.

She was dangerous once more.

She found Cynewulf waiting for her in the great hall.
Many of his people were still sprawled in sleep upon the
benches and floor. Taras lifted her hem and stepped over
them.

Clad in his mantle and a brown leather hauberk,
Cynewulf looked more like a huntsman than the master of
Ilovar. He sat motionless in his chair, watching her come.

The passion luster in his eyes made her tremble. She'd heard him tossing upon the mattress all night while she lay by the fire, fearing he'd crawl into the furs with her. If only she'd known the vial was within reach, she could have slept without fear.

"Sit down and eat," he said. She dropped onto the stool and began to eat sops left from last night's feast.

The rising sun struck the east windows and turned them to jewels. Grumbling, the carls crawled from their pallets. Taras saw their eyes widen when they noticed her beside their lord. Did they think she should be crawling around with a scrub brush?

Denholm came in and Cynewulf rose to speak to him. Out of the corner of her eye, Taras studied his bowl. Would he return to finish the sops? She pulled out the vial and removed the stopper. A few drops in his food and he would be finished. Trying to dissociate herself from the terrible thing she was doing, she leaned close to the bowl and started to tip the vial.

"Are you finished?" Cynewulf asked.

Taras gasped and rammed the cork back into the vial. Thrusting it out of sight, she twisted on the stool and found Cynewulf right behind her. There was a perilous light in his eyes.

"F-finished?" she stammered. Had he seen the vial? Did he know what she'd tried to do?

"Have you finished eating?" Without waiting for her reply, he caught her arm and escorted her across the hall. Taras's legs wobbled like a newborn calf's. If he let go of her arm, she was sure she'd fall.

At the door he stopped and looked her up and down until she felt naked. She shivered. Her reaction had nothing to do with the cold air and everything to do with fear. Fear at nearly being caught trying to transform him. Fear of his powerful touch, his raw masculinity. His stare was purely sexual, a master's bold perusal of his prize.

"Shall I strip bare," she demanded, "lest your imagination be overly taxed?"

"I do not have to see your breasts again, Taras. It is no strain to summon their image."

She whirled toward the door, but he caught her shoulder and pulled her against the wall. For several long seconds he held her there, then he slid his hand along her collarbone. She knew he felt the cord hidden in her bodice. Would he take the vial again?

He smiled and followed her curves to her waist. "You're shivering," he said. He whipped a red mantle from a peg and wrapped it around her.

She wrenched away and stalked out the door. Cynewulf didn't touch her as they crossed the bailey to the curtain wall. Finding the gatekeeper asleep, Cynewulf set his own shoulder to the portcullis winch.

As he raised the heavy iron gate, Taras watched the awesome play of his muscles. She pictured his naked body sheened with sweat. She remembered his taut form as he dressed by the window yesterday morning. How spectacular he was, how—by the sweet saints, what was she thinking of? He was the man she'd sworn to kill, yet she was thinking of him as a bedmate.

Cynewulf finished lifting the gate and turned to take her arm. He stood like a big, randy buck, his muscles swollen from exertion, his pulse beating in his throat. Excitement roiled in her belly and made her dizzy. Blast the cur, how did he raise her blood so?

She rejected his hand and strode past him, but when she heard him chuckle she knew he'd sensed her lust. "Anyone can open a gate," she said. "You needn't act as though you've slain a herd of dragons to lay at my feet."

Cynewulf smiled, looking immensely pleased with himself. Taras tried to walk off, but he diverted her to the stable. Eboracum bucked and whinnied when they walked in but soon settled down to nuzzle Taras's cheek. "Lovesick knave," Cynewulf groused. He stood beside Taras and bridled the horse.

The Viking's nearness made Taras's pulse pound harder. Closeted in the warm darkness with the smell of beasts rising around her, she suddenly wanted to lie down in the hay with Cynewulf.

Exclaiming under her breath, she ducked under his arm and strode to the feedbox. "Is it customary for you barbarians to feed your horses so much grain and apples? My horses would suffer colic and, mayhap, joint illness."

Cynewulf rushed to the box and looked in. In English he yelled, "Mechalah! Show yourself!"

Someone scrabbled in the loft, then hay showered down on Taras and Cynewulf. A lad skittered down the wall pegs, but before his feet touched the floor, Cynewulf jerked him up by the tunic and shook him like a rat. "Are you trying to kill my horse?"

"Nay, lord!"

"Then why have you given him this?" He rammed the boy's head into the box.

"He hungered, my lord," came the muffled reply.

"You should have given him hay and only a little grain." Cynewulf set him back on his feet. "Empty the box."

While Mechalah worked, Cynewulf bent and pressed his ear to Eboracum's belly. After a minute he ran his hands down the horse's legs and probed the joints. Taras caressed Eboracum's muzzle and waited anxiously for the verdict. Cynewulf finally straightened and looked at the young groom.

Taras caught his arm. From Mechalah's speech she knew he was a Briton; she feared what the Viking would do. "Be merciful, lord. He's but a lad, with a lad's lack of judgment."

"His lack could have slain my horse."

"Was there never a time when your judgment was flawed? Never a time when a creature suffered for it?"

She saw him glance at the scar on his hand; then he gazed at the groom. "Eboracum has labored this year on rations of the rudest kind," he said. "To suddenly fill his belly with riches will ruin him."

"Aye, lord," the lad said. " 'Twill not happen again."

"See that it doesn't, or I'll bury you to the eyebrows in horse dung. Now go saddle the mare and bring her to the girl."

Taras held the destrier's head while Cynewulf saddled him. Soon Mechalah came back, leading a gray mare with a black mane and tail. He handed the reins to Taras.

"She's lovely," Taras said.

"She's Arabian," Cynewulf said. The saddling done, he led Eboracum outside. Taras followed with the mare.

As soon as they reached the bailey, Eboracum thrust his nose under the mare's tail. She lashed out with her hind hooves. Neighing, the horse danced back, only to return to his lecherous play a moment later.

"By my father's gray beard!" Cynewulf swore. He leaped onto Eboracum and forced him away from the mare. Eboracum bucked and kicked, defying his master's efforts. House carls and servants ran to watch the show.

"You're the son of an ass!" Cynewulf twice told his horse. At last he brought the beast under control and turned him toward the gate.

Mechalah helped Taras mount and sent her after Cynewulf. The Viking slowed beyond the gate. "Go slowly across the stone bridge," he said. "It is a very long fall."

Taras looked over the balustrade at a waterfall thundering into a ravine. Spray wet the bridge and rainbows colored the air. Taras took a death grip on the reins and tried not to look down again.

The keeper of the barbican swung open the outer gates. Eboracum, the scent of the mare firing his blood, pranced through like a crab and tossed his mane.

Cynewulf felt only a little less randy than his horse. As he led Taras down the mountain, he twisted in the saddle again and again to watch her. His insides felt like a volcano about to erupt. With the sun gilding her face and hair, the wench was too beautiful, like some mountain witch of legend. By the thunder of Thor, how could he endure the day without yanking her off the mare and subjecting her to his passion?

In all his years he'd never stopped himself from acting on carnal desire. There had never been any need to stop. Never until Taras entered his life.

He was getting soft-hearted.

He studied his captive as though the wind might blow off her clothing. He pictured her bare, as hungry as he, a prisoner of her own yearnings and his.

She lifted her emerald eyes and gazed at him. A tenuous smile claimed her lips. He saw a softness about her that he'd noticed in unguarded moments. She was as helpless as an eyas taken from the nest, utterly dependent upon his mercy. If he used her, he would snatch away the very innocence that so enflamed him even as it aroused his protective instincts.

Whatever else he did today, he would not take her.

He hoped.

It was going to be a long day.

Chapter Ten

Taras held the mare half a dozen yards behind Cynewulf, thinking how easy it would be to crash into his horse's quarters and plunge him over the cliff. She wouldn't have to worry about frog potions and grinding him underfoot. Ethelred wouldn't care how the Viking died, just so long as she killed him.

People said he was invincible, yet Taras knew he could be slain. Hadn't he been bitten by one of the very wolves he was purported to rule? And didn't he bear a scar from an English sword?

Yes, she could kill him. She could succeed where others had failed. She could blot him from the earth and free her people from his curse. After he was dead, she could return to London. There would be one less legion of Vikings to swell Forkbeard's ranks in the spring. There would be one less fell leader to lay waste to villages and strike fear into the hearts of children.

There would be one less barbarian in her life.

She lifted her gaze to the Viking. The wind snapped his wolfskin mantle around his wide shoulders, blowing it aside to display his narrow waist and hips. He was an incredibly large man, as big as a statue. She'd heard his servants whisper that he was of the race of the gods, that Thor was his grandfather.

Ridiculous. His followers had built a pagan religion around him. But what would they do when they discovered his broken body in the valley below? To whom would they turn when Ethelred sent his armies north? Would their women and children suffer even as the English had?

That last thought nearly swerved her from her purpose. She didn't want innocent folk to suffer—but the Viking had to die. He had to. She was the sword in Ethelred's hand. Surely God would concur that she must smite her enemy while she could.

She kicked the mare to a faster pace. Eboracum's black tail tossed in the wind just a few yards away. His hooves slung up stones and dirt clods. She'd have to smash into him with enough force to push him over the cliff or cause him to lose his balance and fall. The mare might fall, as well, carrying her along. All four of them might end up crushed on the boulders below.

She waited until Cynewulf approached a sharp bend in the road. Gripping the reins, she jabbed her heels into the mare's flanks. The animal jolted toward Eboracum's gleaming black quarters. In an instant she'd strike him and it would all be over.

An instant before impact, the mare shied violently, rising on her hind legs and twisting toward the cliff, her hooves pedalling over the edge. In that horrible instant Taras sought and found Cynewulf's gaze. He was already turning in the saddle, dragging Eboracum around, reaching for Taras's reins. Eboracum's off-hind hoof slid in the loose dirt. On three legs Eboracum scrabbled on the very edge of the cliff. Cynewulf kicked him, strained for Taras.

Before he could touch the reins, Taras jerked the mare's head and shifted her weight. Her horse's hooves thudded onto solid dirt, inches from death.

Cynewulf caught the reins and dragged her to the safe side of the road. His face was pale, his eyes fever bright. "What happened?"

"We—we slipped," Taras gasped. She thought her heart would burst from her chest, it pounded so hard.

Did he know what she'd tried to do? Dear God, what madness had possessed her to try something so wicked? She had nearly killed herself and the mare, yet all she could think of was what she'd almost done to Cynewulf and Eboracum. Even now they could be tumbling end over end into the terrible void. She could almost hear the thud of their bodies. Her stomach heaved.

He stared at her in silence. Had he guessed her intent? He had tried to save her even though she'd placed him in mortal danger, but now that he'd had time to think about it, he would know it had been no accident. Would the barbarian drag her out of the saddle and shove her over the cliff?

He dropped the reins and caught her chin between hard fingers. For a long moment he held her still, looking into her mind. Taras trembled, trying to hide, feeling him unlocking her secrets. Dear God, he would surely cast her from the mountain.

But his eyes filled with tenderness and pain. He dropped his hand to his thigh and continued gazing at her. Unable to bear his regard, she lowered her eyes and sat with bowed head. He knew what she'd done. He didn't need to say it.

"Let's have no more excitement today," he said quietly.

She looked up. He knew, oh yes, he knew. He understood foes mightier than she was. "Yea, lord," she said in a small voice.

"Come, then. There's work to be done."

He wheeled and continued around the bend. If he worried that she would try to kill him again, he didn't show it. He rode all the way to the bottom of the mountain without glancing back. Taras rode meekly, holding the mare well behind him.

In a village nestled at the mountain's foot, peasants stopped working and greeted their lord. Two lads ventured to pat Eboracum's nose. Taras was afraid the big stallion would react to their touch, but he dropped his head to the grass beside the road.

A few minutes later they rode across a low hill and stopped to view a lake bearded with hemlock trees. Trailing a net behind his boat, a fisherman slowly rowed across the lake. A hawk swooped to rake a fish out of his net, missed, and flapped on.

Cynewulf led Taras through a hillside vineyard. The grapes were already harvested and most of the leaves fallen, yet Taras saw beauty in the twisted wreaths of vines. "I have sold my wines as far away as Antioch," Cynewulf said.

Taras was afraid to talk to him after what she'd done, but since he seemed to desire conversation, she said, "A skald came to Widnes Keep one time. He sang of Danish voyages."

He looked at her out of deep blue eyes. She could imagine this golden Dane standing at the helm of a great longship, storming waves like castle towers. She bit her lip and told him no more of the skald's song. *Don't get carried away. He is no romantic legend. The man is an enemy.*

He seemed to catch her thoughts because for an instant he scowled; then a smile warmed his face. Taras's heart hammered against her breastbone. She hated her fickle body. Only half an hour ago she had tried to kill him, and now she wanted to lie with him in the vineyard.

Fearing he would again guess her thoughts, she said, "If I am to be your scribe, what records shall I keep?"

"We'll attend them tomorrow. Today you'll see the harvest."

He led her on through pastures dotted with sheep and rough-haired cattle. Trees shimmered under leafy mantles of red, gold, and purple.

"My father used to say the gods walked here before man came to be," Cynewulf said.

Taras's hand tightened on the reins, breaking the mare's pace. The gods? Might Thor be Cynewulf's grandfather, as the people whispered? Then how would she deal with him?

Cynewulf told her his father had come here many years ago and wrested the land from the barbarian tribes. His deep voice harmonized with the wind as he described Viking conquests. Each time he fell silent, Taras listened breathlessly for his next words. It was as though her old life existed only in dreams, as though the Viking were weaving a magical spell around her.

Cynewulf stopped several times to talk to peasants stooking wheat. Taras couldn't help but compare the people to Ethelred's serfs. The king's serfs hated and feared him. There was no affection between them.

How ironic that a pagan warrior could somehow be kinder than her own civilized family. Could he really be the bloodthirsty conqueror she'd heard he was? From what he had just told her, it was his father, not he, who had been the fell conqueror. But then she remembered Sweyn Forkbeard and his chieftains. There *was* blood on Cynewulf's hands. English blood.

Cynewulf dismounted by a field of straw flowers and helped Taras down. He tied the horses some distance apart, then walked her down the hill to a longhouse. Goats grazed on the sod roof; frost-nipped flowers and roses blanketed the foundation; vines bearing long, velvety seed pods crawled up mossy stone walls and poked into eaves. Taras was more interested in the women carrying earthenware crocks into the house.

"They've honeycomb in those crocks," Cynewulf said. "They robbed the hives this summer. Now, with winter near, it is too late to rob the hives again, but the women are extracting the honey from the comb. Do you want to go inside and watch?"

"I know how it's done," Taras said. "We kept bees at Widnes."

"Then I'll show you the hives."

He led her to a field dotted with beehives. Cynewulf squatted down to stroke the tattered wings of a worker bee too worn out to fly home. "I have oft traded my honey in far ports," Cynewulf said. "The honey of Amandolar is the sweetest in all the world."

"I doubt it can compete with mine. Widnes's clover is better than yours."

Cynewulf laughed. "I'll raid your hives someday and find out. Come, wipe that frown from your face. I was jesting."

"A pillager jests of his trade?"

He touched his forehead in mock shame. "You have me, my lady."

They walked among the flowers. Pollen dusted Taras's bliaut. Bees hummed and fumbled among the petals. Cynewulf picked a white flower and stuck it into Taras's plait. She plucked it out and dropped it underfoot. Cynewulf did not comment, but she saw the corners of his mouth draw down. She lifted her nose and walked on. If the Viking thought to gain her friendship through small gestures, he could save his energy.

They climbed over a stone wall into a pasture. Cynewulf

stopped to talk to an elderly shepherd. Although Taras couldn't understand their conversation, she heard Cynewulf's respectful tone and saw joy in the shepherd's face.

After they had returned to the horses, Taras said, "Your serfs seem content, even merry."

"That is because they're not serfs, but free men and women."

"But they work your fields and tend your flocks!"

"Of course. I hire them."

"So? Everyone gives serfs a wage," Taras said.

"You call the pittance English lords give their serfs a wage? Those poor wretches seek death as a welcome release."

She looked at him in dismay. This was not the fell Viking of legend, the one who slew suckling babes, but a man offended by cruelty.

Again he seemed to read her thoughts. "You're surprised? But we Danes do not wear devil's horns upon our heads, Taras."

"There is more to being a devil than outward appearances." She urged the mare to a trot.

Cynewulf rode up beside her. "You've told me nothing of yourself, Lady Taras, but I know your kind. You English use up your land until it is barren and the poor slaves starve."

Taras cast about for a way to defend her way of life, but he had spoken the truth. Ethelred didn't give a fig for his serfs. Even her own father had regarded them as less than draft animals. Many times she had sneaked grain from the underground storehouses of Widnes to save them from starving.

"There is only so much land to work," she said. The excuse was feeble. She shouldn't have offered it.

"We Danes made like mistakes many generations ago in

121

our homeland," he said. "But we learned. Now we tend our properties with a father's care, as you see here. And our ships sail to ports you have never dreamed of, selling our goods to make our people prosperous. Each man is his own master, exercising dominion over his own wealth."

"That's not true. I've seen slaves in your castle."

Cynewulf's eyes darkened. "You saw Britons captured at Manathilim and Hlaverin Towne. They will repay the debt they incurred by raising their swords against me. For the next three years they'll sweat upon my lands. When the Althing meets, they will be freed according to our custom. They may then return to their kindred or stay here. I will grant them land or a place in my army, whichever they desire. Many of my carls were once my slaves."

Taras didn't want to hear this. She could no longer deny that almost everything she'd known of the Vikings was false. The revelation wrenched a small gasp of protest from her lips.

"Are you ill?" Cynewulf asked. He caught the mare's reins and dismounted. Over Taras's objections, he pulled her off and carried her to a stone bridge. "I'll get you water."

Before he could descend into the stream Eboracum tried to mount the mare. Cynewulf dashed back to save her. Eboracum began to buck but backed off as his master grabbed his reins. In making good her escape, the mare stepped on Cynewulf's foot. She trotted down into the stream and stood blowing. Taras took small pleasure in Cynewulf's grimace of pain.

He tied Eboracum to a stout branch, then limped over and flung himself down on the balustrade. Yanking off his sandal and hose, he frowned at his bloody foot.

"You should soak it in the stream," Taras said. She could make him a poultice of mud and linden, but—

Cynewulf hobbled off the bridge and down into the

water. The mare nuzzled his jaw. "Move over, nag," he ordered. "For one silver kufic I would let Eboracum get you with foal."

"The mare is a lady gentle born," Taras said. "She should not be forced to rut."

Cynewulf grinned up at her. "It is more enjoyable when the female begs first?"

"You are odious!"

His smile deepened. "I will not mate her with Eboracum—he is too large and randy."

Like you, Taras thought. Shame burnished her cheeks, although she couldn't remember why she was angry. He looked so handsome, so virile standing in water swirling to his knees. She couldn't stop her body's response.

He came up out of the water and stood on the bridge in front of her. She knew she should stand, but she couldn't force her knees to straighten. He took her hands in his and held them close to his thighs. With just a little more pressure he could guide her to him. She awaited his will. In another moment he would pull her against him, and then there would be no quenching the fire.

The Viking's jaw tightened until she could see every cord in his throat. His great chest rose and fell. Heat radiated from the place beneath their locked hands. She parted her lips and breathed a single word: "Please."

A tremor coursed through him. She knew exactly what he wanted to do. It was the same thing she desired. The thing she must fight with all her strength . . . if she could find any left.

The Viking's eyes changed to midnight, his hands to iron. She remembered standing naked before him yestermorn while he sat looking at her. She had displayed herself with brazen disregard of the consequences. And now, inches from his pleasure, she knew it was time to pay.

Cynewulf dropped her hands and stepped back. He

gripped the hem of his hauberk to raise it, then let his hand fall to his side. Rage burned in his eyes. Abruptly he turned on his heel and strode into the thicket.

Taras began to tremble. How could she have allowed her imagination such license? Had he sensed her besotted thoughts and refused them just to humiliate her?

A sense of rage overcame her shame. She couldn't do anything right where the Viking was concerned. She couldn't turn him into a frog, she couldn't push him off a cliff. She couldn't even fight off his advances . . . or hold his interest when he was aroused. She was worse than useless here. It was time to get away and tell Ethelred she'd failed. He would have to send a warrior to do the job.

She jumped off the balustrade into the water. Vaulting onto the mare, she urged her out of the stream. Once on the road, she sent the mare flying like a bolt from a crossbow.

Cynewulf heard her go. He rushed out of the thicket, cursing. He should have known the little jolt-head would fly the second he turned his back. Damn and damn, he should have taken her in the dirt instead of leaving to regain his self-control!

He mounted and galloped after her. He'd punish her this time, by thunder. He'd be damned before he would hold himself in anymore. The time for mercy had ended two minutes ago.

But as the miles passed, he realized not even powerful Eboracum could catch the mare. The Arabian had been bred to fly like a hawk across the desert sands. She was faster here.

He reined in and swept his gaze across the pasture bordering the lake. The road curved around it. He urged Eboracum down a steep bank, then leaped a ditch. Sheep scattered as they thundered across the field. They jumped a stone wall bordering the woods and skidded into the middle of the road. Eboracum reared and pawed the air, hungry for battle.

"Not yet, my fine lad," Cynewulf said, backing him into the trees.

For five minutes he watched and listened. Had the vixen left the road? Was she slipping into the mountains at this very moment? It might take him all day to find her.

Hooves echoed through the trees. Gripping the reins in one hard fist, Cynewulf waited for the mare to draw closer; then with a terrible war cry he kicked the warhorse into the road.

Trying to stop, Taras dragged the mare down on her haunches. Before the mare could regain her footing, Cynewulf snatched Taras out of the saddle.

"I hate you!" Taras screamed. "Why do you not let me go?"

"Because you are mine."

"You cannot hold me captive forever!"

"When I grow tired of you, I'll sell you. Not before."

She kicked Eboracum's shoulder. Enraged, he reared high. Cynewulf forced him down and, gripping Taras, slid to the road. "You blear-witted savage," he said. "Damn it, stop biting! By the loins of Thor, you will learn obedience!"

"I'll learn nothing from you!" She stamped on his wounded foot and hurled herself backward, unbalancing him. They fell into the dirt and rolled over and over. Taras punched until Cynewulf flipped her onto her back and pinned her wrists over her head.

"Does this make you feel like a man?" she screamed into his face. "The mighty Viking warlord defeats a woman. Mayhap your glaziers will stain a window honoring this fearsome contest, you prideful cock-a-hoop!"

Cynewulf gave her a furious shake. She made him sick with lust, sick with the frenzied urge to tear off her clothing and engage in the sanguinous combat between warrior and virgin maid.

The mare gave a sharp whinny of pain, and Cynewulf knew Eboracum had finally gotten to her. He saw Eboracum mount her in all the fire and might of a warhorse. Their hooves hammered the ground as the mare fought to break free. Cynewulf dragged Taras over the stone wall to safety.

Taras slapped him across the face. "That's your fault!" she screamed. "If he kills her, it's your fault!"

"I've had enough of your venom!" he thundered. He tore the mantle off her shoulders and pulled her hips savagely against his. White-hot passion increased his rage tenfold. The mare's screams reverberated in his ears. He was no better than Eboracum. What he wanted he would take.

He threw a glance at the horses. Eboracum buried his teeth in the mare's withers, holding her against her attempts to rear.

Cynewulf glared down at Taras and found her weeping. Her hair, free of its plait, swirled around her body. Her torn gown and chemise revealed her breasts.

He ought to tear off the rest of her clothes and do to her what Eboracum was doing to the mare. He pushed his rock-hard length against her belly. With one motion he could shove through her skirt and make her his slave in very truth.

"Let me go!" she wept.

He cast his eyes upon the coupling beasts. Would the mare beg Eboracum in those same words, had she a voice? Would the big stallion release her? "By Odin's blood," Cynewulf swore, "I am near angry enough to send you naked from my lands."

"Near angry enough to send me away?" she demanded through her tears. "What can I do to bring your wrath to a fullness?"

"Is there no dulling the edge of your tongue? Should I lock you in my dungeon a twelvenight with naught but rats to slander?"

"You would find my tongue still well-honed when I ventured forth!" she said, but her words lacked fire. He felt her trembling in every limb. Her tremors only served to massage the very thing she feared. He moved back, breaking the contact.

Because he couldn't trust himself, he walked down the road. He knew she would still be there when he returned.

Eboracum finished at last. Shaking his mane, he unleashed a triumphant whinny and trotted down the road to his master. Cynewulf caught his bridle and stood glowering at him. "I hope you're satisfied, you brute," he muttered. "At least one of us isn't suffering. Come, let us go see what damage we've both wrought."

Taras was leaning on the wall where he'd left her, holding the mare's bridle and stroking her muzzle. Cynewulf went around to check the mare. Satisfied that Eboracum hadn't truly hurt her, he bade Taras mount.

"I will not, after what she's been through."

Cynewulf's patience had long since reached its end. "Don't be a fool. Mount the damned nag or I'll strip you bare, tie your heels to her tail, and drag you back to the castle."

"You wouldn't dare!"

He caught the mare's reins and jerked her broadside to Taras. When she made no move to mount, he leaned over Eboracum's neck and glared at her until, with an angry sob, she grabbed mane and pulled herself into the saddle.

"There," she said, "now hand me the reins."

"Do you take me for a fool?"

"Aye, and a calf-lollied goosecap."

"Your English insults inspire me to lay you in the dust and cool this hellish fire in my loins."

Through slitted lids she matched his glare. Snorting in disgust, he wound the mare's reins around his fist and set off at a trot, pulling her helplessly in his wake.

What was the matter with him? Had he gone so long without a woman that he'd forgotten how to use one? Had he lost every jot of sense, that each encounter with the wench became a battle between his own mind and body?

Denholm was right. The wench wanted to kill him. She'd proven it on the mountainside. He hadn't feared her futile attempt to murder him, but what caused him worry was his own stupid reaction to her womanhood.

He must somehow determine her fate. It would be easy to break and sell her. He looked down at the scar on his thumb. But instead of the eyas falcon, he could see only Taras's troubled green eyes.

Her fate lay somewhere in the future, but he wouldn't decide it yet. He was a damned fool.

Chapter Eleven

Cynewulf galloped back to the castle and stormed across the stone bridge. He reined in before the keep and leaped off his horse. Before he could lift Taras from the saddle, she jumped down and dashed into the keep. She ran upstairs to the bedchamber and slammed the door.

The servants had laid the furs upon the bed again, so she yanked them off and made her pallet by the fire. She crawled in and lay watching the door. He did not come, even when the shadows lengthened and she stoked the fire against the chill. Good, she didn't want him to come. She was mad enough to bash him in the head with the fire iron.

Each time she closed her eyes she saw his handsome, angry visage. All too well she remembered the iron clasp of his hands, his hot breath ravishing her throat. The thought made her weak with longing. Curse him, in what fire had he forged the shackles binding her to him?

She should have thrown the potion into his face instead of trying to escape. She wished she'd transformed him into a frog. How grand to have seen him hop into the stream to join his new subjects! She would have let him go. What danger would a frog prince pose to England?

At last she fell into a fitful sleep disturbed by frogs and croaking and war. She dreamed that legions of frogs overwhelmed England.

Denholm slammed into the chamber before cock's crow. "Get up. There is to be a *moot* and a tournament. You will work beside everyone else to prepare."

Taras worked all day in the scullery, scrubbing pots with sand and gravel. Denholm didn't say anything about her working as Cynewulf's scribe. She had destroyed that chance, she supposed. Cynewulf did not appear all day, nor at the evening meal. Exhausted, she retired to her pallet late that night.

The next morning, Ardeth set her to dressing the game the huntsmen brought in. It was hot, messy, disgusting work. The smell of blood and death made her sick with the desire to avenge herself. She abandoned the idea of merely turning Cynewulf into a frog and letting him swim off downstream. Nay, she would grind him under her heel and take his remains to the king. He deserved it, after humbling her so. She no longer thought of the good of England. This was a personal matter.

In the chamber that night she prepared a draught of warm wine and sprinkled in half a spoonful of potion. She set the silver chalice on the chest beside the bed and settled herself by the fire to wait.

At midnight she heard soft footsteps in the hallway, a scrape at the door, then silence. She jabbed her nails into the palms of her hands and forcibly stilled her sudden trembling. When he came in, she'd get up, greet him with a submissive bow, then serve him wine. And that would be the end of him.

She watched the door anxiously. Why didn't he enter and get it over with? *Open the door.*

It slowly opened. Taras wanted to get up and greet him as she'd planned, but she was too scared to make her muscles work. She lay on the pallet and feigned sleep.

He came into the room. She felt him stop beside the pallet and look down at her. *The wine. Go drink the wine.*

As though sensing her command, he turned toward the bed. Taras ventured to open her eyes a crack. By the dim firelight she saw him standing with his fists on his hips, looking at the cup.

Just drink it, Viking. You're thirsty, you know you are. Drink the wine. Transform yourself.

He lifted it and turned toward the fire. The chalice sparkled as he raised it to his lips.

Nay, don't drink it. It's poison!

He lowered the cup. Taras could see him staring at her. Could he see her in the gloom? Had he sensed her thoughts? Terror gathered at the base of her skull and held her fast. She could hear her own tortured breathing.

He set the cup on the chest and swiftly left the chamber. She heard his footsteps fade down the hall. She flung her arms wide and lay panting. So close. Why hadn't he drunk it? Had he sensed her hatred? Had the Wolf's keen sense of danger saved him yet again?

Or had he read her mind?

She bolted upright clutching the furs to her breast. If he could see her very thoughts, he owned her soul as well as her body. She could never kill him. She could never break free of him. She was his slave. She, a lady of England, a barbarian's slave!

She was doomed to drudgery, of toiling in his castle, of doing his bidding. What had he said when she'd demanded he let her go? *I'll let you go when I tire of you. Then I'll sell you.*

Sell her, as though she were an animal of no more importance than the mare. At any moment he might stop holding himself in check and come back to the chamber. She remembered the mare's agonized screams as Eboracum mounted her. She imagined herself on hands and knees while the Viking rode her hard and fast and his sweat fell upon her naked back. She could feel him opening her, holding her in arms of steel. He would do it to her without mercy. He would repay her for trying three times to kill him. And when he'd tired of punishing her, he would take her in to his men and sell her to the highest bidder.

She buried her face in her hands and wept. He did not come back that night. Taras did not sleep. In the morning, she cast the wine into the fire. An evil green flame shot up and was gone.

At midmorn, the watchman's shouts sent the household rushing to the circular barbican. On the dusty road far below, warriors by the score wound toward the castle, their chargers' silk trappings nearly sweeping the ground. Ladies plumed in brilliant mantles and headpieces formed islands of color. An army of servants, children, and dogs plodded behind the long caravan.

When they reached the mountaintop, Taras ran to the stone bridge to watch them parade past. None of the beautiful blond women so much as glanced her way. Taras felt like a sparrow perched there in her ragged clothing. She was relieved when Ardeth pushed through the throng and grabbed her arm. "Get back to work, lazy twit!"

"It's not necessary to order me about," she answered. "I'll help make these folk welcome."

"I can scarce believe my ears. Why, until this moment you've shown not desire to serve, but fear of the seneschal."

"I fear no one," Taras said. "I'll serve, if only to repay the debt your lord thinks I owe him."

"Ha! He finds your work of insufficient value to justify feeding you, much less to grant your freedom."

Taras controlled her temper. The Viking had mocked her for giving in to her baser urges and attacking this woman of low station. She vowed not to make a fool of herself again. "There is much to be done, Ardeth. I am at your bidding."

Hours later, Taras sat in the shade outside the keep to eat a bit of horsebread. She heard a merry uproar through the open doors. Other troupes were still arriving, bringing with them tons of baggage and hundreds of children and servants. Pallets and possessions crowded the castle chambers, galleries, and towers. Servants erected cloth pavilions in the baileys to house the overflow. The older children were sent down to the village to stay in the longhouses.

Late that evening as she moved about the great hall pouring wine and nabid, Taras felt warm fingers on her shoulder. She didn't have to look around to know it was Cynewulf. She stood with bowed head, waiting to know his will.

"Look at me, Taras," he said in Danish. By now she was familiar enough with the language to guess his meaning. Blood surged into her cheeks as she lifted her gaze to his.

Garbed in dusty leather, he smelled of horses and sweat. His sword pommel brushed her hip as he stepped closer to her. "For a chit who hardly knew how to scrub a floor just days ago, you've done well in your duties."

"I need no flattery from a man whose words are as hollow as his head."

Instead of scowling as she'd thought he might, he smiled. She wanted to touch the deepening clefts in his cheeks. Instead, she gripped the wineskin until the leather creaked.

"I can see you've missed me," he said.

133

"Aye, as sorely as the pox."

"Tch. Such sharpness. You haven't blunted the edge of your tongue. Denholm has been too lenient with you."

She spun away, but he caught the wineskin strap over her shoulder and jerked her near. He changed his grip to her upper arms. She tried to twist away, but he pulled her pelvis against his. From all over the hall men raised a lusty shout. Taras continued to writhe against him.

"My retainers are watching," he said.

"I do not care!"

"You provoke them with your delicious movements."

She provoked *them*. Not him. A frisson of anger charged down her spine. Was she nothing then, in this roomful of rich, beautiful women?

She didn't care that he didn't want her, she told herself. She didn't want him, either. Remember the mare. Don't excite this warhorse of a man.

"Leave me be, Lord Cynewulf," she said, daring to address him by name. "I despise you with all my soul!"

"Then it is not desire for me, but hatred that paints your cheeks the color of ripe quince?"

"Of course!"

"And does hatred cause your heart to hammer thus?" He took her left breast into his hand and flicked his thumb over her nipple.

Snarling, she clawed his wrist. He let go and stepped back a pace, planting his fists on his hips. His dark look made her tremble. "Go to my chamber, Taras."

"I would sooner sleep in the dungeon!"

"I will not give you that remedy."

Stamping her foot, she cried, "I will not go to your chamber!"

"Am I obliged to carry you there and lock the door behind us for the night?" He closed in until he filled every

134

corner of her vision. "If I do, I won't even try to stop myself from taking you in the furs."

"Will you leave me no choice, Viking?"

Dropping his voice so low she could scarcely hear it, he said, "Methinks you do not want a choice, my lady. You tease me as a young cat teases a lion, hoping to feel the kiss of his velvet paw."

"I hope for no such thing," she said, but she couldn't look him in the face. If she did, he would see the lie written there.

"Go now, young cat, and bar the door against me, else it will be more than my velvet paw you feel tonight."

Taras stumbled back a pace, dropped the wineskin, and fled upstairs. She barred the door and burrowed deep into her pallet. For a long time she lay listening to the noise from the great hall, not quite understanding why her cheeks were wet.

The *moot* lasted three days. In a large chamber off the great hall Cynewulf and his warriors met to discuss politics, war, and God knew what else. Taras endeavored to eavesdrop but could rarely make out what they were saying. She was sure Cynewulf was laying plans for the spring. If she could discover what they were, she'd escape and tell Ethelred everything.

Of course, the Viking's plans would change if she managed to transform him into a frog. Despite her nightmares, she didn't think a frog prince could lead a charge against armored knights.

At night Cynewulf slept somewhere else—she was too proud to ask where—and by day he avoided her. When at last the tournament began, the seneschal didn't allow her to go to the field to watch. She divided her time between the scullery and caring for children.

Around noon the next day, she slipped away to the southwest tower and climbed to the topmost room. From there she could hear faint shouts, but a hill hid the tournament field from sight. Even the folk traveling up and down the road were too distant to recognize. She couldn't see Cynewulf's black and silver colors. Disappointed, she returned to the scullery.

A cart rattled into the bailey. Denholm and a group of men rode behind it. As they passed under the portcullis, Taras caught sight of wounded men in the cart. All of them were big and blond. The cart was smeared with blood.

Taras dropped a kettle and bolted after the cart, which pulled up before the keep. She reached it as Denholm lifted the first injured man.

"Cynewulf! Is he here?" she cried. One of the men shoved her out of the way and cursed her. Taras ducked under his arm and climbed into the cart.

"Odin's beard, wench, get back to the scullery!" Denholm roared. He jerked her out of the cart, then shouldered one of the wounded. "He is yet on the tourney field."

She ran after him and seized his sleeve. "Is he hurt?"

Denholm released a great sigh and handed over the sufferer to two carls. "He rests after the melee. Already he has won many horses and arms. Now get back to your duties ere I take the whip to your backside."

He stomped up the steps into the keep and yelled, "Someone fetch the herbalist from the village, if he can be found!"

Taras dashed after him and seized the skirt of his chain mail. He turned, growling, upon her, but she didn't give ground.

"Will he fight again today?" she demanded.

The seneschal's eyes narrowed. " 'Tis no concern of a thrall woman, but aye, he will fight."

"But is he not weary after fighting the English for so long? He's done nothing but war."

"Bathing his sword in the blood of Ethelred's henchmen gave him strength, Briton, not weakness. None will defeat him in the game of spears. Now back to work!"

"My work is here, with the wounded," she said, and scooted away.

The servants and wives of the injured were already settling them on pallets before the fire. Taras hurried from one to another, assessing their wounds. She stopped beside a young warrior who lay curled on his side, gasping for breath. No one seemed to know how to help him. The herbalist had not arrived.

Taras quickly undid the warrior's mail byrnie, but when she tried to ease it off him, his face contorted and he groaned piteously. Taras snapped her fingers at a manservant. "You there, help me undress him!"

The servant stared at her without comprehension.

"Hurry up!" Taras cried. "Oh, why can't you learn English?"

"I will help with young Harrod," Denholm said, crossing to her. He removed the young man's byrnie and padded undertunic.

Taras caught her breath in horror. A fragment of a lance protruded from his left side. A swelling bruise extending from navel to armpit told Taras that he had lost much blood. Pockets of air crackled beneath his skin when she touched him.

At Taras's soft command, Denholm eased Harrod onto his left side. He breathed a trifle easier in that position. His lung was pierced, she was sure.

She didn't know how to save him. If only her mother were here! The lady's herb skill was much greater than her own; she could surely heal this boy. Taras squeezed her eyes shut and tried to remember what her mother had taught her about the lungs.

"I need hot water and a bowl of goose grease, and—and

a knife, and some clean cloths for bandaging. We haven't much time." While servants hastened to obey Denholm's translation, Taras bathed Harrod's face and whispered comforting lies. "We'll have you right enough to enjoy the feast tonight."

Inside, though, she simmered with anger. Cynewulf had done this. Death and suffering followed his every turn. Not only did the barbarian slay the king's men, but his very own. None can best him in the game of spears, Denholm had said. The cost didn't matter.

Denholm came back with the grease and bandages. He bade three men hold Harrod's arms and legs, then he laid hold of Harrod's pelvis and applied traction. "Pull it out," he told Taras. "He won't move."

But Harrod cried out in agony as soon as she touched the splinter. He arched and spasmed until the men could hardly hold him. When the fragment finally slipped free and blood frothed from the wound, Taras clapped a cloth laden with goose grease over it. The men placed him on his left side again.

Harrod's eyes rolled back in his head and he stopped screaming. Taras thought she had killed him. Then she heard him draw a ragged whisper of breath. Cold sweat sheened his ashen face. He was so young, and so very close to death.

"I need herbs," Taras told Denholm. At this point she didn't know what good they'd do, but she couldn't think of another remedy. "I need dandelion—perhaps you call it 'piss-a-bed'—and elder and bearberry and wormseed. Can you find them for me?"

"The herbalist has what you need. Thunder, where is that old man? He ought to be here by now!"

He got up and left the hall. Taras knelt beside Harrod and laid one hand on his forehead, the other on his breast.

138

He was growing colder, his breathing fainter. Ardeth came over and covered him with a blanket.

"Where is the herbalist?" Taras whispered.

"Who can tell? The old madman keeps to himself," Ardeth said with a snort. "He's sampled so many of his decoctions that he's less than worthless. People are afraid to go to him with their sicknesses. He'll do young Harrod no good."

But Taras wasn't listening. Whether or not the herbalist was worthless mattered little; she needed his herbs. If Denholm didn't return soon, she and Ardeth would go raid the old man's stores.

The door slammed open and Cynewulf and Denholm entered on a blast of cold wind. The Viking was wearing full battle gear. He hurried over and squatted beside the carl.

"Denholm says his lung is pierced," Cynewulf said.

"Aye, perhaps you remember the incident!" she spat.

Cynewulf narrowed his eyes in thought. "The shadow of death hovers over him. No herb will dispel it. Denholm, go to Beldor's forge and bring me the smallest bellows you can find."

Cynewulf pulled his sheath knife and began to cut away the bandages.

"What do you mean to do?" Taras asked, seizing his wrist.

"Leave be, Briton."

"If he dies, it will be your fault! Doubly so, since you doubtless pierced him on the field."

"You wist not the affairs of men. Be silent."

Soon Denholm returned with the bellows. Cynewulf squeezed the wooden handles together until air puffed out of the leather bag. Understanding his intention at last, Taras raised shocked eyes to him.

"Replace the bandages when I tell you to, woman," Cynewulf said. "This is the only way to save him."

Horror snaked up and down Taras's spine. Cynewulf inserted the mouth of the bellows deep into the wound and puffed in short bursts of air. Taras could see no change in Harrod's condition, no motion in his chest.

"It won't work," she whispered. "You'll only fill his last moments with more pain!"

Cynewulf's mouth tightened. He continued to puff air into the hole. Harrod groaned. Suddenly his chest rose.

"Seal the wound!" Cynewulf said.

Taras clapped on the cloth and smeared over it another thick layer of goose grease. With Cynewulf's help she layered bandages around Harrod's chest. They propped him on pillows.

Cynewulf sat back on his heels and touched Harrod's cheek. His hard hands moved so gently that Taras could scarcely imagine them curved around a spear. "He does not sweat with such coldness," he said at length. "Perhaps we have cheated death for now."

They sat watching him in silence for a long time before Taras spoke. "Denholm said you won many horses in the melee."

"Aye."

"You were not injured?"

"Nay."

"Oh. You only *did* the injuring, then."

He glanced up at her. "It's late. I don't feel like fighting. Retire to our chamber."

"I will not leave this boy until I know if he'll live."

"You care so much for a barbarian?"

"I do not understand your meaning."

"He is a Dane. A pagan. You despise us, or have you forgotten?"

"I despise some of you."

"Some few fortunate ones."

Taras nearly choked on a wave of anger. "It is a shame you do not lie in his place. It would be a pleasure to watch you die."

"And I desire always to pleasure you. Mayhap I'll be killed tomorrow."

"One can always hope."

Cynewulf sighed. He gestured at Harrod. "He is not so gray now. And see, his chest rises on both sides. A good sign."

Taras touched the warrior's cheek. Harrod opened his eyes and groaned. "What devilment happened to me?" he whispered.

"You forgot that the game of spears is also played with shields," Cynewulf said.

"Stupid of me, lord." His lids fluttered closed.

United in their concern, Cynewulf and Taras leaned over him. Taras gradually became aware of the Viking's scent in her nostrils. Without moving her head, she raised her eyes to study his rugged profile. She made no effort to blow away the golden strands of hair brushing her face.

Cynewulf turned his head and stared into her eyes. His breath flowed like a lover's caress over her face. He held her thus for a long moment before his lips drew back in a smile.

"You would not scratch me tonight, were I to carry you to my bed, my feisty young cat."

Taras's longing turned to dismay. Scooting away from him, she backed into a man lying on a pallet.

"By the old gods!" he roared, rearing up to clutch his splinted leg. "Send the bedwench away, lord, I beseech you!"

Taras slapped him across the face. He bellowed and changed his grip to his jaw. At Cynewulf's chuckle, Taras rounded on him.

"Is this the gratitude I receive, sir? Insults and recriminations from you and your filthy man? A pox on you both then, and may the devil drag you on tenterhooks to your eternal damnation!"

Still chuckling, he fastened his gaze upon her breasts. "Go to bed, Taras."

"Nay!"

"You have naught to fear."

"Ha!" From the way he was staring at her bosom, his thoughts were far from the tournament field and the men he'd laid low. No chamber door could withstand the pressure of his great shoulder should he desire to enter. And desire it, he would. Taras needed no soothsayer to divine the lust in his eyes.

"I'll stay here and watch Harrod," she said. "You can join those revelers of yours."

Cynewulf rose and stood over her. She stared back boldly, though inside she trembled like a newborn foal. Damn him and his power over her!

"Stay then," he said at last. "Ardeth will fetch you victuals. I will come back later."

"Don't trouble yourself. I'll be content without you."

"Your welfare doesn't interest me. I'll return to check on my man."

He stalked off to the feast. Wenches hurried to surround him, exclaiming over his prowess on the tourney field. Trying to contain her wrath, Taras laid a cool cloth on Harrod's head.

"How do you fare, lad?" she asked when he opened his eyes.

"Nigh dead," he gasped.

She fetched him wine and helped him drink. He shut his eyes and slept again. Taras stole a glance at Cynewulf.

He sat in his chair on the dais, looking at her through a

screen of maidens. He lifted his cup to her in a silent toast. Taras looked away. She wouldn't pay any more attention to him. She hated the very sight of him and wished him dead.

Murderess. If Lord Cynewulf really were the grandson of Thor, one of the Viking's fell gods might wipe her from the face of the earth for thinking such thoughts.

She clasped her arms around her knees and bowed her head. If only Ethelred would send his warriors to rescue her from the terrible deed she was about to do. If she killed Cynewulf, she would never know another moment's peace. If she let him live, her beloved country would never be secure.

She fingered the pewter vial hanging around her neck. It was as heavy as a millstone.

Chapter Twelve

Cynewulf gazed across the crowded hall at Taras. Curled on the floor near Harrod, she'd fallen asleep at last. He should carry her upstairs, but then she'd awaken and begin fighting him again. The wench deserved a few hours' peace.

He tried to force his attention away from her, but his feet betrayed him. He crossed noiselessly to her and covered her with his wolfskin mantle. He listened to Harrod's pained breathing, then settled into a chair close to the woman.

By his father's whiskers, what should he do with her? For days he had watched her, wanted her, resisted her. All today he had pondered what to say to win her regard. He was naught but a foolish knave trying to grope his way through the maze of a woman's heart!

And just how would he find his way through the maze while forcing her to work as a slave? Such a woman should be clothed in silver and ermine. She should command men and kings. She should rule beside him—

Great Thor, where was his imagination taking him now? He passed his hand over his eyes. It was one thing to spare her the sweet agony of his ardor, but quite another to entertain such soft feelings toward her. She was his enemy, by thunder, an enemy who had tried to kill him on the mountain road. And then there was last night, when he'd come to his chamber to find the silver chalice waiting for him. He'd nearly drunk it when, out of the darkness, he'd sensed his beautiful enemy's thoughts. *Poison.* For that she deserved to die, yet how could he bring himself to harm her? He frowned at the scar on his thumb.

Denholm came over and sat in a chair beside him. Cynewulf didn't feel like talking. Amid noise and confusion, he could be alone as long as no one spoke to him. But he knew the seneschal wouldn't keep his mouth shut.

"How fared you at the close of the melee, lord?"

He shifted in his chair and stared into the fire. When Denholm repeated his question, he answered softly lest his hated voice arouse the wench: "I was holding Beogar's Bridge. I'll fight there again tomorrow."

"And I will be at your back."

"Suit yourself."

Denholm chuckled. "You nearly shared young Harrod's fate today. Where were your thoughts, that you let Svenson touch you with his spear?"

Cynewulf glanced at the woman. He remembered exactly where his thoughts had been. On Taras. When Eboracum leaped into combat, he'd spared a glance at the stands to learn if she was watching. He could still feel the blow of the spear against his ribs. *Callow youth. Imbecile.*

"You should be abed, lord, not mooning over the wench."

"Your reflections are as brilliant as dirt. Keep them to yourself."

The seneschal chuckled again. In a soft baritone he sang, " 'Take care, young ladies, and value your wine. Be watchful of young men in their velvet prime. . . . Deeply they'll swallow from your finest kegs, then swiftly be gone leaving bitter dregs—' "

"You take too great a burden upon yourself, seneschal, to try to read my thoughts. You're neither skald nor soothsayer."

"Ah, but have you not said you will use her at will, and discard her in like fashion?"

Cynewulf laid his head against the back of the chair. "One of these days, old knave, I'll get the spell weaver to swell up your tongue and choke you. She knows all manner of poisons."

Denholm only laughed and offered him wine. Cynewulf took the cup, started to drink, then dashed it to the floor. The wine seeped like blood into the rushes.

Taras awakened the next morning snuggled into Cynewulf's mantle. She sat up and looked around, but he was gone. She thrust the mantle away and crawled over to Harrod. He had improved enough to growl and curse when she tried to turn him.

"Evil vapors will settle upon your chest if you lie so still," she said. "Now roll over!"

She checked the other wounded men, changed several dressings and poultices, then went outside to the kitchen for a kettle of broth.

Ardeth stopped her on the way back to the keep. "Here, where do you think you're going with that?"

"To feed the sick. Now stand out of my way."

The maid stepped close and raised her voice to be sure

the carls saddling their horses heard her. "You think to win the master's favor by pretending to care for his men."

"I do care. Now stand aside."

"He'll be interested to know how you spent last night, then, won't he?"

"And exactly how was that?"

"Why, don't tell me it wasn't you I saw crawling from pallet to pallet, offering the slut's breed of comfort."

It wouldn't do any good to try to defend herself. She ought to turn the hot broth over Ardeth's head. Instead, she stepped around her and walked on. Ardeth ran and grabbed her skirt.

"Aye, Harrod and the others feel much better this morn," she said, "after the tender care you gave them in the furs!"

Taras set the kettle deliberately on the ground and straightened. "I surely did not hear you correctly. Mayhap the difference in our accents accounts for it."

"I called you a whore."

"So I wasn't wrong, then." She bent as though to lift the kettle, then suddenly jammed her right shoulder into Ardeth's middle and lifted her into the air, stumbled a few feet across the bailey, and dropped her into a stone horse trough. The watching housecarls roared with delight. Ignoring them and the spluttering maid, she retrieved the kettle and hurried away.

It was a small victory. To live among warlike people, a maiden had to be strong. To kill their master, she had to become a warrior herself. She set her jaw and walked into the keep.

She did not see Cynewulf all that day. The wounded poured into the hall seeking stitches and splints and compresses and bindings. Most of them went back to the tournament field. Others packed up what few possessions remained to them after their losses and journeyed home.

Cynewulf did not come near her at the feast that night.

For the next three days Taras hardly saw him. Strangely, as his fame grew, he took less and less interest in feasting and song. The skalds sang of his prowess and everyone said he grew richer and more fearsome with every passage of arms.

His luck wouldn't last forever, Taras told herself. One of these days, the bloody man they carried home would be Cynewulf. She didn't need the frog potion. If he kept fighting, someone else would slay him. Ethelred would soon breathe easier.

Yet she could scarcely breathe at all. By day she pictured him risking his life on the tournament field, by night she pictured him in the arms of some noblewoman.

At the feast on Wodin's Day, Cynewulf decreed that on the morrow they would rest. Taras felt such a sudden, shaky sense of relief that she had to hurry from the great hall.

She went to the cistern in the outer bailey and began to winch up the bucket. Starlight stippled the dark water. For an instant she held the heavens in a bucket.

"You shouldn't venture into the night alone, spell weaver."

"Oh!" She dropped the bucket back into the well.

Cynewulf stood only a few feet away. The stars which had glittered in the water now traced the sword in his hand. Clad in black leather and a winged helm, he looked like a pagan god of war. His beauty seemed to suck the very marrow from her bones.

"I might have known you would follow me," she said unsteadily. "Mayhap you feared I would climb the walls and escape your army."

Saying nothing, he stepped close to her. She saw his eyes glint; then he thrust Damfertigénen into the ground between them and rested his hands on the jeweled crosspiece.

Taras couldn't bear his nearness. She turned away to the

149

cistern and caught the handle, then cranked furiously until the bucket reappeared. Before she could catch it, he leaned over and lifted it off the hook.

"I need no help," she said, grabbing the handle. He didn't let go. She tugged with both hands.

"You're weary," he said. "Let me help you."

"Throw yourself into the well, then."

Cynewulf released the bucket so abruptly that she stumbled back into the stonework. "I see you enjoy your role too much to relinquish any of its duties."

"What role would that be, Viking?"

He slid Damfertigénen into the scabbard before answering, "That of my slave."

"Ha! That I'll never be!"

"I thought you would come to cherish it, in time. It is the measure of a Briton to serve the children of Odin."

"You're a conceited lout!"

Cynewulf caught her chin between his fingers and turned her face up to his. He spoke against her lips. "Were I the devil you think me, I would rub your backside raw against my bed."

He'd spoken the truth. She could not understand why he had restrained himself thus far, surely he possessed no fine feelings for her, nothing that made him cherish her virginity. He was unlike the stories she'd heard of Vikings. Very unlike them.

He was gazing into her eyes, his own alight with promise, and perhaps a question. Did he seek her permission to bed her? Did he, after all, cede her some portion of free will, slave though she was?

Her treacherous thoughts shifted to the hard body so close to her own. She felt his hand close over the bucket handle, capturing her fingers. He brought his other hand to the small of her back and pulled her hips against his. He was hard and strong, too warm and big and male to resist.

She tipped back her head and watched him out of half-closed lids. Her breath came fast, and her belly burned with fire. Why resist anymore? Why pretend hatred toward this man who had taken more than her freedom when he'd stolen her from the forest? He'd taken her heart, reluctant though she was to give it. She could not deny that.

"Your beauty overwhelms me, Lady Taras," he said. "In all the earth I cannot conceive of another like you. What is this spell you've woven about me? What have you done to steal the very marrow from my bones, to turn my thoughts to water and my heart to a quivering moth's wing?"

Sharp, pained surprise and guilt seized her, held her speechless. Before she could answer, he cast the water bucket aside and enveloped her in his arms. His mantle fell over her, and he kissed her mouth, her eyes, her cheeks, her throat. She moaned and strained against him, wanting to give him everything, yearning to breathe acquiescence in his ear. She could make him love her, she could!

And what of England? a cooler part of her mind demanded. She had no right to take his love, no right to bend his heart to hers when she knew he must die.

"Dear God, no!" she gasped, breaking from his kiss. "Please let me go!"

She tore from his arms and sped from the bailey leaving him cursing into the well.

He did not come to the chamber again that night. Through the dark, lonely hours Taras wept and paced to and fro. She had to kill him. There was no other way. She could not, would not love him. But though she couldn't love him, she couldn't betray him, could she?

She wanted her mother; surely the lady could tell her what to do. Her mother could weave a seeing spell to show her the future. And if the spell failed and showed only darkness, what then?

Then she needed a priest. A priest could absolve her of the ghastly sin she must soon commit. She knelt and prayed for peace, but when daylight encrusted the frosty eastern battlements, she was no closer to forgiveness. When she looked out the window she saw a gyrfalcon speed across a field on quicksilver wings.

Cynewulf was out there somewhere. She could feel him. The gyr was a sign.

She went and washed herself at the basin, taking a long time. Then she plaited her hair and donned the red mantle he had given her. Through the fabric she felt the pewter vial. It was time.

In the great hall, the tables still groaned under the remnants of last night's feast. She tied a loaf of bread into a corner of her mantle and took a small wineskin and two wooden cups.

She hurried outside and stopped in the shadow of the keep. Fumbling in her haste, she pulled the stopper from the wineskin, then with shaking fingers uncorked the pewter vial and trickled all but a little of the potion into the wine. She sealed both containers and hid the vial in her bosom.

In the outer bailey she tried to keep to the shadows of the curtain wall, but she had to step over people curled up in pallets. The stable was just ahead. She felt sure she could bribe Mechalah to give her the mare she'd ridden the other day. If she offered him half the loaf of bread, he'd probably give her the mare and tell her where to find Cynewulf.

She jumped over a young woman asleep in the furs and landed on someone else's hand. The sleeper awakened with a roar. To her horror, she saw she'd stepped on the seneschal.

Denholm thrust aside the furs and rose quickly, grabbing the ax in his belt. His face relaxed when he saw who had fallen over him. "You are about early this morn, Briton."

Cold with fear, Taras clutched the wineskin behind her back beneath the mantle. "I—I looked for you inside, seneschal."

"Wherefore?"

"I thought . . . um . . . I thought you would take me to see Lord Cynewulf."

"He will summon you if he desires your presence."

"But I desire to speak with him."

"Then by all means, Your Highness, let us interrupt his pleasure."

"Pleasure?" She suddenly felt sick. Last night, after she refused his advances at the well, had he sought comfort with another woman? Was this what the seneschal meant?

Why should it matter? She wasn't here to serve his needs, but her king's. The proof of that was hidden behind her back.

The seneschal studied her with the keenness of a hunting dog. She tried to mask her emotions behind a brittle smile. To her surprise, he said gently, "He seeks not his pleasure in the furs, lady, but in the field with his raptors. Come, I will take you."

He clapped his spangenhelm on his head and strode off. She had to run to keep up with him. Reaching the stable, he ducked under the doorway and quickly saddled a huge brown destrier. A crooked grin bisecting his face, he led Taras past the Arabian mare and pointed out an ancient roan of uncertain lineage.

"Your steed, my lady," he said dryly, and doffed his helm. "This is Shemaby-Alflender. I cannot translate it into your tongue, but some call him Dragon Crusher. Shall I saddle him for you?"

Taras might have smiled if she had not murder in her heart. Perhaps it was best she wasn't allowed to ride the Arabian; she was too shaky to control her. "Please."

After saddling the roan and leading the horses outside,

Denholm helped Taras mount, then trotted his horse off to the stone bridge. The wind howling up the ravine shook the bridge so hard that the destrier balked, but Shemaby-Alflender plodded across without a qualm.

"Nothing can surprise you anymore, can it?" Taras whispered, patting his gray-flecked withers. She wished she shared his confidence. The wineskin felt like a stone against her side.

Two hours later, they passed through a narrow gorge and forded a stream. Soon they entered a windswept field framed by gray stone walls. Clouds crowned a vast fell on the northern end. A lake lapped its foot.

Taras spied Eboracum grazing with several other horses. As she rode closer, she discerned servants and house-carls resting beneath a giant oak.

"There is your master," Denholm said.

Against the reeds on the lake shore, Cynewulf stood nearly invisible. Taras felt her heart lurch. She jerked the old roan to a halt.

Denholm reined in beside her. "We're in luck," he said. "Watch the lake."

They heard a splash, then Cynewulf's big wolfhound exploded out of the rushes. A flock of ducks leaped into the air and flapped for a distant stand of trees.

"Look up there!" Taras cried, pointing out a gray flash.

A peregrine falcon stooped out of the sun and hurtled straight down the fellside. It slashed one of the ducks with its talons, tumbling it for several yards. The fowl recovered enough to evade the next strike.

For many seconds the falcon spiraled after her quarry, maneuvering with such violence that Taras thought her wings would snap. Again and again she stooped on the larger bird, but at last the duck managed to ring up into the clouds.

Rounding her wings, the falcon soared past the cliff

screeching, the bell jingling on her leg. At last she swooped down and perched on Cynewulf's gauntlet.

Taras sent Shemaby-Alflender into a jerky trot across the field. Denholm followed at a slower pace. Cynewulf did not turn or indicate that he was aware of their presence, not even when Taras reined in only ten paces away. He tied a short leash to the bird's jess, slipped a plumed leather hood over its gray and white head, then settled it into a light wooden cadge on a servant's back.

"We will fly her again tomorrow," Cynewulf told the cadger. "She may do better then."

"She's young," Taras said. The bird's brownish-gray coloring and heavy stripings told her so.

"The eyas will learn," Cynewulf said to the cadger.

"She will have no choice," Taras said, looking down at him from the horse.

Cynewulf gestured to his dog. "Warf, come!"

The wolfhound splashed along the water's edge and sped across the field to plant his muddy paws on Cynewulf's chest. The Viking pushed him down and fed him a portion of meat. "Good lad."

Determined to make Cynewulf acknowledge her, Taras said, "I've never seen a wolfhound flush birds."

The Dane looked up at her then, his eyes like cold bits of glass. A muscle throbbed in his jaw; then he turned on his heel and stalked off. Taras sat her horse, scowling.

One of the cadgers brought him a white gyrfalcon twice the peregrine's size. Cynewulf caught its gess and tugged gently. The gyr stepped onto his arm and waited while he removed her hood.

Blinking against the glare, the gyr stretched out one snowy wing and ran its beak through the flight feathers. Then it assumed an alert posture on its master's wrist, digging its talons into his gauntlet.

"Warf, seek!" the Viking commanded.

The wolfhound made a wide sweep around the field. Waiting on the gauntlet, the gyr watched the dog out of fierce, unblinking eyes. It tensed when a grouse leaped chattering into the air.

Cynewulf released it. Speeding over the ground like an arrow, it chased the grouse for half a minute before striking it to earth.

Caught up in the excitement, Taras set heels to her horse's flanks and galloped after the gyr.

"Eboracum!" Cynewulf shouted. The stallion flung up his head and charged across the field. He slowed just enough for Cynewulf to vault into the saddle, then pounded after Taras. Cynewulf threw her a glare as he thundered past.

Cynewulf dismounted and approached the gyrfalcon. Mantling over its prey, it screamed at him in possessive fury and dug its talons into the grouse's breast.

This was the moment when he might lose it, this moment of exhilaration when the falcon owned the kill and the instinct to fly off and never return ruled its heart. In this moment Cynewulf was not her master. No man could own a creature born to the wild. This was the time when will matched will, when the force of his nature alone must conquer its thirst for freedom. This was the part of the hunt he relished most.

Cynewulf extended his arm and waited with glittering eyes.

The gyrfalcon screamed again—a raging burst of surrender—then leaped off the grouse onto the gauntlet. Cynewulf held it high for a moment, offering it one last chance at freedom. It bored its talons into his gauntlet, seeking his naked flesh. Its dark eyes took on a fiercer radiance as it stared into his.

"So you come back of your own will once more, my lady," Cynewulf said. He took its jess between his fingers, smoothed its snowy breast plumage, and went to retrieve the grouse. He turned to mount Eboracum.

The warhorse was several yards away, his muzzle against Taras's neck. Shemaby-Alflender grazed nearby. Cynewulf looked for Denholm and found him loafing under the tree with the other men.

"What the devil are you about, wench?" he demanded of Taras.

"I came to speak with you." A gust of wind blew her mantle off her shoulders and molded her bliaut to her breasts.

Cynewulf had to draw in a deep breath to steady himself. "We have nothing to talk about."

"You prefer to set me free without discussion, then?"

"I do not intend to free you."

"I've earned my freedom. Denholm says so."

"Denholm is an old woman with a loose tongue."

"He lauded my labors with the wounded. Even Harrod is recovering."

"Denholm often flatters slaves, thinking to appease them."

His words lashed her like a whip. Remembering just in time the real purpose for her visit, she bit back a retort.

Cynewulf slipped a blue hood over the gyr's head and tied it before it could rake it off. He slid his fingers down its feathered legs to check them for injury.

"Is that the gyr we saw on the mountain?" Taras asked.

"Nay, it is a haggard I captured in Denmark three years ago." He shut his mouth tightly, as if unwilling to tell her more, but when she waited in silence, he added, "The gyrs here are grayer in color."

"Oh . . . Are you hungry?"

He looked at her without replying. She pushed Eboracum away and brought out the bread and wine.

"Have you poisoned it?"

Taras's heart nearly failed her. Did he know she'd mixed

in the potion? With a boldness she didn't feel, she pulled the birch stopper and raised the wineskin to her lips. "Do you think I would be stupid enough to slay myself to get you? Shall I drink half the draft to prove its purity?"

Before he could reply, a cadger rode up to take the gyrfalcon. While Cynewulf was distracted, Taras lowered the skin. Her hand shook so violently that she could hardly replace the stopper. *Dear God, what if he'd bidden me to drink?*

She tried not to look at him, but his naked, muscular arms drew her gaze. When his wolfskin whipped in the breeze, she glimpsed a dirk strapped to his bare thigh. He cut a barbaric figure against the savage fell.

By the Virgin, how could she kill such a man? She had to enchant him, yet it seemed he had already enchanted her. Why else were her senses confounded by passion and rage, ardor and enmity? Most of the time he seemed completely unaware of his effect on her, but this was a sham. He well knew how to flush her cheeks and start a fire in her loins, damn him. That was reason enough to kill him.

The cadger rode off with the gyrfalcon. Taras said, "Will you eat, my lord?"

"Since you've taken the trouble to bring it."

With studied calmness she took off her red mantle and spread it upon the ground. She laid out the bread, wine, and wooden cups. "Will you sit?"

He stared down at her, one lid half closed in suspicion. Suddenly he caught her plait and twisted the end around his fist. "You dare much in seeking to manipulate me," he said.

Her heart jolted. He knew! He knew what she wanted to do to him! Her knees gave out and she sank into the grass. He did not release her hair. As she looked up his sinewy arm to his face, she knew he could break her with little effort.

"The—the morn is far spent," she whispered. "I would not toy with a hungry man."

He switched his gaze to her bosom until she felt her nipples tingle. Smiling wickedly, he tightened his grip on her hair. Between his teeth he said, "Mayhap you cause his hunger, wench."

Before she could stop herself, she touched the vial at her breast. Cynewulf's gaze followed her hand. "Your amulet?" he said. "You still seek its fragile protection?"

"There is no protection from you, Viking! You've taught me that again and again!"

He yanked her against his thighs and held her there. She could feel his hardness against her breast and cheek. What if he lifted his tunic? What would he make her do? He could drown her in a pool of rage and sensual desire.

She almost wanted him to do it.

Chapter Thirteen

"Almost, wench," Cynewulf muttered, staring hard into her eyes. "Almost I shed my control."

He thrust her away and sat down on the mantle. Taras fell onto her hands and glared up at him, breathing between clenched teeth. What foul madness had seized her, that she'd desired him to take her but moments ago?

Watching her out of unblinking eyes, he stretched his legs before him, reclined on one elbow, and peeled off his gauntlets. With the tall grass waving around him, he seemed half-lion. She could almost feel his velvet caress.

"Will you stay on your hands and knees like a dog, Briton, or put aside your barbaric manners and sit?"

"One of these days," she gritted out, "I'll teach you just how barbaric I can really be."

He tossed one of his gauntlets on the mantle between them. "Any time you're ready, I'll receive the lesson."

Taras folded her legs under her and sat back. In a moment he'd swallow the terrible potion and his crowing would change to croaking. She visualized his face going green and horrible.

But first, she must calm his rage and dull his wits. Food would work; it always did with a man. "I need your dirk," she said.

"Indeed? The lesson begins now?"

"Not the lesson you hope for. I need to cut the bread."

"Too bad, I would have enjoyed your instruction." He thrust aside his mantle, revealing the knife strapped to his thigh. "Take it."

She wrapped her fingers one by one around the handle and slowly withdrew the gleaming blade. As she slid it over his naked skin, she sensed his tension. His breathing changed to short bursts. Did he suppose she would try to stab him? Drat it, she was doing nothing to dull his senses.

Her little finger brushed his hot skin. Fire shot up her arm to her breast, filling her brain with wild imaginings. She wanted to drop the knife and caress him, to slip her fingers up under the leather tunic and see just how much he wanted her.

Instead she slid the dirk free and with a violent motion sliced the loaf in half. Although he didn't move, she perceived his surprise. Didn't the fool know she dared not take him on like a warrior? Didn't he know she had to kill him in the coward's way? She bit her lip and looked down to hide her tears.

"Weeping over horsebread?" he said, low. It was not a question but a gentle mockery. Without looking at him, Taras handed him a piece.

She heard his men laughing from across the field. The sound seemed irreverent, like laughter at a funeral. She wondered if they would laugh when their lord turned into a frog and hopped into the lake.

"Wine, Taras," he said, holding out one of the wooden cups.

Now that the time had come, she didn't want to pour it.

Like a person in a dream, she picked up the wineskin and pulled the stopper. She watched the red wine stream into the cup. Cynewulf raised it to her in a silent toast. She gazed back at him in wide-eyed horror.

"But it would be wrong of me to drink alone," Cynewulf said, "seeing that you've brought two cups."

Cynewulf picked up the empty cup and held it out. She dared not refuse. She dribbled wine into it, but her hand shook until she spilled a portion over his wrist.

"So skittish you are," he said. Instead of wiping the spill onto the mantle, he flicked it off with his tongue. Taras clutched the wineskin in both hands and tried not to show emotion. She felt frozen from end to end.

Cynewulf handed her the cup. "Let us drink together, Lady Taras, as befits two enemies under a flag of truce."

"Truce?" she said through dry lips. The cup felt like a sleeping viper coiled in her hands. She remembered the evil vapors after she'd decocted the potion. How in her maddest dreams had she thought she was brewing a love potion? How could she have made herself belief that a decoction of such dangerous herbs could provoke one to venery? And how could she now obey Ethelred's rule?

"Even enemies must occasionally rest from hating each other," he said.

"Must they?" she whispered.

He lifted his cup. "A toast to you, Briton. May your beauty never fade."

She laughed out loud, a hysterical burst of sound quickly stifled. Beauty? What beauty would he find in a she-frog? Would they lanquish together in the lake until some duck snapped them up?

Cynewulf clicked his cup into hers, then quickly swallowed. He lowered the cup and looked at her, waiting.

She shut her eyes. She'd done it. By all lights, she'd killed him. Dear Lord, she didn't want to see the transformation, didn't want to hear him scream as his flesh festered and boiled, melting into monstrous greenness. She didn't want to see his lips stretch wide and hideous, his eyes turn yellow and bulge from their sockets. She remembered Sir Osric the Frog's coldness when Ethelred pressed him against her breast.

Dear God, forgive me. She needn't drink with him now. She could pretend to drink, and pour the poison into the grass. Then she could keep watch until the transformation was over. When the Viking sat before her, a frog prince, she would run away to England. She'd kill another frog and give it to Ethelred.

Cynewulf took the wineskin and replenished his cup. He drank deeply, then poured and drank again. Taras watched him for signs. She didn't know how long it would take. No one had known how long Sir Osric lay in his bed before his squire found him. She thought again of Sir Osric's trust in her, his desperate need to be loved. She had failed him.

The Viking needed her for nothing. She was his plaything, a tarnished treasure he alternately craved and despised. Since he expected nothing but her hatred, she could not fail him. She could only give him what he deserved.

"I am grateful for how you've treated my retainers," he said, breaking the silence. "You've wrought miracles, spell weaver."

She wanted neither to hear that name nor the gentle way he said it. Didn't he know how stupid he was to praise her, the woman who had just taken everything away from him? Didn't he know what it had cost her to set aside every shred of decency and destroy him with a fiendish trick? Didn't he see that she'd tossed away heaven to send him to hell? Only a woman who hated with her whole soul could take the life of another.

She had never hated like that before . . . she didn't think she hated so now. His life was not hers to take. If God willed Cynewulf dead, he would smite the Viking himself. She was no shield-maiden to war on a man. And then she thought, *Nay—I am an assassin.*

She wished she could drown in the swirling wine in her cup. She couldn't live with herself anymore, not after using enchantment to destroy this man she was coming to . . . love.

Love. It was a fearsome emotion, worse still than hate. If she despised the Viking, she could someday, perhaps, forgive herself for what she'd done. But love? Nay, surely she didn't love this brutal enemy. Please Lord, not that.

She locked eyes with him, searching for a bit of yellow in the sea blue depths. She saw none, yet soon he must shrivel and become a loathsome, slimy thing belonging to the swamp. She would see his long, powerful legs bend and contort, his mouth twist into a foul, lipless grin.

She couldn't bear it, nay, never. The scene would haunt every moment of her life. She'd never forgive herself for transforming a vibrant being into a creature of hell.

In a voice strange to her own ears, she said, "I must join you, Cynewulf." She lifted the cup and drained every drop. The draught burned a fiery track to her belly. She wondered how long it would be until her fingers grew webbed and warty. She folded them tightly together and waited for the pain.

"The wine will settle your fidgets," Cynewulf said.

Tears trickled down her cheeks. "You don't understand, do you?"

"Understand a maiden's tears? What man alive does so?"

"Certainly not you."

"I understand more than you think," he said with a mysterious smile. He took her empty cup. "It's not necessary for you to drink again. You've proved the wine isn't poisonous."

165

She felt her breath catch on a laugh that was no laugh at all, but a cry torn from her soul. "Don't you understand yet what you've done? What I've done to you?"

The smile faded from his eyes. "I know damned well what you've done to me, spell weaver. It causes me grave concern."

"Concern? Is that all? You sit here smiling and—and drinking while my ungodly enchantments wreak destruction inside your body?"

"Ach, I do not think I'll be destroyed." He leaned forward on one elbow and grinned. "In fact, since I drank that potion of yours I've felt quite randy. Perhaps your witch's brew wreaks some other effect on a man. I suddenly can scarce contain the urge to tear off my clothing and chase you naked across the meadow. What say you, spell weaver, will you strip down to your soft white skin and let me chase you? I'll be the falcon and you be the pigeon." Cynewulf threw back his head and laughed.

Taras raised her brows in amazement. The wretch wasn't growing green and warty at all, but ruddy as a young buck. She'd seen such lust in the eyes of drunken men. Worse yet, she was becoming light-headed and unlike herself. Low in her belly she felt the red flower of passion bloom. She wasn't turning into a frog, but a hot-blooded bedslave.

She finally understood. "You took the vial of potion!" she accused. "You guessed it contained poison, so you poured it out and filled the vial with something to bring on venery—to make me want to leap into bed with you, didn't you?"

Cynewulf wagged his finger at her. "Nay, your potion is the same. I believed you wanted to kill me, so I bade my herbalist test the stuff on a pig. The pig did not die as I thought it would, but became so enamored of a goat that, well, you can imagine what ensued."

"Oh my heavens!" Taras cried. She stared at the vial, aghast. The fire began to fade from her belly, replaced by cold rage at his trickery.

Cynewulf talked on, oblivious to her anger. "The herbalist said he'd never seen such venery in a pig, so he tried it upon himself, and him not a day under seventy winters old! No wench was safe from him for two days. He desires to know your secret to brewing such a love spell, thinking he'll become rich as well as . . . popular. And I, of course, wonder why you gave me such a fiery potion." Smiling in a meaningful way, he ran his fingers down her arm from shoulder to wrist.

Taras snatched herself away and slapped him across the face. She jumped to her feet and ran to the horses. Cynewulf's laughter followed her across the field.

Eboracum thrust out his muzzle and slobbered against her neck. She pushed him away and reached for Shemaby-Alflender's bridle, but the roan kicked up his heels and capered around her like the Dragon Crusher of old. Again and again he jerked the reins out of her hands until, her temper a flaring comet, she grabbed his mane and tried to vault onto his back. He sprang sideways, tumbling her to the ground.

She lay there gasping. Eboracum trotted over to nuzzle her face. Even the wolfhound ambled over to sniff. Cynewulf came and squatted beside her, amusement etching his handsome face. "Are you hurt, spell weaver?"

"Go jump in the lake!" How dared he make a fool of her? The next time she tried to kill him, she wouldn't settle for changing him into a frog—she'd poison him with something deadly painful. He could die in screaming agony, as he deserved.

He took her hand, but she jerked away and clambered to her feet. "I need no help from you!"

"Yea, that I can see."

"If you begin laughing again, I'll split your gullet from stem to stern."

"I do not intend to laugh." He produced her mantle and slipped it around her shoulders.

Taras stalked off and grabbed the roan's bridle. She began to walk him toward the gorge. Denholm and the others saddled up and mounted to follow. Cynewulf rode over to speak with them. Taras walked on, pretending not to notice him, but when she reached the gorge he rode up beside her.

"Would you rather ride?" he asked.

"The horse wore himself out just now."

"He's recovered enough for you to sit him."

"He might drop dead," she said, in a tone that included her hope that Cynewulf would, too.

"He's a tough one. He'll not die under you."

"He will if he's pushed too hard."

"He likes to be pushed; it makes him feel young." Cynewulf reached down to tug the old destrier's forelock. "He was my father Beogar's warhorse. He would carry you to the moon, if you asked him."

"You've had a touch of the sun to entertain such fantasies."

"Mayhap it was your sorcerer's brew. Tell me, just how did you hope I would react to that love potion?"

Taras raised her nose and did not reply. She couldn't understand why Sir Osric had been transformed, while she and Cynewulf remained whole. And then there was the matter of the pig and the herbalist. It seemed she'd decocted a love potion, after all.

Perhaps Cynewulf had lied about the herbalist. And yet, why question what she saw for herself? She was grateful that her hands were still her own and not those of a frog. She glanced at the Viking and grinned. In spite of herself, she was glad he wasn't a green frog prince.

They made a peculiar party, she thought, this band of Vikings following her, a would-be frogmaker. She heard the men talking and laughing among themselves, and guessed she was the object. Cynewulf let them prattle on in their heathen tongue. She wondered what he thought of her now that he knew she'd tried to murder him.

Nay, he didn't believe she'd tried to kill him. The conceited lout probably thought she'd tried to endow him with the instincts of a pig. Perhaps he thought she'd wanted to bind him to her with lust because she was jealous of the Viking women he dallied with—God's mercy, she couldn't bear him to think so of her. Better that he think her an assassin.

Before the roan could try any of his tricks, she swung into the saddle and stared Cynewulf in the eye. "I was trying to kill you, Viking, in case you thought otherwise."

"I divined as much."

"Oh." She felt her cheeks flush. Perhaps she'd just made matters worse. After all, she'd voluntarily drunk the enchanted wine. It must have looked as though she'd been willing to die with him. She had been.

Not anymore.

"I have the wine if you thirst," he said with a smile.

She didn't reply.

"Of course, we've almost reached the stream. Do you prefer a drink of water?"

"I'll leave every drop where it flows to be sure it's of sufficient depth to drown you."

"Ho! You are a cold wench with a tongue sharper than the Damascus steel of Damfertigénen."

"Would that it were that sharp that I might slay you!"

"Better that it be soft that I might kiss you."

How dared the brazen rogue speak of kissing her, when she'd just sworn her enmity? Had he no respect for her ability to slay him? "If you ever try to kiss me again," she said with quiet menace, "I shall bite off your lips."

"That should make the kiss more memorable than others I've had." Cynewulf urged his horse into the stream. "Much more memorable, indeed."

"Memorable because it would be your last," she said, turning the roan into the water behind him. The Viking warriors fanned out on either side, which she didn't mind until their horses splashed cold water all over her. She covered her head with her mantle, but within seconds she was drenched from crown to foot.

Cynewulf rode up the bank and reined in to wait for her, controlling Eboracum with his knees. He looked like a centaur out of legend.

"It is a shame you forded without drowning," she said when she'd gained the bank. Her hair tumbled loose from its plait and streamed over her face like sodden weeds. She flung it out of her eyes and tried without success to wring the water from her mantle.

Cynewulf chuckled at her distress. "Briton or not, I enjoy you," he said.

"I don't enjoy you. Not one particle."

"Good, it will keep things lively between us."

Taras kicked her horse ahead of Eboracum and said over her shoulder, "One might think you've enough liveliness, already, to occupy you. Your lady guests find your vigor most gratifying."

"Do I detect envy in your tone, spell weaver?"

"Envy! You may forswear yourself of that notion for all time, you rooster!"

"The thought flew ere it had gained firm footing," he said, touching his forehead in mock apology.

He was insufferable. How could she have imagined for one moment that she loved him? The thought must have been born of the tension of imminent death.

The wolfhound loped on ahead and was soon lost around a bend. Taras lifted her gaze to the battlements of mossy stone rearing a hundred feet high on each side of the path. Through the gloom she could see swallows' nests crouched on ledges a finger's-breadth wide. Insects and frogs croaked shadow songs from pools hidden in the rocks, and misty ferns curled from fissures. Shivering, Taras drew her wet mantle more closely around herself.

Before they'd reached the bend in the path, the wolfhound's great bark echoed down the corridor. Taras instinctively dragged her horse to a halt. Shouting a warning, Cynewulf grabbed Taras's reins and forced her behind him. The Vikings closed ranks and unsheathed their weapons.

The wolfhound rushed back down the trail, his fur rigid over his spine. Behind him hooves pounded, then a dozen British warriors rode into view and reined in. One of them threw a spear that landed barely six feet from Cynewulf. The shaft stood quivering, a mute challenge.

Instantly Cynewulf spurred Eboracum to the spear and reined in. He knew that within seconds the factions would join in bloody combat. There was nowhere to secret Taras, no time for her to run. All he could do was try to shield her when the larger force attacked.

His voice reverberated against the stone walls in a challenge: "Who among you will be the first to die?"

A knight built like a siege tower rode forth, his sword jouncing in the baldric slung over his mighty shoulder. His smile was an ugly gash in a flat face scarred by the pox, his eyes a hideous yellow. " 'Tis no fight we're after today," he said, "but an errand of peace."

Cynewulf snatched the spear out of the ground. "This is your way of heralding peace?" His voice thundered up and down the gorge. Swords and spears ready, his men faced the enemy across twenty feet of dirt.

The Briton shrugged. "The spear slipped out of my hand."

Cynewulf thrust its tip into the ground and with one kick broke it in half. He dropped the shaft into the dirt.

The giant's face twisted with rage. He raised his sword and opened his mouth, but Cynewulf spoke first. "I would not charge, were I you." He seemed to grow in the saddle as he gestured at the grim Vikings behind him. "Mayhap you have seen what berserkers do to appease their bloodlust."

Another voice rose within the English ranks. "I would speak with the Viking."

The giant kneed his destrier aside to make room for a knight in black mail and a red overtunic. He doffed his helm, releasing a tide of dark hair. Cynewulf heard Tara's voice a soft cry. He glanced back at her face; she'd gone white as marble. No time to wonder why.

"Lord Camlann at your service," the knight said. He was handsome despite a scar that twisted his mouth into a sneer.

"What do you want, Briton?"

Camlann's eyes glittered, but in a smooth voice he said, "We would join you at the *moot*. There is much to discuss."

How had he known of the *moot*? Cynewulf wondered if there were a spy among the Britons in his household. Perhaps the wench? Bah, she'd had no opportunity.

"I've oft heard of your hospitality," Camlann said. "You would deny the stranger nothing."

"I owe my enemy nothing."

"Ah, but I am not your enemy, lord. I am not the first Briton who's seen the logic in coming over to your side. I would form an alliance with you."

"To what end?"

"To break the yoke of kingly oppression. Ethelred and I—well, his rule threatens to leave me penniless. One more season losing battles will see me ruined. I cannot afford to fight for him any longer."

"Turn your horses around," Cynewulf said. "This interview is at an end."

Anger flickered along Camlann's scar. "It surprises me to find a warrior of your renown refusing an alliance. With my men at your back you could—"

"I want no English strangers at my back," Cynewulf said. "It is a most foolish way to stand."

He saw Camlann's gaze flicker to Taras, and his lips tighten almost imperceptibly. Cynewulf felt the hairs lift along the back of his neck. Was there some connection between them? He forced himself not to look back at his captive. He would as soon smite the head off the Briton as blink an eye, but then he might not find out the truth about Taras.

"If you are in good faith," Cynewulf said, "tell your men to drop their swords and spears. You may then come to the castle. We'll talk tonight."

The knight inclined his head. "Done." He snapped his fingers, and one by one his men dropped their weapons and turned their horses about. Camlann lowered his hand to his sword pommel and let it rest there.

"You may keep your sword, Lord Camlann," Cynewulf said. Contempt shimmered just under the surface of his words. "I think you know the way to my castle. We'll follow you."

Camlann jerked his warhorse about and rode after his men. Cynewulf bade his cadgers to collect the Britons' weapons; then he followed with his Vikings a short distance behind. Taras rode close to Denholm, who gripped his battle ax and stared longingly at the back of Camlann's skull.

No one spoke all the way to the castle.

Chapter Fourteen

They reached Castle Ilovar at sundown. Cynewulf ordered the servants to house Camlann and his Britons in the outer bailey. Taras hurried off to the keep.

"The wench is not what she seems," Cynewulf told Denholm as they unsaddled their horses.

"And this surprises you, my randy young buck?" Laughter burst from his chest. "I've told you all along that she would kill you, but you're too full of conceit to believe me. One of these days she'll ram a dagger into your heart."

"She tried to today."

Denholm's smile faded. "Stupid wench. One would think she'd have the sense to wait until you slept."

"It wasn't a dagger of steel. She tried to poison me."

"I no longer want to laugh," Denholm said. "When will you sell her?"

"She is not for sale. I won't give her up."

"Not until you lie dead?"

Cynewulf shook his head. "Do not worry. I understand

the wench and her little charms and potions. I've blunted her fangs."

"Have you? You did not see how she gazed at that damned Briton today. I would swear she knew him."

Cynewulf hid his surprise. So the seneschal had noticed something amiss, too? Then it had not been his imagination.

"Methinks the knave is a lover come to reclaim her," Denholm said.

"Because she looked at him? You've been too long without a drink, my friend."

"She didn't just look at him. She *looked* at him. She quivered like the last leaf of autumn."

"She was afraid," Cynewulf said. He didn't want to accept Denholm's assessment. The wench recognized a fellow Briton, that was all. "We nearly joined battle."

"Methinks you deny the truth, lord, that mayhap Camlann had her first."

"Bah! Even if it were so, it makes no difference to me whose furs she warmed in the past."

"Mayhap it matters that she's warming no one's furs now."

Cynewulf cast him a look that would have sent a lesser man running for his life, but Denholm only threw back his head and roared. Cynewulf watched him in pained silence until, recovering, Denholm said, "You have enjoyed not a moment's peace since capturing the chit. If she has lied and played you for a fool, then sell her to this English bastard and have done with her. If, though, you secretly love her as I think you do, marry her."

Cynewulf stalked past him out of the stable. Chuckling, Denholm followed him to the keep.

Taras poured hot water into the bathing tub and sank into it. Everything was wrong. She felt that she'd taken up her life and thrown it down again. Now that her cousin Camlann was here, she could not return to Ethelred and fool him with lies. Ethelred must have sent Camlann to make sure she'd fulfill her end of the bargain. But how could she? The frog potion was nothing but a love spell. And as for other means of killing the Viking, why, she couldn't. She wanted to go away and never look back at the mighty castle on the hill.

But what to do about Camlann? He surely wouldn't take on Cynewulf himself. If he'd planned to attack him, he would have done it in the gorge. Nay, she and her cousin were very alike. She hadn't the stomach for killing; he hadn't the courage.

But what was it Camlann had said? He'd seen the wisdom in coming over to Cynewulf's side because he'd soon be penniless if he continued to support the king. Mayhap Camlann's motives weren't sinister, after all. It wouldn't be the first time her cousin had betrayed another's confidence. Camlann loved money. He needed bushels of it to run his huge estate and man its keep.

Taras raised her knee out of the water and began to soap her leg. If Camlann were here to better his lot, she needn't worry about his trying to force her to kill the Viking.

She needn't worry about Camlann trying to kill him, either.

The curtain suddenly snapped open. Taras gasped and crossed her arms over her breasts. It was Cynewulf.

"You might have knocked, sir!"

He rapped his knuckles on the side of the tub. "Does this suffice?"

"Flinging yourself out the window would do so better."

His face hardened. "Always the shrew. A peculiar thing in a woman of your type."

"And what type would that be?"

Instead of answering, he left the alcove. After a moment he returned holding a bliaut of white silk. Along its low neckline and pendant sleeves glittered flowers stitched with pearls, amber, and precious stones. The chemise was cut from jade green silk.

"You shall wear this to the feast tonight."

Taras raised her chin. "I won't go to the feast. Give that rag back to whichever of your whores it belongs."

"I do not take the rags off one whore's back to give to another." She reached out to slap his leg, but he imprisoned her shoulder between his fingers.

"Let go!" She raked her nails down his arm. He ignored the pain.

"I want you to look well in front of your countryman tonight," he said. "I want him to see what I've taken from him—taken from his country."

Taras's pulse raced. Did he know she and Camlann knew each other, that they were related by blood and intrigue? "You—you are mad!"

"Mayhap I am. Mad to keep a murderess under my roof, mad to let her friends into my stronghold."

"I do not understand you!"

He bent over and stared into her eyes, as though to draw the secrets from her soul. His breath raised icy prickles on her wet skin, although the blood in her veins felt hot and thick.

"Would you like me to kill him for you, Taras of Widnes?"

"Why would I want that?"

"He craves you. I saw it in his eyes today."

Taras caught her breath. He didn't know the truth, then. He was guessing. But if she denied the charge, she might give him reason to look further. Her attempt on his life had amused him because he'd thought it was personal, not an act of war. She dared not let the Viking figure out that the plot went all the way back to Ethelred. If he knew she'd come here at the king's bequest, he would slay Camlann and her.

The Viking was still staring at her, still holding her shoulder. "Shall I kill him tonight?"

"N-nay, leave him be. He is nothing to either of us."

His eyes turned to frost. He straightened slowly, and just as slowly began to undress. His hauberk hit the floor. His muscular arms and chest rippled as he unlaced his braies.

"What are you doing, Viking?"

"Joining you in the bath."

"My bath is finished. Turn your back that I might dress!"

"Modesty in a whore? How droll."

"I am no whore!" She scrambled out of the tub and held the wet towel around her.

He dropped his braies and stood naked, staring at her. Scandalized, Taras stared back. There was not a particle of fat on him, nothing but satiny hard flesh and a manly spear jutting from his dark mantle of hair.

Flushed from crown to sole, she sprang to the fireplace and seized a poker. "Stay away!"

"I require your services in the bath."

"You won't get them."

"Indeed I will. You will come to me of your own accord or I will come and get you. If you choose the latter, I may not bother to bathe."

She could try to flee into the hall, but where would she go clad in a towel? She would make herself a laughing-stock. She hurled the poker onto the hearth. "I am no strumpet!"

Cynewulf stepped into the bath. "The water is cold. Fetch the kettle."

"It's nigh empty."

"Bring what is left."

Holding the towel with one hand, Taras reluctantly obeyed. She nearly dropped the towel as she struggled to balance the kettle and pour. Before she could leave, he seized her wrist and made her kneel beside the tub.

"I did not give you permission to go."

"What do you want of me?" She feared he would pull her in on top of him and finish what he'd begun the other morn. "What do you want?"

"Your services. Bathe me."

"What?"

"I spoke your foul English tongue. If you cannot comprehend your own manner of speech, it is time you learned your master's."

"It's not the difference in language that hinders our communion, but your cruelty. I shall never understand the mind of a Viking. Never."

"I require your obedience, not your understanding." He released her wrist, yet his expression declared that he had in no wise yielded his dominance. "Put aside your tears and wash my back."

"You are a—a sea monster!"

"And you are a whining complainer with a barbarous lack of manners; but then, I expect that from a Briton."

She seized a washrag and swiped it across his broad back, her ire rising until at last she burst out: "Only a barbarian treats a woman so!"

"Scrub harder."

"You demand much for nothing."

"And what would you have me give? A few moments ago you rejected the gown I brought you."

"I will not accept your gifts. Besides, I refuse to go to the great feast and have you shame me before my own countrymen."

"Then mayhap you yearn for a feast of a different sort." He jerked her halfway into the tub and pressed her to his chest. When she tried to scream he caught her jaw. Against her lips he said, "Feast at my table, wench."

He took her mouth in a deep kiss. She could do nothing to stop him from sliding his hands inside her towel. She heard him groan, a deep-throated, animal sound almost of pain. In spite of herself she began to pant, to press against his mouth and chest, to slide her hands up and down his hard flanks. She suddenly wanted him to take her, to ravish her, to devour her in his feast of fire. She spread her knees and pushed against the hard metal tub as though to make him penetrate her straight through the brass.

He released her mouth but held her face close, staring savagely into her eyes, reading her fear and desire. Damn him, how did he move her to such base lust? She despised him—she did! If she could find the right herbs, she would slay him this time, for certain.

"What spell have you woven about me?" he demanded hoarsely.

"You've woven a spell of your own madness, Cynewulf. I've done nothing to you."

"Bah!" He pushed her off his chest and lay back against the tub. Taras heard his heavy breathing and saw the pulse in his neck. She looked down at his iron-hard member protruding from the bath. A pulse throbbed there, too, disturbing the surface of the water. For several minutes he lay thus, his big hands gripping the sides of the tub until the metal groaned.

Taras sat back on her heels and shut her eyes. There was nowhere to run, nothing to do but keep still until the berserker rage in him passed. She wondered how long it would take for her own battle lust to flicker out.

"Taras."

She jumped, expecting to feel his hands upon her again, but he did not move or open his eyes.

"Wash me, Taras."

"Nay, please—"

"There is very little sanity about me now, my lady," he said in a voice she sensed in every inch of her spine. "Obey me."

She took up the rag and glided it over his chest. His dark golden hair whorled under the cloth. His breath sent wicked currents up her arm and fueled the fire in her veins. She could not ignore his unyielding muscles, or the scars proving his valor. She could not ignore her response to him.

He was like new wine in her belly. Intoxicated, she closed her eyes and let her head fall back. The towel slipped down to her waist. She began to wash his rigid abdominal muscles.

Cynewulf groaned.

She raised her head. Naked, raw passion looked back at her. His desire licked her like a fiery tongue, and again she pressed against the tub. Her nipples hardened and throbbed until she thought she would burst.

She felt his hand slide down her spine and slowly peel away the towel around her hips. He caressed her cheeks, each brush of his fingers making her start in uncontrolled need against the tub. What wizardry was this, that he could own her passions and bend her to his rule?

"You're hungry, Taras. Yield to me." He thrust his hips upward, exposing every male inch of him. "Yield by taking."

Had she lost all decency? Was she no better than a she-dog, to rut with a man, a bitter enemy? She struggled to find honor within the boiling caldron she'd become. She must not yield to this most vile temptation. She must not go on touching and being touched. She must not let this go one step farther.

She must not, yet all at once she lowered her mouth to his hot sword. She heard him gasp, and heat seared her lips. She opened her mouth slightly, letting the tip of her tongue touch him. It was a kiss, an intimate kiss that she'd never believed she could give. It thrilled her, heated her, shook her. She felt his hand slide down to her knees, then up between her legs to touch her, pull at her. His fingers ignited her need. She opened her mouth and went down over him, enclosing half his throbbing length. He felt like hot wet satin slipping over her tongue.

Groaning, Cynewulf caught her hair in one hand and led her through the dance, pulling and slipping and filling her mouth with his maleness. Meanwhile his fingers played a song inside her. Taras moaned as she served him. She couldn't bear another moment; he had to release her long enough to let her climb into the bath and mount him. She wanted him to fill her up, to stretch and force and knead her until she exploded with desire.

He was panting now, his breath ragged and harsh as his hips jerked against her mouth. Warm water splashed in her face and ran over her breasts, trickling down to the wet flame between her thighs. His fingers explored every sensitive place. She moaned and at last, unable to think or see or reason, she closed over him until her lips touched his belly and he erupted and there was a wild taste and stickiness in her throat. Convulsively she swallowed and his fingers brought her against the tub in a wild surfeit of passion. She felt she was melting, her breasts molded to the tub, her mouth forever closed around the quicksilver beat of his loins.

At last, her passion finished, she released him and sank down against the tub to the floor. She knelt there panting, her head bowed as though in supplication, her hands clasped in his.

"You are mine, Lady Taras," she heard him say. "You carry part of me inside you now. I own you always."

"Nay, I am no slave," she said, but her voice was weak

and not her own. She knew she lied as she spoke, and an overwhelming sense of shame had replaced the lust. "No man owns me. I have no master."

"You crossed the line tonight. Your life has changed forever. When I bid you lie in my bed, you'll come and we'll enjoy each other. I have not yet shown you pleasure."

Taras pulled her hands free and staggered naked to the door. He sank deeper into the water and watched her out of eyes alight with heat.

"What a tempest you are, my beauty," he said, looking her over from head to toe. "What a magnificent young falcon you are."

Sensing his passion was expended for now, Taras ventured to the fire and wrapped herself in a pelt. She picked up the poker and watched for signs of danger. She despised herself for giving in to her desire, yet if he tempted her again, she wondered if she could say no. Perhaps she couldn't. Perhaps she had indeed crossed a line into a land from which she couldn't return. Perhaps she was, after all, nothing but an enemy he would use for his pleasure until he tired of her. And then what would happen? Would he hand her over to his men?

In a fit of despair she sought to reclaim some measure of dignity. "You're a petty despot whose only ambition is to build up his rude little kingdom and rule over a herd of barge rowers," she told him. "I—I abhor you to my very marrow!"

Cynewulf rose suddenly and cocked his fists on his hips. His great muscles turgid, he looked like a golden god of war. His stare reached across the chamber to hold her captive.

"Taras, come here."

His masterful tone shook her resolve. "Nay, I'll not! You may demand until your throat grows hoarse as a frog's and you choke upon your own tongue!"

"Come to me. Now."

How could she fight him? He'd toss aside the poker like a dry reed. He was too powerful for her to fight, too full of ire. And heaven help her, she wanted him. Honor fled on the wings of desire. Her will did not belong to her anymore, but to him.

As though in a trance she moved across the cold stone floor. He stood still, watching her come. When she was half a foot away, he caught her behind the jawbone and gently pressed his thumbs against the corners of her mouth.

"Why do you do this to me?" she whispered.

There was no kindness in his voice as he said, "It is my right. You are a stringed instrument in her master's hand, Taras. You will sing under my touch."

He closed the gap between them and engulfed her in molten heat. He tossed the pelt aside and pressed his spear against her belly. Like a shaft of white heat consuming her bones and sinews, he tongued her mouth. Her knees turned to water and she would have fallen, but he caught her into his arms and laid her on the bed.

"I won't lie with you!"

"You already are." He lay down beside her and stretched one leg over hers to hold her still, then slid his hand up her thigh and over her belly to her breasts.

"You care naught for me!" she cried. She could hardly draw breath through the tempest in her breast; his rigid flesh against her thigh made her ache for release. "I am nothing to you!"

Cynewulf held her in a hawklike stare: merciless, hungry, predatory. "It matters not what I feel for you. You are mine."

"I am a free woman."

"You are my thrall, as I believe we've just proved in the bath. The next time I call you to me, you will come immediately or I'll do this to you again. Nay, I'll do worse." He swung off the bed and went to the chest for his clothing.

Through tears of rage Taras said, "The next time you call me, Viking, I'll take a knife to your cursed heart!"

Cynewulf flung his clothing over his shoulder and strode naked from the room without deigning to reply.

Taras jumped up and ran after him intending to push him down the stairs. Just in time she grabbed the door frame and held herself back. He was already gone. She stood in the doorway until a womanservant came down the hall and giggled. Taras slammed the door in her face.

"Just wait, Lord Cynewulf," she said to the door. "Just wait until I get my hands on you again. You won't find pleasure in my touch next time."

She tore the pewter vial from her neck and hurled it out the window.

Chapter Fifteen

The lamp glow fell over the folk gathered to feast. Musical notes from horns and lyres floated down from the loft. To the feasters the final day of the *moot*, tomorrow's clash of steel, seemed distant, as though the merrymaking could go on forever.

Cynewulf harbored no such illusions.

He gazed at the two men seated below the salt, the position of least honor. Camlann and his giant, Tabor, seemed relaxed and pleasant. Although they spoke to some of his British subjects, they focused most of their attention on the Danes. Cynewulf thought they acted too much at home. He wondered about their true purpose. Mayhap he would find out on the field of honor tomorrow, when he engaged them.

Scowling, he turned to look over his shoulder at the staircase. Where was his captive? Two hours had flown since he'd left her. She knew he required her tonight.

He sought out Camlann again and found him staring.

The Briton's expression was cold, but when he caught Cynewulf's eye he smiled like a fox, exposing sharp yellow teeth. Was he waiting for Taras, as well? Or awaiting the opportunity to stick a knife into her master's back?

Cradling a cask of nabid, Denholm dropped onto the chair beside him. With owlish interest he examined Cynewulf's tunic of blue wool, his armlets of silver encrusted with amber gripping beasts, the circlet of golden hawk's wings upon his brow.

"Methinks you could win the wench's favor clad in such finery," Denholm said, "were our friend Camlann's rags less extravagant. Mayhap you should garb yourself in red silk and ermine, too. And why not diamonds like the pea-sized ones sparkling on his hands and earlobes?"

"Bah." Cynewulf quaffed ale. He would give Taras only a few minutes more before he went after her.

"Even without such raiment," Denholm said, "Camlann is a fine-looking devil. See how the wenches hover over him? They find his scar appealing."

"He is not the only one who bears a scar," Cynewulf said.

"Perchance you speak of scars not readily seen, those of the heart?"

Cynewulf winced. Seizing a pitcher, he refilled his cup and drained it without drawing breath. Tonight he sought the solace of drunkenness. It was not his wont.

"Tabor the Yellow-eyed looks like a hungry lion," Denholm said. "You should not drink so much, lord. Your enemies would eat you, finding your faculties slow."

"The morrow's battle of spears will prove whether or not they'll feed," Cynewulf said. He did not feel drunken yet. He refilled his cup.

" 'Tis like letting a wolf among the sheep to lodge him and his master in the hall."

Cynewulf looked around at his retainers and chuckled.

"These sheep have terrible fangs and fleeces of iron. The wolf would break his teeth at the first bite."

"Unless he pounced on the sheep's unwitting neck."

Cynewulf waved his hand. "A sheep who takes no heed of a wolf in the fold deserves swift death."

"Mayhap."

Cynewulf glanced at the staircase again. How long would the chit's stubbornness persist? For the twelfth time he wondered how she would react when she saw Camlann. Would her gaze lock with his, or would she cast down her eyes? Either way, Cynewulf knew he'd suspect the worst. He squeezed his cup until the pewter molded to his fingertips. For an instant he felt Camlann's throat in his hand.

Ardeth came over to pour his ale. She licked her lips and gazed up at him. "Is there aught else you desire, my lord?"

"Aye, the Lady Taras. She delays."

Ardeth tossed her head. "Mayhap she admires her dainty reflection in the bath."

"She is not the sort to engage in such vain pursuits."

"Who can divine a woman?" Denholm interrupted. He reached over and squeezed Ardeth's right breast, roaring with appreciation when she saucily offered him her left. Encouraged, he pulled her onto his lap and buried his face in her bosom.

Cynewulf swallowed his ale in one long gulp and sat back in his chair. His head reeled, and for a moment spots danced before his vision. He didn't like Ardeth's brazen displays, yet he wished Taras shared a tiny portion of her wantonness in public instead of trying to shame him.

Angered by his lapse into fantasy, he brought himself up short. Perhaps Taras *was* a wanton, but simply did not wish to do it with him. She had given him wild pleasure this evening, but immediately afterward she'd shown her disgust. What a fool he had been to accept her maidenly shame when she might have but lately come from Camlann's bed! But for her wide-eyed aura of innocence, he would have taken her long ago. What a ninny-lobcock he'd been—he set his jaw as he caught himself using one of her epithets—to fall for a harlot's lies.

He was drunk, he felt it in his veins and head. The sensation did not calm him; only sating his taste for Taras would bring him peace. After he'd purged his blood of her witchery, he'd let her go. Nay, he'd sell her to the grinning ass seated at his table.

He smiled ominously at Camlann. This time his foe did not pretend to smile, but raised his goblet in a silent challenge. Cynewulf lifted his own cup, unaware of his fierce grip until the stem snapped and the bowl crashed to the table. The small violence heated his blood another degree. If Taras so much as looked at the knave, Cynewulf would slay him where he sat.

"The lord's meditations arouse him to battle frenzy," Denholm said to Ardeth in a voice meant for Cynewulf's ears. "If he but looks, he will see scores of noble wenches ready to hie to an alcove and spread themselves for his pleasure!"

"I am not a buck in rut," Cynewulf growled.

"Nay? Whom do you seek to convince?"

"Heed to your own rutting, and leave me to mine."

"Too late, lord," the seneschal said. "Just this eve I admitted Dame Frisia to the feast. You remember her. See, there she is, sporting with Camlann."

Cynewulf switched his gaze to the Briton. A noblewoman clad in furs and a pointed headpiece slid between Camlann and Tabor. She smiled when Camlann raised her hand to his lips, whispered to him for a few moments, then slipped out of his grasp and made her way to Cynewulf. Fluttering her lashes over her dark blue eyes, she dropped to one knee.

"My lord," she said when he did not speak, "I am very glad to see you again."

She looked older than he remembered, her florid skin showing the effects of a life enjoyed a bit too well, but she was still damned beautiful, especially to Cynewulf's ale-sopped mind. He stood and took her hand to raise her to the dais.

"Come, sit beside me."

She thrust the tip of her tongue between her teeth in a cat's smile. "It has been too long since last we supped at this table, Lord Cynewulf."

"Aye. They say you've married since."

Frisia glanced down the table at a Dane of medium build and smiled indulgently. Holding a maiden on each knee, he nibbled at their bodices. "Yea, I have married," Frisia said. "I could not wait forever for your return."

"I had not realized you were waiting, else I would have dispatched the English into the North Sea and hastened back to your arms."

"I daresay."

"You doubt my veracity?"

"Damn you, Cynewulf," she said, and leaned over to press her right breast against his arm. Running her nails down his chest, she smiled into his eyes. "I'll forgive you anything, you cloddish ass, if you will but take me to the furs. 'Tis been too long since last I felt your knightly spear."

Cynewulf glanced down at her breasts. At one time an invitation to her bed—husband or no husband—would have aroused him immediately, but tonight he could muster only faint interest. He'd drunk too much, he told himself.

Frisia drew back and frowned. " 'Tis true, then, what they say about you!"

"And what is that?"

"That you're tied to the skirts of a waspish little wench of few years and even less intellect!"

"Which vexes you most, her youth or her lack of worldliness?"

"You are intolerable."

"Then why do you dig your nails into me with such hunger?"

"Because, my Lord Cynewulf, you are the most irresistible man I've ever known. I could eat you alive."

Cynewulf shook his head. "Your husband would favor other wenches less, were you to expend your womanly charms on him."

She laughed in derision. "We have an understanding, he and I. We each do whatever we want. 'Tis the natural order of things."

Denholm, still fondling Ardeth, leaned over to say, "More the natural order among cats and other creatures of the night."

"I am surprised, Cynewulf, that you allow this ill-mannered vermin to toy with his trollop at the table!" Dame Frisia snapped.

As Denholm bellowed with delight, Cynewulf's attention caught on Camlann. He was gazing toward the staircase. Cynewulf instantly knew the source of his interest. He turned to see Taras descending the stairs, her figure superbly displayed in the jeweled gown. A golden girdle studded with emeralds scintillated on her hips. Entwined about a circlet of gold, her hair shone like the rising sun. In a hall filled with lovely women, her beauty overshadowed them all.

Cynewulf rose and shrugged off Frisia's clutching fingers. She cried, "Please, lord, go not to her! She is a child, a damned barbarian!"

But Cynewulf set her aside and shouldered his way through the merrymakers. He stopped at the foot of the staircase and waited for his captive. His anger at her tardiness vanished like a puff of smoke.

She stopped on the bottom step but did not take the hand he offered. Instead, she looked at Frisia out of wide, angry eyes. A muscle quivered in her jaw, then she suddenly turned to retreat upstairs. Cynewulf caught her wrist and drew her toward him.

"My lady," he said in a voice he hardly recognized as his own, "you are a jewel beyond the flawed imaginings of men."

"Pretty words, my lord," she said, glancing at Frisia again. "But then, I'm sure you've practiced them often tonight."

"Let us not quarrel again. Come, feast with me. I would have you at my side."

"Is there enough room for two in your lordly lap?"

"You envy Dame Frisia, I see."

"Envy her? Indeed not. It gladdens my marrow to find you otherwise engaged."

"And does it gladden you to find Camlann at the table, as well?"

Taras flushed to the roots of her hair. Rage burst upon Cynewulf's senses. Tightening his grip on her wrist, he said, "Just as I thought—gladness is written upon your countenance."

"You are mad, sir."

"It's no longer necessary to pretend—this man has come for you."

"And if he has, let me go with him!" she flared. "I cannot bear another day under your roof!"

"You'll go nowhere until I decree it," Cynewulf said. He pulled her through the crowd and seated her beside him. He saw Camlann's resentful stare and heard Dame Frisia huff with annoyance. Good, now everyone was as happy as he.

Denholm shoved Ardeth off his lap and bellowed, "Welcome to the feast, my lady!"

Taras glared at her hands.

"My seneschal bade you welcome," Cynewulf said. "Answer him."

Taras cast him a look calculated to melt iron before she said, "Thank you, seneschal."

But when a servitor set a three-footed silver mazer by her elbow and filled it with mulled cider, she ignored it.

"Drink," Cynewulf said. "It will sweeten your disposition."

"I would sooner drink gall with a leper than honeymead with you, Viking."

Frisia leaned toward her. "You ought to be grateful that my lord suffers you at his table. 'Tis not often that a bedwench sits at table with the quality."

"I am sure you're overjoyed then, that he made an exception in your case," Taras said.

Hissing, the dame raised her hand, but Cynewulf caught her wrist before she could strike. "The harlot slandered me!" she shrieked. "I demand that she be punished!"

"She gave back what you offered," Cynewulf said. "Now go to your husband ere you make an ass of yourself."

Frisia thrust off his hand and shoved through the crowd. Instead of sitting by her husband, she went to Camlann. He wrapped his arm around her waist and pulled her close.

Cynewulf studied Taras and smiled in spite of himself. The fiery glint in her eye revealed her pleasure in routing Frisia. She laid a portion of *mawmenye*—lamb and lentils—on her trencher and drowned it in mulled wine sauce.

Denholm lurched to his feet and shouted, " 'Tis time the company heard the tale of Discoftomb. Skald! Let us hear how the lord slew the British bastards at Hlaverin Towne!"

Taras put down her knife, folded her arms, and stared at the rafters. Cynewulf knew she did not want to hear a song recounting his exploits against her people. Right now, he didn't, either.

Denholm reached over to touch her arm. "You will

enjoy the entertainment, my lady. The skald often travels with the master and records his battle deeds in song."

"I have heard them each evening," Taras said, throwing Cynewulf a challenging look. "They are tedious."

"I agree," Cynewulf said. He enjoyed her look of aggravation. He picked up his linen napkin and handed it to her. "Stuff it in your ears, my lady."

The skald drifted down the musicians' gallery staircase, plucking a lyre. At Denholm's nod, he began to sing.

> "Comes now the light and fog of morn
> O'er ruins of Hlaverin Towne,
> Where lay the men of Discoftomb
> In seeming sleep.
> What fiendish army laid them down
> Forevermore—
> Ne'er to raise the crown of worthy men?
> In battle to defeat they went
> With sword and shield to die
> For honor of the Lord of Discoftomb."

Taras looked at Cynewulf. Although he stared back at her, the pain in his eyes told her that his thoughts were far away. She dragged her gaze back to the skald, steeling herself to the images his words conjured. She had not heard this song before.

> "Comes now with bloodied sunlight,
> O'erpowering mists and sorcery
> The vengeful Wolf, fell enemy.
> His eyes traverse the scene of cruelty
> His countenance quells hearts
> As he views a fallen people

Made to pay a price
By the blood of Thor, too high!
Great evil has befallen here
That no man can abide.

"Now, not too far afield there rides
The Knight of Solway Moor,
The one who slaughtered Hlaverin Towne—"

Out of the corner of her eye, Taras saw a flash of red. Tabor was on his feet beside Camlann, gripping the edge of the table in white-knuckled fists. His mouth worked as he glared at Cynewulf. Taras glanced at Cynewulf and saw his eyes narrow.

"The evil knight looks up to see
His weird upon him:
All fate conspires to put the Wolf
Across his only path.
And now, with no retreat at hand,
This Knight lifts the sword
Called Lifedrinker,
And speaks a deathly curse—"

Taras's skin crawled. Tabor stared at Cynewulf through slitted eyes, grinding his teeth as though devouring bone. Enmity hotter than Ethelred's war flared between the men.

"—two great armies join at Manathilim,
The Wolf with fifty-fifties,
And the Knight an hundred hundreds—"

Again Taras lost the thread of the tale. Cynewulf was openly hostile now, his eyes clashing with Tabor's.

"—the evil Knight of Solway Moor
Kneels vanquished before his fate—
Damfertigénen, Sword of Justice,
Descends upon his unrepentant head."

Tabor clawed at his empty baldric, seeking his sword. "So, bastard of Ilovar," he shouted, " 'twas you who killed my brother!"

Without haste Cynewulf rose. Taras could almost hear the slow, steady thud of his heart. Her consciousness became one with the fire pulsing in his veins, the sharpness of his vision.

"Give back my sword, Viking!" Tabor demanded. "Give back Lifedrinker, my elder brother's sword, that with her I may avenge his death!"

"If it is your desire to bring about your own end, you will have the blade in the morn."

Tabor's lips fluttered back from his teeth. "And then I will slay you before your misbegotten tribe!"

"The morn will see whose blood waters the field of honor, my friend," Cynewulf said. His smile did not touch his eyes.

Growling, Tabor struck his chair a blow, sending it flying. He stalked out of the hall. Camlann did not stir, but sat shaking his head. "My apologies, lord," he said at last. "My man was shocked by what he learned just now. It does not change matters between us two."

Taras could hardly look at her cousin. What evil designs had he, that he would respond with such false humility? She had never heard him apologize to anyone; it was not his way. Was he really here because he'd betrayed King Ethelred, or did he intend to kill Cynewulf? She wished she knew the answer.

Should she tell Cynewulf what she suspected? Nay, that

would make her a traitor to the king, as well. She could say nothing. She dared not admit to Cynewulf that she even knew Camlann, no matter what he suspected. All she could do was watch Camlann . . . and Cynewulf's back.

Aye, she could do that. Cynewulf did not realize the plot against him, and so had no true concept of the danger. If Camlann really planned to kill him, it would be by stealth. It was up to her to watch her cousin. If possible, she would find a way to speak to him and discover his intentions. If they were harmless, she could let him go his way and become part of the household. But if he designed to kill Cynewulf . . . well, she'd have to think about that.

She twisted her fingers together in an agony of indecision. Her heart felt as though it would beat itself to death against her ribs. If and when the time came, would she betray her country and kinsman, or the enemy Dane?

She started when Cynewulf placed his hand on her shoulder. He looked her full in the face, his eyes dark with an emotion she could not identify. "My lord, you require something of me?" she asked. Her voice shook.

"I require everything of you, Taras," he said. "When I take it is my decision."

"You dare speak to me thus, after what I'm doing for you—" She cut herself short and looked away.

"What are you doing for me?" he asked, low and dangerous.

"Nothing. I'm doing nothing for you. And you will forever demean me."

"Did I demean you when I paid gold coin for that gown you wear? Do the emeralds studding your girdle lower your worth?"

"Now, just a moment—"

"Did I degrade you in allowing you to sup with me tonight, when any one of these wenches would sit at my feet, nibbling crumbs from my hand?"

"Why, you overbearing coxcomb! Do you think I'm a harlot to be bought with gold, or a slave to be commanded to your table? Your very thoughts defile me!"

Cynewulf sat in silence for half a minute, his eyes sinister. "Mayhap you came to me defiled by another's hand."

Taras barely controlled the impulse to spring at his throat. "You are vile! I know nothing of this—this *Camlann* you've allowed into your hall."

"Indeed? And I am supposed to believe his tale of treachery against his own king?"

"Why not? Look how many other English traitors have already rallied to your standard. You've filled half your hall with them. Why not one more?"

Denholm leaned forward and caught Cynewulf's forearm. "I would tender a suggestion, my lord."

"What is it?"

"Marry the wench."

Taras threw up her hands and sat back in her chair, shaking her head. Cynewulf glowered at his seneschal. "You have taken leave of your senses once more."

"Aye," Denholm said. He took a swig of nabid directly from the cask. "But defiled or not, I have never seen a wench rule your thoughts so—outside the bedchamber, anyway."

Taras leaped to her feet. "Why you lop-eared, barnacle-shriven son of a rower, you!"

"Mercy, lady!" Denholm said with a laugh. "A moment's peace, I pray."

"I'll give you a moment!" Taras snatched a roast pig from a tray and swung it into the seneschal's head. Before the drunken man could defend himself, she hurled a ewer of cream into his face.

Raising a deafening shout, the merrymakers plunged into combat. Wine, tripe, venison, and boar steaks flew thick in the air. Dodging flying victuals, ladies screamed and ran.

Cynewulf made a grab for Taras, but she leaped off the dais. Knowing Cynewulf was only a few steps behind her, she bunched her skirts above her knees and sped across the room and up the staircase. Within seconds she reached the gallery. In another moment she dove into the bedchamber and slammed the door. She dropped the bar an instant before his shoulder struck the panels.

"Open to me, wench!"

"Nay! Go drown yourself in the putrid river of your imagination!"

The door shuddered under his fists. Taras pushed the heavy chest in front of the door, then ran to the fireplace for the poker. Just as she grabbed it, the door exploded into the room and slanted over the chest. Cynewulf sprawled on top of it and lay inert.

"Cynewulf!" Her anger fled as swiftly as it had ignited. Rushing to his side, she grabbed his hair and turned his face toward her. Blood streamed from a cut in his forehead.

"What have I done?" he asked groggily.

"You've broken your thick skull at last, you infernal Viking. Here, I'll help you up."

Too dizzy and blinded by blood to stand, Cynewulf crawled over the wreckage and collapsed onto the floor. Taras pressed her hand against his wound to stop the bleeding. "I'll get the needle," she said. "I must stitch this at once."

"You would likely stitch shut my mouth, as well, you mad little Briton." He pushed her away and sat up. "How is it possible that such a snip of a wench wreaks such havoc in my home?"

"I did naught but defend my honor—heaven's mercy! Behind you!"

She screamed too late. Tabor launched himself over the broken door, his dagger arcing at Cynewulf's back.

Chapter Sixteen

Cynewulf thrust Taras out of the way and rolled right. Tabor's knife jabbed the floor next to him. Cynewulf could scarcely see through the blood from his cut forehead. Relying on instinct, he scissored his legs and swept his assailant's feet out from under him. Tabor crashed to the floor. Cynewulf sprang up, only to fall over the door behind him. He twisted to land on one knee.

Tabor came after him, slashing. Cynewulf vaulted backward and hit the doorpost. Tabor struck the wall beside him, causing a shower of sparks, then the giant reversed his grip to drive the knife at Cynewulf's throat. "Die, Viking!" he roared.

Taras smashed the poker into the side of his head.

For an instant Tabor stared in wide-eyed shock; then his eyes turned up and he crashed into the wall beside Cynewulf. He slid to the floor and lay still.

Dashing blood and sweat out of his eyes, Cynewulf

stepped over the huge knight to Taras, who stood with her feet braced apart, clutching the poker with both hands. Cynewulf took the iron from her and flung it onto the bed, then slid his finger into the notch beneath her chin to raise her face. He saw tears in her eyes.

"That was quite a blow," he said. "My little falcon is forged of iron."

Trembling, she pulled away. "Did he stab you?"

"He missed, thanks to you."

She stared at the body. "Is he . . . dead?"

Cynewulf prodded him with his toe. "Nay, the thick-pated villain merely sleeps."

"Thanks be to God," Taras said, crossing herself.

"If you care so much for this Briton, why did you strike him down?"

"I care nothing for him," she said. "I just did not wish to kill a living being."

"Because his master once shared your bed," Cynewulf said before he could stop himself. Odin's beard, why could he not keep his envy to himself? He gave her power every time he accused her of something.

He saw her eyes narrow, then she said, "I believe the great Lord Cynewulf, the master of Castle Ilovar and all the land of Amandolar, is jealous. How quaint."

"Jealous of that thing's master?"

"Aye."

"Ha!" He moved to the kettle to wash his face. "Your past matters not a whit. You are my captive, and so it will stand."

She smiled and folded her arms.

"You're a vain little fluff," he said, "to think you incite envy in a warrior's heart."

Her sudden flush of anger proved his arrow had struck home, but before she could retort, Denholm wandered into the chamber. He was plastered with food, his hair and beard clotted with cream.

"I thought you and the knave planned to break spears tomorrow, my lord," he said, ogling Tabor. "Did you brawl over his brother's death, or did he fight for the wench on behalf of his master?"

"My lord did not brawl over me, seneschal," Taras snapped. "As he has just informed me, a thrall cannot incite passion in a proud Danish warrior."

Cynewulf scowled at her. She seated herself on a stool and folded her hands in her lap. Feigned serenity masked her face.

Several manservants arrived to drag Tabor away. Taras rose and went to the window to stare into the blackness. She hoped Cynewulf could not detect the terrible seed of jealousy germinating in her own heart. Dame Frisia had planted the seed, although it was Cynewulf who had watered it with his cruelty. He felt no passion for her; he had stated it in so many words. He had simply been using her and feeding her own illicit desires.

She reminded herself that she was a captured prize, not one of his bedwenches. She had turned from the king's mission and, in so doing, had allowed the enemy to seize upon her very soul. Stupid dreamer!

She heard Denholm leave the chamber. Without turning around she knew Cynewulf had not followed him; she felt his gaze on her back. Fire kindled low in her spine and spread to her belly.

Sweet Mary, why could she not control her feverish impulses? She had risked her life again to defend his. Gripping the casement with both hands, she shut her eyes and remembered Cynewulf with Dame Frisia. That image cooled her blood.

When she finally looked around at him, her pulse was

almost steady. "If you would sit by the fire, I'll tend that cut."

"It's nothing." He pulled off his bloody tunic and dropped it on the floor.

Taras's pulse quickened at the sight of his naked chest. Feeling weak, she went to the fireplace and stretched for the small box on the mantel where she'd discovered a needle and a ball of fine silk thread several days ago.

"Come," she said, "you're cut to the bone. Your wound will heal faster with a stitch or two."

He sat down on the hearth. "Do your worst, then."

He didn't move or speak while she inserted three stitches and knotted the thread. Denholm came back and stood in the doorway. "Has the wench become a chirurgeon as well as a scullery maid? Such talent."

Cynewulf ignored his drollery. "Is Tabor outside the walls?"

"Aye, and mad as the devil's dog. Why did you not kill the rogue when you had the chance?"

"Why didn't you guard my back to keep the reptile from slithering after me?"

Denholm indicated his messy clothing. "I was otherwise engaged, hurling victuals about the hall. Young Taras started a splendid engagement—I did not miss a moment of it."

Taras sighed and began putting away her suturing materials. Tabor had been able to attack because she had distracted Cynewulf and his men. She would never have guessed the Viking love for food fights.

"Tabor wears a beautiful lump on the side of his head," Denholm said. "Your fist?"

"Nay." Cynewulf rested his gaze on Taras. "Her fire iron."

"Well struck, my lady," Denholm said, bowing. "May-

204

hap you should guard the master's back and leave me to pursue the pleasures of old age."

"I wouldn't dream of usurping your duties. You dotterels deserve each other."

Mirth touched Cynewulf's eyes. Denholm said, "We dotterels should have slain the blackguard while he slumbered."

Taras snapped the box shut. "Killing a senseless foe is a pagan practice."

"And one which enables a pagan to live longer," Denholm said.

Cynewulf took the box from Taras and placed it on the mantel. "The seneschal jests. Tabor will have his turn tomorrow, if he can put aside his cowardice long enough to engage in a fair fight."

"You will break spears with him?" Taras asked.

Instead of answering, he lifted the door and set it against the wall. "See that the hinges are mended, Denholm, that Lady Taras may sleep in safety tonight."

"You will not sleep with her?"

Tense silence greeted his words. Taras tightened her lips and glared from the seneschal to his lord, daring him to comment. Cynewulf merely touched the stitches on his forehead, bowed, and walked out.

As his footsteps faded down the gallery, Denholm said, "He will sleep in the stable tonight, I suppose."

"Aye, with a dame to keep him company, no doubt!" It did no good to tell herself or anyone else that she didn't care, because she did. The only way to rid herself of this contemptible sense of envy was to rid herself of *him*.

The question was, how?

The morning dawned cold and bright. Mountain wind tore leaves off the trees and hurled them onto the vast tournament field to mingle with the champions' snapping pennants.

At Cynewulf's command, Taras had dressed in a bliaut of rare black velvet embroidered with gold, and ridden a white palfrey to the field. Her guards seated her on the front row of the *berfrois,* or grandstand, then took their seats behind her.

Shading her eyes, she searched for Cynewulf among the combatants warming up on the field. She saw her cousin Camlann, garbed in a mantle of ermine and red silk, galloping up and down the lists. Tabor rode beside him on a great brown destrier.

"Where is Lord Cynewulf?" Taras asked an old man beside her.

He pointed to a string of tents some distance away. Taras picked out a large one draped with silver and black. Cynewulf's shield hung on a spear outside the door.

Camlann trotted over to the stands and reined in, his horse's nose touching the draperies beneath her seat. Taras pretended not to notice him.

"You try without success to ignore me, my lady," he said. He doffed his helm and cradled it under his left arm. "A strange thing, considering."

Fear touched her heart. The fool was about to reveal that they knew one another. What madness was this? She leaned forward and hissed into his face, "Silence! Do you not understand the game you play? He'll kill you if he discovers we know each other. He'll deduce the worst!"

"Are you afraid for my life, little cousin, or yours?" he murmured. "Pshaw, do not look so afraid. Your Viking lover would not harm you."

"Go away, Camlann! Go before he comes out!"

Camlann grinned like a satyr. "Again, do not fear. Soon he will writhe in the dirt, food for vultures. You will be glad, will you not?"

His gaze bored like icicles into hers. She read death in his eyes. Not an honorable death, but some twisted, hideous demise known only to him. Camlann was no traitor to Ethelred at all. She had not killed Cynewulf, so here he was.

"Little fool," he breathed into her face, "I have come to do what you were too stupid to accomplish. You and your potions!"

"What about them?"

"Sir Osric the Frog, indeed. Ha!"

She half rose from her seat and reached out to grip his ermine collar. "What is it? Tell me!"

"He never turned into a frog, you young charlatan! Your potion did not win him his lady's love, so he slipped off in the night. A frog hopped into his chamber and assumed his place—"

"Oh, thank God!" She dropped back onto the chair and buried her face in her hands. She hadn't ruined her friend, after all. Even though Cynewulf's herbalist had claimed her potion harmless, she'd still believed she'd transformed Osric.

Coming to Castle Ilovar had all been a dreadful mistake. She shouldn't be here. She'd never held the power to transform Cynewulf. She could leave without guilt, without—

"I hate to think what the king will do to you when I bring you back to England, tied to my horse's tail," Camlann said.

She stared at him through her fingers. "And why would you do that?"

"The answer is plain. You sought to gain fortune through your trick with the frog. No doubt you discovered Sir Osric's departure and placed the frog there on his bed yourself, hoping you'd be hailed as a mighty sorceress. It was your bad luck that Ethelred sent you here."

"You're a madman!" She could hardly keep her voice low. Between her teeth she said, "You're angry with me for shaming you in the woods, when you feared some trifling herbs brewed into a harmless potion! Remember how you begged for the Peace of God? Coward!"

Camlann kicked his gelding as though to drive it over the wall into the *berfrois*. The horse reared and planted its forefeet on the rail, thrusting its head into Taras's face. A guard sprang forward and rapped its nose with his knuckles to drive it down.

"You'll see what happens today, my lovely!" Camlann shouted. Laughing, he wheeled and galloped off to join Tabor.

Shuddering, Taras sat back in her seat and stared after him. He was cocksure and deadly. This would be no ordinary game of spears. Her cousin was certain of his ability to kill. No Briton alive could feel so confident of slaying the Wolf of the North. If Cynewulf died, it would not be because of Camlann's skill. She looked beyond him to Tabor, who was swishing a sword through the air as though smiting off invisible heads.

The two of them planned some trickery. She had to warn Cynewulf. It didn't matter now that he'd find out she was here at Ethelred's command. Sooner or later, she would have told him the truth. Now was the time. No more delays.

"I must see Lord Cynewulf!" she said, standing up.

A guard pulled her back into her chair. "The lord has other concerns than you today."

Before she could retort, the old man beside her put his finger to her lips, then left the stands. She saw him push his way through crowds of people, then stoop into Cynewulf's tent.

Before long, a messenger came and whispered to the guards. One of them caught Taras's elbow and raised her. "It seems your master would entertain you."

Within minutes they were standing outside Cynewulf's tent. "Go on," the guard said. "Be quick about it."

He pulled open the flap and pushed her inside. She stood blinking, trying to see after the brilliant sunshine. It was a moment before she saw Cynewulf.

Naked save for a narrow loincloth, he stood with his hands clenched behind his neck and his feet braced wide apart. Slowly he twisted back and forth, shifting his weight from foot to foot. Sweat darkened the hair under his arms and burnished his powerful muscles the color of copper. His eyes were closed.

Taras caught her breath in sudden fear. She should back out the door now, before he saw her, but her feet froze to the rug. She struggled to lift her gaze from his body, from the heavy symbol of dominance bulging against his loincloth.

"You've come to oil my body, then." His dark blue eyes rested upon her. It was too late to run.

"I wondered when you would," he said. He forced his arms down behind him, stretching his chest and sides until his muscles stood out in gleaming bulges.

"I—I came to ask you not to fight, lord."

He did not change expression. Catching up a rag, he wiped sweat from his throat and chest. He waited for her to speak.

She twisted her skirt in her hands. "I have no wish to watch the game of spears," she said in a low voice. Dear God, how could she tell him the truth? "The priests say it is a wicked sport."

"You know my opinion of your priests."

"You're nothing but a—" She broke off, biting her lip.

"What? A pagan? A blasted rower? A barbarian? Which of your insults will you spit in my face this time, Lady Taras of Widnes?"

Looking down at the velvet crushed in her hands, she said, "I didn't come to defame you, but to reason with you, if such be possible."

He stepped close to her. Taras's nostrils flared at his

incense of heat and leather. Deep in her belly an ache grew. Afraid, she twisted her skirt into a matted effigy of her own emotions.

"Reason with me, Lady Taras," he said at last, his voice so low it bypassed her ears and went straight to her heart. "Tell me that Camlann means nothing to you, that never has a man touched your soul but I."

His gaze was too intense to bear. She stared at her hands and tried to speak. She had to tell him that he was right, that Camlann was her cousin and desired to murder him. She had to admit her part in the plot. "I came here to kill you . . . " she began, but her tongue stuck to the roof of her mouth and stifled speech.

"Again?" he asked, his voice hardening. He grabbed her wrists and forced open her hands. Finding them empty, he pushed her back a step. "And what weapon would you have used, your tongue?"

Did he think she'd come here *just now* to kill him? She hadn't meant that at all; she'd meant—

"The anointing oil is on the table yonder," he said. "Fetch it, slave."

"It may stay upon the table until it grows rancid!" She'd come here to save his life, damn him. And what was his life worth, this man who lived to shame her?

"Anoint me, Briton," he said.

She turned on her heel and strode to the table. Her hand strayed to Cynewulf's knife, then she snatched up a flask of oil and pulled the wooden stopper. The scent of sandalwood filled the tent.

If he wanted to be anointed for death, so be it. Someday she could stand before the gates of Heaven with a clear conscience. It wasn't her fault he refused to listen. She'd tried to warn him.

She tipped oil into her palm and set the flask on the table. Rubbing her palms together, she came back to the

210

Dane. His eyes dared her to try something foolish. Instead, she slid her hands up his arms. His muscles felt as hard as steel, his gaze even harder.

She tried not to look into his eyes as she caressed the great muscles bridging his shoulders and neck. As she smoothed oil down his chest, she heard sharp little intakes of air. It took her a moment to recognize the sound of her own breathing.

"Now my back, slave."

She moved around him. Her hands trembled as she massaged his spine to his lower back. Her fingers brushed his loincloth.

"I want to feel your breasts on me," he said. His low growl sent shock waves into her belly. He raised his hands to the back of his neck, opening his sides to her touch. "Reach around me."

"Nay," Taras whispered, yet she moved against him until her velvet-covered breasts pressed his back. She slid her hands down his sides, then around to his navel. She could feel her breasts slide against him.

Cynewulf groaned and lowered his elbows to lock her arms against his waist. She felt his hands on her hips, pulling her tightly against him.

Tears stung her eyes even as desire gripped her loins. To hold this man was to chain a smoldering volcano. It was impossible. She could not love him—he would never love her.

But what madness was this, to talk of love? She'd come here to save him from Camlann's treachery. "You must not fight today," she whispered. She felt him tense.

"Do you fear for your British champion?"

"He isn't my champion. He's my—"

"Your voice quivers. You lie."

She yanked her arms free and spun toward the doorway, but he gripped her savagely by the upper arms. She tried to stamp on his foot. He lifted her off the ground and held her effortlessly against him, forcing her to stare into his eyes.

"You desire me to set you free, slave?"

"Aye, for this moment and forever!"

"That you might run to your precious knave and spread yourself for his pleasure."

"How dare you say such a thing? You know nothing of the truth! Why don't you listen to me?"

He set her on her feet. She felt his fingers tighten on her shoulder, then with a savage jerk he tore her sleeve off her arm. Half of her bodice came away, as well. She stumbled back with a cry.

He caught her again and thrust her into a chair, holding her in place with a heavy hand. In helpless rage she glared at him. A ruthless light burned in his eyes as he raised her torn sleeve to his nostrils and inhaled her scent. Then he dragged the black velvet down his oiled chest and tucked it into his loincloth.

"I will wear my slave's favor into combat."

"May it bring you bad luck!"

"Is that why you came here, then, to offer bad fortune?"

"That, and other things!"

Muttering an oath, he snatched her off the chair into his arms. "You mean naught to me, Briton. Naught! My family would yet be alive had not your precious Ethelred the Unraed. . . . " He clenched his teeth on the name and pushed her away.

Taras tripped over a woven rug and fell. She sprawled on the ground, looking up at the Viking, astounded by the fearful transformation of a man she had almost come to regard as civilized. She saw berserker rage in his dilated pupils, in his flaring nostrils and grinding teeth. His pulse pounded in the distended veins of his neck and chest. Fury balled his fists into hammers.

"You don't know what you're doing, Viking." She heard

her own voice as though from a distant sphere. She knew she took her life in her hands to speak to a warrior fired by the divine rage of Thor. "The battles of men are not mine. Though English blood flows in my veins, part of me remembers the frozen North."

His lips drew back in a snarl. She wondered if he'd even heard her. Dropping her gaze to the velvet protruding from his loincloth, she said, "Wear my favor upon your right arm, lord, and know that there is one Briton who decries the shedding of innocent blood, whether it be Danish or British."

He could not hear her. His rage was too strong, his memories too vivid. She needed no soothsayer to divine his thoughts. He was the Lord of Discoftomb beholding his kinsmen dead upon the field of Manathilim, and she was the enemy. There was no escape, yet she would not beg.

Feeling in every part of her his desire to exact the blood *weregeld,* she rose to her knees and prepared to fight for her life. Yet even as she waited, the rigidness went out of him. He blinked twice, and recognition dawned in his eyes. He turned on his heel and strode to the back of the tent.

Relief almost sickened her. She sat on the rug, trembling in every limb. Soon he came back bearing his wolf-skin mantle. He pulled her up and held her until the dizziness washed through her system and departed. Wordlessly he wrapped his mantle around her, covering her ruined gown. Then he led her to the doorway and pulled back the flap. He pushed her outside and dropped the flap between them.

Chapter Seventeen

Seeking again the inner peace and fluidity of movement his rage had banished, Cynewulf resumed his exercises. The wench should not have come to him . . . Odin's breath, did she not know how perilous it was to anger a warrior preparing for battle?

He dragged her tattered sleeve to his nose and held it there with both hands, picturing it molded against her skin. By the thunder of the gods, she shook him! She would never know how close he'd come to pulling her down in the furs and expending his passion upon her.

"Lord, may we enter?"

His squire and half a dozen armorers peered through the doorway. Cynewulf nodded once, then stood silently while they arrayed him in leather and buckled cuir bouilli greaves to his shins. Grunting under the tremendous weight, two armorers fastened him into his split-skirted coat of polished mail. They girded him with a leather-and-silver baldric studded with onyx and lodestone.

As Cynewulf took up Damfertigénen and tested its edge, Denholm ducked into the tent. Garbed in leather and chain mail, he stood grinning.

Cynewulf's aggavation found a focus. "What meaning do you attach to that odious leer, seneschal?"

"It is but pleasure occasioned by taking the lovely Lady of Widnes back to her seat, my lord."

"One should ware how he takes pleasure, my friend," Cynewulf said in a dangerous whisper.

"Aye. It would be an outrage to glory in a barbarian thrall," Denholm said, "when it is only meet to impress her lowliness upon her. A prideful captive is a ticklish creature."

Cynewulf slammed his sword into the scabbard, seized his winged helm from an armorer, and clapped it into the crook of his left arm.

"There comes a time in a man's life when he must do his duty," Denholm said.

"I keep my people well. In what sense have I failed in my duty?"

Denholm removed his spangenhelm and pretended to examine the rivets joining the iron bands to the leather. "There is the matter of an heir."

"My heir is none of your concern, seneschal."

" 'Twould distress Beogar to find himself without a grandson."

"My father is dead, and my mother. *And* my brother and sisters."

"The Lady Taras did not murder them."

"She is Briton," Cynewulf said. "The Unraed is her kinsman."

"It is not meet that you exact the *weregeld* upon her for Ethelred's sin."

Without taking his eyes off the seneschal, Cynewulf shoved his hands into leather gauntlets studded with iron. "The vengeance I exact will be upon Ethelred, himself."

"As you say, lord."

"Indeed, as I say." But Cynewulf could not resist asking, "What brings you to her cause, when you've cautioned me to beware her time and again?"

The seneschal shrugged his massive shoulders. "She is brave, lord, as brave as the shieldmaidens of old. That is enough for me to believe she's worthy. And I cannot help but note your bemusement in her presence. You've never been in love before."

"This isn't the talk a man going into combat needs."

Denholm raised his hand. "Nevertheless, you asked why I've come to her cause. You've had many women, lord, yet not one has touched your soul as this one has. I made your father a promise that his seed would not die with you."

"And so you desire to be a matchmaker, is that it?"

"I would see an heir to Amandolar before I die."

"You have a long life ahead of you, if I don't break your foolish pate."

Denholm shrugged again. "The Lady Taras loves you, even I can see that. I've observed her as she goes about her labors with the wounded. Always she fears she'll find you among them."

"Bah, she fears that I will *not* be among them." Cynewulf wanted to hear no more of Taras. He could still feel her hands on his body, and sense the tingling pleasure of her nails against his spine as she massaged him with scented oil. He shouldn't have allowed her in the tent. She distracted him.

The squire fastened a sable cloak to Cynewulf's shoulders. Denholm went to munch grapes from a bowl on the table. Turning to Cynewulf, he said, "Do not forget the giant Tabor. He will seek to kill you today."

"He may seek what he will."

"Beware of treachery."

"When dealing with Britons, it is foremost in my mind."

217

Cynewulf drank ale from a brass mazer and wiped his mouth. "Did you restore to Tabor his elder brother's sword, Lifedrinker, as I bade?"

"Yea, though why you returned the battle prize I do not understand. Why, the rubies in its hilt are worth—"

"Bah! I do not care for wealth. Let the varlet fight with it. The thing is marred with the blood of the murdered."

"Lifedrinker has defeated worthy opponents, too, lord," Denholm said. "Pray, do not let your thoughts stray far from *weregeld* vengeance."

"It seems that is the only place my thoughts dwell these days." Cynewulf stalked out of the tent.

Denholm followed at a slower pace. As they walked into the sunlight, the seneschal could see only darkness around the proud figure in silver and black. Today all would change in Amandolar. Nothing would ever be the same again.

With a heavy heart the seneschal went to mount his destrier.

As soon as Cynewulf stepped into the light, the folk leaped up with a shout that rolled across the valley and echoed from mountain to mountain.

Eboracum squealed with rage, and reared. His pedaling hooves raked his groom's tunic to tatters. Clinging to the reins, Mechalah screeched in terror. The big horse reared for another try at him.

"Eboracum! Get by!" Cynewulf shouted. He shoved Mechalah aside and seized the destrier's upper lip, pinching until the horse stood still. "There now, lad, you'll fly into battle soon enough. Stand still while I check your armor."

He took a firm grip on the reins before releasing the horse's mouth. He glanced around at Mechalah and found him sitting on an overturned water bucket, inspecting his ruined tunic. His rags reminded Cynewulf of Taras's torn gown.

Grimacing, he seized Eboracum by the straps of his leather face shield and said, "If you and I do not temper the wind of our wrath, all our folk will soon be naked."

He moved over the horse, adjusting his barding: the hardened leather cruppers, chain apron, and fetlock-length sable trappings. Satisfied, he vaulted onto the wooden saddle.

His squire handed him a long, teardrop-shaped shield. Catching up his spear, Cynewulf shook out the ceremonial *gonfanon* until its black wolf sprang upon the snapping silver flag.

"May Thor ride with you this day," Denholm said, reining in beside him.

Cynewulf raised the spear. "And with you, seneschal. May you gain wealth this day."

Wheeling, he spurred Eboracum within fifty feet of the *berfrois*. He saw Taras in the front row. She stared straight at him, her face betraying nothing.

"Kneel, Eboracum."

The warhorse folded one knee to the ground and lowered his head until his chamfron's black plume brushed the dirt. Cynewulf raised his spear. The roar of his people fairly shook the heavens.

"Present, Eboracum!"

Neighing, the destrier stood on his hind legs and pawed the air. The people shouted again. Taras stood up with them but maintained her silence.

Cynewulf pressed his knees against Eboracum's sides, sending him charging down the field, his black trappings billowing after. He turned and came back for a second pass.

As he drew abreast of the stands, a trumpet fanfare ushered more than two hundred combatants onto the field for the coursing of horses. They fell in behind Cynewulf, their colorful *gonfanons* declaring many noble houses.

Taras watched them circle the field. Arrayed in black, his spear jutting skyward, Cynewulf looked like one of the Vikings in her nightmares—the ones who'd surged onto the shores of England so long ago. Like them, he hungered for conquest. Like them, he would show no mercy.

No mercy. No mercy to *her*. He would not consider her conquered until she crawled to his feet. She drew a ragged breath that carried with it the scent of his anointing oil. Fire kindled in her breast until her cheeks grew hot.

Beneath the wolfskin mantle she touched her naked arm. *Savage*. His barbarism kept her enthralled. What a fearful hold he had on her.

He was closer now. She tried to draw a mask of indifference over her face, but as he rode by, his glance shredded her resolve. She was sure he saw her blush. Could he sense her desire to touch him, to hie with him to a place far away from the battleground?

Every warrior on the field was there to win prizes and glory. Felling the Wolf would bring both. *Cynewulf, come away with me before it's too late*.

And then Camlann and his men rode into view. Camlann wheeled and reined in just in front of her. He cast her a mocking stare, then doffed his helm and treated the crowd to a smile that fairly put the sun to shame. Touching his fingers to his lips, he tossed a kiss to the ladies. Several shouted and threw their tassels at him. He tucked the favors under his decorative surcoat.

Taras wondered that they did not sense his coiled hatred, the poisonous fangs waiting to strike. Didn't they know he'd delight in killing them, as well as their lord?

Camlann rode on. A woman behind Taras said in English, "Do you not think it a disgusting spectacle, to find a bedwench flaunting herself before quality folk? Yonder rides her lover. Methinks Lord Cynewulf wonderfully perverse to tolerate her drooling over a British knight."

Taras swung around and spied Dame Frisia seated above her. The strip of ermine around her throat looked like the one Camlann had worn less than an hour ago.

Smiling maliciously at a thin woman beside her, Frisia said. "I hope you've brought a scented cloth, Allison, to shield your nose from the whore-stench in our vicinity."

Allison fanned herself. "Faith, I've just thrown my kerchief to the fair Lord Camlann. What shall I do to temper this abominable odor about us?"

Taras bit her tongue. One of her guards grinned at her, then turned to Allison. "Mayhap you should take a seat down here by Lady Taras, where the air is pure and sweet."

Everyone within earshot twittered. Frisia leaned over and slapped him across the cheek. The guard only laughed.

Taras turned away. Despite the guard's defense of her, she did not feel she'd won a victory. A sickening sense of envy flooded her throat when she remembered the look in Frisia's eyes last night. For the manna of Cynewulf's body she would have forsaken food, drink, and honor. Taras wondered if Cynewulf had sought her out after leaving their chamber last night.

She forced her attention back to the field. The coursing of horses done, the squires rushed to take their masters' cloaks, to adjust saddles and harnesses, to shrug *ganfonons* from spears, and to perform a dozen other duties. In the confusion, Taras lost sight of Cynewulf.

"I should like to sit with you, my lady spell weaver."

Taras twisted around in surprise. "My lord, I thought you were on the field—oh!" Instead of Cynewulf, the young warrior whose lung she had helped treat lowered himself into the seat beside her. She blinked away sudden tears. *Spell weaver.* Only Cynewulf called her that.

"Are you ill, my lady? Is there aught I can do?" Harrod asked.

"I am quite well, Harrod. I—I was just surprised to see you."

"Surprised or disappointed?" Harrod asked. He followed her glance to Cynewulf's tent. "I am not annoyed that you favor another over me. Were I a wench—and I thank the Lord I am not—I would esteem him over a clumsy oaf like myself."

Taras felt her face burn ever brighter. Was she so transparent, that even a youth could see into her heart?

Harrod gestured at the warriors. "They will divide into two teams for the grand melee. Though they use rebated—blunted—spears and do not fight to the death, it is a damned bloody affair if one is not used to seeing it."

"I have seen a melee," Taras said. "It is a bloody affair, whether or not one is used to it."

He touched his wounded side and grimaced. "It's a bloody painful business to be part of, as well."

"You should be lying down, not coming out here in your weakened state."

He smiled as though warmed by her sympathy. "Aye. Perhaps."

"Cod-headedness is not a thing to be proud of," she said. "I do not understand why you foster it."

"To watch my brethren crack their skulls together makes my own pangs seem slight."

Taras bent on him a cold look. "Delighting in the art of war is a pursuit likely to land you in hell."

"The Norseman hopes to land himself not in hell, but in Valhalla," Harrod said. "He must die in battle to be carried hence in the arms of the Valkyries."

One of the guards leaned over her shoulder. "Aye, there is no higher purpose in life."

"You think so, do you?" Taras said. "Then you're as witless as Harrod, for your precious Valhalla is nothing but a mystical sphere dreamed up by your bloodthirsty forefathers! A man's purpose is not to seek death, but to serve God in meekness all the days allotted to him."

Dame Frisia unleashed a scornful laugh. "So our ignorant little bedwench seeks to instruct warriors on the meaning of life, does she? And will she bring in her friars to tell Lord Cynewulf to beat his mighty sword into a plowshare?"

"It would be better than for him to spill his lifeblood on the ground, chasing an empty dream."

Harrod touched her hand. "You needn't worry. The Iron Wolf cannot be defeated in battle."

"That is a myth you Danes have concocted!" Taras nearly shouted. "He is a man, and a man can be hurt . . . or killed."

She kneaded her forehead. Why couldn't she tear Cynewulf out of her brain and relinquish his memory to outer darkness? It wasn't fair that he disarrayed her emotions so. How could she hate him, yet love his very life?

When she looked at the field again, she saw that the riders had formed up on opposite sides. His spear thrusting at the sky, his horse's hooves shaking the ground, Cynewulf galloped to his place before his men and reined in.

Taras thought of the terrible injuries she'd treated all the past week. The game of spears was no game at all.

The marshal raised his red pennant. A hush descended over the field. Against the mountain backdrop, the contenders waited in eerie silence, players on a stage.

The pennant fell. Weapons flashed. The silence held for a heartbeat, and then a great war cry shivered the air. The ground quaked under the hooves of warhorses on a collision course with death. The battle roar gathered volume in its race across the field and burst upon Taras; she felt it in every fiber of her being. With a thousand others she sprang to her feet. She gripped the rail in front of her and held on. The spectators roared until Taras couldn't hear her own screams.

223

In dread alarm she watched Cynewulf surge ahead of his men. When he was ten paces from the armored wall riding down upon him, Taras clapped her hands over her ears and screwed shut her eyes.

Half a second later, the shock of impact hit the *berfrois,* shuddering the boards. Taras opened her eyes and searched for Cynewulf in the roiling mass of horses and men.

Cynewulf surged through the horde's center and unseated three enemies. All around him, men and horses cartwheeled. Spears shattered like glass. Through the choking cloud of dust he saw Tabor and one of Camlann's men plunging toward him. Tabor's monstrous horse mowed down others in its path.

Cynewulf fought his way out of the pack and galloped straight at Tabor. When the tip of Tabor's spear nearly touched his shield, Cynewulf swerved into the other knight and knocked him out of the saddle.

He heard steel swish behind him. Instantly he wheeled Eboracum, bringing up his shield just in time. Tabor's longsword bit into the edge next to his face.

They were too close for Cynewulf's spear to be of use. He cast it aside and clawed for Damfertigénen, but before he could unsheath it, Eboracum stumbled over a fallen horse and crashed over sideways. Cynewulf jumped clear and wrenched free his sword.

"Die upon Lifedrinker!" Tabor yelled.

Cynewulf threw off his shield and laid hold of his sword with both hands. Tabor struck a savage blow at his head. With leopard quickness Cynewulf dodged and sprang almost into Tabor's face. He grabbed the giant's shield and hurled him to the ground. The huge Briton immediately gained his feet.

"Now we are even again," Cynewulf said with a nasty smile and struck Tabor's blade.

Tabor snatched his sword back and struck a scything blow at Cynewulf's knees. Cynewulf leaped over the blade and smote Tabor's mailed shoulder, but the blade slid harmlessly off the links.

Again and again they struck and parried without gaining the advantage. Finally, thigh to thigh, arm to arm, they locked swords and glared into each others' eyes.

"For my brother, the Knight of Solway Moor!" Tabor said.

Cynewulf saw his eyes flicker almost too late. He snapped his fist down and deflected the dirk Tabor had slipped from a sheath. He caught his enemy's hand. Their swords crossed in front of their faces, the dirk wavering between their bellies, they strove in mortal combat.

"For Ethelred and the Knight of Solway Moor!"

"For Beogar and my kindred dead!" Cynewulf said. With a mighty heave he rammed the dirk up through chain mail into the giant's heart.

Tabor's sword fell out of his nerveless hands. He stared at his slayer for several seconds, then at the blood splashing over his fallen sword. Then, with a soundless curse, Tabor released his soul to the darkness.

At noon the marshall called a halt to the fighting. Tabor's body was dragged off the field and given to his companions. Camlann had already limped off to his tent.

Taras felt ill. She'd seen Cynewulf slay Tabor, then reclaim his horse and fight at the bridge. He hadn't looked hurt, but he'd been too far away to know for sure.

"I must see Lord Cynewulf," she told her guard.

"He has men to attend him."

"He may be hurt."

The guard laughed. "All the more reason to keep you away, then. A woman like you makes a strong man weak."

Before Taras could respond, Harrod intervened with an

easy smile. "If she cannot see the lord, let her go and tend the wounded."

"They have wives and daughters, and the old herbalist is there."

"He hasn't the adroitness of the spell weaver. She's set more bones and healed more wounds than the old man can spit upon. Let her go."

"All right, but she only goes to the tents of the wounded. I've orders not to let her near Lord Cynewulf. He does not wish to be disturbed."

All afternoon Taras worked her healing in the tents. The shadows lay in long streaks across the field by the time she finally left. Her guard had wandered off, so for a time she mingled with the crowd. Shouts and dust rose from a distant melee. Taras wondered if Cynewulf were involved.

Mayhap he'd been wounded while she tended the others. The thought made her mouth dry and her legs weak. She had to know. The longer she delayed, the worse she felt.

She hurried through camp to Cynewulf's black and silver tent. Since there were no guards, she ducked inside.

Denholm lounged in a chair, drinking from a wooden bowl. Cynewulf sat cross-legged on the woven rug, Damfertigénen across his knees. A muscle tensed in his jaw, but he did not vary his rhythm as he sharpened the sword.

Denholm lurched to his feet and bowed. "My lady, I thought you had returned to the castle."

Taras looked only at Cynewulf. "And you, lord? Did you think I had returned?"

"I gave no thought to your whereabouts."

She felt her face redden. Stalking past him, she stared up at Denholm. "What happened to you?"

He lifted his hand to a gash on his forehead. "You did not witness me fall off the bridge? My own cousin knocked me arse backward into the water!" He shouted with laughter and slapped his belly. "I spent most of the day in the *recet,* nursing this damned head."

The *recet* was the place of refuge on the field where warriors could take fresh horses, rearm, or hold prisoners. Women were not allowed there. Too often, men died who went to the *recet* because their women couldn't nurse them.

"You and your lord will bear matching scars, seneschal."

"It matters not, compared to the loss of my horse."

"You'll win him back," Cynewulf said. He jabbed his sword into the ground and shoved to his feet. He wore a loincloth and nothing else.

Taras swiftly perused him for injuries, found none, and looked away. She could not still the impetuous murmuring in her veins that his seminakedness wrought. She wondered what he had done with her torn sleeve. She risked a peep at his loincloth.

He caught her looking. Immediately he turned away and said, "Why have you come, Taras?"

She elevated her gaze with guilty haste, and for a moment found herself voiceless.

"I suppose you've come to ask me not to fight again," he said.

"Would it do any good?" she managed to say.

"Nay."

"Then I will reserve my breath for more useful things."

"Like quarreling," Denholm said.

"I have no desire to quarrel," Taras said. "There are enough stupid men outside doing just that, and worse. If my lord does not halt his gaming soon, his retainers will be too damaged to fight a real battle."

Cynewulf's eyes darkened to midnight. He stepped close to her. "A real battle? Does my captive lay plots with her lover, then? Has he concealed an army within my borders?"

"Had I a lover with the power to wage war against you," she said, "you could stake your life I would aid his cause in every way imaginable."

"Mayhap you already have," he said, in a voice pitched low as a lion's growl.

She returned his glare, but inside she trembled as though ice-water filled her.

"If you are finished, woman," he said, "you may go."

"I will not be dismissed like a dog. I am a lady gentle born. I'll leave when I'm ready."

Cynewulf moved even closer. She smelled his hot warrior scent. His breath burned her face like an August wind. She stared defiantly into his eyes.

Cynewulf's visage hardened. His breath blew harshly between his teeth, then he caught her against his body and forced her lips open in a brutal kiss. With his tongue he explored her mouth, delving until she could scarcely breathe.

Taras could not muster enough strength to break his iron embrace. His hard muscles pressed every part of her, bruising and marking her his possession. He slid his hand down her spine and pulled her against his pelvis. He was steel, a hot blade forged of desire. She wanted him as she'd never wanted anything else in life.

He released her and stepped back, his chest rising and falling, sweat sheening his muscles. Pressing her hand to her bruised mouth, Taras stumbled away. Her mantle fell open, exposing much of her body through the remnants of her bodice. She trembled under Cynewulf's hot-eyed stare.

"Are you ready to leave now?" he asked roughly. "Or should I dismiss you once more?"

She recoiled as though he'd struck her, then turned and fled outside. Her single, choking sob quivered against the eardrums of the Vikings she'd left behind.

Denholm released his breath in a long sigh. "To think of

the pains I took during your youth, teaching you to charm wenches! An ill-tempered bull possesses more charm than you. I wasted my time!"

Cocking his fists on his hips, Cynewulf gave a snort. "Aye, you should have spent your time teaching me to avoid their cunning snares."

"This wench sets no trap for you, lord. Your pride blinds you."

"If any other man had said that, he'd be searching the rushes for his teeth right now."

"Aye, and his head also," Denholm said with a shrug.

Scowling, Cynewulf pulled on his tunic and tied the laces at his throat. Confounded by his own emotions, he had wanted to confuse and hurt Taras. Still hearing the echo of her sob, he knew he'd succeeded. Why did he feel no pleasure?

Denholm turned to go. Cynewulf caught his arm and said, "Send a search party into the forest. See if the bastard Camlann has an army hiding there."

"You do not think—"

"I don't know what to think. Mayhap the wench is a spy. If Camlann is here seeking vengeance for Ethelred's defeat at Manathilim, he may have sent her ahead to feel out our defenses."

"Your wits are addled," Denholm muttered as he stalked to the tent flap.

"Eh? What's that you said?"

" 'Tis the way of a man in love," Denholm called over his shoulder as he disappeared outside. "All I can do is humor you until you regain your senses."

Chapter Eighteen

Taras stayed in the warrior camp that night, in a lean-to beside the blacksmith's forge. It was a terrible place to try to sleep. While Beldor pounded iron, warriors and women danced and sported by the bonfire. She peeped out of the cloth doorway to watch them. She couldn't see Cynewulf.

She lay back on her bed of straw and gazed up at the hemlock bough roof. Mice squeaked and skittered in the straw, but she scarcely cared about that. She didn't care about the guard outside, either. All she wanted to know was why Cynewulf had detained her tonight. The knave hadn't spoken to her directly, but had sent Denholm to do his dirty work.

She jerked up onto one elbow and splashed wine out of a pitcher into a small mazer. The mice started fighting again. On an impulse she dumped wine into the straw where the loudest noises were coming from. The squabbling ceased.

"Mayhap a bit of wine-bibbing will settle us all," Taras said. She drew another draft and drank it quickly.

Beldor began pounding again. Knowing she'd never sleep, Taras lifted the flap and propped her chin on her hands. The folk looked like devils dancing around the fire, screaming and laughing, urged on by the pagan drumbeat.

She couldn't see her guard anymore; he'd probably joined the revelers. It would be simple to crawl out of the lean-to and set off into the night . . . if Camlann weren't lurking somewhere in the forest with his men. Besides, Cynewulf was probably watching. She wouldn't get far.

She recalled his brazen fondling of her in his tent. By the saints, he'd nearly taken her before his seneschal! Only his desire to humiliate her had saved her. There was bitter irony in that. His hatred was stronger than his lust, though if it suited him, he would vent his lust to prove his hatred.

She must avoid him. No matter what, she had to stay away from his tent. And if he tried to come to her tonight, she'd crash the wine pitcher over his head.

Would she? In the back of her mind she knew her vinegary actions aroused his battle lust. It was as though she wanted him to molest her.

She was a fool, a calf-lollied fool.

She finally slept, but it wasn't long before a manservant shook her awake. He was a captive Briton, a slave until the Althing met. She crawled out of the shelter groaning with stiffness.

"The lord bids you wear clean vestments," the manservant said. He pushed a linen chemise and white wool bliaut into her hands.

"I must bathe first. Take me back to the castle."

Alarm flickered in his eyes. "Nay, he forbids it."

"Then I'll bathe in the stream." It was cold this morning; frosty clouds formed on every breath.

"Water weakens a body, m'lady. With winter nigh, a good layer of dirt insulates one from the cold."

"Just show me to the stream."

The servant motioned to Taras's guard, who was standing by the fire eating from a bread trencher. "The lady wishes to bathe," the servant said. "We should stand guard."

" 'Tis freezing this morn, wench," the guard said.

"Then I won't take long." Taras strode off toward the trees.

"Well, come on," she heard the guard say. "The master will flay us alive if some rogue attacks her in the forest."

Cynewulf stepped out of the stream into sunlight filtering through the trees. He ignored the breeze pricking his wet skin as he squatted down to shave, staring at his reflection in the shield propped against a tree.

He and Denholm had found no English army hiding in the forest last night. Camlann and his men had come alone to Amandolar, which seemed to bear out his story that he'd deserted King Ethelred. And Taras hadn't tried to slip out of the lean-to and go to him, even though the guard—at Cynewulf's order—had left her alone most of the night.

The knife slipped, nicking his chin. He cursed as he flicked away blood. By thunder, he'd convinced himself that Taras was part of a plot against him. Was she as innocent as she claimed? Not since his youth had a wench so confused him! Was he growing daft, as Denholm thought?

He swore again and stood up. He pulled his clothing over his damp skin and gathered his weapons. It was time he cast aside his vain meditations and set his thoughts on the tournament field. He would not allow the wench to fog his wits.

As he started up the trail he heard voices. He slid behind

a tree just before Taras and her escorts came into view. Taras was muffled to her chin in his wolfskin mantle. She set a bundle of clothing on a rock beside the stream and shot the men a withering look. "You are dismissed."

"Nay," the guard said, "we will go into the wood and keep watch."

"So long as you do not watch *me*."

She waited until the pair disappeared, then shrugged out of her torn garments and stepped into the water. Vapor rose from the surface, and a thin film of ice crackled along the stream's edge. Gasping with cold, she immersed herself to her shoulders.

Cynewulf came out of hiding and slipped up behind her. "It seems my finest memories are made of your baths, spell weaver."

"You! Can you never leave me alone, you cursed rower?"

"If I leave you alone, you might run away."

"And why should that disturb you?" Her teeth chattered until she could hardly spit the words. "I should think you'd gladly be rid of one who despised you so."

"It pleasures me to toy with you."

Anger flashed in her green eyes. "Turn your head. I'm frozen to the bone."

"There is much I could do to warm you, Taras."

"My loathing for you warms me."

"Methinks you are not quite warm enough," he said, but he stood up and entered the forest. As he strode back to camp, he wondered if their strange relationship befuddled her as much as it did him. It was an odd notion.

Taras claimed her seat in the front row to watch the coursing of horses. Cynewulf rode by, doffed his helm, and smiled gravely. She saw that he'd tied her black sleeve around his right arm. She did not smile back.

Gonfanons fluttering, Camlann and his retainers rode by and waved at the crowd. Camlann was popular with the ladies, Taras thought, judging by the shrieks. She settled back in her seat and looked elsewhere.

Camlann broke away from his men and rode over. There was no kindness in his smile. In a murmur meant solely for her ears, he said, "Today I'll make an end of him, little cousin, and you will return to England with me to face your punishment."

"Cocky knave, you'll return alone, if you manage to return at all!"

He smiled like a serpent. "You ought to speak politely to me, that I might soften our cousin the king's wrath."

Taras lifted her nose and looked off into the distance. Camlann shoved on his helmet and galloped off to join his men. His knights moved to flank him.

Again the warriors divided into two teams for the grand melee. Taras watched through her fingers as the marshal dropped the red pennant to send them plunging at each other. She saw Cynewulf leading the charge, then the two sides came together in a cacophony of noise and dust. Swords arced and flashed. Spears splintered and men fell screaming from their horses.

Taras jumped up, striving with all her might to see Cynewulf. It seemed a long time before she saw him forge through the fighters and smash two horsemen into the stream. He captured their horses and drove them toward his squire.

And then, out of the sun, she saw three riders closing on him like a wolf pack that had long run together. She screamed his name even though it was impossible for him to hear her.

He turned on them. At that instant Taras recognized Camlann in the center. Cynewulf didn't wait for them to come to him; he spurred Eboracum into the knight on

Camlann's left, tearing him out of the saddle. Before the others could turn, Cynewulf wheeled and went after them. With the butt of his spear he knocked down the second knight, then reversed his grip and attacked Camlann.

Instead of engaging, Camlann set his heels to his horse's flanks and galloped toward the *berfrois*. He cast aside his spear and drew his sword, swinging it overhead. Women screamed in joyous fright, thinking Camlann wanted to thrill them with a taste of battle.

But something in the malevolent set of her cousin's face warned Taras that she was the target. She saw desperate rage in Cynewulf's eyes as he whipped his horse after Camlann. The great destrier's hooves seemed to fly above the grass.

Did her cousin intend to kill her? Not waiting to find out, Taras turned to run, but her guard jerked her into her chair and held her. The roar of the crowd drowned out her shouts. In a moment Camlann would plunge his sword into her heart and the spectators would get a thrill they hadn't expected. She twisted and fought, but the guard only clamped down harder, holding her for Camlann.

Then Cynewulf rose from the saddle and hurled his spear. The blunted tip slammed into Camlann's armored back. He crashed to the ground and rolled against the draperies below the stands. Women screamed and wept.

Cynewulf dragged hard on Eboracum's reins to slew him away from the stands. Dust rolled over the spectators. For an instant Taras stared straight into Cynewulf's angry eyes, then Camlann jumped up and swung his sword at his foe.

Cynewulf leaped off Eboracum and met Camlann's sword with his own. Sparks showered his face. The men twisted and turned, their swords ringing and crashing off shields and helms.

For minutes too long to count Taras watched them fight. The crowd hollered and clapped each time the opponents clashed. They thought this wasn't a fight to the death, but

Taras knew better. If Camlann could kill him, he would. Judging from Cynewulf's expression, he felt the same way.

Cynewulf lost his shield. Now he had to parry Camlann's mighty strokes with the flat of his sword. Safe behind his shield, Camlann struck viper-fast.

Taras could see Cynewulf weakening. He swung Damfertigénen ever more slowly. The crowd's roar lessened, then stopped altogether. Now the only sound was steel on steel, and the men's tortured breathing.

Suddenly Cynewulf lunged and flipped Camlann's shield up with the tip of his sword, tearing it off his arm. Before Camlann could react, Cynewulf smote his side with the flat of his sword. Camlann screamed and stumbled back. Cynewulf pressed his advantage while Camlann fought back with desperate strength.

But Taras noticed something strange. Instead of maintaining a two-handed grip on his sword, Camlann sometimes tried to slap Cynewulf with the back of his hand. Taras saw his rings sparkle in the sunlight. Did he intend to gash Cynewulf with his jewels?

And then she knew. Camlann hadn't tried to kill her at all. He'd rushed at the stands to draw Cynewulf close so that she could see him die. Camlann was wearing a poison ring. For some sick reason, he wanted Taras to witness the killing.

She slapped away the guard's hands and jumped up. "Cynewulf! The ring! Don't let him touch you!"

But the crowd was yelling again and Cynewulf didn't hear her. Again and again the swords rose and fell, ringing like hammer blows on an anvil. Taras screamed until she was hoarse, but Cynewulf fought on, oblivious to the threat. She tried to jump onto the field, but her guard held her back.

Suddenly Camlann parried a blow and got inside Cynewulf's guard. Instead of smiting with the sword, he struck Cynewulf's cheek with his fist. Taras screamed in horror and tried again to jump over the draperies. The guard dragged her back and clamped his hand over her mouth.

Cynewulf shoved Camlann back, then closed on him, striking him to one knee. Before Camlann could raise his sword again, Cynewulf pressed Damfertigénen against his throat and stared coldly into his eyes. "Yield, varlet."

Camlann's breath hissed between his teeth. Cynewulf increased the pressure on his throat. How he longed to kill this bastard who had ridden at Taras, but tournament rules restrained him. "My sword is called 'Slayer of the Damned,' Briton," he said. "To send another to hell on its teeth would not disturb me."

"I yield," Camlann said, and dropped his sword. A corner of his mouth lifted in a tiny smile.

Cynewulf slowly lowered his sword and jabbed the tip into the ground. In some way, his enemy acted as though he'd won a victory. "This day I have spared your miserable life," Cynewulf said. "Beware, if ever our paths cross again, I will kill you. Now take yourself and your pox-ridden horde from my lands. Begone!"

He did not move as Camlann rose stiffly to his feet. For a moment the Briton stared at him, and Cynewulf read triumph in his eyes.

"You've won no victory," Camlann said. "In the spring, your precious Sweyn Forkbeard will ride without you. The army of Ethelred will crush him and scatter his bones in the sea!"

Cynewulf raised his sword, then remembered Taras's words: " 'Tis a pagan practice to kill a senseless foe."

He said through his teeth, "Begone from my lands. Whatever you've sought to accomplish here has won you naught. Return here, and die."

Camlann stood up and spat on the ground between

them, then walked off the field. Cynewulf's people leaped up to cheer their lord, but he looked only for Taras. She was on her feet again, her face twisted with fear. She shouted at him and touched her cheek, but he could not hear her words. Cynewulf lifted his hand and started to walk toward her, then blackness drifted across his vision and he knew no more.

Chapter Nineteen

He would die this time. He could not fight the terrible floating sensation invading every pore of his body. This wasn't like a sword wound, sharp and fiery; he could conquer pain like that. This was pain of a different sort, a pervasive evil that beat him like the wings of some awful vulture.

He tried to resist, but the vulture pulled him out of his skin and flew his body into cold, thin clouds, where he breathed his own blood and death and decay. He could not overcome this.

"Please, lord, wake up. . . . Open your eyes and sip this."

He heard Taras calling through the fog. Her voice was soft, urgent, kind. Nay, it could not be her. She despised him.

The vulture's beak ripped into his belly, spilling his bowels to the earth. He screamed.

And then her gentle hands held him, pried him out of the bird's grasp, slipped under his neck to raise his head. Miracle of all, he felt her lips on his mouth, warm and soft, pressing and urgent. He parted his lips to take her tongue, but she withdrew. An instant later, an unholy brew filled his mouth. He gagged and tried to spit it out, but she held his head hard against her breast and massaged his throat until his muscles convulsed.

"Swallow it, lord. Swallow it lest you die! There, that's not so bad . . . yes, yes . . . drink some more. Oh, such a frown . . . "

He didn't open his eyes, but gradually his limbs felt lighter and his skin settled over his frame once more. A curious warmth stole through his system, and his heart beat again.

She made him drink more, then laid his head on the pillow. For a moment he thought she'd gone away and he became afraid that the vulture would get him again; then he felt her massaging the soles of his feet. The scent of cyprus and birch oil filled his nostrils, chasing away the stench of mold and death.

"Spell weaver," he whispered, though his mouth felt too cracked and dry to utter the words.

"He spoke—did you hear him?"

"Aye, lady. A good sign." It was Denholm's voice.

"Take the leeches off now, seneschal. He's bled enough, I think. I'll rub some oil into the places where they drank."

Cynewulf forced open his lids and stared up at the seneschal who leaned over him with a candle, burning and plucking long black suckers from his chest. Denholm's face split in a huge grin, and for an instant Cynewulf feared the seneschal would kiss him. To avoid this, he pushed his chin against his chest and gazed down at Taras kneeling beside the bed, massaging his feet. Her hands stilled when she saw him looking at her. Her lips trembled in an uncertain smile, then tears coursed suddenly from her eyes. She brushed them away and hurried to give him a drink of water.

"How do you feel, lord?" she asked.

Like he'd been torn apart by a bird of prey and stitched back together by someone who'd never sewn before. He didn't say it, though. Instead, he pushed himself to his elbows and looked for his sword. By the light of a tallow candle he saw it hanging from the central tent pole. When he tried to sit up to take it, his head reeled and Denholm made him lie down again.

"Camlann—what of Camlann?" he said through parched lips.

"After the fight, I ordered my men to escort him and his horde beyond our borders," Denholm said. "Would that I'd known what he'd done to you!"

Cynewulf pushed the seneschal away and sat up. His head felt as though it were compressed between blacksmith's pincers, but his dizziness had eased. "What did he do to me?"

Instead of answering, Denholm nodded at Taras. Blushing, she examined her hands before replying, "He poisoned you. Did you feel him scratch your cheek with his ring?"

Cynewulf raised his hand to his cheek and felt dried blood. "What kind of poison?"

"Monkshood and henbane, I think. And belladonna—I gave you tannic acid along with other herbs."

No wonder his mouth tasted like a tannery. He took a long drink of water and spat it into the dirt. "Did you know he planned to scratch me?"

"How could I have known? I saw him strike and guessed his intent."

"It was not . . . planned?"

"You think I decocted the poison for him? If I did, then tell us why I saved your miserable life. Go on—the seneschal and I would like to hear it." She folded her arms and glowered at him. Denholm mirrored her actions.

But Cynewulf couldn't shake his suspicions—or the horror of his dreams. "How did you know the poison and its antidote?"

"Your pupils grew large as ha'pennies, your tongue dry as a dead raven's wing. Any simpleton would know it for belladonna," she snapped. "And then you rambled and raved about flying. A decoction of monkshood and henbane, and perhaps other poisonous plants, creates such a delusion. You don't have to take my word for it—your own herbalist confirmed my guess."

"And where is he?"

Denholm cleared his throat. "He's drifted back to the nether regions he loves, the madman. I think he's trying to recreate the spell weaver's love potion, though she won't tell him how she made it. However, he gave Lady Taras the herbs and leeches she required to cure you."

Cynewulf scowled at his seneschal. After all the mischief Camlann had done, Denholm had trusted his life to another Briton!

"Summon the herbalist," Cynewulf said. "Call him away from his damned brewing—I want him here."

He saw Taras's eyes take flame; then she jumped up and strode out of the tent, snapping the flaps closed with a violence that shook the poles.

"Have I mentioned upon occasion, lord, that you are a fool?" Denholm asked. Chuckling, he moved to the table and poured wine for them both. He held a goblet out to Cynewulf, who reluctantly took it, drank, then massaged his aching head.

"Mayhap you're right," Cynewulf said at last. "But it takes a still bigger fool to coddle a serpent to his breast."

"Lady Taras is no serpent."

"Does my memory fail me, or were you not the man who warned me to watch my back? 'She'll kill you, lord,' you told me time and again. And now you're her champion." He struck his forehead with the heel of his hand, and instantly regretted it when a bright shaft shot through his eyes. "By Thor, you won't rest until I marry the wench."

"I can think of no worthier lady to stand at your side. You should have seen her tonight, struggling to save your ungrateful skin. She was kind when she said your herbalist helped her determine the poison—that one-wheeled wagon stood scratching his head and weeping. Without the Briton, you would most certainly be dead and ready for the funeral barge."

Cynewulf leaned back and pillowed his arms behind his head. "A less trusting soul might say she'd concocted the whole thing. What greater way to gain my trust than to get her countryman to poison me, then fly in to save my life?"

"Bah—it's the monkshood talking. Perhaps next time Camlann will give you a larger dose, and you can flutter off to Valhalla with your suspicions."

"Desist! You make my head hurt worse."

"If I were you, I'd rush off to marry her this very night before some swain steals her from under your nose."

"The swain would win himself a bellyful of Damfertigénen, were he to behave so rashly."

"Indeed? How many of your own men would you kill, lord? They're all in love with her. Old Beldor the blacksmith works day and night in his forge, linking the wench a chain mail vestment as though he would armor her against you. Young Harrod has taken to following her about like a puppy, as do a hundred others."

Cynewulf uncurled from the bed. "Do you, too, share their sentiments?"

"I am an old man, but if the wench were free to choose me, I'd gladly take her to the wedding furs."

Cynewulf's hands found Denholm's neck and for a moment all he could see was red. Denholm's smile faded as he was forced to fight for breath. His energy spent, Cynewulf planked down on the cot and scowled at the seneschal.

"I was but teasing," Denholm finally said. He rubbed his neck before going on in a hurt tone, "Do you think that I, who fought back to back with you against the Saracens, would cuckold you? Verily, you cut me to the quick."

"Not even Damfertigénen could cut your barnacled hide to the quick."

Denholm waved his hand. "In truth, the poor blind girl hardly notes anyone else's existence. She loves *you*. Why, I cannot imagine."

Cynewulf gripped his fist in his left hand and lowered his head in thought. Her feelings should make no difference to him. He could not forgive her for what her people had done to his. She aroused his lust, that was all. Lust was not enough to make him forget. Not enough to make him wed the enemy.

"Go away, seneschal," he said. "The night is far spent. I need sleep."

"Shall I summon your herbalist to care for you?"

"Nay. I need no nursemaid."

"You need the stuff in the flagon beside you, though. Mayhap in addition to clearing the poisons from your body, it will clear the stupidity from your brain." Denholm turned and stormed from the tent.

Cynewulf scowled after him long after he was gone. Finally, he swept up the flagon and sniffed it. The acrid stench of tannic acid filled his nostrils. He got up and flung the mixture outside.

For a moment he stood in the doorway, looking across the camp. He could hear Beldor pounding away in his forge. The mute blacksmith should be shoeing horses and repairing armor. Was he working on the chain mail vestment, instead?

Cynewulf rubbed the back of his neck and blinked the

pain from his eyes. What was he going to do with Taras? He owed her a debt of gratitude for what she'd done, yet he could not humble himself to a Briton. The wall between them was too high.

At last he turned and went back to his cot. In the morning the world would look different. The brush of the vulture's wing would flee his mind, and he would be strong again. He would figure out this woman he owned.

Cynewulf slept again, this time without dreams, and awakened at the first brush of dawn. His sickness had fled, leaving in his core only a hollow, dry feeling. He swung out of bed and flexed his muscles to purge the last bit of soreness.

Along with the poison his anger was gone, and though he tried to summon his pride, he couldn't. The wench had saved his life, and for that he owed her something. Freedom, perhaps? Nay, he couldn't bear the thought. Neither could he be honest with himself. It was best not to examine his reasons for keeping her enthralled.

He dressed quickly and strode into the daylight. The camp was already awake. He smelled food and for a moment his stomach rebelled, but he swallowed and moved on. Perhaps the spell weaver could give him an herb to settle his gut.

Perhaps he should reward her in a way she'd understand. He could give her an occupation solely her own. Aye, he'd give her the herbalist's job, along with a fine title. He imagined her pleasure when he told her.

Hurrying now, he strode to the lean-to near the forge and jerked aside the curtain. Empty. Was she bathing in the forest again? He hastened to the stream but found no trace of her. Back at camp, no one remembered seeing her since last night. He sent a messenger to the castle to learn if she'd gone back, but the man returned with no news.

Dame Frisia, obviously pleased, reported that one of the

palfreys and a saddle were missing. "Perhaps your little sorceress has run off to weave spells with Lord Camlann."

He'd already thought of that. "She'll be caught."

Denholm brushed Frisia aside. "By now our men have had time to drive Camlann well across the border," he said. "If Lady Taras has followed him, they'll catch her."

"I'll catch her myself," Cynewulf said with an oath. He saddled Eboracum and tore out of camp. Denholm went after him.

But by noon they'd found no trace of her. Hours later, they met the warriors coming back. Camlann was gone, and no one had seen Lady Taras. Cynewulf dug his heels into Eboracum's flanks and sped back the way he'd come.

Denholm shook his head and galloped after him. "Lovesick knave," he said, "he'll kill the horses."

The hunt was on.

Taras wrestled with Cynewulf's memory. She'd fled him three nights ago, yet it seemed he rode beside her through these northern mountains. She could almost see him astride Eboracum, devastating her with his smile. She ground her fist into her forehead in a vain attempt to expel him.

Why should she care for the knave after what he'd done? He'd taken her heart in his hands and squeezed the blood into the dust at his feet. Had she despised him, she could have borne his suspicion and slander, but God help her, she loved him. She could not have saved his life without that love.

What a fool she'd been, to think that if she snatched him from the jaws of death, he would open his eyes and realize he loved her. When he'd recovered enough to look at her, she'd seen only the predator in his soul. She was nothing but a conquest. He would never trust her, never believe she was anything but his enemy.

She could not live such a life. She refused to be his

slave. She would not come at his beck and call to be used according to his need, nor would she sit in a corner waiting for a call that would never come. His every word and action proved she was less than nothing to him. It was true that she'd tried to turn him into a frog only a few days ago, but he should have realized she'd repented of that. He even thought she'd tried to help Camlann poison him, when he should have seen that she cared for him. He wore blinders of prejudice and hatred.

What would she do if she managed to get back to Ethelred's court? If Ethelred didn't lock her up as punishment, he'd doubtless force her to marry some cod-head loobie. Dependent on the king, her mother would make her do whatever he said.

But where else could she go? Widnes Keep? It was so near the Danelaw that it might, even now, lie in Viking hands. Dared she take a chance and return home? Could she even find it?

She leaned over the palfrey's neck to avoid a branch, and thought about when her father was alive. They'd been happy in Widnes. But that was long ago, before Ethelred had called upon her father to serve him. Even so, perhaps she'd find refuge at Widnes Keep. If any of her people still lived there, they'd take her in. She'd be safe from the Viking who so despised her.

A cold gust of wind tore at her mantle and swirled leaves into her face. Huge, bruised clouds were gobbling the sunset. Lightning prodded the darkness falling fast across the mountains.

She hated storms. All her life she'd feared them. They were like battles—a clamor of drums and pipes and death. She kicked the palfrey into a trot and scanned a nearby bluff for shelter. Icy rain struck the back of her neck and trickled inside her mantle. She pulled the mantle over her head, but rain pelted her face and made the reins slip through her fingers. The trail soon became a muddy stream, swirling fetlock-high. The wind and water pushed the palfrey to and fro.

A white-hot sword of lightning slashed the mountainside, deafening her. A second bolt struck an oak, sundering it in a mass of flame. It fell across the trail in front of them. The palfrey reared, then crashed off the path into the trees. Taras lost the reins and nearly fell. Blinded by rain and tree boughs, she wrapped her arms around the horse's neck.

White fire exploded out of the clouds and uprooted a tree beside them. The lightning crackled and flared, chasing them to the bluff. Spurred by the wind and lightning, the horse sped along the rocks until Taras dragged it to a halt. She jumped off and led the palfrey under a shallow overhang.

The rain poured over the lip of the shelter and spattered horse and rider. Taras held the shivering animal close against her side. Both cringed with every thunderous blast.

Cynewulf led Denholm up a game trail deep into an evergreen forest. Hoofprints marked the ground here and there. Although too small to belong to one of his warrior's destriers, the tracks might not belong to the palfrey Taras had stolen. The tracks weren't old, though—no more than a day.

Cynewulf cast an anxious glance at storm clouds gathering in the west. Rain would wash away the trail. He pressed his heels into Eboracum's flanks, forcing him to greater speed. Every minute was precious. He had to find her before another night passed into day. There were great beasts in the mountains, both four- and two-legged. What chance had a lone woman against them?

He remembered her fighting the wolves to save his life the night he'd taken her. God's mercy, the wench had saved him more than once. He'd been cruel to treat her as he had, after she'd cleansed him of Camlann's poison. His own herbalist could not have saved his life, yet he'd insulted Taras by demanding the old man's services, instead. *Fool.*

So many times he'd told himself that her feelings didn't matter because she was a Briton, an enemy, a slave. She had not deserved kindness. Hadn't she tried to kill him with the potion in her pewter vial? It had been harmless, but she hadn't known that. Her intention was to kill him, and for that he owed her no mercy. Still, his heart said otherwise.

He could hardly believe she'd eluded him. With every passing hour his chances of finding her seemed more remote. It was now almost too dark to see.

Were they chasing wild geese? Mayhap she had circled round and returned to the castle to warm her feet before the fire. Nay, he knew it wasn't so. He'd marked their trail so his housecarls could find him if they discovered Taras.

"Mayhap we shouldn't try to find her," Denholm said.

Cynewulf twisted in the saddle. "What? Do you not know the dangers to a woman alone in the forest?"

"She's been alone before. Remember when you captured her."

"And was I not a danger?"

"A very big one, I'm afraid. Mayhap you still are."

Cynewulf stared at him a long moment. "You think I mean to harm the wench for fleeing me?"

"You have a temper," he said, and looked deep into Cynewulf's eyes, weighing him.

"If I had wanted to harm her, I would have done so long ago," Cynewulf growled. "I would have punished her when I guessed her ploy."

"And that was?"

"I think she wanted me to capture her in the forest. It would not be the first time an enemy engaged in such a practice. Remember the Saracen assassins? They allowed themselves to be taken as slaves so they could get into the enemy camp."

"And you think Taras allowed herself to be taken? Hmm."

"Consider it. She probably knew who I was when I captured her, and after we reached Ilovar she set about trying to kill me. She tried to plunge me off the mountain road one morning, and then she attempted to poison me with that damned silly love potion. I suspect Ethelred sent her. You warned me early on that she was trying to kill me."

Denholm threw up his hands, startling his horse. The big warhorse tossed his head and pranced sideways until Denholm controlled him. "If this is true, then all the more reason for you to harm her after this latest sin. I've come to like the chit, lord. I would not see her come to grief."

Cynewulf threw him a look colder than the north wind. "I would not, either, which is exactly why we're here."

They rode on for a while, but before long the darkness closed in and rain began to fall. They followed the trail until it disappeared into blackness. Cursing, the Viking vaulted to the ground and began to unsaddle Eboracum. "Thor, how I wish for cat's eyes, that I might follow her through the darkness!"

Denholm laid his hand on his arm in a manner strangely gentle for the grizzled old barge rower. "I'll go catch us something to eat," he said. "I'm fair sick of dried mutton."

Cynewulf led the horses to a clump of grass and hobbled Denholm's destrier. When it was Eboracum's turn, the horse objected and tried to rear, but Cynewulf forced him down and tied his front feet. "You're not the only brute who's hobbled," Cynewulf growled. "I swear, the wench has placed cords around my very heart."

He built a small fire, then set about gathering hemlock boughs for a shelter. The low growl of thunder in the distance told him they were in for a heavy storm.

He hoped Taras had found shelter.

For a moment his hands stilled on the boughs he was fastening together. He'd tried to let her go. Time and time again he'd considered sending her back to her people. But each time he'd invented some excuse to keep her. He scowled as he thought back to his most recent excuse: making her his herbalist, complete with a title. As if she'd care about titles.

He bent a thick branch into a bow and stabbed the ends into the ground. Was love the emotion that waged war in his soul?

The thought made him shudder. The chit had deluded him and made him look a fool. He'd be a greater fool to love her, yet Taras of the flaming hair was as easy to ignore as a spate of locusts scourging the fields of his soul. If he couldn't master himself, he'd have no choice but to bind her heart to his own until the end of time. A man could drive himself mad with such thoughts!

"You need an heir, my lord." Denholm materialized at his side, holding a hare. "What better wench to give you a son than the strong young vixen?"

"A child out of her would be half-Briton."

"And therefore flawed, I suppose."

Cynewulf's anger flared. "I have sworn to drive the slayers of my family into the sea."

"Taras has slain no one."

"She is bone of bone, sinew of sinew, of those who slaughtered my kindred. She's Ethelred's own kinswoman. Would you see our houses joined?"

Denholm dropped the hare into the dust at his feet. "There is more than one way to end a war."

"Bah—all reason has deserted you." *And me.* He yanked off his helm and flung it aside. The wind whipped his hair free of its plait and stung his eyes. Soon the rain would cause the tracks to disappear into the mud.

By the wings of the Valkyrie, how could he bear to lose her to the dust? To enfold her now in his arms and see the fire of love in her eyes, he would give half his domain—nay, all of it. "She drives me mad, I fear!"

"No man maintains his reason once the sacred fire kindles in his loins," Denholm said. "The things are mutually exclusive."

"In just what seer's crystal did you divine such lore?" Cynewulf muttered, barely able to control his voice. "I have yet to see you swept away by the sacred fire, though you've stoked it often enough."

"I've never laid claim to reason, lord, where wenches are concerned."

Cynewulf rested his hand on his sword and looked toward the west. Lightning pierced the sky, and he knew the storm raged some miles away. He smelled ice in the wind. Was Taras caught in the blast?

He yearned to leap onto Eboracum's broad back and race into the tempest. He imagined finding her in the rain, her clothing torn and plastered against her body. He would take her in his arms and shelter her. After awhile, neither of them would feel the cold.

Blood pounded in his brain and coursed through his veins. He wanted her more than anything he'd ever wanted in his life. More than wealth and power. More, even, than revenge.

Whether she wanted him in return mattered not. He could make her love him, make her comply with his wishes. Make her bear him sons and daughters.

But a cooler portion of his brain decreed that he could force nothing upon her. Whatever he desired between them, he could win only with gentleness. He must temper the wind to the shorn lamb.

Temper the wind . . . ah, Taras, where are you? Have you hidden from the storm? I would ride to you now, if I

*knew your hiding place, and shelter you in my arms. Great
Thor, protect her. God of thunder, defend her 'til I come.*

Freezing water pelted his face. He threw back his head
and stood defiant against the driving wind and rain. Over
the fury of the storm he raised his voice in a Dorian
melody, haunting and pained.

> "Deeper than the hunger of famine
> Is my soul's yearning in your direction,
> You've fled far beyond my ken
> And run from my protection.
> Unknowable, too dark, too cold
> My mind when you are not near.
> The bonds of reason cannot hold,
> Only your call will I hear.
> Soft fire that burns
> Strong woman self-reliant
> I seek your return,
> E'en love compliant:
> For you I would raise my arm
> Lest you should suffer harm."

He would find her, he silently vowed. If he had to turn
over every leaf on the continent, if he had to cross the
oceans and wander the wastelands of Arabia in parched
solitude, he would find her. And when he did, he would
never allow her to leave him again.

Chapter Twenty

She was lost. Though she'd wandered the forests for nearly a fortnight, Widnes Keep eluded her. She passed through villages where ragged, listless women and children crouched by dung fires brewing turnip and acorn broth. Mounds of fresh earth marked the graves of those who had already succumbed to the starvation and disease bred by the war that had gone on too long.

What a great contrast this was to Amandolar, a land which now seemed the stuff of fairy tales and legend. Here were no sleek herds of cattle and sheep, no wheat pouring into granaries. Here was only want and suffering, the heritage of an unwise king.

This was Ethelred's fault. His avarice had hurled England into this war, and even the peasants said the terror would not end until the Danish Sweyn Forkbeard sat on the English throne.

Another week passed before she happened upon a town on the shore of an iron-gray lake. A stone keep brooded on a promontory high over the town. An old Roman firebeacon near the keep had long fallen into disuse, but the path meandering down the slope looked like old leather, beaten soft by many feet.

Taras stayed just inside the treeline, watching. Soldiers walked the walls surrounding the keep, but peasants came and went freely, bearing burdens almost larger than themselves. A small girl herded a flock of goats along the top of the cliff.

She looked closely at the soldiers. They weren't clad like Viking warriors, but they didn't look like Ethelred's men, either. In whose hands did the town lie? Dared she go past the keep and down to the village to seek food?

She suddenly wished Cynewulf were here. He'd know what to do. With him at her side she could wander wherever she chose.

Fool! She must be faint from lack of food to entertain such idiotic notions. If Cynewulf were with her, she wouldn't be here.

Heaven help her, why must he haunt every minute of the day and night? The farther she fled, the closer he loomed in her imagination. She did not feel free at all. Invisible shackles bound her to him.

Something stirred the brush behind her. She twisted in alarm, but before she could bolt, an elderly monk stepped out of the bushes. She relaxed a little.

"You are a stranger here," he said.

"You're English!"

"Aye."

"And is the town held by the English?"

"Aye, though the Danelaw lies not many miles behind you. Ethelred still holds the whole of York, thanks be to God. The Viking pagans dare not attack this garrison. Our monastery lies within the walls."

Monks and their prayers had never stopped Vikings

before, Taras thought, but she held her peace. She didn't want to provoke the man; a monastery meant food. Still, she was painfully aware of how little she had to offer. She had no money or possessions worthy of trade. Her palfrey had broken its tether and wandered off days ago; she'd worn out her shoes; she'd broken the hunting spear she'd brought.

"Father, I need food. I'll work for it."

His stark blue eyes flicked over her, and she thought he would refuse her request. "How long since you've eaten?"

"Yesterday morn I ate acorn soup with a peasant. Nothing since."

"You're better off than many, then." His face twisted, as though he'd tasted alum. "The king's people must go hungry that his army might eat. Our safety is foremost."

Taras remembered the starving peasants she'd encountered. Had Ethelred's army taken what food remained to them, that this town might be safe?

"Come along to the priory. I'll tell the kitchener to give you a crust." He started toward the keep.

"I—I'd rather not go in there," she said. Hungry or not, she was afraid to enter the fortress.

The monk looked at her strangely. "Go into the village, then, and speak to the fishermen who supply our needs. Tell them to give you a fish meant for the priory. Hurry, 'tis nearly Vespers. You should not be on the path when night falls."

Taras hurried down to the village. Even with night fast approaching, oxen, pigs, goats, and people jammed the narrow streets. Muck lay in heaps and rats skittered over the feet of passersby. Vast fishing nets upon the walls threatened to drop into the street and trap them like flies.

Taras elbowed her way down the street and finally emerged on a stony beach. A fishing boat lay at anchor, and several ketches rested upside-down along the shore. A group of fishermen sat on driftwood stumps around a fire, mending nets. Smoke drifted from a fish-smoking shack.

Before she could approach the fishermen, a big, ugly fellow detached himself from the group. Taras took a backward step. Beggars were often beaten, or worse. This man looked as though he'd enjoy teaching her a lesson.

"The monk from the priory told me to ask for a fish," she said.

"Liar. I'll lay he sent you to me for a thrashing."

One of the men spoke up. "Come, Gil, give the wench a fish. A rich man like yerself won't feel the lack. Besides, the priory'll pay ye for it."

"I don't feed beggar wenches—begone!"

But Taras darted around him to the shack. She yanked open the door and grabbed a fish from a spit, burning her hand. Before she could eat it, Gil caught her by the arm and flung her onto the stones.

"Thief! I'll thrash you and pack you off to the sheriff!" he roared.

"I'll pay for it—I'll work for it."

"Work? Can you mend nets?"

"Nay, but I can cook."

"So can we all," he said. He gazed at her ankles, showing beneath her skirt. He moistened his lips with his tongue. "What else can you do?"

"Gather firewood."

"Ah, now, that's something the smallest child in the village can do, and I wouldn't have to give up a fish for it." He waved his hand at the fishing vessel. "I'd put you to work on her if you knew aught about sailing."

Should she lie and say she could work the vessel? Nay, he would know it in an instant and throw her overboard.

He dropped his eyes to her breasts. "Mayhap there is one skill you know. It might be worth a fish or two."

Taras scrambled to her feet. "Hire me and I'll scrub

every plank, muck out the hold, and mend the ropes, but I'll not defile myself with you!"

One of the other men said, "Leave her be, Gil. A slight wench like her can eat but little. She won't hurt your profits."

"You are quick to judge what hurts my profits," Gil snapped. He shot out his hand and wrenched the wolfskin mantle from her shoulders.

"That's mine!"

" 'Tis payment for that fish you stole." Gil examined the fur. "From what fine lord did you steal it, beggar?"

For answer, she began eating the fish.

"I wonder what reward a comely runaway serf fetches these days?" Gil said.

"I am not a serf!" When the men laughed, she demanded, "Do I look like a serf?"

"Nay," Gil said, "you look like a royal consort in those rags." In a nasty undertone he said, " 'Tis my duty to return you to your master."

"I have no master, and there is no reward for you to reap."

"Then why do you come here, alone and starved, like a deer with hounds at her heels?"

"There is war in the land, in case you've paid no heed! I am not the only one the Danes have run off her lands."

"Who are you, then?"

"Taras of Widnes. I am a cousin of the king."

The fishermen chuckled. Gil said, "A fine tale, and one you cannot prove."

He was right. She had neither purse nor script, neither seal nor letter. At any moment the ugly fisherman might haul her off to the sheriff and imprison her for stealing. She had to think up a suitable lie, one with just enough truth to make it plausible.

"I—I was a prisoner in Amandolar," she said, "in Castle Ilovar. While I was there, I saw a great army gathering. The servants said the Vikings would sweep down upon London and burn it to the ground. The king will die. Cynewulf decreed it." That last part, at least, was true.

"Cynewulf?" one of the men blurted. "You escaped the Iron Wolf of the North?"

"That fur belongs to him. I was taking it to the king as proof. Everyone knows Lord Cynewulf wears the fur of the great wolves. And see, his mark is inscribed inside."

Gil snatched open the mantle and stared at the rune branded in the soft leather. Taras didn't know if it was Cynewulf's mark, but from the look on Gil's face, he believed it was so. Strangely, his hands began to shake and his face paled.

"You're a clever one to have outwitted the Wolf," Gil said at length. "We all know of him, though none of us has crossed his path."

"Or we wouldn't be alive to tell it," another chimed in.

Taras reached out to take the mantle from Gil, who did not resist. She wrapped herself in it and sat down by the fire. She wanted to run away, but Gil was likely too fast for her. She wolfed down the rest of the fish and wiped her mouth on her skirt.

"You're naught but trouble," Gil said. "You'll be lucky if I decide not to have you thrown into prison."

"Lucky?" Taras jumped up and stabbed her finger into his breastbone. "Will Ethelred feel so lucky when Cynewulf and his berserkers arrive without warning? Will the king lie in a dungeon until he grays and his teeth fall out, feeling lucky? Will England feel lucky when Sweyn Forkbeard the Dane ascends the throne and sets his thieving Vikings upon her daughters?"

"And what would you have me do?" Gil shouted.

"Nothing," Taras said, dropping her voice. "I require nothing of you. If you care not for your country, what could a maiden possibly expect of you?"

He regarded her in silence. She could see her words had struck their mark; at any second he would bid her go, and she'd flee back into the woods where she belonged. She shouldn't have dared come to this village, and certainly not down to the beach.

Gil's lips fluttered in a wicked smile. Before Taras could run, the fisherman caught her arms and swung her into the air. With a shriek of rage Taras kicked him, but he tossed her over his shoulder and strode toward the village.

"Let go, you verminous fishmonger!"

"Nay, not until I've tucked my little treasure trove into an inn for the night."

"Treasure trove!"

"Aye, you're worth a king's ransom, wench. You and I will journey to London Towne to see the king. Your knowledge of Cynewulf's plot will win us a hefty reward."

Taras struggled to break his grip, but he only held her tighter against him. His shoulder dug into her belly and robbed her breath. "There is no plot!" she gasped. "None!"

"You lie." He hurried into the same street Taras had traversed not an hour before, and made his way to the common room of an inn. He flicked a copper at the householder, who seized a rushlight and led the way up three flights of stairs.

He carried her into a room under the eaves and dropped her onto a thin straw mattress. Dirty rushes littered the floor, and a slops bucket reeked in the corner. The cold wind gusting through the unshuttered window nearly blew out the rushlight. He shoved the light into a wall sconce.

Taras ran to the window and looked down at the street far below. There was no escape. She rounded on the big fisherman. "I won't stay in this room with you!"

He shrugged. "I would carry you home, but my wife would take a broom and knock your ears off."

"Don't you touch me!"

"You would have me believe you a chaste young virgin after belonging to a murdering Viking?"

"Cynewulf has nothing to do with this!"

Gil rubbed his thumb and forefinger together as though fondling gold. "Yes, he does. He's the key to my coming wealth."

"Out!"

"Oh, I'll take myself out. There's a strumpet calling my name. She hasn't your beauty, perhaps, but I prefer a harlot's charms to a witch's tongue."

He went out and slammed the door. Taras rushed to open it but it wouldn't budge. Trapped!

Taras stood holding her breath until she heard his footsteps recede down the hallway, then she hurried to the window and looked out again. A few vertical timbers had been added to the wall to shore up some rotting boards. It was too dark to tell if the timbers reached all the way to the street.

She stepped onto the sill and stretched for one of the timbers. She couldn't reach it. Before she could lose courage she let go of the window frame and flung herself at the timber, catching the rough wood with both hands. She slammed into the wall and struggled to hold on, her feet scrabbling against the planks, splinters jabbing her flesh. The timber groaned in protest. Nails popped out of the wall.

Taras began climbing down as fast as she could, but chips from the rotten planks showered her head. Horrified, she looked up to discover the timber splitting away from the wall, nails clattering to the cobblestones far below. She tried to hurry, but the timber shook and creaked until it seemed the whole building would tumble down.

Suddenly the timber bowed over the street. She thrust her legs forward just as the beam snapped in two, hurling her screaming through the air. She landed heavily on the rooftop across the street. The loose clay tiles slid toward the edge, carrying Taras with them. She heard people shouting and tiles crashing into the street. Her feet slipped into space.

With desperate strength she lunged up to the roof peak, slid down the far side, and jumped onto a lower roof. More tiles gave way. She slid over the edge and for one terrifying moment twisted through naked air. She landed on her back in a bush. Struggling to catch her breath, she fought her way clear and ran down an alley.

Although the street was dark and deserted, she heard music coming from one of the houses. She slipped past an alehouse door to a gelding hitched to a post. The horse snorted softly when she ran her hands over his neck, but he didn't move when she untied him and vaulted into the saddle.

"Go, old warrior," she shouted, kneeing him.

He dropped his head to a thistle. The singing inside the alehouse stopped and Taras heard running feet.

"Come on, move!" she screamed furiously, kicking him.

The door burst open and a man stumbled out. He took one look at Taras and lunged at the horse. Before he could touch the reins the gelding bolted. Taras heard him shouting, but in an instant she hauled the horse around a corner, splashed through a gutter, and jumped over a beggar lying in the street.

"Go, old warrior! Run!"

Ears back, neck stretched long, her reluctant steed thundered out of town into the wilds of York.

It was evening as Cynewulf and Denholm rode up a lake shore toward a town. On the cliff above them a stone keep glittered in the last rays of the sun. Cynewulf knew he imperiled himself and the seneschal by riding into an enemy town. No matter. He had to find the wench.

"I would fill my belly with ale and my lap with a broad-hipped English wench," Denholm said.

"I would question the people first."

"Give Eboracum a rest, lord," Denholm said. "His hooves are nigh worn to the quick. If you won't rest yourself, at least let the beast take a bite of grain."

Cynewulf knew the seneschal was right, yet they could ill afford to dally. Already villagers were pointing at them from their houses. Others hurried into shops and slammed doors. He thought uneasily of the soldiers on the hill.

Still, an alehouse was the best place to ask after the wench. If she was in town, somebody would know it. He fingered his leather purse tucked inside his belt. For a piece of silver these English curs would murder their own mothers.

They reined in before a low stone building where, on a weathered signboard over the door, a cat rode a rooster. As they dismounted, a boy shuffled out of the shadows and offered to feed and water the horses. With a great deal of misgiving, Cynewulf allowed the horses to be led away.

Inside the dark, smoky Cat and Cock, peasants played nine-men's morris. The host waddled between the horse-and-saddle tables with a keg, refilling wooden flagons.

Noticing the Vikings standing in the doorway, the host dropped the keg and crossed himself. The noise ceased as though by magic, the silence broken only by the slosh of beer running out of the keg.

Resting his hand on Damfertigénen's hilt, Cynewulf studied the malevolent, fearful expressions on the English faces. He noted without surprise that many of them bore rusty swords and wooden cudgels. He'd run into similar arms over the past weeks.

In English Cynewulf said, "We've come for food and ale, naught else."

Striving to arrange his face into a smile, the host righted

his keg and wiped his hands on the dirty sacking around his waist. He bowed clumsily. "If my lords would sit, I'll bring out a bit of pork."

The Danes crossed the room and sat with their backs against the wall. They did not remove their helms. The peasants crowded to the opposite end of the table. No one spoke until the host returned.

"The beer's f-fine," he said, edging toward them. He set a trencher of salt pork on the table and slopped beer into two flagons. He managed to grin until he upset one of the flagons into Denholm's lap. Looking as though he would faint, he stammered apologies and swiped Denholm's chain mail with the tail of his own tunic. As he tried to refill the flagon, he cascaded more beer onto the seneschal.

Cynewulf flicked a silver kufic onto the table. "Just leave the keg, there's a good fellow."

The host whisked the coin into his bosom and fled. Cynewulf tipped beer into Denholm's flagon. The seneschal said, "Being the enemy brings us—if not excellent service—eager service, anyway."

Cynewulf did not reply, but looked from one Englishman to another. He brought out another kufic and dropped it onto the table. "I have five more of these for the man who can tell me about a certain wench. She's—"

A clatter of hooves cut him off. He and Denholm sprang up as one, unlimbering their swords. The door burst open and seven knights stalked into the room. They stopped when they caught sight of the Vikings.

Their leader, a monstrous man in black mail, swept his sword from his baldric and yelled to his men. All seven rushed upon the Vikings. The peasants scattered. In escaping, someone knocked down a torch, which rolled upon the floor and set fire to the rushes.

Cynewulf and Denholm met the English charge with

steel. Denholm felled one of the knights almost immediately and Cynewulf wounded a second.

Fanned by the wind rushing through the door, the fire quickly raged out of control. It exploded the oily wall timbers and set the thatched roof ablaze. A flaming beam broke loose.

Distracted by the English leader's two-handed blows, Cynewulf barely dodged the falling beam, but his sudden movement spoiled the knight's violent cut at his head. The knight stumbled into one of his own men, pushing him into the flames. The roaring inferno swallowed the man's screams.

As the flames spread, the English lost their taste for battle. Denholm smote two trying to squeeze past each other out the window. He turned to help Cynewulf against the big leader, but a beam crashed down between them and caught his beard afire. Yelling, he dove out the window.

Oblivious of the flames, the leader wielded his sword like an executioner. "You won't get away, you Viking bastard! I'll have your heart and roast it!"

Cynewulf parried, spun, and missed his follow-up thrust. He could scarcely see his enemy's blade through the smoke and falling debris. The air felt like dragon's breath, and his chain mail seemed melded to his skin. Twice he felt hot English steel graze him.

A section of roof collapsed into the room and glanced off Cynewulf's shoulder. Struck to one knee, blinded by smoke, he heard the big knight's battle cry. Instinctively he shoved his sword straight up and felt it strike home. He rammed and thrust with all his strength, then jerked free his blade.

Screaming, the English knight staggered backward into the fire. In desperate haste Cynewulf sprang over blazing wreckage and dove through the window. As he hit the ground outside, the inn collapsed. Sparks and debris roared into the night.

Denholm yanked him to his feet. The seneschal's eyebrows were singed off and his front teeth bloody. His mouth widened in a grotesque smile. "You've just added another verse to your legend."

Cynewulf gulped air into his scalded lungs. "We must get to the horses!"

They were tethered at the end of the alley. A crowd of peasants had gathered around them. Cynewulf needed no palm reader to tell him that they meant to kill him and his friend.

Locking eyes with the peasants in the front row, the Vikings strode down the alley. The crowd shifted and growled, then suddenly a hole opened and they began to retreat.

Cynewulf was surprised to see the innkeeper holding the horses. He made no move to follow the peasants, but pointed a shaking finger at Cynewulf's breast. "Who will pay for my inn?" he cried. "You've destroyed me!"

Denholm pushed past him and took the horses, but Cynewulf stared at him for a long minute. Abruptly he pulled three golden coins from his purse and shoved them into the host's palm. "Rebuild, Englishman," he said, and moved to mount Eboracum.

The man scowled at the coins, then swung around and threw them at Cynewulf's back. "I'll not take your filthy Viking money! Begone from my village! Begone to hell, from whence you sprang!"

Cynewulf jerked Eboracum's head and set his heels to the destrier's flanks. A sudden scream from the host twisted him in the saddle. The man stood in the middle of the road, shaking his fist. "You'll be sorry! Twelve thousand men of Ethelred wait to trap your precious Forkbeard!"

Cynewulf yanked Eboracum around and jerked the host up by his scruff until his feet kicked air. "Where?" Cynewulf roared. "When?"

The man screeched in terror and fought to get down, but Cynewulf pinned him to the saddle with one hand and glared into his eyes. "Tell me when and where, or I'll crush your windpipe and leave you to gasp like the damned codfish you are!"

"Nay, nay! Don't hurt me! They're at the River Wiltham, not four days' ride from here. 'Tis said Forkbeard approaches from the north!"

"You lie," Cynewulf said, squeezing his throat. "Forkbeard is done fighting for the winter."

"Nay, lord, I swear it!" he gasped. "I overheard soldiers speak of it only yesterday. Why do you think only seven knights came after you? The keep is nearly abandoned—all gone off to the fight! They say they'll trap Forkbeard between the mountains. But there is nothing you can do."

Cynewulf dropped him into the dust and slapped Eboracum with the reins. The great warhorse stood on his haunches, then galloped away from the burning inn. Denholm hot on his heels. Peasants poured out of the buildings and pelted them with rocks and sticks, but the Vikings soon rode clear and galloped up the stony beach.

"We must warn the king," Cynewulf said after several miles' hard ride. "I came too late to save the folk of Hlaverin Towne. I will not come too late to save my king."

"And your quest for the wench?"

Cynewulf could not answer that. *I will not come too late to save my king . . . I will not . . .* he repeated like a litany, forcing away the image of a woman with hair the color of the setting sun.

But in his heart he knew that in serving his liege, he had lost his love to the flames of war.

270

Chapter Twenty-one

When Taras forded the northernmost branch of the River Wiltham she knew she was almost home. After weeks of wandering, she'd found a peasant who'd known where Widnes Keep lay. Late the next evening, she rode out of the forest and saw the keep on a low hill.

She reined in sharply and sat staring at the empty ruin of her once beautiful hall. The roof was gone. Smoke stains crept like black fingers from every casement. Blackened stumps replaced the fruit trees that used to grow across the hills.

In her heart she'd known she'd find it so, but the dismal reality sickened her. She dismounted and walked to the wall. The gates were shut fast.

"Who are you?" demanded a gruff young voice.

A lad stared down at her from the parapet. His eyes bulged from a thin face, and his mousy hair looked as though it had never seen a comb in all its years.

"Toby? Is it you?"

The boy's eyes grew even larger, then his mouth opened in a shriek of delight. "Lady Taras! You've come home!"

He disappeared, and after a moment Taras heard him scrabbling at the gates. After a great deal of rattling and banging, he managed to pull open one side. He shot out of the gate and into her arms.

"Where is the castellan, your father?" Taras asked when he stopped squeezing her neck.

"Dead! Burned by the Vikings."

Taras pushed him to arms' length, gazing at him in shocked sorrow. "And your mother?"

"Dead, my lady. 'Twas the plague. The Vikings brought it."

"Who were these Vikings?" Taras cried. "Tell me—was there a warrior named Cynewulf among them?"

"I do not know. My mother hid me in the cellar, in a wine cask. The Vikings broke open many casks, but they did not get me."

Only a few of the serfs still lived in the keep, he told her. They eked a living from tiny gardens within the walls. They had no place else to go.

Taras raised her gaze to the ruined walls, the windows staring like eyeless sockets. She wept to think of the men and women who had served her family. She'd deserted them.

She should have slain Cynewulf with the bitterest poison she could concoct. Perhaps it was not too late.

"Come, Toby," she said in a hard voice not her own. "Let us go down to my mother's secret chamber. Perhaps there is something left that will someday prove valuable to us."

King Ethelred stood upon a hill looking across the river. Five thousand Danes swelled Forkbeard's army. Although the distance was too great, he fancied he could see the forkbearded old devil, himself.

He slammed his fist into his thigh. "How did that cursed Dane discover our plan, Harold?" he demanded of one of his captains.

"How is any plan discovered, my liege? There are spies, traitors, deserters. Who can tell? 'Tis a shame we have not the advantage of surprise, though our superior numbers will surely carry the day."

Would his more than two-to-one advantage be enough? God help him, it had to be. The champions massed with him on the hill represented his last hope. His own people despised him, calling him *unraed*: the uncounseled, the unwise, the stupid. If he lost this last battle, there would be nowhere for him to hide.

"They draw their lines, my liege," Harold said.

The archers and levies had deployed along the river, waiting for the Vikings to ford. They would catch the mongrels in midstream and turn the river to blood.

Ethelred's squire helped him mount his charger, then stood holding the bridle to prevent the horse from rushing into battle after the others. The king and his household troops would watch from the hill until the battle was decided. If victorious, he would ride down to accept Forkbeard's head. If not, he would escape to the rear.

King Ethelred raised his hand. All England seemed to hold its breath in that moment, waiting for the king's white hand to fall. Sunlight danced off the helms and shields of the five thousand carls waiting to join the seven thousand levies at the river.

Ethelred dropped his hand and the soldiers sallied forth. English arrows hissed over the river. From Ethelred's vantage point he could not see the feathered barbs strike, but the sight of a Viking falling from the saddle bubbled laughter from his throat.

Viking berserkers surged into the river, their archers covering them with volleys of arrows. Within five minutes the leaders had reached the bank and engaged the English.

Ethelred ordered his cavalry to engage. By this time the Danish halberdiers were marching across the field. Since the warhorses would not charge the bristling formations, the carls had to wait for their infantry and archers to break the line.

Forkbeard's axmen came out of the river, spinning long-handled axs until they looked like the spokes of a wheel. They mowed down the English like so many sheaves.

"Hold them, you dogs!" Ethelred roared. "Push them back into the river!"

Behind him rose a terrible war cry. As he twisted in the saddle he heard the shouts of his personal guard. There, silhouetted on the hilltop behind him, was a golden-haired pagan on a black horse. The Viking set a winged helm on his head, raised his jeweled sword, and bellowed, "Thor be with us!"

His war cry shuddered into silence; then a deep rumble shook the mountain and a thousand Vikings surged over the hilltop. From whence had these others come?

"They'll catch us in a vise!" Ethelred screamed. "After me!"

Followed by his household knights, the king of England plunged down the slope into the forest. He hoped his army could stave off defeat long enough for him to escape.

Taras awakened and went to the garden just after sunrise. The weather had turned colder. Ice encased the reeds in the pond and diamondlike strands shimmered in the tree branches hanging over the water. It was lovely, but she had only to turn to see the blackened ruin of her family home.

She waited for the starlings to awaken, but they

remained silent. Was a storm approaching? She knew animals could hear murmurings long before humans.

She walked down the garden path and climbed the worn stone steps to the top of the wall. Continuing along the parapet, she saw Toby below her, curled on his mantle just inside the gates.

Taras felt the hairs rise on the nape of her neck. There was something out there beyond the hills, something silent, yet vibrating along the edges of her hearing. She felt as though she were holding her head underwater and clapping her hands, not hearing but feeling the vibrations. She strained to see into the forest, but it was still dark beneath dawn's first glimmer.

She ought to organize the few serfs still living there. They could place barrels of rocks on the walls, and take turns keeping watch.

Smoke appeared above a distant hill. Taras knew there were no dwellings within several miles of the keep. The smoke shifted and the wind began to curl through the trees. She listened until her brain translated the keening. It was not the voice of the wind but the shrill cry of pipes, the rattling thud of armored horses.

War had come again to her land. There was no time to defend her home. Burning with fear, she hastened down the steps and shook Toby awake. "We must hide, lad! I think soldiers are coming here again. Hurry—let us run and warn the others."

They dashed into the keep to rouse the serfs and hustle them down into the cellar. Taras wished she could barricade the keep, but most of the shutters had burned and the doors were broken. They rolled empty wine casks in front of the cellar door.

Toby seized her arm. "Come, Lady Taras, you must hide, too."

"We'll go to my mother's secret chamber," Taras said.

"I'll lead the way!" Toby grabbed the torch and ran ahead of the serfs.

Taras didn't immediately follow. Working in pitch darkness, she rolled more wine casks in front of the door, then turned to feel her way after the serfs. She stepped carefully down the staircase and through a wine cellar. At the far end, she turned right into a short passage and went down another level. Water dripped from the black walls and turned the flags to glass under her feet. She fell once and struck her forehead. Gasping with pain, she struggled on through the darkness, turning and twisting by feel and memory.

At last she saw a rectangular glimmer of light and knew she'd reached the chamber. Its stone door was open. Taras slipped through the opening and pushed a stone above the door. A counterweight dropped, turning the door on its axis. When it clicked shut, the door looked like part of the wall. But would it fool anyone?

Taras forced herself to smile at the serfs huddled between the shelves in the small room. There were six women, two elderly men, and several children. Toby affected a brave expression.

"Try not to talk," Taras said. "There is plenty of air, so no one need be alarmed, but those same vents that give us air might also reveal our voices."

"Do you think they'll come here?" a woman cried.

"Nay, they've burned the keep already and stolen every drop of wine. What more could they want?"

"Us," Toby said. "They'll make us slaves." The others murmured in fear.

"Hush!" Taras snapped. "We don't know that they're Vikings. Perhaps they're some of our own people. We're here as a precaution, that's all. Please be calm."

But the chamber smelled like a crypt, and the thought

that they might be trapped forever in the bowels of the keep made her sick with dread. She began to collect some of the wooden bottles from the shelves, unstoppering each and sniffing. Then she went into the corner and began to mix powders and liquids in a pewter bowl.

For a long time she measured and poured, stirred and measured again. The serfs watched her in silence. Water dripped from the black walls into puddles on the floor. Rats scrabbled behind the shelves.

There was a crash and the chamber trembled as though rocked by an earthquake. Bottles fell off the shelves and rolled across the floor. Taras knew someone had managed to shove open the cellar door. The noise must be from the wine casks tumbling downstairs.

"From the fury of the Norsemen deliver us, O Lord!" an old man whispered. Toby hid his face in Taras's skirt.

She deliberately turned her back on the secret door and continued mixing her potions. Her hands shook, but she tried to keep fear from showing in her expression. "Toby, fetch the torch and stand near me," she said, low. He obeyed at once.

There was more crashing; then they heard shouts. Steel rang against the stone walls. Whoever they were, English or Viking, they were not friends. Taras poured the potion into a vial and rose to face the door.

She heard them just outside the secret door, shouting and crashing. One of the serfs let out a cry. Taras recoiled when something heavy hit the stone wall. The counter-weight began to rise and a thin crack appeared between the stones. The door was opening!

Taras sprang forward and seized the weight, but the game was up. With a mighty shout the men crashed against the door, forcing it open six inches.

"Come and help!" Taras screamed at the serfs. "Hold it shut!"

They threw themselves against the door, but it continued sliding inward. A hand thrust through the opening and seized a woman's hair. Toby shoved the torch against the intruder's wrist. He let go with a howl, but it was too late. The door burst open, hurling the serfs to the floor. For an instant Taras stared into the crazed eyes of Viking berserkers. Beneath the torches their faces loomed like fleshless skulls.

She dragged potion into her mouth and spat it at them. At the same instant she knocked the torch into the spray. It ignited in an explosive blast. Fire seemed to stream from her mouth, searing her enemies.

"Who dares come into the witch's chamber?" she shrieked, raising her arms and curling her fingers into claws. Her own people screamed in terror and retreated to the back of the secret room. The Vikings were hardly more courageous. Unnerved and in pain, they plunged back into the cellar.

Taras knew her advantage could only last a second or two. She took another draught of potion and again spat fire. "Who dares come down into this hell of mine?"

She grabbed the weight to shut the door, but someone struck her from behind and she fell onto her face. The terror-stricken serfs ran over her, grinding her into the flagstones. She had scared her own people.

"No! No!" she cried, trying to struggle up. "I won't harm you! Please!"

But they were more afraid of her than the Vikings. She heard shrieks and blows, and saw them clubbed to the ground. Before she could rise, someone came and stepped on her neck, holding her against the stones. She recognized the hiss of a spinning ax. In a moment her attacker would lift his foot clear and chop off her head.

"Nay!" a voice thundered in Danish. Taras understood enough of the language to hear him say, "The witch is Hornfoot's!"

Her captor seized her by the neck and jolted her off the floor. He locked his forearm around her throat and forced her over to Hornfoot, a huge man with long white braids. His beard was singed and his nose charred white.

"What do you want with us?" Taras cried.

He did not reply, but thrust out his thumb and jabbed her under the ribs. She cried in anguish, jerking against the warrior holding her.

"Give me your gold, witch," the old man said in gutteral English. "Give it!"

"I'll give you nothing until you set my people free and leave this place!"

His expression darkened. Stepping close, he breathed into her face, "I'll roast each one slowly on a spit until you give me the gold."

What could she do? Her mother had dug up the gold they'd kept under the hearthstone and taken it with them to London. She had nothing with which to bargain—nothing. But if she told the Viking, he would torture them all to death.

Feigning disdain, she raised her chin. "A witch knows better than to hide gold in her own keep."

For the first time she read confusion in his eyes. "Let my people go and I will take you to its burial place."

"You'll tell me where it is, witch, or I'll roast *you* over the fire."

"I *am* fire," Taras bluffed. Dear God, if only she could take another draft of potion and burn up his ugly face!

He seized her chin in iron-thewed fingers and snarled, "Then I shall strip you naked and rape you on the cold floor, witch."

"Go ahead—burn that carrot of yours. Do it if you care never to be a man again!"

The Viking stepped back, clutching his groin as though afraid it would catch fire. "What guarantee have I that you'll deliver the gold?"

She stared at the man. "Only I know where the mountain of gold is hidden. If you harm my people, the secret dies with me."

The Viking caught her arm and wrested her from the man holding her. He forced her ahead of him through the cellars and up the stairs. She could hear the serfs stumbling along behind them. Toby's angry sobbing punctuated their shouts and cries.

When they reached the yard Hornfoot flung her onto a horse and tied her feet to the girth. He bound her hands behind her, then mounted his big destrier. At his command, his men released the serfs and went to mount their horses. Taras counted fifteen men in the party.

They rode out the gates and, at Taras's nod, headed southwest. She didn't know where she was taking them, but she had to get them far away from Widnes. What would happen to her when Hornfoot discovered she had no gold she dared not contemplate.

They rode all day and into evening. Again and again Hornfoot demanded to know how far they had to go, but each time Taras put him off. When at last he seemed ready to strangle her, she said, "It is a secret place among the mountains. There is no day and no night."

"What do you mean—no day and no night?"

"It is a riddle you must solve before the gold will allow me to reveal it."

"What! You've set me a riddle? A trick?"

"I am powerless before the gold—it possesses magic greater than my own. It has sworn me to secrecy. To reveal its hiding place, I must play it a trick."

He cursed her then, low and furiously. Taras heard fear in his voice. Magical gold was a good trick. She must expand upon it.

But then she wondered how long she could keep him

guessing before his gold lust departed and he went in search of easier loot. She tried not to think of how he would kill her.

"Hail, my Lord Sweyn."

King Sweyn Forkbeard, warming his hands before the communal bonfire, rounded on a warrior riding into camp on a black horse. He let out a whoop as the warrior dismounted.

"Cynewulf, you young pup!" He swept the younger man into his embrace. "Where have you been? I thought you'd fallen after that charge on the hilltop."

"Nay, I went after some Englishmen, thinking one was Ethelred." Sighing, he doffed his helm and cradled it under his arm.

Sweyn Forkbeard laid his hand upon his shoulder. "I feared you were dead, and was envious. To have fallen after turning the tide of battle as you did would earn you a place at Odin's right hand."

"It is better to tarry and fight for you, lord, than to drink mead in Valhalla."

"Ha, well spoken, and loyal as always." Forkbeard pulled Cynewulf down beside him as he sat. "Now then, tell me of Ethelred."

Cynewulf spat into the fire as though he'd tasted bile. "He managed to save his miserable hide. He is probably halfway to Normandy, the coward."

"The villain has the luck of the gods," Forkbeard said. "He will outlive us both, coddled in the arms of fat wenches. May we all suffer such a fate!"

"You have but to command it, once you are crowned king of England."

"Aye, it would take a royal edict. English wenches are cold snow caves."

Not all of them, Cynewulf thought.

"But would it not be delightful if they flocked to me like ripe partridges?" the king continued, grinning.

Cynewulf stared at the wrinkled seal's-hide face above the forks of his beard. The King of Denmark was as old as the earth, and as strong. Women would flock to him, indeed. They loved power, and Forkbeard had the stuff to his eyebrows.

Still, the English were stiff-necked. They would not easily accept defeat. Sweyn Forkbeard's battles were not yet over. Neither were his own.

He was surprised when Forkbeard seized his wrist and stared at him out of ice-blue eyes. "I desire you to tarry with me, Cynewulf. Do not return yet to Amandolar. You've a gift for making men see reason, and as I rule this country, I'll need it. You and my son Canute shall be my ministers."

Cynewulf lowered his gaze to the fire. "I cannot, my liege. I am . . . questing. I cannot abandon it."

"Is this quest more important than my kingdom?" the old man flashed back.

"To me, lord. Only to me."

"A woman, then. And I thought you were a man of reason!" Forkbeard exclaimed, though already his anger had cooled. "But perhaps that is the difference between you and me. You are yet able to love."

The old man had seen into his heart. Cynewulf didn't like it, but he was not wholly surprised. "I would swear, lord, that the Allfather's black ravens, Hugin and Munin, rest upon your shoulders and whisper to you the turmoil in my brain."

"Bah, the black ravens whisper nothing to me. I need the flesh and blood counsel of you and Canute. But if you must abandon me, you must."

And I must be chasing a ghost, Cynewulf thought, *so completely has she vanished*. He imagined himself bent with age, riding across continent after continent in search of a woman who existed only in his memory. Yet she must be alive . . . he could almost feel her nearby.

Cynewulf shoved to his feet and bowed, but as he turned to go, Sweyn Forkbeard caught him by the tail of his cloak. "Come back to me, Cynewulf, if you fail to find her."

"If I fail to find her, my liege, there is no coming back," he said and strode into the darkness.

Chapter Twenty-two

When night fell, Hornfoot had no choice but to dismount his men. He snatched Taras from the saddle, untied her hands, and dragged her behind a bush, where he watched her take care of her needs. He did not try to touch her, though, probably fearing she'd burn his most precious member.

Humiliated, she stalked back to camp and sat down with her back against a boulder. She choked down a bit of half-cooked squirrel and determined to stay awake all night. If anyone tried anything, she'd take his ax and lop off his head. She'd had enough of Vikings.

Despite her intentions, she dropped off to sleep and didn't awaken until morning. Hornfoot gave her a crust of bread, allowed her another trip into the bushes, then lifted her into the saddle. But before he could tie her, a deep voice resounded through the forest.

"I see you've found my spell weaver."

Hornfoot grabbed his sword and glared into the dark

woods. His men drew steel and waited for his command to charge the invisible foe.

Taras sat the mare as though frozen. She felt as though she'd run up a mountain and fallen into a cloud. Her tongue stuck to the roof of her mouth, denying her even a small cry.

"Who are you?" Hornfoot demanded. "Show yourself, or my men will shoot you full of arrows."

This time the voice came from the opposite side of the clearing. The warriors rounded in astonishment. "I've searched far and wide for her, my old friend Hornfoot."

Cynewulf rode out of the woods and reined in. Denholm trotted up behind him and drew his horse to a halt. Taras thought she'd faint. Surely she was imagining things. Cynewulf was in faraway Castle Ilovar, not here in this glade.

He did not look at her, but smiled at the old Viking. Hornfoot scowled, then suddenly his face split in a grin as he recognized the man. He rode over and punched Cynewulf hard on the shoulder. "Imagine slipping up on an old sea serpent like me! I ought to cut off your feet!"

Taras shifted uneasily in the saddle. She hadn't understood much of the Danish conversation, but they obviously knew each other. If the two were friends, Cynewulf was no better than the barbarian who'd captured her. Her heart sank.

She was afraid of the big, armored warrior. More than ever, clad in shiny mail and a scarlet cloak, Cynewulf emanated power and life and sexual hunger. He was dangerous, yet she needed him to free her of these others.

"I'll take the wench off your hands now," Cynewulf said.

Hornfoot backed his horse and stopped smiling. "The witch belongs to me," he said.

"Witch?"

"Aye, witch. Do you not see the scorched faces of my men, and this nose of mine? In truth, the witch burned us with the breath of her mouth."

Cynewulf laughed. "She's done it to me a time or two."

"And has she burned off your carrot, as well? Why do you want her back?"

"What do you want with her, my friend?"

Hornfoot gazed at him for half a minute. The Vikings shifted restlessly, fingering their weapons. Taras's mare whickered and stamped.

"It would not hurt to tell you," Hornfoot said at last, "since my men and I could easily slay you and Denholm. The witch has gold."

Cynewulf lifted a brow. "Indeed? And where is this treasure?"

"Where there is no day and no night," one of the Vikings sang out. Hornfoot scowled at him.

"She's set you a riddle, then," Cynewulf said with a chuckle.

Taras noticed Eboracum edge a little nearer her. His nostrils flared in a soft snort. He seemed interested in her mare. He was randy again, the brute.

"She is no witch," Cynewulf said. "The spell weaver is incapable of breathing fire."

"Explain my beard, then," Hornfoot roared, seizing its singed ends. "Explain my nose!"

"A trick."

"She's a dragon," Hornfoot said. "Now ride off, Cynewulf. We have business with her."

"And after you've found her gold?"

Hornfoot shrugged. "I'll sell her to you, since you desire her so much."

"Then you'll let me ride with you and your men?"

"Set your own lights in the firmament," Hornfoot said, acceding. "But beware, my friend, that if you try to just take her, I'll kill you. It matters not to me that we fought together against Ethelred. The wench is mine."

"And rightly so, since you found out her secret."

Hornfoot nodded, then turned to command his men. At that instant Eboracum lunged at Taras's mare and stood on his hindlegs to mount her. Taras screamed and jumped off. The Vikings roared with laughter. Cynewulf hurled a cloth ball into their midst.

The ball hit the ground and exploded in a dense red cloud. Blinded, the Vikings screamed and tried to mount their horses, which bucked and plunged in terror.

Taras was blinded too. She shrieked when strong hands snatched her up and flung her belly-first over a horse's withers. Then the rider spun and galloped into the forest.

Taras bounced and screeched until her captor righted her, setting her astride before him. It was Cynewulf, she realized. Only he smelled and felt like this. She buried her hands in Eboracum's black mane.

"Ride faster!" Denholm shouted from behind them. "I hear them!"

An arrow thudded into a tree right beside them. Eboracum swerved around a tree trunk and leaped a fallen log. Taras felt herself leave the saddle for an instant before Cynewulf tightened his grip. She heard him laugh.

"You're enjoying this!" she shouted.

"And you're not?" He kicked Eboracum into a dead run. Taras was sure that at any second they'd crash into a tree, but the destrier flew with the sureness of an owl. She heard Denholm grunt as he smacked into branches, but he remained close upon Eboracum's heels.

"They'll kill us!" Taras cried. "Throw more of that red smoke!"

"I have no more—it was all I could find in your nasty little cellar. Perhaps you should smite them with your fiery breath," Cynewulf said.

"You were at Widnes Keep!"

"Aye. Where is the gold?"

"If I had gold, do you think I'd be riding here with you—look out!"

Eboracum nearly crashed into a boulder. He spun and took off again, his mighty hooves churning up great gouts of earth. Taras tried to see behind them, but she couldn't look past Cynewulf's wide shoulders. "Where are they?"

"Not far, I think. Keep your head low and don't talk."

They tore around a giant heap of boulders and Cynewulf reined in. Bidding Taras to keep her seat, he sprang to the ground. Denholm helped him bend a large tree limb back and hold it behind the boulders. After a minute or two they heard hoofbeats. Hornfoot rounded the corner at full speed. Three of his men flanked him.

Cynewulf and Denholm let go of the branch. With a vicious snap it caught Hornfoot across the chest and slammed into his cohorts. The four men flipped off their horses and hit the ground. Cynewulf leaped up behind Taras and galloped off.

When they'd traveled a quarter of an hour without hearing sounds of pursuit, Cynewulf directed them into a stream. They followed its course for over a mile before climbing out onto rocky ground, where hoofprints wouldn't show.

A stiff wind picked up and the day grew cold and cloudy. Rain began to fall, and as the temperature dropped, ice encased every limb. The horses slipped and slid in the mud, spattering the riders.

Taras pulled Cynewulf's mantle close about herself and leaned against his chest. He'd been silent for a long time. She wondered what he would say when he finally decided to speak. Was he angry with her? She'd caused him a great deal of trouble. She did not doubt he'd make her pay.

"Are they following us, do you think?" she ventured.

When Cynewulf didn't answer, Denholm said, "Nay.

There is other gold to find. Hornfoot is probably licking his wounds and preparing to seek his fortune elsewhere."

She straightened in sudden fear. "Do you think he'll return to Widnes Keep?"

"If he does, he'll find no one there," Cynewulf muttered. "We sent your serfs into the forest to hide."

"And Toby?"

"The urchin with the blackened face?"

"He's a fighter, that one," Denholm interrupted with a chuckle. "He nearly put out Lord Cynewulf's eye with a stick."

Taras twisted around and, for the first time, stared at Cynewulf. A bright red welt extended from his forehead down to the corner of his right eye. "What did you do to him?"

"I took the stick away, what do you think?"

"Did you hurt him?"

"Mayhap his vanity. I wore out his backside."

Taras tried to slap him, but he caught her wrist and pulled her hand down, pressing it against his thigh. "You had no right to touch him!" she yelled. "He's an orphan, thanks to you!"

"I had naught to do with that," Cynewulf growled.

"You're a Viking! How do you think Widnes Keep ended up in ruins and my people killed?"

"That is one of the tides of war."

His coldness infuriated her. It did no good to speak to him; he was utterly without mercy. "You should not have come after me, Cynewulf. The day will come when I drive a knife into your black heart."

"Mmm. Fear will haunt my every waking hour."

She jerked her hand off his thigh and hid it in her lap. Cynewulf laughed without mirth. Taras heard Denholm chuckle. The old seneschal sounded as though he were enjoying the conflict very much, curse him.

At noon they stopped by a stream. Denholm started a fire and filled a small, three-legged copper pot with water. Cynewulf dropped in lentils, dried pears, and salt coney and handed Taras a stick. She squatted down and began to stir the stew.

Soundless as a pair of lions, the Vikings disappeared into the woods. Taras stirred the pot and feigned indifference to their absence just in case they were watching.

Cynewulf came back and dipped into the pot for a bit of coney. He shook his head and began to feed twigs to the fire to make the pot boil faster. Taras tried not to pay him any attention, but as she watched his muscular hands she pictured them tracing her body. She raised her eyes to find him staring at her, longing etched in his face. Firelight flashed off his chain mail and white teeth until he looked like a creature enchanted.

Nay, he wasn't enchanted. She held no sway over his heart. He'd taken her because it pleased him to do so. She was the one enchanted. He fired her blood and stimulated her senses until she couldn't bear to live inside her own skin. He'd cast a spell over her. Perhaps he'd discovered something in her mother's secret chamber in addition to the red smoke powder, something that made her want to drop the wolfskin mantle on the cold ground and lie down upon it, waiting for him to cover her.

Please, Cynewulf, don't force my love. Don't look at me out of those dark blue eyes as though you'd draw out my soul and wrap it in silken chains. Don't make me recant my oath. . . . Don't enchant me.

"What will you do with me?" she whispered. "You've trapped me like an animal."

"You're a dangerous animal, Lady Taras," he said, low. His warm breath stirred her hair and made her tremble. "But I could take you here and now."

"I . . . know that." Why didn't she get up and move away?

He dropped his hand to her hip and let it rest there, setting her blood pulsing wildly through her veins. She did not retreat, but raised her chin and gazed at him without emotion.

"You would not fight me, Taras."

"You're horny as an old stallion's hoof, lord, and as dull of intellect."

He pushed his face close to hers and said very quietly, "Your words do nothing to sate the hunger in my loins. You belong to me, as you did from the moment I captured you on my land."

His hand drifted along her hip and over the top of her thigh. She felt his fingers come to rest beside her secret place. Through her garments she could feel his heat; it swelled the discordant song of anger and desire in her breast.

"Do not shame me, Cynewulf."

"A slave lives for her master's pleasure."

"Then her shame is his shame."

"You seek to curb me with words?"

"Is it possible to curb an old warhorse, then?"

The pot bubbled over, spilling broth into the flames. Thankful for the distraction, Taras wrapped the hem of her skirt around her hands and reached for the pot.

Cynewulf beat her to it. With his bare hands he lifted the pot off the fire, cursed at the heat, and set it down quickly. Broth slopped onto the ground. He glanced up when Taras chuckled.

" 'Tis a shame your noble herbalist is not here to tend your burns, lord," Taras said. "My, my, how those blisters will hurt when you hold the reins."

"Who holds your reins?" he said, scowling.

"I hold my own, thank you."

Denholm came out of the forest and sat down beside Taras, who nodded at the pot. "Eat hearty, drink deep, live long, seneschal," Taras said. She handed him a piece of bark to use as a spoon.

Giving her a grin, he dipped into the pot and conveyed the soup to his mouth. "Ah, lady, your cooking skill will soon restore my strength."

"Not a moment too soon, I think. Just look at you." She touched Denholm's scalp. Out of the corner of her eye she saw Cynewulf glare at the older man. "Stitches. And how did you manage to burn off your hair?"

Denholm smiled and launched into a description of the battle at the Cat and Cock, and then at the River Wiltham. He shamelessly exaggerated his deeds while glossing over Cynewulf's part in the fight.

Taras grew sick at heart. Ethelred, defeated? The English army routed? Then nothing stood between Sweyn Forkbeard and the throne of England. Would her mother be safe? Would the court go into hiding?

She lost her taste for the stew and stood up, locking her hands over her stomach. Denholm stopped talking. Both men looked up at her; Denholm in surprise, Cynewulf in speculation. She wanted to knock their heads together.

"You are a fine pair of Viking pillagers and murderers," she said in a voice shaking with rage. "How dare you come after me when the blood of my people stains your armor? How dare you think to amuse me with your tales of bloodshed? What filthy, misbegotten swine you are!"

Cynewulf rose and towered over her, his countenance dark as a moonless night. "You think I should let *my* people perish to the English dogs waiting to set upon them? You think Forkbeard should bow to an army two or three times his size, and offer up his head to the pike? Nay, lady, the war is over. Your miserable race has lost, and a new king rules this land."

Taras smacked him hard across the cheek, but he only glared down at her, his hands at his sides. She stumbled back a pace and screamed at him, "May a pox of hell descend upon your conquering army! May your own gods look down on you and mock your puny vanity! May your—"

Cynewulf turned on his heel and strode into the forest. This time he did not retreat soundlessly. Branches cracked and swayed, then a young tree crashed down into the stream.

"Go ahead—take out your wrath on the helpless trees!" Taras shouted. "Don't stop until you've razed the whole forest!"

Denholm stood and took her by the shoulders. "If I may tender a suggestion—"

"When I desire your advice I'll read your entrails!"

He spread his hands and bowed slightly, stepping back. "As you wish, my lady."

"Since when have my wishes mattered a whit to anyone?"

"Sit down, Taras," the seneschal said. His manner was no longer kind. Taras sat, drawing her knees against her chest. "You see what you want to see, hear what you want to hear, think what you want to think. But the truth is, your lord's heart has belonged to you since first he saw you in the forest."

"Ha!"

"Look at the side of that pot." Again his voice brooked no argument. Taras obeyed. "Do you see yourself?"

"Aye."

"Is it really you?"

She nodded testily.

"Then you are quite ugly, with four eyes, cheeks wide as a badger's, a flat pate, and the thinnest neck imaginable."

"My thanks for the compliment."

"You have eyes, Briton. You can see I am correct."

"The pot is curved," she said. "The picture isn't true. It doesn't reflect what I am."

"Just as your picture of Lord Cynewulf does not reflect what he is. He is not the brute you think him."

"He behaves like one."

"He is a warrior, which explains his deeds at the River Wiltham. He is also a man, which explains his anger toward you. You led him a merry chase. Do not expect him to sing you chansons of love. His pride is sorely stung."

"His pride? And what of mine, tossed from man to man like a worthless trinket?"

Denholm threw back his head and laughed. "A worthless trinket? Have you no idea what price he paid to find you? The gold he gave to one and all for worthless information? The sleepless nights and anxious days, thinking he'd find you dead?"

"Seneschal, be silent!" Cynewulf came out of the forest, his countenance terrible to see. Denholm turned and walked stiffly to his warhorse, where he fussed with bit and bridle.

Feeling unaccountably guilty, Taras got up to rinse the pot in the stream. While she worked, she sensed Cynewulf's gaze on her back. Trembling, she got up and strode past him to Eboracum. She rammed the pot into the leather bag tied to the saddle, and waited for Cynewulf to help her mount. This he did without speaking. Cold mist shrouded them as they rode away.

Darkness came early that night. Cynewulf led them into a shallow cave in the hills. While Denholm built a fire and handed Taras food to cook for supper, Cynewulf saw to the horses. Taras dared not look at him as she worked.

Denholm perched on a rock and began to sharpen his ax. With each stroke his good humor gradually returned, until he burst into song. Taras couldn't follow the Danish, but she could tell by his lusty laughter that the song was a bawdy one. As they dipped their evening meal from the pot, he regaled them with tales of his trips to the brothels. Taras and Cynewulf spoke not a word.

Taras knew the seneschal was trying to dispel the anger between them. She sensed Cynewulf's rising irritation, and was glad. After Denholm's speech today, she had almost felt ashamed of her actions. She needed to brew her anger afresh; Cynewulf deserved no goodwill.

With a feeling of bitter satisfaction, she crawled deep into the cave where the roof sloped low, and rolled herself up in the wolfskin. Moisture dripped off the stone onto her face, so she pulled the fur over her head. When she peeped out she could see the men sitting by the fire, talking in low tones. Strangely comforted, she closed her eyes.

After a few minutes she heard a slight sound. She opened her eyes and found Cynewulf's big shadowy figure crouched beside her. Backlit by the fire, his hair burned like a halo. Before she could move, he pressed her shoulders against the stone and growled, "What about the damned fisherman? I heard the tale as we travelled." Cynewulf said. "The man even offered a reward for you. It was not for stealing another man's horse, I'll wager. Mayhap you collect men as other women collect jewelry."

"What do you mean by that?"

"Is it such a mystery, fair one? You had to support yourself somehow after running away from me. Mayhap by whoring—"

"You!" Taras slapped his face and drew her hand back to hit him again. He seized her wrist, his fierceness both frightening and exhilarating her. She read injury in his eyes, and knew he was jealous. She'd make him suffer more for insulting her.

"Did you give yourself to him, Briton?"

"That is none of your concern."

"Curse it, I want the truth, hard as it may be for one of your race to tell it."

"And would you believe me?" she demanded, suddenly close to tears. That this savage should question her virtue outraged her. She'd be damned before she'd answer his question. Let him writhe on a spike of envy.

He tightened his grip. "Did you give yourself to him?"

She tried to burst free and could not. "Unhand me, barbarian!"

He let go of her wrist and caught her chin between his fingers, turning her face to catch the firelight. "I am your lord and master, Lady Taras of Widnes. I demand the truth from your lips."

"If you wish truth, wrench it from me if you dare!"

He rolled on top of her, the stone roof mere inches above his back, and slanted his mouth across hers, forcing her to open to his deep kiss.

Taras tried to claw his face, but he seized her wrists in his left hand and pinned her arms over her head. She felt his right hand slide down over her body and yank up her hem. She tried to buck him off, but he gripped her bare thigh and clasped her to him. His chain mail rasped her breasts.

She twisted away from his lips and cried, "I have never known a man. Leave me be!"

But he thrust his tongue into her mouth and, at the same time, thrust the skirts of his chain mail byrnie aside. She felt his hardness through his leather braies. He rubbed himself against her, sliding over her softness until she hungered for air and her breath came in sharp, needy gasps.

He broke off the kiss and dropped his mouth to the hollow of her throat. Releasing her wrists, he pushed down her bliaut and chemise to bare her bosom. He found the tips of her breasts and licked until she begged him to stop.

He wasn't through with her yet. Slipping his fingers between her thighs, he touched her as no man had ever done. The world was exploding and there was nothing she could do to put it back together.

"Damn you, Cynewulf," she gasped. "Leave me be!"

"Not this time, wench. I'm done holding back."

Raising himself slightly, he untied his braies and slid them down to his thighs. Taras jolted against him, the velvet length of his arousal pressed against her, and she tried to thrust him off. He held her still, then she felt a sudden, sharp pain. She screamed and strove against him with all her might, but he was already inside her, thrusting against her frantic movements, covering her face and throat with tender kisses.

"My heart's blood," Cynewulf said. "My love, my love . . . "

She had never suffered such pain before. He was tearing her apart, this big, hungry animal. In a moment she would die and he'd be sorry.

But in that moment the agony transformed into a roiling fire of pleasure. She wrapped her arms around his neck and held on, arching and moaning. Spasms shook her until she could not hear the sound of her own cries. The world shrank until she could see nothing but the handsome face above hers, the blue eyes hot with passion.

"Cynewulf, you're consuming me!"

He held her against his mailed chest and called her name over and over, carrying her on a flaming tide. She clenched her muscles and rode the wave down into a fiery trough, questioning whether she'd ever breathe again. His answer echoed deep and hard inside her. She thrust back at him with all her strength, her wordless voice echoing in the firelit cave.

And then they were still, their limbs entwined, their

bodies hot and trembling after the storm. Their breath rose in white tendrils on the cold air.

Cynewulf stroked her hair away from her face and kissed her eyelids, nose, and mouth. Her loins quickened again with longing.

"Cynewulf."

Her whisper broke the spell. He rolled onto his back and glared up at the stone roof. His anger chilled the fire in her belly.

"Curse it, Taras, why did you play me for a fool?" he whispered. "You have never been touched before."

She flinched at his words. *Heart's blood,* he had called her a few minutes ago, yet now, his passion spent, he made her feel dirty.

"I told you I was innocent," she said. "You chose not to believe me."

"You told me too late," he said.

"And that excuses this?" She pushed herself up on one elbow and struck his chest with her fist, bruising her hand. "You might force yourself upon me again, my lord pillager, but you'll wrest naught but curses from my lips. I loathe you! I shall be your enemy forever!"

Tears came then, burning her cheeks and wetting her naked breasts. Cynewulf left her without a word. She saw him framed against the mouth of the cave, and then he disappeared into the night.

She cursed herself then. She should have told him the truth about the fisherman. Playing games had gained her naught but this.

Damn it, why did she blame herself? He'd had no right to touch her. No right to make her burn for him, to wrest shouts of abandon from her throat, to peer into her soul at her secret longings. He'd had no right to awaken her body to the hot joy of his flesh in hers.

He had no right to make her yearn for him even now.

She despised herself for wanting to crawl to his feet and beg for his touch once more. She wanted to feel him engage her, to pour into her his liquid fire. By the high heavens, what was this spell of madness he'd woven about her?

"May the angels carry you down to hell, you cursed Viking," she screamed into the empty cave, "after I carve my name on your soulless heart!"

This time she'd make him pay. She swore it.

Chapter Twenty-three

They rode north all the next day. Cynewulf and Taras hardly spoke. Denholm kept his own counsel, though when he looked at Taras he seemed amused. She wondered if he'd been in the cave last night when Cynewulf had his way with her.

Cynewulf did not come to her in the furs that night. He lay just outside the rim of firelight, where the shadows hid all but the glimmer of his eyes watching her like some great, fey wolf. Taras was afraid to sleep for fear he'd come to her, after all.

She almost wished he would.

She hated herself for her weakness. Try as she might, she couldn't stifle the memory of his face above hers in the cave, the rhythm of his body like the dance of the night wind. She could not forget his words: *heart's blood* . . . *my love, my love.* What had it meant?

The next morning she cooked rabbit meat in the copper pot. Cynewulf treated her with the politeness of a stranger,

thanking her gravely for the meal. Denholm sipped broth
and patted her shoulder once, when Cynewulf wasn't looking. She pretended to ignore his touch. She needed no sympathy from her master's companion. She needed no one's
sympathy at all.

That night they took refuge under the limbs of a towering walnut tree. Snow began to fall. Bitter wind cut
through Taras's wolfskin mantle. Too stiff and miserable to
cook supper, she nestled against the roots of the tree. Soon
she slept.

Denholm built a fire and prepared a stew. Cynewulf gazed
at the beauty sleeping under the tree. Rubbing his hands
together for warmth, he felt the raised scar on his thumb. He
could almost feel the falcon's beak tearing his flesh, could
almost hear her wing snap as he jerked away. Had he, in his
brutish impatience, broken Taras as well? Curse this iron
heart of his!

"I could not help but notice her countenance these two
days past," Denholm said. "Methinks you betrayed her."

"It is impossible to betray a slave."

"You speak too quickly to be wise, lord. She is no
slave."

"I've had enough of such talk," Cynewulf snapped. "I
had the right to take her after the trouble she caused me."

"Of course. She is ungrateful, that one. Not every master spends gold to track a runaway, then forces the precious
gift of his seed upon her in a cold cavern. The chit ought to
appreciate your sacrifice."

Cynewulf barely controlled his urge to knock out Denholm's teeth. "It is time I got something in return."

"You got her hatred, I deem."

"Her feelings are her own plight." But were they? Was
Denholm right? Nay, he had done what any man would do
after capturing a haughty slave. He'd tamed her.

But again he glanced at his scar.

On the third evening they rode out of the forest into a snowy field. A keep brooded upon a hill, its lines blurred soft by the snow. As the trio drew near, Cynewulf raised his right hand to the watchers on the palisade wall.

"Sorelvelden," Cynewulf said to Taras. Before the gates were fully open, he trotted into the bailey and reined in. A crowd gathered before they could dismount. Someone lifted Taras out of the saddle.

"Cynewulf, my lord!"

An old man stood in the doorway, his gnarled hand uplifted. A squire steadied his elbow.

"Lord Sorel," Cynewulf said. He hastened through the crowd and sprang up the icy staircase to embrace him. "May two warriors and a maid beg the hospitality of your hall this night?"

"My household is honored to receive its liege lord. You are welcome, indeed! Come."

The great hall looked like Widnes Keep had before the fire. Taras caught her breath in sudden longing. Since Cynewulf was speaking to his retainers, she went across the hall and sat down on a fur-covered bench by one of the fireplaces.

Strange that she should suffer homesickness. There was nothing for her in Widnes, now that the Vikings had destroyed it and driven away her people. She was without lands and property. In making her his slave, Cynewulf had taken even her name. All she had left was pride. She would not relinquish that, at least.

A servant brought her a *hanap* of sops with almond milk. She ate the sops and drained the last drop of milk. She would have eaten more, but sleepiness weighted her eyelids. She curled onto her side and listened to the drone of voices from across the hall, where Lord Sorel and his men entertained Cynewulf and Denholm. They spoke an odd mixture of English and Danish, enabling her to understand some of the conversation. Cynewulf spoke of defeating Ethelred at the River Wiltham. While he talked, a nearby skald strummed a lyre. Taras knew the skald was already inventing new chansons to sing. The Wolf's fame would grow.

She wondered what tomorrow would hold for her. In escaping him, she had angered the Lord of Amandolar. What sort of life could she expect to lead once he'd gotten her back to his castle? Would he make her just a bedwench, using her to satisfy his desires, yet speaking no kindness to her? Would she warm his furs until he tired of her and gave her to another man?

Her chest heaved on a sob. Why had the saints allowed him to find her? And why did Heaven still soften her thoughts every time she looked at him? She needed to loathe him, yet the memory of his strong arms made her weak.

A hand pressed her shoulder. Overwrought, she bolted off the bench with a screech of alarm. Lord Sorel stumbled back into the arms of his squire and dropped a goblet onto the stone floor. The color fled his face, leaving him gray as old limestone. Taras was instantly sorry; she saw he'd been bringing her the wine.

She started to apologize, but Cynewulf stormed over and caught her by the arms. "What are you about, frightening an old man so? Go upstairs at once and tell the chambermaid to put you to bed!"

"I'll do nothing of the sort, you precipitate knave!"

She saw his nostrils flare and fire come into his eyes. He dropped his hands and stepped back, muttering, "Denholm, put her to bed. I cannot trust myself to be kind."

"You, kind! How could you expect to change your stripes now?"

She turned and sped for the front door, but Cynewulf caught her and pinioned her arms to her sides. "Not so fast, you wildcat. I'll not have you shame me before my vassals."

"Release me, you bloody dotterel!" She kicked his shins and tried to wrench her arms free.

Cursing, Cynewulf swept her onto his shoulder. The people fell back as he strode to the staircase. Taras pounded his back and called down the fire of Heaven upon his head.

"Let go of me, you beetle-browed tyrant! You thrice-cursed spawn of a cod's-head loobie!"

Lord Sorel cackled. The folk joined in until the hall shook with mirth. Cynewulf cast them a pained glance and took the steps three at a time.

"You riven-pated lobcock!" Taras yelled.

Cynewulf reached the landing and turned to go down the hall. The last thing Taras saw was Denholm, his arm around Lord Sorel, his mouth open on a gust of laughter. He pointed at her and laughed harder.

Cynewulf stalked down the hall and into a chamber, slamming the door behind them. He threw her onto the high bed and turned to bar the door.

Taras snatched up the feather bolster and jumped off the bed, swinging the bolster into his back. Feathers exploded from the seams. Through the fluff she saw him turn on her. She dodged him and managed to snatch the dagger sheathed at his thigh. He grabbed her shoulders. She tried to stab him.

Cynewulf lurched back with a snarl, wrenching the blade from her hand.

Taras's knees turned to water. She slumped onto the bed as Cynewulf hurled the knife at the door, where it stuck quivering. Sweeping Taras a savage glare, he unhooked his mail and slung it after the knife.

He raked off his leather undertunic and stood in only his braies and sandals. Every glistening muscle poised for vengeance, Cynewulf came to stand over her. She trembled under his raging stare but did not try to run. She was too weak.

Cynewulf swept his hand toward his discarded mail. "You think you can stab me? I paid for the best chain mail, for full-proof," he said. "And I paid to find you, may Odin damn me for a madman! I *paid* for you—a railing bundle of misery."

Terror constricting her throat, Taras bowed her head and squeezed her eyes shut. He'd kill her now, she was sure. The silence stretched long, punctuated by the hiss of the fire.

"Taras."

His low voice startled her. She covered her face and began to cry.

"Taras, look at me . . . please."

She glanced up in woeful surprise. She did not know what to expect. Anger. Reproach. Murder.

But Cynewulf dropped to one knee. By the light of the fire she saw that his berserker fury had fled. She could not understand his reaction. What fell enemy was this, to kneel at her feet?

"Are you all right, my lady?"

She jerked her head up and down once. He put out his hand and traced the path of her tears down her cheeks. She saw him swallow and his eyes brighten.

"Do not weep, my shorn lamb," he said. "There is no need to fear me. The lamb has tempered the wind."

She had known it already. Even in his anger over the last days, she'd sensed the wind had changed. Now only her own pride still blew, and that uncertainly.

A sharp blade of remorse stabbed her heart. "Forgive me, lord."

"There is naught to forgive. It is I who must beg pardon. I've been unforgiveable."

He cupped her chin in his hand and drew her mouth to his. His warm breath fell across her face while his battle-hardened fingers cradled her chin with the softness of eiderdown.

"You've woven a spell about me," he whispered, "and enslaved my heart. All that I am, all that I will ever become belongs to you."

"Please don't speak so."

"Wherefore?"

"Because I am a Briton. You'll remember this when your need is not upon you. You'll regret your words then, as you did in the cave the other night. Again you'll see me as your enemy."

She saw her pain mirrored in his eyes for an instant. "The battle is over, spell weaver, the sword of vengeance fallen from my hand. You are not my enemy. I have no enemy. Nay, no more forever."

Would he still think so when he knew the truth about her? Digging her nails into her palms, she said, "I am Ethelred's kinswoman, my lord. I cannot change the accident of my birth, nor can I now change the fell purpose that brought me to you."

"You wanted to kill me then, from the start."

"Yea, in a most dreadful manner. You see. Ethelred sent me to transform you into a frog using that potion in the vial. We thought I'd turned one of his knights into a frog by mistake. Ethelred saw his chance to get rid of you through my enchantments."

"But your enchantment was harmless."

"But I didn't know that, don't you see? I tried to slay you." She hung her head. "Camlann is my cousin. He came to kill you when I failed . . . and just now I tried to draw your blood."

He raised her chin. A muscle throbbed in his cheek, yet she saw amusement in his eyes. "You drew my blood the hour we met, Taras."

"But I might have killed you just now."

"You may kill me yet if I cannot win your love."

Love. The word ran between them, deep and cold as a river she dared not cross. She was his possession. Nothing could erase her shame or make him forget what she was.

Not even love.

Coldness swirled around her heart. She wanted to pull away from the river's edge, to seek refuge in the forest of her own solitude as she had done in the past.

"Do not run away from me again, beloved," he said, pulling her into his arms. "Neither you nor I could stand the pain."

"Please—"

"Believe in my love, only in that. Let its light drive the shadows from your heart."

He brought her mouth to his, probing her like a bee a deep rose. For a moment she resisted the sensual assault, then she accepted his kiss. His liquid heat coursed downward to fill her body. Tendrils of ecstasy unfurled within her, flying on the wind of her lord's desire until she closed her eyes and gave herself over to his caress.

She wanted to possess him, to be possessed by him as she'd been in the cave. To feel him inside her again, no matter what the consequence. No matter if giving in only deepened her bondage. No matter if he despised her tomorrow.

She gave a little growl of need and dragged her nails down his spine, hooking her fingers in his leather waistband. She sought his tongue, fenced with it, implored his ever wilder kiss.

Without releasing her mouth he laid her in the furs and stretched on top of her. She felt the urgent pounding in his loins, the hot waves of need hardening him. She wanted him to tear off her garments and bury himself in her.

"You are a Valkyrie fallen from Valhalla's lofty peak," he said.

"Straight into the arms of a war god," she whispered, and played upon his throat with her tongue.

"You madden me, Taras."

"If you are mad, my lord, may you never be sane again."

"There is great danger in that, spell weaver. Great danger, indeed." Suddenly impatient, he caught her bliaut and tore it down the front. He surveyed her out of hot, marveling eyes. "By Odin's sword, you burn my very soul."

Lowering his head, he kissed her breasts until she panted his name. In an agony of greed, she arched against him again and again, seeking his deepest caress. With his hands he traced a molten path from her breasts to her pelvis. Slowly, intimately, he massaged her.

Taras reached down to free his leather belt and slide his braies down over his buttocks. His thick shaft slid free and rode against her thighs. She tilted her pelvis toward him, entreating him with wordless grace to engage her.

Like a white-hot tide he swept into her, carried her far downriver, plunged her deep into a shimmering pool of sensuality. There he held her while the steaming fires of his love buffeted her to and fro, back and forth, over and over.

At last he brought her to the surface with warm, languorous caresses, calming the trembling currents of desire. "Taras," he murmured.

"Yea, lord?"

"You are the most beautiful creation. I cherish you."

Tears washed her eyes. She didn't know what to say or what to believe. Even after the wild ride down the river of love.

"When we joined in the cave, Taras, I thought I'd lost you."

"How so?"

"I was damnably brutal. You did not deserve such treatment."

She could scarcely believe her ears. Trembling, she lowered her gaze to his chest and whispered, "I would not have run away again, lord. I am your slave."

"You are not my slave, damn it! I've been a fool."

She did not deny it. A quiet melody began in her soul, thrumming and vibrating until she could hardly hold back her joy. Still, she composed her face and looked at him out of wide, serious eyes.

"My young falcon, would you have me lay my soul bare to you?"

"Mayhap you have already, lord, and I've been too blind to see it."

"Mayhap I wanted you that way, lest you came to know you owned my soul. A warrior likes to believe he owns some measure of pride. A foolish thing, pride."

Taras could no longer fight back a smile. "I was the greater fool. In pride I ran away from Ilovar, from the one man I've ever . . . " She wanted to say the word, but her courage faltered under the expectancy flaring in his gaze. "I could not believe you cared for me."

"Cared for you? By the old gods, yes, I cared for you! Day after day I pursued you to exhaustion's gateway, yet by night I lay sleepless, composing chansons like a wine-guzzling skald."

"Chansons? What sort?"

"It is best you do not hear me sing them."

"Were they about me?" she asked, tracing his jaw with her forefinger.

"They were about life."

"My life?"

"You *are* life. There is no life without you."

She breathed in his ear, "It is the other way about, my fierce Viking lord, for I cannot breathe if I cannot love you."

He pulled back his head and stared at her in surprise. "I

never thought to hear such words from you, though I prayed for them not long ago."

"You prayed? You?" He felt the need for a power greater than his own? She could hardly imagine it.

He kissed her temple. "Yea, as I lay one night after the battle, listening to a wolf cry. His voice of desolation was mine. That night I rejected the old gods of war and petitioned your God to lead me to you."

She entwined her fingers in his hair and pulled his mouth close to hers. "He heard you. Now I would hear you, too."

"What would you hear?"

"Those chansons."

"They are intimate," he said with a slight grimace.

"And this is not?" She glanced down at their bodies. "Your reticence astounds me. Your tongue was not so reserved moments ago."

"You are a saucy one," he said. "Very well, I will assault your ears with one verse. You will not soon beg for another. The skald's art evades me." A solemn look overcame his smile as he began to chant in a soft, deep baritone:

> "When I look into the deep green eyes of my love I
>   am lost.
> The fires of hell could not dissuade me from her
>   temptations.
> There is no reckoning: I cannot imagine the cost!
> Without her life is naught but sorrow and lamentations
> For her voice sings in my soul
> Her touch kindles my desire
> Her look weakens my control.
> When we kiss I become one with her
> When we touch I am free
> She is open to me and I am a wild creature
> All thought, all reason leaves me."

Roxi Ashe

The chanson vibrated in the air an instant after he fell silent. She laid her head against his heart to hear the echoing voice of love. He tightened his arms around her and whispered, "You are mine this day and forevermore. Truly, you've broken the cold iron bands that held my heart for so long."

She opened to him again, giving freely to the passion that evolved into a mighty storm. Cynewulf was the fire-maker god of old, riding her like a flaring comet. He was heat, he was light, he was fire. She belonged to the fire-maker, belonged to him for all time and eternity. Belonged to him until eternity ended.

And then coolness brushed her consciousness as he carried her from the bed to the window and flung open the shutters. There he stood holding her, looking out upon the snowy fields.

"Have you come back to me, spell weaver? You were worlds away."

"You are my world. I shall never leave you for another."

Midnight rushed into his eyes. "Does this mean you'll become my wife?"

His proposal stole her breath. She could not utter a sound.

"Will you?"

"I'm dreaming."

"We both are."

Faintly she said, "Then let us wed quickly ere we awaken."

"We shall not awaken, you and I, so long as you spin your enchantments about my heart."

She felt giddy, intoxicated, gripped by the wizardry *he* had wrought. "Together we'll spin them for a hundred years, and a hundred after that."

"Let us spin them now, love," he said in a husky voice. He carried her to the bed. "Let us spin them now."

* * *

Denholm was in the stable when Cynewulf entered from the hawking fields late the next afternoon. Pointing at Eboracum, Denholm said, "He would have preferred hawking with you today, instead of keeping to this dingy stall."

"He needed the day of rest," Cynewulf said, patting the warhorse's neck.

"And you did not?" Denholm laughed. "From the noises coming from your chamber last night, methinks you closed your eyes not once, yet tonight you'll marry! Your bride will be sorely disappointed when you carry her to the marriage bed only to slumber and snore."

"I will not slumber tonight," Cynewulf said, chuckling. "What news of Lady Taras? Has she rested since I left her this morn?"

"How could she rest, when Lord Sorel and an army of seamstresses plagued her every moment?"

"I should not have allowed the old man to shoo me off to the hawking field," Cynewulf said. "It was a mistake to announce the marriage this morn."

"And miss the look on everyone's face? You could not have confounded them more had you sprouted wings and flown off the house top, although I, of course, was not amazed at all."

"What is this? I remember your face, in particular, set in the drollest lines of astonishment right before you spit your wine upon the tablecloth."

"I spewed wine because it was sour! As to astonishment, I knew from the day you brought the wench to Ilovar that you'd wed her. You surely cannot think I've endured these hardships to bring home a mere slave."

"Of course not."

" 'Tis only meet that you wed her immediately," Denholm went on in fatherly tones. "If aught were to happen between here and Ilovar, you would be sorry you had not."

"Naught will happen. I'll make her mine forever tonight, and that is an oath. Now I'll go up and see that she's keeping well."

The seneschal caught his arm. "Not until the marriage feast. It's Lord Sorel's rule, not mine."

"A poor thing, indeed, when the bridegroom cannot see the woman he loves!"

"Easy, lord, you'll be sewn into a fur with her soon enough. Come, in the tack room is a hot kettle and a sliver of soap. You'll feel better for a wash and a shave. I've laid out clothing from Forkbeard, as well."

"Clothing from Forkbeard?"

"Aye, gifts from the grateful new king of this land. I've been saving it since we left him, thinking you'd need it for just this occasion."

Cynewulf stalked into the tack room. Ducking around the harnesses and bridles hanging from the rafters, he washed and carefully scraped away his whiskers with a knife, combed his hair and plaited it, then dressed in a black silk tunic embroidered with gold.

The silk slid over his muscles like the sensuous glide of Taras's fingers. He remembered her attack on him last night just before they made love. Had he been dressed then as now, he would be dead.

"Thor's tool, what a woman she is!" he murmured, feeling himself stiffen at the recollection of the wild night in the furs. He could hardly wait until the marriage feast was over to carry her upstairs again.

He drew on ankle-length braies of dark green silk, cursing when he tugged them over his arousal. He had to stop thinking of his bride before he burst with the wanting.

Setting his teeth, he concentrated on crossing leather strips over his calves, then pulled on soft boots. He thrust back his sleeves and snapped golden armlets around his biceps and wrists. He girded himself with his broad leather belt, then clasped his wolfskin mantle over his left shoulder with an emerald-encrusted box brooch. Finally, he slung his baldric and affixed Damfertigénen.

He was ready. Passion lighting his eyes, Lord Cynewulf of Amandolar strode out of the tack house to the great hall to claim his bride.

Chapter Twenty-four

Taras came out of her chamber and stood at the top of the staircase to look upon the crowd. She wore a bliaut of midnight blue silk over a pleated chemise set with amethyst beads. A circlet of pearls and gold crowned her hair. Below her, Denholm stopped in midstride and raised his horn of nabid.

"Lady Taras!" He rushed upstairs, enveloped her hand in his huge paw, and bowed unsteadily. "By the holy shinbones of Odin, if only I were a younger man!"

Taras thanked him gravely, fighting a chuckle. The scorched tufts of hair protruding from his scalp made him look silly, though she would sooner boil herself than tell him so. Taking his arm, she walked beside him down the long staircase, her girdle of carved amber strands clinking like chimes.

She smiled and bowed when Lord Sorel's people raised a great shout: "Hail to the Lady Taras!" They were kind and gentle. All day they'd seen to her comfort, stitching clothing and fussing with her hair.

Lord Sorel waited by the main fireplace. Despite his squire's supporting hand, he sagged under his heavy ceremonial robes and furs.

Taras surveyed the folk gathered at the sideboards and trestle tables. The tall, ornate salt wrought of gold marked the liege lord's place at the table. His chair was empty.

A cadre of servants began to lay the first course of cold duckling and boar's head. Rushlight played upon the cutlery and goblets, mazers and hanaps, carafes and silver ewers. All was ready for the marriage feast.

All except the bridegroom.

A chord of doubt vibrated in her brain. He had left her this morn with a kiss. . . . Was it all mockery? Mayhap he had reconsidered his declaration of love. Mayhap, in his eyes, she was still Ethelred's kin, the woman who had come to kill him. Had last night been his way of evening the score, after all?

She suddenly felt tawdry in her borrowed gown—a cheap imitation of a bride. The chord of doubt became a loud, discordant call to retreat. She forced herself to stand still, to nod to the folk paying their respects, to mask her inner battle behind a polite little smile.

This was nonsense. Something had delayed him, that was all. The seneschal would tell her so. She turned to question him, but he was whispering in a maid's ear. The query died in her throat.

Cynewulf would not play cruel games with her heart. Still, she could not stave off a cold fear of betrayal. There was no reason Cynewulf should love her. She was a Briton and therefore his enemy. And an attempted murderess, she added. Mayhap he was taking his revenge right here in front of his people.

This was madness. He'd said he had no more enemies, that she had tempered the wind of his wrath. He wanted no more barriers between them, yet here she was, erecting the same prickly wall of doubt she'd built so many times in the past.

Yet her walls had not kept him out. He had traveled hundreds of miles in search of her, loving her when she could not fathom her desire for him. Loving her when she screamed and railed at him. Loving her when she attacked him with his own knife.

To lose faith in him would be to throw away happiness with both hands. He was unlike any man she'd ever known. He would not use her to satisfy some twisted end. She had built the thorny wall; she would raze it. Once it lay in ruins she would never resurrect it. She believed in Cynewulf.

She caught Denholm's shoulder, turning him from the maid he'd begun to kiss. "Where is he, seneschal? I've kept him waiting long today. I should go to him."

"He'll come to you soon enough. He is near as mettlesome tonight as his damned warhorse—my lady, where are you going?"

Taras hastened through the crowded hall to the vestibule and called upon the man-at-arms to open the door. Before he could reach for the latch, the door burst open, rebounding almost into his face. Cynewulf stood on the threshold, his wolf furs whipping on the cold wind sweeping the courtyard. Clouds swirled from his nostrils and raced off into the wind.

His gaze settled upon her with predatory fierceness. Taras wanted to touch him, but instead she clasped her hands in the folds of her gown and waited for his words. There was still a chance he did not mean to marry her, after all.

He looked her over slowly, visually stripping off her garments until she felt naked and heated under his stare. There was no disguising the desire burning in his eyes. Awareness tingled her nerve endings.

"By the winged Valkyrie, you are alluring, my love," he

said. Stepping into the vestibule, he kicked the door shut and bent over her hand. His lips brushed her fingertips for one hot, intimate moment before he took both her hands in his and straightened to his full height. He brought her fingers to his mouth again. "I could slake my thirst with you."

"And so you shall, lord, and your hunger also," she whispered. "As I shall slake mine with you. Forever."

A muscle undulated in his cheek. His fingers tightened possessively over hers, drawing her close to his chest. Desire curled up and down her spine.

"Let us marry with haste," he said, "for I am sorely afflicted."

Then he masked his desire behind a solemn expression, drew back, and raised her right hand high in his left. As he escorted her through the great hall, every man and maid bowed low.

"Lord Sorel is Christian," Cynewulf murmured. "He was a priest many years ago before he fell in love and married his late wife. Mayhap the ceremony will be to your liking."

"Will it be to yours, lord?"

"Even a pagan enjoys ceremony upon occasion, my lady," he said with a hint of the old mockery.

"Methinks you are not as pagan as you would have me believe," she said. "Remember who answered your prayer."

They stopped before Lord Sorel at the fireplace. At the old man's nod, Cynewulf lowered Taras to a red cushion, then knelt beside her. The folk dropped to their knees.

Lord Sorel crossed his breast, then took a silver chalice from his squire. "Drink, my lord and lady."

Cynewulf drank deeply of the wine, then pressed the chalice to Taras's lips. He gave the chalice back to Lord Sorel, who threw the dregs into the fire, then laid his hands on their heads. He chanted a prayer in Danish, then in English. At last he said, "I bid my lord and lady drink deeply of life. Let their judgment be distilled from charity and long-suffering. Let them renounce evil even as dregs of wine are cast aside and burned."

He fell silent for a space; then in a voice stronger than his frail body, he said, "My lady, may you be quickened by every gift of God. May you and the children you bear find protection in your husband's arms. Lord Cynewulf, may the Father of us all guide you in his paths. May you rule righteously all your days, that when snow crowns your head and earth bows your back, your people will rise up and call you blessed."

After making the sign of the cross in the air, Lord Sorel said, "Lady Taras, it is fitting that you covenant to honor your lord. What say you, my lady?"

She looked into Cynewulf's dark liquid eyes. Love flowed forth to perfuse her soul. Unable to speak above a whisper, she said, "Lord Cynewulf, beloved, I covenant to stand under your shield arm, to hold sacred my love for you as long as breath quickens my frame. . . . All that I am or ever will be, I give to you, my protector and companion, as my oath and covenant. I, Taras of Widnes, swear it forever."

Lord Sorel touched Cynewulf's shoulder. "And you, lord?"

Cynewulf took both of Taras's hands and held them against his heart. His voice dropped a full measure as he said, "Taras of Amandolar, I covenant my strength to be your strength, my honor, your honor. To you I pledge my sword and shield, my fortresses and lands, my warriors and defenses.

"Upon my arm you shall walk; upon my loins you shall conceive; upon my heart you shall write your name. I, Cynewulf, the son of Beogar, Lord of Amandolar and Discoftomb, covenant this before your God and his heavenly armies forever."

He took an armlet of gold from his wrist and clasped it around hers. "I have borne your face in my heart for time unmeasured, beloved. Accept this band of gold in token of my eternal love."

The golden cuff bore his heat, transporting his promise into the center of her being. Tears coursed down her cheeks as she gazed into the eyes she'd come to love so well.

In ringing tones, Cynewulf said, "This day, a conqueror of England joins with its choicest daughter. May our union be a sign of peace unto our peoples."

Lord Sorel ceremonially raised them. "Let all who witness this joining ever defend it."

Cynewulf pressed Taras's hands to his lips. The people raised a great shout, and suddenly he laughed and swept her into his arms to kiss her.

"I love you!" she said against his lips, and repeated it three times before he silenced her with another hungry kiss. It was a long time before they broke apart to accept everyone's kisses and embraces. Lord Sorel bade the feast begin.

Much later, the newlyweds sat at the high table with Lord Sorel and Denholm. Over the second meat course of peacock and roast coney, Cynewulf whispered to Taras, "Shut your eyes a moment."

"Can I trust you?" she asked, smiling.

"Mmm, we'll see."

Taras shut her eyes and waited, expecting a kiss. Instead, she heard the melodious tinkle of amber, then felt him place a necklace upon her. She opened her eyes and there, spread upon her breast, was the silver necklace he'd fastened upon her long ago in Castle Ilovar, the day she'd fought with Ardeth and scrubbed the great hall. The amber gripping beasts clutched their paws and grinned up at her.

Taras touched the whimsical beasts, and smiled. "I

thought I'd lost it, Cynewulf. Where did you find it?"

"In the cistern. It must have fallen in when you drew water that day. I've been carrying it around with me ever since, wanting you to have it." Cynewulf's brows drew down in concern. "But perhaps it brings bad memories— you don't have to wear it."

"Of course I will! I didn't admit it then, but I was sad I'd lost it. Something about these carved beasts' droll little faces reminds me of yours."

Cynewulf pulled a face. "I'm often told I have a silly grin."

"No, you haven't. You have a silly nose."

Cynewulf kissed her then, smothering her giggle. Denholm hardly waited for the kiss to end before he said, "Lady Taras, I am glad this knave finally cast off his mantle of stupid pride."

"And I'm glad I cast off mine!" she said with a laugh.

"Ah, but your beauty made up for your stubbornness."

"I'm still stubborn, seneschal. I'll not rest until I see you wed, as well."

Denholm choked on his beer. Cynewulf pounded him on the back until he regained his breath and said, "Pray, do not curse me, lady. I am an old man unused to shocks."

"He's right, my love," Cynewulf said, raising his voice to include those below the salt. "He is too old to think of marriage. A maiden would be sore disappointed in the furs, with his vigor grown soft as a cat's tail."

Denholm reddened at the roar of merriment, then shrugged and returned to his beer. Before long he joined the housecarls in singing ditties. The songs grew more ribald as the wine flowed and the women danced.

Cynewulf stiffened when Taras brushed his thigh through his silk braies. He glanced at her, but she had turned to talk to Lord Sorel. Her touch was accidental, then. He was conveying a knifeload of roast coney to his

323

mouth when he felt her hand on his thigh again. Heat wrenched his gut and he looked at her sharply.

She was still talking to the old man, though when Cynewulf sat forward in his seat he saw a dimple at the corner of her mouth. It was no accident, then.

Her hand slid boldly under his tunic and enclosed him. He nearly came out of his chair. At that moment, one of the women approached to pay her respects. Striving to give no clue of the turmoil taking place under the tablecloth, he mumbled replies.

Taras had him between her thumb and palm, sliding her fingertips over him in a subtle, maddening rhythm. Wave after hot wave pulsed in his groin. Beads of sweat burst upon his brow, but the woman was still talking to him. He knew his replies made no sense.

He choked when Taras closed her fingers tightly around him. He stole a glance to see if she were betraying herself in any way, but her shoulder was steady, the tablecloth hiding her mischief. She was smiling openly now, though not looking at him.

Just when he thought he must surely leap to his feet with his manhood bursting from his clothing for all to see, the woman left and Taras relaxed her grip.

"Odin's breath, wench," he gasped, "would you have me lay you upon the table for the final course?"

In wide-eyed innocence she said, "Was it not your intent, lord? I believe you wanted to slake your thirst and hunger with me."

"Aye, and so I will. Lord Sorel's fare can't compete with the feast I would make of you."

"Devour me then, my lord," she whispered, leaning toward him until her breast pushed against his arm. Lightning jolted deep into his bones.

"I'll devour you in private," he said. Shoving his chair

back, he snatched her into his arms and carried her to the staircase. Everyone sprang up, cheering.

"This is most undignified!" Taras said, and linked her arms around his neck. "Lord Sorel will believe me incapable of climbing the steps under my own power."

"I prefer you going upstairs under my power," Cynewulf said.

"You randy old lion!"

"Mmm, and you are a tender young doe. Delicious." He mounted the steps as though she weighed no more than a fawn, then turned to grin down at the people. With their cheers reverberating in his ears, he hurried down the gallery to the chamber.

As Cynewulf barred the door, Taras nibbled his ear with mock ferocity. "Now that you've dragged me into your den, what do you intend to do with me?"

"Gobble you for a morsel, of course!"

He laid her on the bed and cast off his sword and mantle. Then he stretched out beside her and took her face between his hands. Slowly he ran his tongue around the edges of her lips, then down over her throat to her breasts. He tugged down her bodice and clasped her left hip in his hand to control her amorous movements.

Taras slipped her fingertips along his back, feeling the taut muscles beneath his silken tunic. The sensation reminded her of stroking him under the table a few minutes ago. There was the same miraculous softness over hardness, vulnerability over strength.

"How do you do it, lord?"

"Do what?"

"Manage to be so fierce, yet so tender all at the same time."

"It is not at the same time, spell weaver. I do not feel tender now."

He opened her mouth with his tongue, filling her with heat, impelling her thrusts until his silken hardness began to penetrate her clothing and he was almost inside her.

She caught the ties of his braies, freeing them, sliding the silk down to his thighs. Then she boldly clasped his buttocks, delighting in the heat and strength that promised powerful, intimate thrustings. Round and hard as an iron staff, his manhood probed her through her skirts.

"Take me, lion," she said against his lips. "Devour me."

He pulled off her clothing. Caught up in the elemental rhythm of desire, he kissed her throat and breasts. His fingers laid bare her secrets until every organ in her body took fire. There was nothing in the world but the splendid feel of him, a swirling tempest invading every portion of her being.

Outside the window, a storm bore down on Sorelvelden. The lovers ignored the wind. For them, the storm was inside, roiling them in ectasy.

Taras awakened at first light to find Cynewulf leaning over the bed, smiling at her. Soft light shone through the open casement behind him. Snowflakes dusted the floor.

Shivering, Taras pulled the furs up to her chin. "You're naked as Adam. You must be freezing. Don't you want me to warm you, my love?"

"Aye, in a moment. I want you to see something first." Tucking the furs around her, he plucked her out of bed and carried her to the window. "Feast your eyes. Look!"

Snow shrouded Sorelvelden. Hemlocks bent close to the drifts like tired old ghosts. Strange white light shone through the clouds.

"Bewitching," Taras said. She wriggled until he let her down in front of him, then instantly regretted it when her bare feet touched the stones. Clenching her teeth, standing on the balls of her feet, she leaned back against him and surveyed the unblemished bosom of earth.

"There was a blizzard last night," Cynewulf said.

"Odd that we failed to hear the wind."

"We were blowing a tempest of our own." He tightened his arms around her and kissed the hollow between her shoulder and neck. "Mmm, you're a warm little bundle this morn. I ought to wrap up with you in that fur."

"I would let you," she said, giving him a saucy smile, "but were I to move the robe, the air would slip in. So I suppose you must bear the cold like a warrior."

"Cold? What cold? Ah, you mean *this* cold!" He snatched off the furs.

Taras shrieked and dashed for the fireplace, but he intercepted her, laughing like a fiend. Within seconds he'd snuggled her into bed and pulled her against him.

"Let me warm you before you catch cold, little warrior maid."

"It'll take a lot of warming!"

"You'll be surprised at how much warmth I can generate."

Later, after they had gotten warm, they came downstairs, bypassed the folk huddled around the fireplaces, and went outside to trudge through the snowy courtyard.

In addition to the clothing Lord Sorel had presented to Taras for her wedding, he'd given her a striped bliaut of heather and green. Over it she wore a white woolen mantle and a fox fur snood. She wore sealskin and rabbit fur half-boots, and warmed her hands in a wolfskin muff.

Beneath his mantle and woolen overtunic Cynewulf wore chain mail. Damfertigénen slapped his side as he strode into the stable.

There Denholm and four of Lord Sorel's carls sat around a charcoal brazier, toasting cheese and bread. The seneschal heaved to his feet, winced, and clutched his lower back.

"What the devil ails you?" Cynewulf demanded.

"A touch of lumbago." Denholm smiled and said, "The

maids would not leave me be last night. My back gave out on the seventh, to the lass's everlasting disappointment."

Taras hid a smile, but Cynewulf clapped his seneschal's shoulder in sympathy. "A man your age should exercise caution. Not for you a stableful of fillies. A lass of eighty winters with hips like yon barn door would give you a gentler ride."

"I prefer the lumbago," he said with a grimace.

Chuckling, Cynewulf walked into a stall and brought out a pony for Taras. He flung a blanket over the animal's back and hefted the saddle. Denholm came to lean over the crumbling stone partition. Frowning, the seneschal asked, "Where do you intend to ride this morn, lord?"

"Nowhere in particular. Lady Taras asked me to show her the land."

"I'll call an escort."

Cynewulf shook his head. He wanted Taras to himself. He imagined her resting upon his mantle beneath a snowy tree, her skirts raised just enough.

"My lord, mayhap you were asleep when Lord Sorel mentioned the rogues ranging the countryside hereabout. It is unsafe to go out without an escort."

Cynewulf cinched the girth with enough force to rock the pony on its feet. "I saw no one yesterday when I was hawking."

"One can't see everything."

The other carls muttered agreement. Cynewulf scowled when he noticed Taras's dubious expression. In another moment these dunderheads would rob her appetite for adventure.

"I would go, myself," Denholm said, "were my back not twisted into knots. These carls can go in my place. They four almost make up for me."

"Cynewulf, mayhap we should let them come," Taras

said. Her voice trailed off when he raised his hand in exasperation.

"Let it be as the seneschal wills," he said. He glowered at the carls already saddling up. Denholm hobbled off to oversee them. "Damned wet nurses."

"Do you think there is danger?"

He sighed out his breath. "Nay, Denholm is an old woman. We'll be the only ones abroad with snow this deep. Only fools would venture into the cold when they could sit by a fire, instead."

"By that reckoning, I know who the fools are today," she said, touching his cheek. She parted her lips to show the tip of her tongue in a catlike smile, enjoying the sudden fire in his eyes.

"There are other ways of getting warm than sitting by a hearth," Cynewulf said, dropping his hand to her shoulder. His lean fingers followed the course of her collarbone to the cleft between her breasts. There he lingered, watching her nipples grow taut against her mantle.

A glow rose where he touched her and spread through her veins. She wanted to feel his hands inside her gown, teasing until need overruled control.

She glided her fingers over the rugged planes of his face to his neck and wide shoulders. There she inched along the fine tunic and chain mail overlaying his powerful chest muscles. His strength excited her. It seemed impossible that she had once feared this big Viking warlord; she could no longer imagine a day without his touch.

After stealing a glance around his shoulder to make sure the carls were engaged elsewhere, she rose on tiptoe to whisper, "I wish you were still wearing only those silk braies from last night."

A muscle throbbed in his cheek. He caught her against him and said in a voice that echoed through her system like a whisper in a mountain cavern, "And what would you do were I so near naked?"

"I would . . . " She stopped, caught in a mixture of passion and embarrassment. Passion won out, and she told him.

Drawing her fingertips to his lips, he kissed them one by one, then tongued her palm until her fever rose another degree. "I ought to order my men out of the stable and lick more than your fingers," he said. "By Thor, my blood is hot!"

She caught his jaw and kissed him until, knowing she was playing with fire, she stepped back.

"Let me mount you," Cynewulf said.

"Here? Now?"

"I mean, let me help you mount," he said, chuckling. He helped her onto the pony. "It will take but a moment to saddle Eboracum."

He was wrong. The destrier stamped and flinched, shook his mane, and refused the bit until Cynewulf rapped him under the chin and forced open his mouth.

"The horse is angry that you left him here to rot yesterday," Denholm said, coming in to watch. Eboracum skittered from side to side, resisting blanket and saddle. "Damned if I would not feel the same way, in his hooves!"

"Sometimes I fail to see which of you is more mad," Cynewulf said. He managed to sling the saddle onto Eboracum's back. As he stooped to cinch the girth, Eboracum swung around and knocked him into the dirt, the saddle on top of him.

Cynewulf didn't get up right away. He sat and cursed the horse with great feeling. Taras giggled and Denholm vented a hearty laugh, but glared the carls into silence when they joined in. Eboracum capered and tossed his mane.

Taras slid off the pony and caught Eboracum's bridle.

She spoke into his left ear. Shivering like a gigantic pup from nose to tail, he snuffled at her neck.

"I ought to give the beast to you," Cynewulf said. "I've never seen man or woman so canny with horses."

"We speak the same tongue," she said. "Don't we, Eboracum, my darling old ninny?"

Eboracum stood docile. Cynewulf said, "You've spoiled him, Taras. He'll never suffer himself to be saddled without your caresses."

"Hmm, it will keep you from rushing off without me."

"I cannot imagine rushing off without you," he said. If his men overheard his sentimental talk, they dared give no sign. He didn't care, anyway. "When you have been mine for fifty winters, I shall still delight in your nearness every second of the day and night. I may stop going off to war."

He lifted her onto the pony, mounted Eboracum, and led the procession out of the courtyard through the gates. He cast the escort a stern look over his shoulder, warning them to stay back. Taras, knowing the pony would be hard pressed to break trail through the snow, followed in Eboracum's swath.

Overnight, the forest had become a fairy world. Gargantuan white dragons kept company with gnarled old wizards, snow giants and longships. Steep scarps and battlements stretched between towering trees. Between two boulders a monstrous snowdrift had formed, then its center had collapsed, leaving a trembling expanse of ice. The shock of horse hooves set the bridge quaking until it crumpled, spinning crystal into the air.

Cynewulf reined in for Taras to draw up beside him. She smiled up at him, her cheeks ruddy with cold and her green eyes sparkling elvishly.

"It's magic," she said. "Let us go on."

After riding another quarter of an hour, Cynewulf reined in and frowned back at her. She raised her brows.

"Do I annoy you, lord?"

"Nay, it is the distance you keep that bothers me. I cannot stand the separation, or the idea that you may be freezing back there and are too pigheaded to tell me."

"Pigheaded, is it? I suppose it would do no good to mention your own intractability, or the fact that your gruffness no longer fools me. Who would have guessed that a warrior's heart could be soft as a rabbit's cheek?"

"A rabbit's cheek?" he said, as though he wasn't sure he'd understood her English.

He looked so annoyed that she took mercy upon him and said, "If you are concerned about my being cold, you should take me onto Eboracum's back with you."

"Mayhap I should lay you on my mantle in a snowdrift and ensure you are quite warm. I can build you a snowhouse."

Taras glanced over her shoulder and discovered that the men had halted many yards back. Clever men, their escorts. She elevated her chin and said with mock hauteur, "Lay me on your mantle? That sounds like a challenge."

Battle light flickered in his eyes. "I crave a challenge."

"Then I'll hurl the gauntlet." She flung her wolfskin muff at him and leaped off the pony, sinking up to her waist in snow. She screeched in dismay and tried to run.

Cynewulf vaulted off Eboracum and plunged toward her. After half a dozen thrashing steps Taras fell down face-first, thrashed some more, and bobbed up just as he reached her.

"Ha! I've got you!"

"Ha! I've got *you!*" she cried, and dashed snow into his face.

Cynewulf stumbled back, wiping his eyes. With a triumphant laugh, Taras lunged off. He plowed after her again. When her fox-fur snood flew off her head he thought she'd go back for it, but she plunged on through the drifts, laughing. He unpinned his mantle and sailed it after her. She tripped on it, recovered, and bolted again.

"Give up, Taras! You know I'll have my way with you!"

"You'll have to catch me first, Viking."

Cynewulf unbuckled his baldric and flung it aside with his sword. Without slowing, he snatched up the mantle. Timing his leap, he hurtled over a drift and caught her around the waist, twisting to bear her down on the mantle he'd strategically cast upon the snow. She tried to smear snow in his face, but he blocked her hand and began to kiss her.

She returned his kiss, twisted her fingers in his hair, thrust her hips against him. The air was very cold, the sky a pale void, the trees swathed in virgin white—a delight-some counterpoint to the hot, brazen swordsman holding her down. There was no sound but their labored breathing.

The earth began to shake. Snow toppled from the hem-locks, splashing her face with burning cold. Without understanding why, she felt Cynewulf twisting to get off her, seeking the sword no longer at his side.

Snow exploded from the trees and ground. Warhorses pounded into view, whirling snow shrouding their riders. Taras thought they were the escort until Cynewulf shoved her under some low branches, burying her in snow.

Half a breath later, two horsemen fell upon Cynewulf, bowled him over, then wheeled for a second pass when he lunged to his feet. He ducked beneath a sword and caught its wielder by the foot, twisting until the ankle snapped. The attacker tumbled screaming to the ground.

Pouncing upon the fallen sword, Cynewulf twisted to engage the other horsemen. He heard the sound of steel through the trees and knew his men had also joined the combat.

An ax swished past his face, cut through his tunic, and sang off his mail. Before the axman could strike another blow, Cynewulf thrust the sword through his gut. The axman screamed in agony, blood and filth splattering his horse.

Cynewulf spun and hacked off someone's sword arm. Before the rider could scream, Cynewulf jerked him out of the saddle and vaulted onto his horse.

Kicking the horse into a swirling frenzy, Cynewulf sought to fend off four horsemen. Two fell stricken to the ground and lay writhing.

And then he heard a sharp crack. The world turned to blood. He scrabbled for the horse's mane, but his nerveless fingers slid through the hair. He dropped into the black arms of the angel of death.

"Taras," he whispered, and then he was gone.

Chapter Twenty-five

Taras struggled out of the snowbank into the midst of a seething, bloody tapestry. Blood painted everything—snow, horses, men, trees, her.

And Cynewulf. God in Heaven—Cynewulf had fallen. Her very marrow seemed to freeze when she beheld his body crumpled on the ground, blood seeping into the snow around his head.

She fell to her knees beside him, gathered his head onto her lap, and went still. The screams of the men he'd wounded did not penetrate her consciousness.

Cynewulf. Dead? God's mercy, he'd been alive less than two minutes ago, enveloping her in the torrid strength of his arms.

Snow began falling again, great heavy discs that stuck to his face and gathered in the corners of his eyes. She tried to brush it off, but the snow kept ahead of her, frustrating her efforts. Tears ran down and froze on her cheeks.

"He doesn't feel the cold, Taras," came a harsh voice.

She dragged her gaze up the legs, chest, and neck of a monstrous warhorse to the knight holding it in check. A hood veiled his face.

"Let the snow bury him," the knight said. "You cannot help him."

The voice haunted her, a memory of malice compounding present horror. She stroked Cynewulf's face, soothing him, keeping him from this half-remembered enemy. Other riders gathered around him like a pack of wolves, clouds of steam from their horses' nostrils freezing on Cynewulf's mail. She hunched over him, taking the cold vapors on her back.

"The others are dead?" the knight demanded.

"Yea, lord. All four."

"How many of ours?"

"Two slain by the escort; three by that dead bastard there. He wounded four others."

"Get the wounded onto their horses. Leave the dead," he snapped. His horse reared, showering bloody snow over Taras and the body she protected. "Bid the spurious knave adieu, Taras; 'tis time we went."

She stared again at the rider, who doffed his hood and bent low to smile at her. It was Camlann.

Hatred choked her. Her own cousin had murdered her husband. How he had found them she didn't know or care. All that mattered was that she kill him.

There was no time to seek absolution, even if she'd wished it. Full of hate and despair, she dreaded neither death nor the certainty that her unshriven soul would wander the earth until Judgment Day.

She saw the sword in Cynewulf's lifeless hand. She would seize it and attack like a falcon, jabbing Camlann's throat before his henchmen could stop her. They'd kill her then, but Camlann would be dead.

"For you, Cynewulf," she whispered. She dropped her

left hand to his throat for one last caress and stiffened in shock.

Feeble as a moth's wing, his pulse fluttered against her fingertips. For an instant her vision blurred and she thought she'd faint. Instantly she clamped off her breath, imprisoning the scream climbing into her throat.

He was alive. God's mercy, he was alive!

Praying she'd revealed nothing to Camlann in that instant of astonishment, she stared into his eyes. One glance, one hint that Cynewulf lived, and Camlann would order him slain on the spot. This time there would be no mistake.

She forced herself to release Cynewulf and stand up. Her legs quivered like willow switches. In an unsteady voice she said, "You've done your murder, Camlann. You've killed the king's enemy. Now begone and leave me with the dead."

"You'll come with me to my castle, you poor excuse for a witch."

She didn't want to leave Cynewulf, but she had to get these men away before they discovered he lived. Even so, he might die of the cold or his wounds before Denholm came looking for him. He was in God's hands. And hers.

With all her soul she wanted to take Cynewulf's broken body into her arms, to bind up his wounds and pray for his life. She dared not even look at him.

Molding her hatred into an iron ball of determination, she said, "Lord Sorel will send his Vikings before long. Your mercenaries will prove no match for their fury when they discover the liege lord dead."

"Grab the witch and tie her on a horse. Move!" Camlann thundered.

She dared not let them get close to Cynewulf. Striding forward, she let them catch her by the arms and mount her on the horse of a dead mercenary. They bound her wrists to the high wooden frontpiece.

Camlann glared down at Cynewulf for a long moment. Taras waited in suspense, hoping the swirling snow would hide Cynewulf's shallow breaths.

Camlann spat upon his enemy's body, then jerked his horse away from the battleground. One of his men caught Taras's reins and pulled her along.

Just before they rode into the trees, Taras glanced over her shoulder at the still figure in the snow. Only then did she allow herself to weep openly. Whether he lived or died, she knew she'd never see him again.

Camlann pushed hard across England for three days, stopping only for a few hours' sleep at night. Despite the cold, he allowed his band to build only tiny fires. Two of the wounded died the second day, and another on the third.

It angered him that Taras never complained. Sometimes he heard her crying at night, but by day she rode in silence, studying him with unnerving absorption. He longed to break her lovely jaw.

He glanced back and found her staring again. His mood grew more brutal. Sheer luck had brought him to Sorelvelden and delivered Cynewulf into his hands. He'd intended to attack and burn the keep, but somehow his plans had gotten all mixed up with vengeance.

Ethelred would be pleased, anyway, the bastard. After the fateful battle at Wiltham and the crowning of Forkbeard, he'd fled to Camlann's castle. In madness borne of power lust, Ethelred had determined to send his loyal vassals against his own people. Disguised as Vikings, they would sally forth to rape and despoil, undermining any confidence in Sweyn Forkbeard's new rule. Ethelred hoped the citizenry would rise up against Forkbeard.

Camlann wasn't sure the plan would work. Since capturing his cousin Taras, he'd developed his own plans. The beautiful spellbinder could blind the eyes of even a king.

She couldn't turn men into frogs, mayhap, but she could certainly brew poison.

Everyone knew Sweyn Forkbeard suffered a weakness for wenches. It wouldn't be difficult to insinuate Taras into his court. He'd have her in bed within two days. There she would deliver the kiss of death: a drop of poison on her lips.

Ethelred would step over Forkbeard's body and regain the throne. In gratitude, he'd elevate Camlann to minister. As the king's own cousin, it was a short step from minister to the throne, itself.

The only snag was Taras. By all the signs, she'd fallen in love with Cynewulf, the man she'd been sent to kill. Angry, he reined in and let her ride up beside him.

"You could have lived like a queen," he said. "Do you know the reward had you killed the Viking?"

She raised her chin and returned no answer. Hatred simmered in her enormous eyes.

"Yet you chose to live like a slattern."

She cast on him a look as cold as a viper's regard. That same poisonous look had stung him so often over the past days that he almost smelled his own corruption. He slapped her face, enjoying the sharp crack of flesh against bone.

She did not cry out, but swallowed hard and transfixed him with glowing eyes. He sensed no fear in her. Damn her, she possessed a warrior's nerve. The black bile of rage congealed in his throat.

But as she continued to stare, Camlann's rage turned to trepidation. He'd seen that look before. Sometimes in his nightmares he saw Cynewulf standing over him on the tournament field, weighing his life in the balance. It was as though Taras bore his image in her countenance.

Such notions were demented! He slapped her again, harder this time. The blow rang on the cold air. His men turned to look. "You shall pay for your haughty airs, Taras of Widnes."

"Taras of Amandolar," she said, spitting the words into his face. "I am married."

He hid his surprise behind an angry scowl. "You *were* married, witch. Mayhap you did not see your lover's blood spilled into the snow."

He made his words deliberately cruel, but instead of distress, triumph showed in her face. A snake of dread coiled around his spine. He dragged air into his lungs to swell his chest into a large, forbidding wall of steel, disguising the weakness that turned his bowels to water.

He ought to just take her in the snow—that would show the spiteful witch . . . if only he could make himself hard.

Her whisper uncoiled from her depths to embrace him and the men who had turned to listen, binding them in a spell of their own superstition. "There is a wolf following your trail of blood and death, Camlann."

He saw madness in her smoldering green eyes. She drew her lips away from her teeth in a smile that was no smile at all, but a threat. "While we fight these snowdrifts, the wolf runs tirelessly through the gloom. At any moment he'll spring out of this cold hell and clasp you in his iron jaws."

"Wolf? There is no wolf!"

"There is a wolf, dark and fey, hunting you down. Hunting all of you down."

His men murmured uneasily. Without understanding how, Camlann knew her next words before she spoke them.

"Do you not see, my cousin?" she whispered. "You made the deadly mistake of leaving him *alive*."

The hairs on his head pricked erect, and cold sweat trickled beneath his mail. Fearful comments sprung up from his men. Surprisingly, he drew strength from their dread.

"I made no mistake. The barbarian is dead. You lie." Because he had to console his men, he raised his voice to a shout. "Liars do not inherit Heaven. If I were to kill you now, you would dwell in that same hell where your lover lies chained!"

"I have spoken the truth. I do not fear the wrath of God. That is your lot."

It took all his willpower not to twist off her head. He forced himself to remember his plans. "Throw in your lot with me, Taras. I can be . . . lenient."

"I do not crave your indulgence."

"You will crave it when you've stood chained to the wall in my dungeon for six days and nights." He ran his forefinger down her cheek and felt her flinch. "What a shame to watch you crumble away, when with a word you could be saved."

"You'll never hear that word, Camlann. I shall never crawl to you."

"You shall crawl to me and to any other man I command you to pleasure . . . the upstart Forkbeard, even."

"You are quite mad."

"We'll see how mad I am when England lies at my feet." He spurred his horse away from her and resumed his position at the head of the line.

They reached Castle MacClesveld that night. Camlann hardly acknowledged the king before he dragged Taras down into the dungeon and chained her to the cold, damp wall. Rats skittered among the broken flagstones and ran over the living skeletons chained to the walls.

He raised his torch and studied her face. Her back pressed to the wall, arms chained over her head, she looked weak and helpless. His loins stirred with desire, yet a frisson of fear held him back. If she were the sorceress her mother had claimed she was, she might wither his precious tool.

"How long will you stay chained among the rats?"

When she did not reply, he squeezed her breasts until she cried out. In a voice devoid of mercy he said, "Do not force me to hurt you, little cousin. What I would offer you is better than this dungeon. All you need do is obey me."

"Nay. Leave me to die, Camlann. I'll not help you."

He grabbed her hair and slammed her head into the wall until she hung limp from the chains. Shaking her, he screamed, "You stupid wench, has your reason deserted you? Answer me!"

He shook and slapped her, but when she did not awaken he became frightened and unchained her. He carried her to the great hall and dropped her upon a rug.

Ethelred arose from his seat before the fire and scowled at him. "The sorceress who cannot weave spells? Is this the reason you've returned so soon, when I sent you to strike terror in their hearts? What is this?"

Camlann was too angry to tolerate the chiding of a deposed king. Muttering oaths, he gathered Taras into his arms and walked out. He didn't know what to do with her, so he climbed the northeast tower and shoved her into a tiny room at the top. Her lids fluttered and he heard her whisper Cynewulf's name. Enraged, he slammed the door, barred it, and posted a guard. If the witch lived, she would serve him yet.

"What shall I do when she awakens, lord?" the guard asked.

"Nothing. Let her hunger a few days. She can watch the world through the window while she rots in the shadows. She'll be of a mind to obey me before long."

He turned and clattered down the steps. It was time to tell Ethelred his plan. Time, too, to negotiate the price.

Taras heard him leave. For a while she could not persuade herself to move. In her shocked state it was too painful to get up. Besides, she didn't want the guard to know she was conscious until she'd shaped a plan.

Holding her throbbing head, she finally got to her knees and crawled to the narrow window. She could see only a few folk in the courtyard far below, but many watchers stood upon the north wall. Beyond the high wall, black grape vines twisted across the snowy fields. There were no trees, no place for a rescuing army to hide from arrows.

She managed to push her head and left shoulder through the aperture. It was a long drop to the ground. She pulled herself back inside and sat down on the dirty rush pallet, leaned against the wall, and let coldness numb her fear.

There had to be a way out. Camlann had erred when he'd taken her from the dungeon. "I'll get out," she whispered to the walls. "I'll get out and come to find you, Cynewulf. I shall come, I swear it." She tried not to wonder if anyone had ever escaped the tower of MacClesveld.

Chapter Twenty-six

Denholm found the murdered escort many hours after the attack. Leaving the warriors from Sorelvelden to see to their dead, he hurried on and found Cynewulf half-buried in the snow. His lord still breathed, although he did not stir when Denholm sought to wake him. There was no sign of Taras, since new snow had obliterated all tracks. He'd have to search for her later.

For five days Cynewulf slept like a dead man despite the efforts of Lord Sorel's herbalists and witches to revive him. All of Sorelvelden despaired for his life. Then, on the sixth day, he awakened. Despite his thundering headache, he arose from his pallet. In silence he heard Denholm's account of finding him and his escort. They had searched several days for Taras, but it seemed the earth had swallowed her up.

Cynewulf couldn't guess who had taken her, but in his heart he knew she lived. He had only to shut his eyes to remember his struggles against the bands holding him in sleep. During those hours Taras had come to comfort him.

Now that he was awake, he could still see her eyes. They were like lodestones calling him forth; through them he'd see the path that led to her. He had to find her; his arrogance had caused all this suffering. His arrogance had lost her to him.

"You must remain quiet a few more days," Lord Sorel told him. "There may be clots in your brain. We've bled you and applied many leeches already, but it may be that you'll die if you move too soon."

"Would I survive only to let Lady Taras die?" Cynewulf answered. He laid his hand on the old man's shoulder. "I must find her, you know that."

"Aye, lord." He sighed. "Already my men stand ready to accompany you."

In grim silence Cynewulf led thirty warriors forth from Sorelvelden. Everywhere they went they questioned villagers. No one had heard of Taras, though some complained that a group of English warriors dressed as Vikings had set upon their flocks and women some days ago.

In growing alarm Cynewulf rode on. Sometimes he felt he could almost touch her. More than once he heard her whisper his name. Oftimes he wondered how it was possible for a man to experience so much love for a woman. He yearned to know this was not the end, that even if he came too late to find her alive, in the heavens she would still be his. There was no justice in life if this was not so. There was no reason to live if the one woman he had ever loved could not be his again.

His thoughts turned toward the God whom Taras revered. He did not realize he'd begun to pray aloud until someone whispered that the blow on his head had unseated his reason. It did not matter. Driven by his imaginings, succored by his prayers to a God he was coming to know through extremity, he plowed on through the cold white world.

One afternoon they met a tinker whose cart had fallen into a ditch. After ordering his men to pull the cart free, Cynewulf demanded to know if he'd seen Taras.

"Ask at the castle over yonder hills," the tinker said, but fear showed in his eyes.

Tight with excitement, Cynewulf said, "Whose castle is it?"

"Lord Camlann's of MacClesveld." The tinker clamped his mouth shut as though he'd said too much and hurried on his way, his tinware clanking.

He should have killed Taras's cousin on the tournament field. Cynewulf had no doubt that Camlann had come back for vengeance, that he had stolen Taras.

Certain now, he charged Eboracum down the road. His men followed at a gallop, slinging snow high into the air. Denholm gripped his ax as though to immediately smite off English heads.

For several hours they raced darkness through the hills. Just at twilight they dismounted and crawled to the crest of the hill. From there they examined the fortress across the valley. It was mighty, built of earthen escarpments and polished stone that looked black in the failing light. Iron bands crisscrossed the great drawbridge defending the north wall. A depression in the snow marked the frozen moat; in the setting sun it looked filled with blood.

Cynewulf quickly outlined a plan to Denholm, who shook his head. "It has been many days since she was stolen, lord," the seneschal said. "Mayhap she is no longer . . ." His voice trailed off under the wrathful look in Cynewulf's eyes.

"She lives," Cynewulf said. "I know it as surely as the beat of my own heart."

"The tinker did not say she was in the castle. He only said we were to ask. You cannot be sure she is there."

"She is there. How else would I have come here, out of all other places? My heart has led me here. My prayers to her God have guided me."

"Short of tying you up, I know of no way to stop you," Denholm said, shrugging.

Cynewulf smiled like a wolf. His veins pulsed with excitement, quickened for battle. He'd need every bit of his strength for the task he'd set himself.

He could not assault the castle with such a small force under his command; Camlann had only to keep the drawbridge closed and set his archers upon them. Besides, if he betrayed himself in a frontal assault, Camlann might destroy Taras. Cynewulf had seen the English throw captives from a parapet to display contempt for the enemy.

Over Denholm's protest, he shed his mail until he was dressed only in a black quilted tunic and leggings. Without his armor, Damfertigénen alone would have to defend him from whomever stood in his way.

"Pity the man who would stop you, lord," Denholm said, reading his dark look. "But do not forget—Camlann's men are legion, and you are only one. Find the wench, then waste no time in opening the gates. We shall be waiting in the shadow of the wall."

Cynewulf gripped his forearm in an ancient salute. "I will not suffer my wife to be locked in that castle another night," he said.

"I am, as ever, on your side," Denholm said. "May Thor lend you his fury."

Cynewulf waited until darkness fell, then rolled down the hill into the hollow. Although the moon was only a fingernail, the snow shone like silver. He hoped the watchers wouldn't see him. He thrust himself up the hill and stood panting in the castle's shadow.

When no one challenged him, he began to climb the wall. The sharp, cold stones scrolled skin off his fingers.

His breath froze on the stones before his face, though he sweated from every pore.

For an eternity he climbed. At last he stole a look at the snow seventy feet below him. Under its soft surface lay the frozen moat. One slip and he'd fall and crack like a walnut.

He pulled himself up another few inches. His fingertips were so cold, he couldn't feel his grip. Cold stabbed his arms all the way to the shoulders. He searched for a toe-hold for his left foot, missed, and sensed his right foot sliding out of the shallow crack where he'd settled it.

Tensing every muscle, he let go with his left hand and stretched desperately for another stone. His right foot slipped out of the crack and his legs swung free. He clung to the wall by one hand, fighting for his life.

Taras hefted the mace she'd fashioned. She'd plaited rushes for its handle and formed the head from a mixture of bread, straw, dirt, and water. Stuffed into one of her slippers, the mixture had frozen rock hard.

When dusk snatched most of the light from her prison, she tied a rope she'd made from her chemise to a metal peg, and threw the other end out the window. She went to the door and began to tap and scratch.

"What are you about, wench?" the guard outside demanded.

She kept quiet until she heard his chair creak, then she dragged her mattress over to the door and began ripping the casing.

"What are you tearing in there?"

She was silent for several minutes, then she began again.

"You're making a rope, aren't you?" His chair crashed against the wall and she heard him cursing. The bar clattered from its rests. "No prisoner escapes!"

He wrenched open the door and barged into the room. Spying the rope disappearing out the window, he hurried forward, shouting, "You think you're smart? I'll have you back inside in two shakes of a lamb's tail!"

Taras sprang from behind the door and hit him over the head with the mace. He bellowed in pain and turned to strike, but he tripped over the mattress and fell into the rushes. She kicked chaff into his eyes, then ran outside, barred the door, and then, holding on to the wall, started down the dark tower on her way to freedom.

For a time she heard the guard shouting and pounding on the door. It wouldn't take long for him to arouse the watchers on the parapet, so she opened a door and slipped into the second-floor gallery. At the end of it she sneaked into a chamber dominated by a huge canopy bed. There was no one in it.

She couldn't guess where Camlann and Ethelred were, but she was certain the great hall was full of soldiers. She needed to distract them.

She seized a torch from a wall sconce and applied it to the bed draperies until they ignited. She ran over and opened the shutters to let in the wind, then dropped the torch on the floor. The resiny wood smoldered, then blazed.

She swiped a silver urn from a chest, then ran back into the gallery. She hurried to the tower and rushed down to the ground floor. Heart hammering, she eased open the door and slipped into an anteroom off the great hall. She heard someone talking on the other side of the curtained doorway. Since there was no other exit, she squatted behind a chair and waited for developments.

Soon smoke began to drift into the room. She could see it oozing through cracks in the timber ceiling. For a while all was quiet.

"Fire!" she heard a maid shout. "Fire in the hall!"

The curtain ripped open and men poured into the anteroom. Some rushed into the tower while others went back for buckets of snow and water.

In the confusion, Taras crawled behind the draperies. The smoke stung her eyes and made her cough. She watched until the anteroom was empty, then hastened out of hiding. Before she could escape, a carl bearing two buckets stumbled into the room. For an instant they stared at each other; then he dropped the buckets and sprang at her.

Taras hit him over the head with the silver urn, felling him. She levered him behind the draperies and undressed him. After clothing herself in his tunic and coif, she crept out, grabbed the buckets, and started outside.

But halfway to the great hall her conscience smote her. Through the soles of her feet she felt the fire-stricken timbers murmur. She dropped the buckets and dashed back to the naked carl, slapping his cheeks until his eyes flicked open. "Get out before you burn, man!"

She ran off before he could catch her, but just as she reached the hall, someone grabbed her elbow and wrenched her against him. Snatching off her coif, he twisted her hair in his fist.

"Why, if it isn't my hapless cousin, Taras," King Ethelred said, and shoved her into the courtyard.

Cynewulf scrabbled for a foothold, jammed his toes into a crack, then reached for the parapet. At the last instant he saw a guard turn and walk toward him. He slid his hand out of sight and found a fingerhold. Pressing his face to the stone, he forced his labored breathing into silence. Every muscle quivered from fatigue. His fingers were frozen stiff, too swollen to bend. He'd have to let go. There were limits to a man's strength.

And then he smelled smoke. The guard cursed and

turned to run down the parapet. Summoning his last reserves, Cynewulf dragged himself to the top of the wall.

Flames were shooting out of the keep's topmost windows. "Taras!" he bellowed, leaping to his feet. He had to get into the burning building and find her.

Halfway to the north tower, he saw a door burst open and a figure stagger out. The man dropped to his hands and knees and coughed as though his lungs would burst. When he raised his face, firelight etched his features. It was Camlann.

"So, viper, you crawl straight into my arms," Cynewulf said.

Camlann scrabbled to his feet and freed his sword. Holding it before him in two hands, he stared in horror at Cynewulf. "You're dead!" he cried.

Cynewulf swept his sword to the ready and strode forward. "Where is my wife?"

"She lies dead, as you will in less than a moment!" He lunged forward, cleaving the air before Cynewulf's chest. "What is this? No chain mail? You make the game too easy!"

He cut viciously at Cynewulf's head, but the Viking parried, sending him staggering. Cynewulf swatted his mailed ribs with the flat of his sword. Camlann stumbled again, gasping for air.

Cynewulf went after him, but the roof timbers exploded, raining fiery debris down on the combatants. Since he was wearing no armor or leather, Cynewulf received the worst of it.

Camlann leaped forward with an overhand chop. Cynewulf dropped to one knee and parried less than an inch above his head. Sword to sword, he rose and pressed Camlann back.

The Briton broke free and feigned a low thrust. At the last second he swept his blade at Cynewulf's face. Sword wind kissed Cynewulf's cheek as he spun past his enemy. He struck Camlann's left calf.

Camlann screamed and staggered back, unable to defend himself. Cynewulf paced after him, pressing the point of Damfertigénen into his breast.

"What have you done with my wife? The truth now! Is she in the keep?"

"Nay—she's with some of my men. . . . I'll take you to her. She's down there!"

Cynewulf followed his gaze to the courtyard. Camlann lurched back, caught up an ember, and hurled it into a vat of oil. Flames roared two feet high. Camlann kicked over the vat, flooding the parapet with fire.

Cynewulf leaped back, lost his balance, and stumbled off the parapet. He clawed for a handhold as he fell, felt his fingers catch a block, and dug in with all his might. A river of fire poured over the wall six inches from his face. He worked his hands along the wall until his toes found purchase.

Cynewulf pulled himself up to safety and saw Camlann crouched down, clutching his leg. "Barbarian scum!" Camlann screamed, lurching to his feet. "You should be dead twice over!"

Cynewulf rolled onto the parapet, but before he could stand Camlann was upon him, his sword scything. There was nothing Cynewulf could do to stop him. It seemed he had used up his last bit of luck.

But as Camlann shifted his weight for the kill, his foot slipped in the oil. He stumbled back, waving his arms for balance. Cynewulf lunged for his hand but caught empty air. Camlann screamed and plunged backward off the parapet. Cynewulf heard a crack and knew he'd struck the icy moat so far below.

Sparing hardly a glance at the still form below, Cynewulf raced along the parapet and hurtled down a narrow flight of steps. He found Damfertigénen in the dirt. The pommel was crushed but the blade intact.

He stormed into the courtyard and found Camlann's mercenaries and followers milling about in panic. The drawbridge was closed and the keeper locked in his gatehouse. Every few seconds a timber exploded from the roof and rained down flaming debris. Someone had loosed the horses, and the terrified animals were racing around the courtyard trampling people.

Cynewulf struggled to the gatehouse and yelled through the embrasure, "Open the doors!"

"Nay, there are enemies outside!"

Cynewulf swarmed up the framework and hacked through one of the cables supporting the drawbridge. It parted with a loud snap, shaking the bridge. Cynewulf ran across the top and smote through the second rope. The great bridge dropped with a thud, knocking people off their feet and stones from the walls. Cynewulf nearly fell off the framework.

Denholm and his men raised a battle cry and charged across the moat. Cynewulf swung down to join the fight, but the demoralized Britons were more interested in escaping the fire than fighting. They stampeded across the bridge and fell down in the snow.

Cynewulf caught a warrior before he could follow them. "Where is the Lady Taras?"

"The red-haired wench? Locked in the north tower!"

Cynewulf reeled as though he'd been struck. The entire keep was afire now, flames spurting from every window. The very stones were turning to glass.

"Taras!" Cynewulf roared. He sprang toward the burning doors.

Denholm galloped through the crowd and flung himself off his horse, tackling his lord. Cynewulf fought him off and stumbled toward the keep.

"Do it! Burn yourself!" called a voice.

Cynewulf stopped in his tracks. He knew that voice. He'd heard it on the battlefields of Manathilim and the River Wiltham. He looked back.

King Ethelred stepped from a passage in the outer wall, holding a knife to Taras's throat. "Aye, burn yourself if you will, Lord Cynewulf. 'Twould pleasure me to see you dead at last. But first, get me a horse or you'll see your pretty witch slain before your eyes!"

"Let her go," Cynewulf said.

"Nay, the horse first." Ethelred dragged Taras's head back until Cynewulf saw the pulse leaping in her throat. The knife blade glinted in the firelight.

Cynewulf saw Eboracum among his men's horses. "Give the king the black horse," he commanded Denholm. "Ethelred, you will go after you have released her."

"And leave you to kill me on the spot? Not likely—do not!" he warned as Cynewulf took a step. Taras's blood beaded up on the blade. Cynewulf stood still, forcing himself not to look into Taras's eyes—huge, silent pools of fear. "One more step and you'll bury your precious witch!"

Cynewulf made himself speak calmly, though he wanted to launch himself at his enemy and kill him with his bare hands. "I will concede, but you must release her outside the gates. We'll not pursue."

"You're in no position to parley. The wench stays with me until I'm safe. Now get me the horse!"

"Do it," Cynewulf commanded.

Denholm led Eboracum forth and dropped the reins ten feet from the king. "There is your horse. A fleeter one you'll not find."

Gripping Taras, Ethelred said, "Stand back, all of you! Nay—further! I'll not have you rushing me." He pressed the knife harder against Taras's throat until Cynewulf and his men had retreated some distance.

"I'll gladly slice your throat," he hissed at Taras. "Watch your ways."

He transferred the knife to his teeth, grabbed a handful of mane, and hastily mounted the horse, dragging Taras into the saddle before him.

Before Ethelred could collect the reins, Cynewulf yelled, "Eboracum, to battle!"

Unleashing a wild neigh, Eboracum reared high. The king fell backward, snatching at Taras' clothing to save himself. The fabric tore, Taras grabbed frantically for the mane, and Ethelred slid off the back of the horse and landed on his feet. He snatched his knife from his teeth and charged Taras. "I'll kill you!" he snarled.

Cynewulf threw Damfertigénen at the king. Taras didn't see the blade strike because at that instant, Eboracum leaped away from the king and bolted through the gateway and across the bridge. Taras held on for dear life, her fingers twisted in the stallion's mane as he plunged down one slope and up another. He was thrashing through the snow on the other side when a long whistle pierced the air.

Eboracum stopped dead, nearly hurling Taras over his nose, then he turned and trotted towards the others. Cynewulf had already crested the hill and was plunging toward them, the deep snow hindering him hardly at all.

Taras rode up beside him and leaped from Eboracum's back. Cynewulf caught her and kissed her hard on the lips, locking his arms around her shoulders and waist. When he finally let her catch her breath she wept, "Beloved, beloved! I knew you were alive—I knew Camlann couldn't kill you! I knew you'd come for me."

Cynewulf couldn't speak. He'd found her and nearly lost her all in a moment. To the end of his days he'd remember how close Ethelred's knife had come to killing her.

Taras caught his handsome face in her hands and kissed

his mouth, long and lingering. "You're mine forever, my darling."

"Come home with me then, wife," Lord Cynewulf said, finding his voice. "Home to Castle Ilovar. Let us begin our eternity."

They looked back at the burning keep. Already the Vikings were herding their prisoners across the draw-bridge. Eboracum stood nearby, awaiting his command. Cynewulf enfolded Taras in his shield arm and looked down the long road at the snowy landscape. With Taras at his side, he never intended to leave home again. He gazed at Taras and smiled, happy at last.

Epilogue

One year later, Lady Taras and Lord Cynewulf sat holding hands before the fire in the great hall of Ilovar. At the long tables their people feasted and made merry. Taras's mother, Lady Gwendolyn, sat in a place of honor above the salt. On her knee perched her nine-month-old granddaughter, Rusalyn.

Taras looked at Cynewulf out of shining green eyes. "I haven't seen my lady mother so happy since Father was alive. Thank you for welcoming her to your household, Cynewulf."

He squeezed her hand. "You've thanked me for that every day for the last nine months, my love, and every day I've reminded you that this is *your* household."

Taras smiled and cut her eyes at a bald knight cozied in a corner with Ardeth, the maid. "Sir Osric the Frog has never been happier, either. Just look at him, wed and soon to be a father."

"Aye, there's nothing like a long draught of love potion to change a frog to a prince," Cynewulf said.

Taras pinched his arm and giggled. "I'm ashamed to think of what I tried to do to you."

"Ah well, we would have been happy living in the pond together. That reminds me, I've a gift for you."

"A gift?"

"To celebrate the anniversary of our wedding, my love. Here." He handed her a wooden box gilded with gold. "Open it."

She set the box on her lap and fumbled the lid open. A grin of delight spread across her face. On a bed of green velvet sat a golden frog, its back studded with diamonds and rubies. Its eyes, made of emeralds, twinkled mischievously in the firelight.

Cynewulf lifted the frog out of the box and pinned it to Taras's mantle. "There, spell weaver, whenever you look at him, think of me."

"I think of little else, my handsome Frog Prince," Taras said, and leaned over and kissed him.

PRETENDER'S GAMES LOUISE CLARK

James MacLonan is in desperate need of a wife. Recently pardoned, the charming Scotsman has to prove his loyalty to the king by marrying a woman with proper ties to the English throne. Thea is the perfect wife: beautiful, witty, and the daughter of an English general. And while she can be as prickly as a thistle when it comes to her undying loyalty to King George, James finds himself longing for her passionate kisses and sweet embrace. Thea never thinks she will marry a Scot, let alone a Jacobite renegade who has just returned from his years of exile on the Continent. Convinced she can't lose her heart to a traitor of the crown, Thea nevertheless finds herself swept into his strong arms, wondering if indeed her rogue husband has truly abandoned his rebellious ways for a life filled with love.

___4514-1 $4.99 US/$5.99 CAN

Prince Of Thieves

Saranne Dawson

Lord Roderic Hode, the former Earl of Varley, is Maryana's king's sworn enemy and now leads a rogue band of thieves who steals from the rich and gives to the poor. But when she looks into Roderic's blazing eyes, she sees his passion for life, for his people, for her. Deep in the forest, he takes her to the peak of ecstasy and joins their souls with a desire sanctioned only by love. Torn between her heritage and a love that knows no bounds, Maryana will gladly renounce her people if only she can forever remain in the strong arms of her prince of thieves.

___52288-8 $5.50 US/$6.50 CAN

ENRAPTURED

KATHERINE DEAUXVILLE

The twelfth duke of Westermere is simply out for a peaceful drive, until the Amazonian beauty tosses herself into his coach demanding he do something about the dreadful condition of his estate. This alone would not have flummoxed Sacheverel de Vries, but when the strange woman in the threadbare cloak babbles something about equal rights and social justice, rips open her dress, and claims he has attempted to ravish her, there is only one thing he can do. Skillfully maneuvered into a betrothal with the handsome aristocrat, Marigold Fenwick begins to regret her impulsive actions. And when Marigold decides to seduce the esteemed duke into an enlightened social consciousness, she hardly knows what she is getting into, for the aftermath will leave her thoroughly enraptured.

___4540-0 $5.99 US/$6.99 CAN

Dorchester Publishing Co., Inc.
P.O. Box 6640
Wayne, PA 19087-8640

Please add $1.75 for shipping and handling for the first book and $.50 for each book thereafter. NY, NYC, and PA residents, please add appropriate sales tax. No cash, stamps, or C.O.D.s. All orders shipped within 6 weeks via postal service book rate. Canadian orders require $2.00 extra postage and must be paid in U.S. dollars through a U.S. banking facility.

Name_____

Address_____

City_____State_____Zip_____

I have enclosed $_____ in payment for the checked book(s).

Payment <u>must</u> accompany all orders. ❏ Please send a free catalog.

    CHECK OUT OUR WEBSITE! www.dorchesterpub.com

BEYOND
Forever
DEBRA DIER

1999. He appears to her out of the swirling fog on the cliff's edge, a ghostly figure who seems somehow larger than life. Dark, handsome, blatantly male, he radiates the kind of confidence that leads men into battle and women into reckless choices. But independent-minded Julia Fairfield isn't about to be coerced into anything, especially not a jaunt across the centuries in search of a miracle.

1818. Abducted from her own time, Julia finds herself face-to-face with this flesh and blood incarnation. Gavin MacKinnon is as confounded as Julia about her place in his life, but after a night of passion, they learn that their destinies are inextricably bound together, no matter what the time or place.

___4623-7 $5.50 US/$6.50 CAN

Dorchester Publishing Co., Inc.
P.O. Box 6640
Wayne, PA 19087-8640

Please add $1.75 for shipping and handling for the first book and $.50 for each book thereafter. NY, NYC, and PA residents, please add appropriate sales tax. No cash, stamps, or C.O.D.s. All orders shipped within 6 weeks via postal service book rate. Canadian orders require $2.00 extra postage and must be paid in U.S. dollars through a U.S. banking facility.

Name_____
Address_____
City_____ State_____ Zip_____
I have enclosed $_____ in payment for the checked book(s).
Payment <u>must</u> accompany all orders. ❏ Please send a free catalog.
    CHECK OUT OUR WEBSITE! www.dorchesterpub.com

Thief Of Hearts

PATRICIA GAFFNEY

Though he is her late husband's twin brother, John Brodie is far from the perfect gentleman Nick had been. His manners are abominable, his language can make a sailor blush, and his heated glances make sheltered Anna Jourdaine burn with shame. But Anna finds herself weakening to her brother-in-law's seductive appeal. Caught up in deceits and desires beyond her control, her future happiness depends on learning which brother is an immoral criminal and which merely a thief of hearts.

___4363-7 $5.99 US/$6.99 CAN

Dorchester Publishing Co., Inc.
P.O. Box 6640
Wayne, PA 19087-8640

Please add $1.75 for shipping and handling for the first book and $.50 for each book thereafter. NY, NYC, and PA residents, please add appropriate sales tax. No cash, stamps, or C.O.D.s. All orders shipped within 6 weeks via postal service book rate. Canadian orders require $2.00 extra postage and must be paid in U.S. dollars through a U.S. banking facility.

Name_____
Address_____
City_____State_____Zip_____
I have enclosed $_____ in payment for the checked book(s).
Payment <u>must</u> accompany all orders. ❏ Please send a free catalog.

A Love Beyond Forever

Diana Haviland

In the solace of slumber he first tempts her—a dark-haired stranger with a feral green gaze—and Kristy Sinclair sees the promise of paradise reflected in his eyes. She swears it is only a dream. But in a New Age boutique, an antique hand mirror shows the beautiful executive more than mussed lipstick—that magnificent man, and a land she has never before known. Suddenly, Kristy is in Cromwell's England. And when an ill-advised remark turns into a brush with the Lord Protector's police, Kristy finds a haven in the solid arms of Jared Ramsey—the literal man of her dreams. But after one rousing kiss from the rogue royalist, Kristy is certain she is awake—and she knows she must learn of the powers that rule her destiny.

___52293-4 $4.99 US/$5.99 CAN

Dorchester Publishing Co., Inc.
P.O. Box 6640
Wayne, PA 19087-8640

Please add $1.75 for shipping and handling for the first book and $.50 for each book thereafter. NY, NYC, and PA residents, please add appropriate sales tax. No cash, stamps, or C.O.D.s. All orders shipped within 6 weeks via postal service book rate. Canadian orders require $2.00 extra postage and must be paid in U.S. dollars through a U.S. banking facility.

Name_____
Address_____
City_____State_____Zip_____
I have enclosed $_____ in payment for the checked book(s).
Payment <u>must</u> accompany all orders. ❑ Please send a free catalog.
CHECK OUT OUR WEBSITE! www.dorchesterpub.com

The Magician's Lover — Fiora Speer

Determined to locate his friend who disappeared during a spell gone awry, Warrick petitions a dying stargazer to help find him. But the astronomer will only assist Warrick if he promises to escort his daughter Sophia and a priceless crystal ball safely to Byzantium. Sharp-tongued and argumentative, Sophia meets her match in the powerful and intelligent Warrick. Try as she will to deny it, he holds her spellbound, longing to be the magician's lover.

___52263-2 $5.99 US/$6.99 CAN

Dorchester Publishing Co., Inc.
P.O. Box 6640
Wayne, PA 19087-8640

Please add $1.75 for shipping and handling for the first book and $.50 for each book thereafter. NY, NYC, and PA residents, please add appropriate sales tax. No cash, stamps, or C.O.D.s. All orders shipped within 6 weeks via postal service book rate. Canadian orders require $2.00 extra postage and must be paid in U.S. dollars through a U.S. banking facility.

Name_____

Address_____

City_____State_____Zip_____

I have enclosed $_____ in payment for the checked book(s).

Payment <u>must</u> accompany all orders. ❏ Please send a free catalog.

CHECK OUT OUR WEBSITE! www.dorchesterpub.com